PURSUIT

PURSUIT

BRIAN GALLAGHER

POOLBEG

Published 2004
by Poolbeg Press Ltd
123 Grange Hill, Baldoyle
Dublin 13, Ireland
E-mail: poolbeg@poolbeg.com

© Brian Gallagher 2004

The moral right of the author has been asserted.

Typesetting, layout, design © Poolbeg Group Services Ltd.

1 3 5 7 9 10 8 6 4 2

A catalogue record for this book is available from the British Library.

ISBN 1-84223-136-7

Typeset by Magpie Designs in Goudy 10.5 pt / 14.5 pt
Printed by Litografia Rosés S.A., Spain

www.poolbeg.com

About the Author

Brian Gallagher was born in Dublin. He is a full-time writer whose plays and short stories have been produced in Ireland, Britain and Canada. He has written extensively for radio and television, and is one of the script team on RTE's successful drama series, *Fair City*.

He collaborated with the composer, Shaun Purcell, on the musical, *Larkin*, for which he wrote the book and lyrics, and on *Songs of Rejoycing*, a collection of songs to celebrate the Bloomsday Centenary.

His novels, *Invincible*, *Flight* and *Payback*, have won widespread praise. He is currently working on a new book.

Outside of writing, his interests include travel, tennis, music and inland waterways. He lives with his family in Dublin.

ACKNOWLEDGEMENTS

My sincere thanks to my editor, Gaye Shortland, to Paula Campbell, Sarah Conroy and Brona Looby in Poolbeg, to Keith Adams and Ber Faughnan who kindly read the manuscript and shared their thoughts with me, and to all of the following for their help and encouragement during the researching and writing of the book: Bernard Farrell, Pat Moylan, Clare and Eugene Garrihy, Chris and Margaret Droney, Dominic Flynn, Mary T Droney, Sian Quill, Eivin Murphy, Anne Crawford, Shay Dolan, Clare Dowling and Claudia Carroll.

Finally, but most importantly, my thanks go to my family, Miriam, Orla and Peter, the best supporters in the world.

This book is dedicated to Peter:
basketball wizard, guitarist, voracious
reader and loyal supporter – what a son.

PROLOGUE

1961
Katanga Province
Former Belgian Congo

Conn Lynch knew that the Baluba tribesmen wanted blood. He could hear the hysteria in their chanting and he sensed that they would soon work themselves up to attack again. They had been on the rampage for the past three days, and on reaching the mining town of Kaburi earlier in the morning they had burnt and looted many of the houses in the hastily abandoned European quarter. It was now just after noon, and the Balubas had been drinking looted supplies of wine and spirits, smashing the bottles, then screeching with laughter. Lynch knew that the laughter and chanting could quickly turn into blood-curdling war cries, and he swallowed hard, fearing the assault that might be launched at any minute.

He wiped the sweat from his eyes, all the while

keeping his Gustav gun at the ready. The Equatorial sun blazed down fiercely, and the fortified dispensary in which he was holed up felt like a furnace. Yet the sweltering heat and the prospect of combat weren't the only things making him sweat. In the chaos that had prevailed since the withdrawal of the Belgians and the secession of Katanga province from the newly formed Republic of the Congo, normal standards of civilised behaviour had been dispensed with. Lynch had heard hair-raising stories of rape and mutilation, and he felt a sense of dread as he glanced over at the two nursing sisters that he was here to protect.

The older one, Mother Benedict, was a severe-looking nun in her sixties. Lynch could imagine her as pious, an efficient but dispassionate medical administrator, yet there was no denying the courage with which she was facing her predicament here. The second nun was much younger. Probably in her mid-twenties, Lynch thought, with a delicately featured face whose prettiness even the harsh nun's headdress couldn't hide. She had large, doe-like brown eyes, and, despite her efforts to match her colleague's bravery, suppressed terror was evident in her expression.

And not without cause, Lynch thought, trying to avoid dwelling on what could befall her were the Balubas to overrun the thin lines of defence. In truth, atrocities were said to be occurring on all sides, and the white mercenaries that President Tshombe had hired to bolster his breakaway state of Katanga had been nicknamed *Les Affreux* – the Terrible Ones. Yet Lynch couldn't imagine the mercenaries with whom he was manning the dispensary's defences raping and mutilating non-combatants.

Being with the mercenaries was unusual in that UN troops and the mercenaries – *Tshombe's Horribles*, as the newspapers called them – didn't normally socialise with one another, much less serve together in the field. But then the situation in the Kaburi area was far from normal, and had become chaotic in the last few days when large groups of Baluba tribesmen had descended on the region. Lynch and his officer, Lieutenant Barrett, had become separated from the rest of their Irish Army colleagues in heavy clashes south of Kaburi. Beating a fighting retreat while pursued by marauding Balubas, they had ended up joining forces with a mercenary unit that had been sent to evacuate those few European civilians who had not already fled the town of Kaburi.

Lynch raised his canteen to his mouth, grimacing at the warmth of the water, then he looked across to where Barrett manned the next window. Barrett was sweating profusely and Lynch could sense that, in addition to the fear that they all felt, Barrett was still smarting from the run-in he had had with Lieutenant Trenet, the French commander of the mercenaries. Lynch had enjoyed seeing his officer being spoken to sharply by Trenet, a handsome and athletic-looking man who, despite a uniform that was stained from the fighting in the bush, cut something of a dashing figure. In contrast Barrett appeared bovine and plodding and there had been a flare-up between the two when Trenet had deployed their force to defend the dispensary. Barrett had objected to Trenet – a fellow lieutenant – giving him instructions, but the Frenchman had a good command of English and had told Barrett that as an officer of the Force Publique, he, Trenet, was responsible for civilian welfare. He stated bluntly that he was in command, and that he hadn't the time to argue with Barrett, whose co-operation he expected.

Barrett had blustered a little, then gone along with Trenet's orders, and Lynch had had to suppress a smile. From their first meeting Lynch had disliked Fintan Barrett, the son of a Mayo shopkeeper, and a man whose rank in the Irish army had more to do with his family background than any obvious leadership abilities. Notwithstanding this, Barrett was always insistent on the deference that he felt his rank deserved, particularly from someone like Lynch, whom he perceived as a social inferior. It was an attitude that rankled with Lynch, but as a nineteen-year-old private he had no option but to endure the officer's petty snobberies.

All of a sudden the chanting stopped, to be replaced by high-pitched battle-cries. Lynch tightened his grip on the Gustav. He knew from the pattern of the previous day's fighting that any second now the Balubas would attack. From the sound that they were making he also knew that the tribesmen badly outnumbered Trenet's tiny force and he prayed that they would be armed only with spears and bows and arrows rather than with captured weaponry.

As if in answer, there was a sudden hissing sound as the tribesmen unleashed a flurry of arrows. Lynch ducked instinctively, and the arrows embedded themselves in the wooden furniture that had been used to barricade the dispensary windows. Another volley of arrows followed swiftly and this time several of them came sailing through the gaps in the fortified windows. Lynch heard Sister Sophie, the younger of the nuns, crying out and he looked around to where she was crouched at the far wall of the room. An arrow had embedded itself in the door frame a couple of feet above her head. Lieutenant Trenet shouted something at her in French and she immediately lay down lower behind the barricaded windows. Seeing her frightened face, Lynch wanted to say something reassuring, but just then there was an ear-piercing, high-pitched scream from the Balubas, and he quickly swung around and aimed the Gustav, knowing this was the main assault.

The dispensary was a one-storey building, strategically positioned at a T-junction at the end of the main street. It was flanked to the rear and on its eastern boundary by a medium-sized lake which meant that the dispensary's defenders could concentrate their fields of fire on a frontal assault and the western approach. Barrett had argued that the Balubas could launch a waterborne attack from the rear, but Trenet had dismissed this as unlikely. They were a marauding band who were travelling by foot, he insisted, and so were unlikely in their present drunken state to seek out craft for a co-ordinated land and water assault.

Lynch hoped that Trenet was right and that they could hold off the tribesmen until the reinforcements that Trenet had radioed for could come to their rescue. Now though he felt his stomach tighten in fear as the main body of Balubas ran screaming towards the dispensary. Although they were armed only with spears, bows and arrows, and highly sharpened machetes known as *pangas*, there were scores of tribesmen in the assault party, and Lynch had to fight hard against a sense of panic.

"*Open fire!*" shouted Trenet.

Lynch gripped the Gustav even tighter in an effort to stop his hands from shaking, then squeezed the trigger. There was a deafening retort as Barrett and Trenet opened up also, and from the far end of the dispensary Lynch was aware of Dutchie and Vince, Trenet's two other mercenaries, who were firing long bursts at another party of Balubas who had come in screaming from the western direction. Lynch had crossed the psychological barrier of having killed his first enemy in yesterday's fighting and so he now raked the advancing Balubas without hesitation. The terrifying high-pitched war cries of the tribesmen were mixed with cries of pain as the first wave was cut down by the concentrated machine-gun fire. Still they advanced however, and Lynch felt a spear whistling within inches of his cheek. Fighting back his fear, he continued firing, the smell of cordite heavy in the hot tropical air. The leading Balubas were now only yards away, their *pangas* glistening in the sunlight as they leaped over fallen comrades.

Lynch heard a click from his weapon, then he ducked down below the window and desperately sought to reload, praying that his sweat-soaked hands could insert a new clip before the Balubas were upon him. He heard the clip click home and he swung the weapon round and raised himself to fire out the window again. As he did he realised that Barrett and Trenet had ceased firing, and looking out the window he saw that in the few seconds that he had taken out to reload, the assault had been halted.

Dead and wounded tribesmen lay all along the approach to the dispensary but the Balubas were now in retreat. The carnage before him was sickening, but Lynch was too relieved at surviving the assault to feel much sympathy for the enemy. *And there was also the thought of what the Balubas might have done to the nuns if they hadn't been driven back* . . .

The firing from Vince and Dutchie had stopped also, and Trenet shouted to them in his accented English. "What's happening?"

"Beaten them off for now!" cried Dutchie, reloading

his machine gun as he spoke. Dutchie was a sallow-skinned Englishman with a friendly disposition and a cockney accent, and although only in his late twenties, Lynch knew him to be a battle-hardened soldier, having served with the British Army in Malaya, Suez and Cyprus. Vince was more deadpan, a lean, rangy Rhodesian in his early twenties, but he too was an experienced soldier, having served for five years in the Rhodesian Army.

"Hang on, hang on!" cried Dutchie. "Listen!"

Lynch strained his ears, then he too heard it. It was the sound of engines, heading towards them at speed.

Dutchie looked out the barricaded window behind which he was crouched, then quickly turned back to the others, his tanned face split in a grin. "It's our blokes! Covering fire, Vince!"

Lynch looked out his window but could see no signs of the approaching Jeeps whose screaming engine sounds were now drowned out by the covering fire laid down by Dutchie and Vince. The vehicles must be coming in via the western approach, he realised, and his spirits soared at the prospect of being evacuated by the mercenary reinforcements.

The Balubas must have realised what was happening, for despite the covering fire they were once again unleashing arrows at the dispensary, then suddenly Dutchie and Vince ceased firing as the Jeeps roared up towards the front of the building. Lynch heard heavy gunfire and reckoned it must be coming from the machine guns mounted on each Jeep, then he saw two Jeeps going past his window at speed. They skidded around the corner of the building, taking shelter out of the Balubas' line of fire on the side of the dispensary that abutted the lake shore. Even before the gunfire had stopped and the Jeeps screeched to a halt, Lieutenant Trenet was pulling back the furniture with which he had barricaded the side entrance of the dispensary.

Vince and Dutchie began firing again in response to the spears and arrows that were still being launched, then Trenet pulled the side door open and the newly arrived mercenaries burst into the room.

There were four of them, and Lynch thought that if this was the extent of the relief column then the situation was still critical.

"'Bout bloody time, lads!" said Dutchie with a wry grin, before he went back to firing short bursts from his barricaded window.

One of the mercenaries, a heavy-set sergeant with a broken nose, began speaking in rapid French with Lieutenant Trenet. The others acknowledged the crouching Mother Benedict and Sister Sophie, then nodded to Barrett and Lynch while taking up positions at the windows.

"All right, Vince?" asked one, in a South African accent.

"Never better."

9

"Still got the poncy haircut, I see," said the South African, referring to Vince's thick blond locks.

"Can't get a decent stylist out here for love nor money," answered Vince, before firing another short burst out the window.

The South African grinned approvingly, and Lynch realised that this was the mercenaries' way of showing each other that they weren't frightened, despite being heavily outnumbered. For his own part Lynch's optimism at the approach of the Jeeps was now fading as he watched Trenet ask a series of questions, the officer's expression suggesting that he wasn't pleased with the answers.

"*D'accord, d'accord!*" said Trenet, ending the conversation with the French-speaking sergeant and turning to face the others. "OK," he said in English, "listen carefully. We've got to get out of here fast – more Balubas are heading towards Kaburi."

"Bloody hell!" said Dutchie.

"Exactly," said Trenet. "So it's time to retreat."

"Are there more Jeeps coming?" asked Barrett.

Trenet shook his head. "No, I'm sorry –"

"But you said! You said you'd asked for enough to take us all and –"

"And now we haven't got them!" interjected Trenet. "Two Jeeps are all we have."

"We won't all fit in two Jeeps!" snapped Barrett, saying aloud what Lynch knew everyone in the room must have been thinking. Yet surely no one could be left to the mercies of the Balubas. *Unless the Frenchman was ruthless enough to decide his own men had priority over UN troops . . .*

Despite the tension, Trenet kept his voice calm and firm. "Two Jeeps are what we have, so the driver and gunner who took each Jeep in, also take it out. Sister Sophie and Mother Benedict leave, one in each Jeep."

Lynch knew that Sister Sophie spoke English and he could see the relief in her face as she translated for the older nun. "Dutchie goes in the first Jeep, Vince in the second. With that much firepower in each Jeep and us giving covering fire from here you should get back out."

"Us?" said Barrett, looking questioningly at Trenet.

"I stay behind with you and Private Lynch, then–"

"What, we stay here on a suicide mission?!"

"It is not a suicide mission, Lieutenant."

"What else can you call it?! If we crowded onto the Jeeps we could all get out."

"No, we need to give them covering fire to get away from here. Also there is another person we have to collect."

"What?"

"The phone lines to here are cut, Lieutenant, so he couldn't get a message directly to us."

"Who couldn't?" snapped Barrett.

"A Belgian – Jean Picard. He was the manager of the Union Minière office here. He was out in the bush when

11

the others evacuated, now he's hiding at his office."

The Union Minière had been one of the most powerful companies in the former Belgian colony, and Lynch reasoned that the manager of one of their branches would still be a person of some significance.

"And what are we supposed to do?" asked Barrett. "Walk over there through the Balubas and collect him?"

"I've orders to get him out. He can't be left behind."

"Even if we got to him, how would we get out of Kaburi?" asked Barrett.

"Picard has the keys to a motorboat," answered Trenet. "If we make for that we can get away across the lake."

"If it's that simple what does he need us for?"

"He's an unarmed civilian. It's best if we protect him, and he provides a way out."

Lynch knew that the lake was about a mile wide and maybe four or five miles long – not much of a head start, he reckoned, even if they got away in the boat.

Barrett looked at the Frenchman disbelievingly. "So, *if* we get through the Balubas, and *if* we get to the boat, and *if* we then get away across the lake, where does that leave us?"

"Better off than we are now – we'll be out of Kaburi."

"About a mile away and with no transport?"

"We can disappear into the bush," said Trenet.

"And what – ask any passing taxi to drive us to Elisabethville?!"

"We travel light, we travel fast –"

"On foot?"

"Obviously. When transport is available, Sergeant Chavant here leads a party back to pick us up."

"For God's sake!"

Lynch saw a flash of anger cross the Frenchman's face. "Enough, Lieutenant! I haven't time to argue with you." Trenet turned away from the Irish officer and addressed his own men. "Let's go!"

The mercenaries quickly hoisted their weapons and withdrew from the windows. Lynch sensed an air of discomfort in their quick farewells to himself and Barrett, as though they were embarrassed at leaving the Irishmen behind, notwithstanding the fact that their own commander was also staying back. Trenet spoke in rapid French to the two nuns, who rose from where they had been sheltering. Both nuns shook hands with Trenet, then the younger nun quickly crossed to Lynch. "Thank you. Thank you for all you've done," she said in accented but good English.

In spite of the circumstances, Lynch found himself smiling at her. "You're welcome, Sister."

"Thank you, Lieutenant," she said to Barrett, and Lynch was relieved when the officer managed to shake off his earlier whining tone and instead responded quietly but sincerely.

"You're more than welcome, Sister."

"*Allez, allez!*" cried Trenet.

The older nun nodded to the Irish soldiers, then

Trenet gave his men some last-minute instructions before swiftly shaking hands with each one. The broken-nosed sergeant opened the door and the party quickly slipped out to the Jeeps.

Trenet turned back to the two Irishmen. "Reload your weapons. We take one window each. As soon as the Jeeps' engines start, we give covering fire. We stop to let them drive past. Then we give covering fire again. OK?"

"OK," said Lynch, and Barrett also nodded assent.

All of them quickly loaded magazines into their guns and Barrett looked round at the French officer. "When do we make our own break?" he asked.

"At my signal," answered Trenet. "I'll create a diversion."

"Yeah?" But before Barrett could ask any further questions the Jeeps revved up at the side of the dispensary.

"Short bursts – open fire!" cried Trenet.

All three men laid down a hail of bullets, then the Jeeps came screaming round the side of the building, and Trenet shouted "Cease firing!" The sound of gunfire was still deafening however with the Jeep-mounted machine guns blazing away and Vince and Dutchie also firing from the speeding vehicles. Before the covering fire from the dispensary, the firing of arrows and spears from the Balubas had become occasional, but now the enraged tribesmen sought to prevent escape via the Jeeps and they unleashed a volley of arrows at the vehicles.

Lynch saw a glint of steel as an accurately thrown

14

spear landed in the rear Jeep. He couldn't be sure if anyone had been hit, and before he had any further time to think about it the Jeeps had gone past and Trenet shouted to recommence firing. Caught in the crossfire from the vehicles and the dispensary defenders, more Balubas were falling to the ground, and Lynch couldn't decide whether the tribesmen were fuelled by sheer unflinching bravery or drink-induced hysteria. Probably both, he thought, then the firing from the escaping Jeeps tailed off and they accelerated away down the road leading out of Kaburi.

Trenet turned to the two Irishmen. "Time to get out," he said. "Reload, bring spare ammunition and wait with the side door open."

"What are you going to do?" asked Lynch as he and Barrett swiftly replaced the magazines in their weapons.

"We need a smokescreen," answered the Frenchman, unclipping hand grenades from his webbing. "Be ready to run fast and low."

"What sort of a smokescreen?" asked Barrett, but already Trenet was moving to the window nearest to the corner of the opposite street.

"Come on," said Lynch, following the mercenary's instructions and scooping up spare magazines before crossing to the door. Barrett looked like he was going to reprimand the private for exhorting him to do the Frenchman's bidding, then instead he too grabbed some spare magazines and joined Lynch at the door.

Trenet had laid out three hand grenades on the window ledge. He peered around a heavy bookcase that was partially barricading the window, then he swiftly pulled the pins and threw all three grenades. The window he had chosen was the one that Lynch had been defending, and Lynch suddenly realised what the mercenary was aiming for. There was an abandoned truck on the opposite corner, and Lynch's theory was confirmed when the first two explosions were followed by a much bigger bang when the third grenade went off. A searing flash of flame erupted in the street outside followed by a thick plume of heavy black smoke, and Lynch knew that the Frenchman had exploded the truck's fuel tank to provide them with their smokescreen.

"Go!" screamed Trenet, then all three men burst out the side door, their weapons raised. The burning truck blazed across the street, but the view was obstructed by a haze of smoke. "Follow me!" cried Trenet, and ran towards the low picket fence where the lake shore met the roadway. He vaulted over the fence and Lynch sprinted after him, keeping himself low but with his gun at the ready. Lynch could hear Barrett right behind him, then both Irishmen were over the fence and running after Trenet as he sped along the road that skirted the lake shore.

Their route was taking them away from the residential European quarter of the town, and towards a more industrial zone. Lynch reasoned that this should bring them away from the main body of looting Balubas. They passed a number of steel-framed factory units that were built by the lake shore, then up ahead they saw the sign for the Union Minière. Trenet kept up his fast pace but was suddenly knocked over when two Balubas ran out of an alleyway between the factory buildings and collided with him. Trenet went down heavily, and the first Baluba fell with him. The second tribesman recovered his balance quickly and brought his spear to bear on the fallen mercenary. Lynch saw with horror what was about to happen and without breaking stride he swung his Gustav by the barrel, catching the Baluba on the side of the head with the stock. The man collapsed in a heap, then Barrett brought up his weapon as the first tribesman swung his *panga* at Trenet. The mercenary stopped the blow by catching his assailant's wrist, then he rolled over, pushing his feet into the Baluba's chest and throwing him in an arc. The tribesman landed heavily but held onto the *panga*, which glistened evilly in the sun. Before he could attack again however Barrett fired his Gustav. Blood sprouted from the Baluba's chest, and he collapsed back onto the ground.

"You shouldn't have fired!" said Trenet as he quickly got to his feet.

"Jesus Christ, how about *thanks for saving my life!*" snapped Barrett.

"I'd have finished him myself! Now they've heard the shots, they'll know we're here!"

17

"Next time they can fucking kill you!" said Barrett, but already the mercenary was making for the Union Minière office.

Lynch immediately followed, knowing that Barrett had meant well, but knowing too that they had now lost the element of surprise and that the Balubas were likely to be drawn to the source of the gunfire. He could hear Barrett sprinting after him, then up ahead he saw the door of the Union Minière office being flung open from the inside. A small, frightened-looking grey-haired man ran out. He had a revolver in his one hand and he clutched a satchel in the other.

"Monsieur Picard," said Trenet, then without waiting to be greeted in return he snapped a question in French at the office manager.

Lynch had no grasp of the language but he presumed that the mercenary was asking where the boat was. Picard pointed to a wooden building, several hundred yards further up the lake shore, then Trenet took the older man by the arm to speed him on his way. "*Allez, allez!*"

Just then all four men heard the high-pitched cries of the Balubas. Lynch spun round to see a group of the tribesmen running along the road after them. "Christ!" he muttered, knowing that Trenet had been right and that Barrett's shots had given away their escape route along the shore road. Lynch felt his stomach tightening in fear at the sight of the advancing tribesmen, but without waiting to be ordered he swung round his Gustav and fired a burst at them. One fell and the others immediately slowed, seeking cover from the machine-gun fire. "Fire and retreat!" called Trenet. "Fire and retreat!"

The Frenchman ran ahead, hurrying Picard in the direction of the motorboat. The Balubas' cries were bloodcurdling and the older man looked terrified, but the mercenary concentrated on shepherding the office manager as swiftly as possible towards the sanctuary of the boathouse. Lynch sprinted after them as arrows whistled through the air. Lynch reckoned that Picard was a man of about sixty, and it was obvious already that he wouldn't be able to outpace the Balubas. *The tribesmen had to be slowed down.*

Even as he thought it, Lynch realised that Barrett hadn't kept up. He glanced around and saw the Irish officer sheltering behind a tree and firing bursts from his Gustav. The tribesmen were being forced to take cover, giving Trenet and Picard precious time to widen the gap as they made for the boathouse. Lynch was impressed in spite of himself. As the son of a poor farm labourer, Lynch had smarted at the class-conscious superiority that Barrett exuded but, despite thoroughly disliking his officer, Lynch had to recognise that Barrett wasn't actually lacking in courage.

The chatter of the Gustav suddenly ended as the magazine clicked on empty. Barrett immediately ran on, and seeing this, the Balubas again took up the chase. This time Lynch was the one who briefly took cover, firing short bursts to slow down the tribesmen as Barrett ran past. Barrett was reaching into his webbing for a fresh magazine even as he ran by, and Lynch fired another couple of bursts, then wheeled away and sprinted after his officer. Once more a hail of arrows flew through the air. And then it happened. Almost as if it were occurring in slow motion, Lynch watched in horror as an arrow embedded itself between the shoulder blades of the fleeing office manager. Picard stumbled, then fell heavily and Lynch heard a roar of triumph from the Balubas.

Already Picard's white shirt was starting to show a red stain, and Lynch winced, knowing that some of the Congolese tribesmen used poisoned arrows of sufficient potency to kill an elephant.

Trenet had stopped his own dash forward and he ran back now to the fallen Belgian, whose face was contorted in pain as he grasped for the satchel that had fallen from his grasp. Despite the terrifying war cries of the exultant Balubas, Trenet dropped to his hunkers, hoisted the wounded man onto his back and then began to run awkwardly forward again. Even as he himself swung around to fire once more at their pursuers, Lynch was impressed at the mercenary's courage.

Barrett was already firing bursts, and now Lynch joined him, both of them laying down a hail of covering fire.

This time two of the tribesmen fell to the ground under the machine-gun fire, but the party of Balubas still numbered more than twenty and no doubt there were scores more of them scattered around Kaburi. *Getting away in the boat was going to be touch and go . . .*

Both Irishmen emptied their magazines, then turned and fled after Trenet and the wounded Belgian, reloading as they ran. Lynch knew it was important not to let their enemies gain possession of modern weapons and so he hastily scooped up the pistol that Picard had dropped, shoving it into the pocket of his fatigues, then sprinted after Barrett.

Running bent over, Trenet was now approaching a wooden boathouse with flaking paintwork. The Frenchman stopped and tried to open the door. He was holding Picard onto his shoulders with his right hand and he still held his gun in his left hand with which he tried to turn the handle of the door. It was locked. Even as he let go the handle in frustration a couple of arrows landed with soft thuds in the wooden walls of the building. Then Barrett arrived at speed. He aimed his gun at the lock, fired a short burst that splintered the frame, then kicked the door in. Trenet stumbled into the boathouse, the bloodied Belgian still hoisted on his shoulders just as Lynch skidded to a halt at the door. Both Irish soldiers turned and opened fire again in an effort to give Trenet time to get Picard into the boat and to get the engine started.

"Grenades!" shouted the Frenchman.

"We've none!" answered Barrett.

"Use mine!"

Lynch left Barrett shooting from behind the cover of the door as he backed into the boathouse to collect the grenades. Trenet had already laid Picard on the ground and he quickly pulled the last two grenades from his webbing. He tossed them to Lynch, then went though the wounded Belgian's pockets for the keys to the boat's engine.

Even in the brief moment when Lynch had been collecting the grenades he had noted two things, one good and one bad. The good news was that the boat looked well maintained and easily big enough to take all of them. The bad part was that Picard looked awful. Already he was only semi-conscious, and blood had seeped from his mouth and run down his chin. Lynch reckoned that even if they got away across the lake and into the bush the Belgian could not survive for long without proper medical attention.

First though the tribesmen had to be kept at bay while Trenet lowered Picard into the boat and got the engine started. Lynch moved back to the door of the boathouse, pulling the pin from the first grenade as he went. Barrett saw what he was doing and stopped firing, then Lynch reached around the door and flung the grenade back towards the Balubas. Nothing happened for a couple of seconds, then there was an explosion, followed by screams. Lynch reckoned that grenade shrapnel would dampen the enthusiasm of the tribesmen for a while but he knew that their blood was up now, and that eventually they would charge the boathouse.

There was still no sound of a marine engine, and when several arrows thudded into the door and walls of the boathouse Lynch held out his Gustav and fired a raking burst in the direction of the enemy. *Save the last grenade for when we really need it*, he thought, then he heard the sound of Trenet starting the engine. The starter motor kicked in but the engine coughed, then spluttered and died.

Sweet Jesus, no! he thought. He fired another burst from the Gustav, reasoning that the Balubas also would have heard the marine engine and that they might launch an all-out assault now to prevent their quarry escaping. *Almost time to use the final grenade*, he decided, as Trenet tried the engine again.

Once more the starter motor kicked in, and this time the engine sounded a little healthier, then once again it spluttered and died. Lynch felt a stab of terror and he gripped the grenade. What would happen if they couldn't get away on the boat? The Balubas would undoubtedly storm the boathouse. And then what? He couldn't let himself be taken alive. God only knew what the Balubas might do to prisoners, but honouring the conditions of the Geneva convention hardly seemed likely. He pulled the pin and threw the grenade.

It would be every man for himself. Lynch was a strong swimmer and he thought about the lake. Before the tribesmen gained access to the boathouse he would dive off the jetty, he decided, and take his chances in swimming for the far shore. There was a loud bang as the second grenade exploded. It was their last one but the Balubas didn't know that, Lynch reasoned, so there was probably a little more time before they became emboldened enough to charge the boathouse. And then he heard the sweetest of sounds. Trenet had started the engine again, and this time it continued running. The Frenchman allowed it to run for a while then gradually built up the revs and Lynch heard the latent power in the throbbing engine.

"Fire again, then jump in!" cried Trenet, and Lynch and Barrett immediately unleashed a withering hail of fire as the mercenary swiftly undid the boat's mooring ropes.

"Let's go!" cried Barrett, and Lynch needed no further urging.

Both men ran towards the boat, a medium-sized cabin cruiser, and jumped down onto its deck. Trenet had laid the injured Belgian chest down on the galley floor and now the mercenary gripped the wheel and put the engine into gear. Even above the engine roar Lynch could hear the cries of the approaching Balubas and he quickly reloaded his weapon, knowing the tribesmen wouldn't meekly accept their escape. No sooner had he loaded a fresh magazine than the first two Balubas burst through the door of the boathouse. Lynch immediately fired a burst at them, but the cruiser had responded to being thrust into gear and the sudden acceleration caused Lynch to miss.

The first Baluba flung a spear and it sailed in a speedy arc. Barrett cried out, and Lynch looked round, then realised that the officer's cry was one of shock, the spear having skimmed past his face. Both soldiers simultaneously began firing their Gustavs, and the tribesmen on the jetty collapsed under the hail of bullets, then the cruiser shot out of the boathouse, picking up speed as it started across the lake.

More Balubas appeared on the jetty, furiously unleashing a hail of arrows, but already the cruiser was drawing out of their range, and Lynch knew that for the moment they were safe.

The lake was about a mile wide and almost five miles long, and Lynch had heard that the bridge at its western end had been destroyed. To get to the bridge at the eastern end and then travel back on the far shore would entail a journey of at least four miles, and Lynch hoped that the Balubas would regard this as too much effort, particularly in pursuit of an enemy who could disappear into the bush immediately after crossing the lake.

Trenet brought the boat up to top speed, then without leaving the wheel he turned round to Barrett. "Lieutenant, there's a first-aid kit at my feet."

Barrett had gone straight to the assistance of the blood-sodden Picard and now he quickly gathered the first-aid kit and returned to the Belgian. Lynch's first instinct had been to offer to help, but he had held back. Barrett was trained in first aid, and Lynch had decided to leave him to it. And in reality he sensed that Picard was actually a hopeless case. The arrow had been notched below the head so that it had snapped off when Barrett had tried to remove it Apart however from the poison likely to be on the arrow tip, serious internal damage had obviously been done, and the Belgian was now unconscious and bleeding more heavily from the mouth.

Barrett injected him with a syringe from the medical kit. Unwilling to watch any further, Lynch looked away.

Despite the trauma of what they had undergone he was struck by the beauty of his surroundings. The waters of the lake sparkled under a clear blue sky and the wooded shore to which they were headed was a riot of bright green foliage. The cruiser was churning up a creamy white wake and a warm breezed buffeted Lynch as they sped along. This was the kind of experience for which people joined the army, he knew, and he suspected that lots of the young Irish soldiers with whom he was serving would talk about their Congo adventures for the rest of their lives.

It was the first time Irish troops had served on an overseas UN mission and their initial naivety and inexperience had been epitomised by the first contingent of troops arriving dressed in tops made of wool – despite the fact that they were serving in Equatorial Africa. They had learned quickly however, and had proven to be effective soldiers who were now playing an important role in restoring order to the Congo.

The whole thing was an adventure far more exotic than Lynch could have hoped for when he had joined the army three years previously. He had just turned sixteen and had joined up on impulse, fed up as he was with hiring himself out to tight-fisted farmers in the west of Ireland. His father had died when Lynch was only three, and his mother had reared a family of two boys and two girls in a tiny labourer's cottage. Both his sisters and his brother had emigrated in the nineteen-fifties when times were bleak in Ireland and jobs were scarce. But for some reason that he couldn't fathom Lynch had resisted the obvious course of emigration that had been the lot of so many of his schoolmates. And now, almost unbelievably, here he was in darkest Africa, terrified yet exhilarated by the kind of adventure he had dreamed of as a boy.

He felt a change in the throbbing of the engine and realised that Trenet was easing off the speed. The Frenchman was steering for what looked like a shingle beach, and Lynch reckoned that Trenet wanted to avoid any rocks or sandbars while trying to get the cruiser in as close as possible to the shore.

Barrett was still tending to the unconscious Picard,

and Lynch went forward to join Trenet as he eased the craft towards the shore. The chances of more Balubas being present in the heavily wooded opposite shore of the lake seemed small, but Lynch nonetheless took up a ready position, his Gustav trained on the shoreline as Trenet eased the boat towards the shingle.

Lynch realised that the waters of the lake must be deep right up to the shoreline, for Trenet managed to bring the cruiser to within a few yards of the beach before there was a shuddering sound as the hull scraped the shingle. The Frenchman cut the engine, then turned to Lynch. "You secure the beach; we'll take off Monsieur Picard."

"Right," answered Lynch, then he made for the bows, climbed over the rail and dropped down into the water, making sure to hold his weapon aloft. Despite the tropical heat, the lake water was cooler than he had expected. He waded quickly through the waist-deep water and scrambled ashore, his Gustav at the ready.

There was a small clearing a few yards inland of the shingle and he entered it, then stopped to look around and listen carefully. Nothing stirred, and he decided that they had gained a respite from the Balubas and that the clearing would be a good haven in which to gather themselves together as they decided on their next move.

He returned to the beach, his weapon still at the ready, but confident now that they were in no immediate danger. Trenet was in the water, and Barrett had Picard propped against the railings of the cruiser, ready to lower the Belgian at the mercenary's command.

"Everything seems fine," called Lynch as he approached them.

"OK," responded Trenet. He quickly slung his weapon over his right shoulder, then indicated to Barrett to begin lowering Picard.

Lynch joined him in the shallow water and together they took the blood-soaked manager from Barrett, then waded ashore carrying him aloft.

"There's a clearing in here," said Lynch.

Trenet nodded and they continued across the shingle, then gently lowered Picard on reaching the clearing. They had just laid the man on the ground when Barrett arrived.

"What do we do now?" asked Lynch.

"It's not good," answered Trenet, kneeling on the ground as he examined the unconscious Belgian.

No, not if we have someone who can't walk, and we've to escape on foot, thought Lynch

"Just before I lowered him from the boat I started to lose his pulse," said Barrett.

Trenet felt for Picard's pulse, checking both his neck and his wrist, then turned back to the two Irishmen.

"Well?" said Lynch.

Trenet slowly shook his head. "He's gone."

"Are you sure?" persisted Barrett, lowering his ear to the Belgian's mouth as he checked for signs of breathing.

"He never had a great chance of surviving, but . . ." Trenet shrugged, a gesture of sympathy yet resignation.

Barrett continued listening for any sign of breath from Picard's mouth, and Lynch felt slightly guilty at the relief he had felt when Trenet had pronounced the Belgian dead. But only slightly. They had miles to go in hostile territory and Picard would have been a huge burden, yet they could hardly have left him behind. Or perhaps they could have, thought Lynch, if the man was certain to die anyway. But now they wouldn't have to make any difficult decisions, he realised, as Barrett turned away from the Belgian.

"He's gone all right," said Barrett softly

Notwithstanding that they had never met before, Lynch suddenly felt a stab of sympathy for the dead man and he reached down and gently closed Picard's eyes. "Lord have mercy on him," he said.

"Amen," responded Barrett.

"We'd better get moving," said Trenet.

Once again Lynch felt guiltily relieved, this time that no one was suggesting the time-consuming heroics of digging a grave. He rose to his feet, as did Barrett, while Trenet removed the dead man's wallet and watch.

"For his family to have . . ." he explained.

"Aren't you forgetting something?" said Barrett.

Trenet slipped the wallet and watch into a pocket of his tunic and looked quizzically at Barrett as he rose.

"Sorry?"

"The satchel."

"The satchel?"

"The satchel that Monsieur Picard had. Seeing as he was fleeing for his life, and seeing as he was the manager of a mining company in a diamond area, it seems pretty likely that it contained precious stones."

Trenet made no immediate response, and Lynch recognised the significance of Barrett's words and Trenet's slowness to answer.

"So?" Trenet eventually asked coolly.

"So I presume that's why you took the satchel from Monsieur Picard and glanced into it when we were fighting the Balubas at the boathouse."

Jesus, thought Lynch, *how did I miss that?* And had Trenet taken the stones from Picard for safe keeping or to make himself rich? He looked at the mercenary and sensed the man's toughness as he stared at Barrett. *More than capable of lining his own pockets*, thought Lynch, *more than capable . . .*

"You're quite right, Lieutenant," said Trenet. "As Monsieur Picard was badly wounded I thought I should look after something that was clearly important."

"Very commendable," said Barrett, not bothering to disguise an edge of sarcasm. "And I'm sure the authorities will be grateful when I return them." Barrett held his hand out, and Lynch saw a hardness he hadn't seen before in the mercenary's eyes as he looked coldly at the Irishman's outstretched arm.

31

"That won't be necessary, Lieutenant. I will return their property myself."

"I think not."

"Then you are mistaken," said Trenet quietly but with an unmistakable tone of challenge in his voice.

"As the ranking United Nations man here I have authority and responsibility. So I must insist you hand over the satchel."

"As an officer in the *gendarmerie* of the Republic of Katanga –"

"An illegal breakaway state –"

"Do not interrupt me again, Lieutenant Barrett!" snapped Trenet. "As an officer in the *gendarmerie* I don't answer to you. I don't take orders from you. Returning the satchel is a matter I will handle. Now get ready to move out."

Trenet went to turn away, but Barrett swung his gun up and pointed it at the Frenchman's chest. "Hand over the package!"

Lynch could see that Trenet was taken aback, but he also saw a murderous look on his face as he looked Barrett in the eye. "Do not ever, *ever* point a weapon at me. Unless you plan to use it . . ."

"Don't make it necessary," said Barrett, and Lynch could hear an anxiety in his officer's tone, yet he knew that Barrett was stupid enough and stubborn enough to back himself into the kind of situation that could end in grief.

"Come on, lads," said Lynch reasonably, "it's enough fighting the Balubas without fighting among ourselves."

Barrett turned on him furiously. "You'll speak when you're spoken to, Private!"

It only took a moment for Barrett to deliver the rebuke but when he turned back Trenet had hoisted his weapon and was pointing at the Irishman's chest.

"Drop your weapon!" cried the Frenchman.

"Drop *your* fucking weapon!" shouted Barrett.

"Drop it! Now!"

"Lower yours or I fire!"

Lynch saw Barrett's finger tighten on the trigger and he shouted no, terrified that this ridiculous schoolyard stand-off could end in both men firing their weapons.

"Lower it!" shouted Barrett, and Lynch could see that his officer was a hair's-breadth from shooting if the Frenchman continued to keep his weapon aimed at him.

"For God's sake – stop this!" cried Lynch, but neither man took his eye off the other.

"Last warning!" screamed Barrett.

"Don't make me kill you," answered Trenet in a controlled tone that was even more frightening than Barrett's hysterical threatening.

"Drop your weapon now or I'll shoot!" cried Barrett.

"No!" screamed Lynch, knowing that the Irishman really meant it, then there was a deafening burst of machine-gun fire.

33

Lynch watched in horror as Barrett's chest exploded, splattering blood all round, then the UN officer fell to the ground. At such short range the mercenary's fire had been lethal, and Lynch knew at once that Barrett had no chance of surviving. He lay unmoving now, and when Lynch looked up he saw that Trenet had the machine gun trained on him.

Lynch looked at the Frenchman, his stomach tightening in fear. If Trenet's intention really had been to steal the diamonds – and Lynch's instincts told him that it had – then the mercenary's course of action was clear. Kill him too so there'd be no witness to the shooting of Barrett. Then he could keep the precious stones and claim that the UN soldiers had been killed by Balubas, who must also have taken the diamonds. His mind raced as he sought a way out of his predicament, then he said the words that he hoped would save his life.

"Let's split the diamonds. Half each."

Lynch could see that he had taken Trenet by surprise. Although the Frenchman still had the gun trained on him, Lynch knew that he had his interest. The longer that passed without the mercenary shooting, the longer that Lynch could keep his interest piqued, the better the chances of coming out of this alive. His mind was in overdrive but already he knew that if Trenet was amenable, then he, Lynch, was willing to forget the killing of his officer. Barrett had been a fool, an arrogant, condescending hothead who had created an unnecessary stand-off that cost his life.

So be it, thought Lynch. He wasn't going to die out of loyalty to a man he despised. And as for stealing the property of the Union Minière manager – why not? Hadn't the Belgians spent years grabbing everything they could get in the Congo? All his life Lynch's family had been honest but poor and where had it got them? Here was a chance to offset all the hardship and poverty that had been his lot until now. *Time to put Conn Lynch first . . .*

He looked at Trenet, quickly gauging how best to sell the idea to him. The fact that Lynch had already spoken of the diamonds and made no reference to Barrett wouldn't have been lost on someone as sharp as Trenet. The best tack now would be to proceed as though Barrett was history, and to find a way to make it more attractive for Trenet to join forces, rather than to kill him also.

"If you killed me too, *and* the diamonds vanished, it would look *really* suspicious," he said. "All sorts of questions would definitely be asked. But if we work together, that's completely different."

"How is it different?"

"We can each back up the other's story. It will be far more convincing."

Trenet raised an eyebrow. "And what would the story be?"

"We keep it as close to the truth as possible. That we

35

were attacked by Balubas, that Monsieur Picard was killed by an arrow."

"And Lieutenant Barrett?"

Although Trenet still had his gun trained on Lynch's chest, Lynch could see that the Frenchman was interested and he continued, his mind racing as he strove to make his pitch as attractive as possible.

"We say he was killed by the tribesmen – using captured weapons. That way when the bodies are eventually found it will all hang together."

"Go on."

"We take Barrett's weapon and any valuables from himself and Picard and throw them in the lake. It'll be assumed the Balubas looted them, and it'll tie in with our story that both men were killed and we had to leave the bodies behind."

"And the missing diamonds?" said Trenet.

"There was chaos in Kaburi. Maybe Picard never got a chance to retrieve them before evacuating. Or maybe he had them on his person and the Balubas got the diamonds with all the rest of their loot. Either way we were in the thick of battle, fleeing for our lives – we certainly weren't going to go rooting through a dead man's pockets to see what he might be carrying."

Trenet gave a tiny nod as though this sounded credible, but Lynch didn't allow his hopes to rise yet, knowing that he still had to persuade the mercenary that it would be worthwhile splitting the diamonds.

"If we work together we've definitely a better chance of getting back from here alive. And when we do they won't be suspicious if we each confirm the other's story to our superiors. And by sharing the spoils we're both involved, so there's good reason for each of us to keep his mouth shut." *He's not arguing*, thought Lynch. *Go for broke now and do the deal.* "Look there's no point in being greedy. This morning we had nothing. This way we can each have half a satchel of diamonds. I bet it's still a fortune – let's halve it and be each other's alibi. What do you say?"

Trenet's face gave away nothing, and Lynch swallowed hard. He had said his piece, and he knew that to try and sell it further would only sound weak. He waited for what seemed like an age, then the mercenary spoke.

"How do I know that you wouldn't shoot *me* – and take it all?"

"I won't do that for the same reason that you shouldn't. It would be greedy and stupid."

"Lots of people are greedy," said Trenet.

"But I'm not stupid. And I know we're a hundred times more likely to get away with this if we confirm each other's stories."

The Frenchman looked at him searchingly, and Lynch could tell that he was swayed by his arguments. He needed to clinch matters though, and he decided to be bold and take a chance.

"Keep these," he said, slowly removing his spare

37

ammunition clips from his webbing and dropping them to the ground. "And this one," he added, very cautiously lowering his left hand and withdrawing the magazine from his slung weapon, then throwing it too onto the ground. "Now I'm not a threat." He watched the mercenary's eyes, gauging that the Frenchman was impressed by the gesture. *No need to hand over the pistol that Picard had dropped,* he decided, *Trenet wouldn't know about that.*

"OK?" asked Lynch.

The mercenary looked at him again, cold blue eyes that seemed to see into his soul, then he nodded. "OK."

"Great," said Lynch, his face breaking into a smile.

"But not half and half. I carried Picard, I took care of the diamonds. We share two to one."

Despite the flood of relief that Trenet was going along with his plan, Lynch couldn't resist the challenge. "Sixty-forty," he said.

The mercenary looked him in the eye, and Lynch realised that he might have gone too far. Then Trenet gave a wry smile. "You have balls. OK, sixty-forty." The Frenchman quickly bent down and removed the magazines from Barrett's webbing and machine gun, then handed the empty weapon to Lynch. "You throw this into the lake, I'll look after his wristwatch and wallet."

"OK. And, Lieutenant?

"Yes?"

"What would you say the diamonds are worth?"

"A lot."

38

"Yeah?"

"Yes."

"How do we cash them?" asked Lynch, unable to restrain his curiosity.

"There's someone I know. He has contacts in Antwerp"

"Great."

"We can do all this later. Right now, it's time to get moving."

"OK," said Lynch eagerly. "Let's go . . ."

CHAPTER 1

May 2003, New York
Maplewood Private Psychiatric Clinic

"I'm stopping the treatment," said Steve Johnson. "I think it's time." He looked across the desk in the plushly appointed consulting room, curious to see how Helena Glasser would react to his decision. She was in her mid-forties – about fifteen years his senior – although with her perfectly coiffured hair, expensive clothes and slim well-toned body she could have passed for ten years younger.

She raised an eyebrow briefly but her voice revealed no trace of surprise. "If that's what you feel is best . . ."

"It is."

"All right."

Steve smiled to himself, aware that he should have known better than to have expected a more significant reaction from Glasser. She was regarded as one of the best psychiatrists in New York, but in the eight months that she had been treating him he had rarely managed to draw her out, rarely got her to reveal what was going on in *her* mind.

"You did say that I could decide when I was better," he said.

"Yes. So – you feel sufficiently better?"

Steve shrugged. "It's nine months since the kidnapping, eight months I've been coming to you. I just feel . . . it's time now to try and start getting back to normal."

"That's very positive, Steve. Very positive."

"Thank you."

"And the nightmares?"

"Still getting them, but . . . well, not as often, and they're not quite so bad."

"Good," said Glasser, nodding approvingly, then she raised a hand. "Though to be realistic, you'll probably still have them for some time."

"I know. And I still get flashbacks, even in the daytime. Still get surges of anger – I've still a bit of a thing about criminals."

"They caused you a lot of trauma," said Glasser, "so that will probably last a while too."

"But you don't think it's too soon for me to stop coming here?"

Glasser thought a moment, then shook her head. "No, I don't think so. If you feel ready to stop, then let's do so. You can always return any time you wish. Or call me if need be. But for now I'm happy to stop."

"There is one thing I wanted to ask you about."

"Yes?"

"I already told you I'm selling the apartment, that I never want to go back to it."

"Yes, and that seems entirely reasonable."

"I'm not ready to go back to the office either, not yet anyway."

"Then don't."

Steve knew that Glasser was aware of his family's wealth and that, if he chose, he need never work, but he didn't want his financial independence to colour her thinking. "I suppose what I'm really asking you is . . . well, is that just a form of avoidance? If I'm ready to stop coming here, if I'm anxious to stake a claim on normal life again, is it avoidance not going back to the office?"

"Not necessarily. Or rather, it's possibly a healthy form of avoidance. You don't have to do everything at once. If you want to try stopping therapy, and easing back into life as you once knew it, maybe that's enough to be going on with."

Steve felt relieved at the psychiatrist's words. "Good. That's good, because . . ."

"What?" answered Glasser gently when he didn't finish.

"Well, if it's not unhealthy to avoid the office, there's something else I might do. I think it could be pretty interesting."

Glasser said nothing as she waited, then when he remained silent she looked at him quizzically. "Are you going to tell me about it?"

Steve smiled, aware that childish as it might be, he sometimes needed to balance the inherently unequal patient/doctor relationship by seeking to be the one in control of their dialogue.

"It's more – more a career choice. Maybe I shouldn't bother you with the details of – well, of my commercial life."

Glasser smiled, and it struck Steve that perhaps she knew that he was teasing her slightly.

"Feel free to bother me," she said with a rare grin. "You've paid me enough . . ."

He smiled back at her. "Yes. I have, haven't I?"

"So?"

"OK," he said leaning forward, "I'll tell you then . . ."

May 2003, County Clare, Ireland

Laura Kennedy savoured the heat of the midday sun on her shoulders as she followed the snaking mountain path. It was a way-marked trail through the Burren, her favourite place in all of Ireland. The blue Atlantic sparkled in the distance, and the limestone-enshrouded fields that gave this part of Clare its unique, magical quality glistened in the bright summer sunshine. Directly ahead of her a herd of goats grazed on a cliff-top, silhouetted against the cloudless sky. Yet despite the beauty and serenity of her surroundings Laura found herself thinking of death.

Her husband, Declan, had loved the Burren, and although it was now over a year since his death, on first arrival she found the landscape an almost unbearably painful reminder of the good times they had shared here. Although they had been married for only sixteen months when Declan was killed in a car crash, they had lived together for two years prior to the wedding, and Laura had been devastated by the premature loss of her partner. She had put off until now the prospect of staying again in their holiday home in Kilfenora, yet despite the trauma of returning there for the first time without Declan, she was glad that she had mustered the courage to reclaim it.

The cottage had once been her aunt's and, as the scene of many happy childhood holidays, Laura had bought it a couple of years previously when her aunt had died. Now it was serving as her base while she took a holiday from *The Sunday Clarion*, the newspaper for which she did much of her work.

Although Eamon McEvoy, the *Clarion*'s editor, had a long-standing contractual arrangement with Laura, she was nonetheless still a freelance journalist, albeit recognised by the public as being associated with the *Clarion*.

In reality Laura could have chosen to work on most newspapers in Western Europe, having written a best-selling book eighteen months previously. She was comfortable with her colleagues in the *Clarion* however and liked working with McEvoy, despite the fact that she didn't particularly need to, her book sales having brought in a good deal of money. As a thirty-year-old journalist making her way in the profession she had been fortunate, she knew, to stumble onto a sensational story in the autumn of 2000 when an Iraqi assassin had attempted to kill every Foreign Minister in the EU at a conference in Harrogate. Laura had shown an unerring nose for a story in following it up, and through a mixture of luck, judgement and raw courage had been centrally involved in the showdown with the assassin. The upshot of it all had been lucrative offers from some of the biggest publishers in the UK, and a book about her experiences that was both critically acclaimed and commercially successful. And then, nine months after the book was published and a mere sixteen months after marrying Declan, her newly acquired world of wealth and acclaim was turned upside down when her husband was killed by a drunken driver.

She knew however that Declan wouldn't have wanted her to mourn indefinitely, and she had tried hard to resume normal living. Now as she moved through the sunlit expanse of the Burren she consciously put the past from her mind and gave herself up to her surroundings.

Not another person was visible in the sweeping land-scape and the only sound to be heard was the distant calling of seagulls. The sweet scent of gorse hung in the summer air and she felt a sense of peace as she followed the trail.

She topped a rise, and paused to look out across the ocean, debating whether or not to take a photograph or merely to savour the vista. Before she could decide, a ringing sound came from her rucksack and she realised that someone was trying to contact her on her mobile. Immediately she regretted having kept the phone switched on while out on her hike, yet her ingrained habit as a journalist had caused her to keep herself open to contact. *Leave it*, she thought. *If it's important they'll leave a message*. Then again if it was important enough for someone to bother her when she was on holidays maybe she should take the call. She hesitated, then swung off her rucksack and withdrew the mobile from a side pouch. "Hello?"

"Hi, kid," said a middle-aged male voice.

"Mac."

"Got it in one."

Although Laura had recognised the nasal tones of Eamon McEvoy, the editor at the *Clarion*, she was taken aback to hear from him only three days after he had wished her a pleasant week's holiday.

"Have you – have you forgotten I'm away on holidays, Mac?"

"No, actually. And I'm sorry to bother you, kid."

Anyone under the age of fifty with whom the editor was on good terms was 'kid' to McEvoy, and Laura had a sufficiently strong rapport with him to adopt a tone of playful outrage. "I was *heavily* communing with nature, Mac. This better be good."

"Wouldn't have bothered you otherwise."

Laura was conscious of a seriousness in his tone and she immediately felt a stab of concern on Mac's behalf. "Is it the take-over? They're not – they're not closing the paper or anything?" Laura knew that the *Clarion* had been acquired recently by an American media group and like everyone else at the paper she was uncertain what the future might hold.

"No, no, nothing like that," answered the editor. "I was actually ringing about a job."

"A job?"

"That you might like to do."

"What sort of job?"

"The kind you're good at. Chasing an interesting story."

"Couldn't you tell me all this when I get back?"

"I could," said Mac enigmatically, "but then you'd have wasted a journey."

"How's that?"

"The story is in the West."

"Let me get this straight. Because I happen to be in Clare, you want me to cut short my holidays?"

"I thought you might want to yourself."

"Really?"

"No offence, Laura, but sometimes holidays can be a little dull. Murder, on the other hand, rarely is . . ."

Laura hesitated a moment, then breathed out. "OK, Mac – you win. You've piqued my curiosity."

"Thought I might."

"I didn't say I want to cut my holiday short."

"Why don't I tell you the background, then you can decide?"

"Fair enough."

"Got a notebook handy, in case you want to jot anything down?"

"Just a second." Laura took a pen and notebook from a pouch in her rucksack, then sat down distractedly on a flat limestone slab, the natural beauty of the Burren forgotten for now. "OK, shoot," she said.

"Right," said Mac. "Old school-friend of mine gets taken to hospital in Galway recently. Had a heart attack, surgery called for."

"Right."

"Needs a triple bypass, urgently, so there's no time to wait till a private room becomes available and he ends up, post op, in a two-bedded unit."

"Very cosy," said Laura, finding herself slipping into the sardonic mode that conversation with her editor always seemed to engender.

"Cosier than he wanted. 'Cause the other guy in the

49

room with him comes out with something he wasn't bargaining for."

"Yeah?"

"Seems this guy also had cardiac surgery, only his wasn't as successful as my friend's. So this other patient is drifting in and out of consciousness, a priest gives the last rites, and then . . ."

"Then what?"

"Well, then the man dies, unfortunately."

"Oh," said Laura, a little ashamed now of her earlier flippant tone.

"There's no family at the bedside when he's dying, and he's drifting in and out of consciousness. But before he dies he blurts out something. Maybe the drugs made him confused, maybe he thought the other patient was a priest, maybe he just needed to say what he did in front of *someone* – who knows? But there was no doubt about what he came out with."

"Which was?"

"That when he was young – he'd been a party to murder."

Despite the warm summer air Laura felt a tiny shiver go up her spine. "What exactly did he say?"

"That someone was killed – no name was mentioned. But he said quite clearly that he'd been party to the murder."

"Did your friend question him about it?"

"No."

50

"Why not?"

"He was taken aback. Then the other guy lapsed into unconsciousness again, and a few minutes later he died."

"Wow . . ."

"Wow is right," said Mac. "Anyway this pal of mine owes me a couple of favours, so he rang me, thought there might be a story here for the *Clarion*."

"Absolutely," answered Laura, aware even as she said it that the journalist in her had been activated, and that her holiday was about to go on hold. "So, what was the name of the man who died?"

"Lynch," answered Mac. "Conn Lynch."

May 2003, New York
Maplewood Private Psychiatric Clinic

Steve Johnson felt elated as he walked down the pathway to the carpark. The grounds of the clinic were beautifully maintained and he looked admiringly at a row of cherry-blossom trees whose fallen leaves formed a pink carpet on the manicured lawns. There was a warmth in the air and a faint scent of roses, but Steve knew that his sense of well-being had little to do with the attractive surroundings.

Top prices were charged by top specialists in this luxurious clinic – "the millionaires' madhouse", as Steve

51

once heard it vulgarly described – but, however cosseted the patients might be, there was no denying that it was a place for people who needed psychiatric care. Steve knew that it was old-fashioned and politically incorrect to attach any stigma to mental ill health, yet during his visits he hadn't been able to shake off entirely an under-current of shame at being a patient here.

His experience at the hands of the kidnappers who held him until his family paid a large ransom had affected him deeply, and it had taken almost eight months of treatment to bring him to the point where he now felt ready to leave what had happened behind and to get on with his life. He had sold the luxurious east-side condo from near which he had been kidnapped – too many traumatic memories there ever to go back, he knew – and he was currently staying in a rented loft apartment near Greenwich Village, until he was ready to commit himself to something more permanent.

And now, to his delight, he felt well enough to end his sessions with Dr Glasser. She had been all one could ask for in a psychiatrist – sympathetic, supportive and skilful at every stage of the proceedings – yet it had felt enor-mously empowering when he told her that he was ceasing their sessions. It was easily the biggest decision he had taken in the last year and although he had wavered and fretted over it, now that he had taken the plunge it felt like it was the right move.

He had sworn to himself that never again would he be

a helpless victim, he had taken one-to-one instruction in unarmed combat and marksmanship, and he now kept a licensed handgun in his apartment. They were measures that had had a positive effect on his confidence and self-esteem, yet deciding to end the session with his psychiatrist had somehow felt even more empowering.

Now as he came to the end of the path and reached the carpark, he activated the remote alarm on his metallic blue Porsche. He opened the door of the car, then stopped and looked back across the grounds. In the early summer sunshine they looked idyllic, and Steve took a long farewell look around, in no hurry to go now that he had reached the end of what he had decided was his final visit.

After he had told Glasser that he wasn't ready to go back to the office, he had made another decision, one that would take him out of New York for a while. At first he had felt slightly guilty about it, but now he rationalised that with his father as chief executive officer and his sister Gretchen as a recently appointed vice-president, the corporation could continue to manage very comfortably without him. Besides, if he was intent on making a return to normal living, then surely spontaneity was a healthy sign. And what was the point in having wealth at your disposal if you couldn't use it? If you couldn't feel free enough to act on impulse occasionally? He had been through the mill, he had earned the right to do something on a whim. His mind made up, he took a final look back at the Maplewood Clinic, then he got into the car and drove away.

May 2003, County Clare, Ireland

It was funny how life went in cycles, Laura thought. She was sitting at the kitchen table in the cottage in Kilfenora, her notes spread out before her. The last rays of the evening sun slanted through the cottage windows and Laura looked at her surroundings reflectively. The only sound to be heard was the soft thrill of birdsong, yet Laura recalled how lively it had been here in other cycles of the cottage's occupation.

She remembered coming to visit with her brother and sister when she was small, and the fuss there had been when she said she hated the taste of the fresh unpasteurised milk. Then when she was eighteen she had spent the summer in County Clare, working as a guide at the Aillwee caves and staying here with Aunt Mary, her mother's sister. Mary had been unmarried and a little set in her ways, but the two of them had got on surprisingly well. Looking back now, she smiled, recalling how by the end of the summer she had her aunt singing "I Don't Want To Talk About It", a popular song of the time that Laura used to sing incessantly. And then there had been the times here with Declan, when they had bought the cottage the summer before last. They had decorated the place themselves and Laura remembered the fun they had had drinking wine and painting the house to the strains of Declan's Bob Dylan CDs before falling into bed and making love. She swallowed hard, the memories suddenly flooding back with a piercing clarity.

No, she thought, she mustn't give in to sadness. The cottage was still a special place and she mustn't let the ghosts of the past ruin it for her now. She consciously turned her mind from times gone by and looked at the papers she had before her, knowing that work was always a good distraction. She had a large foolscap sheet on which she was collating all that she had discovered about Conn Lynch.

He was an interesting man, no doubt about it. Died a millionaire, yet born in a tiny cottage outside Ballyvaughan. His mother had been a chambermaid in a hotel in Ennis, his father a farm labourer who had left his native Donegal and settled in Clare. The father had died when Lynch was two years old and the mother had single-handedly reared two girls and two boys, the youngest of whom was Conn.

All of this Laura had discovered that afternoon by talking to former neighbours of the Lynches. It had helped considerably that Laura herself had family links in the area, links that had enabled her to find the right people to talk to and to ensure that they were forthcoming in a way that they might not have been with someone they perceived as an unconnected outsider.

It transpired that the Lynches had emigrated to America around the late fifties and then sometime in the mid-sixties Conn Lynch had come back to Ireland, with money in his pockets and a swagger in his stride. Just when Ireland's previously rural economy had begun to industrialise he had opened a timberyard in a disused factory in Galway. He had started out supplying local builders, but had quickly expanded into manufacturing wooden furnishings of all kinds. Within five years he had moved to a bigger plant, and had branched out into exporting Irish oak to the continent, and today CL Products, as the company was called, had a large purpose-built plant on an industrial estate on the outskirts of Galway city.

Tomorrow Laura planned to visit the site and also to check out Lynch's home, an architect-designed ranch-style building between Kinvara and Galway, which Laura had been assured was the last word in luxury. It had emerged too that Lynch had been married briefly to an American and – somewhat sensationally for rural Ireland of the nineteen-sixties – they had divorced after only a year, without having any children.

So clearly Lynch had been both colourful and ambitious, but that still left the million-dollar question: *who had been murdered*? And where? And when? And why? Laura looked at her notes, knowing that the answers to many of these questions might also have been buried when Conn Lynch had been laid to rest the previous Tuesday. And yet . . . there was that sixth sense that told her this was a mystery worth pursuing. She couldn't say why exactly, but the prospect of exploring the affair excited her, and she knew from experience that when she got that feeling she couldn't rest until she had the full story.

CHAPTER 2

Steve Johnson knew he was a little jet-lagged, yet there was a spring in his step as he walked across the hotel lobby. He had flown first class across the Atlantic the previous day, then checked into a comfortable suite in Dublin's Westbury Hotel. He had taken a sleeping pill at bedtime and it had helped him cope with the time difference that he knew would otherwise have had his body-clock waking him in the middle of the night. As it was he had still woken fairly early, but a shower and a full Irish breakfast had invigorated him and he felt energised now as he stepped out of the hotel.

He made for Grafton Street, Dublin's premier shopping thoroughfare, its pedestrianised environs already bustling at nine-thirty on a Monday morning. The street was bathed in hazy May sunshine, the staff in the hotel had been friendly, and Steve felt that he had done the right thing in choosing to follow through on his impulse to come to Europe.

He walked through the streets of Dublin, relaxed by the early summer atmosphere, yet looking forward to reaching his destination. Although it was his first time in Ireland he followed his designated route with confidence, reckoning that his journey should take no more than minutes.

He had arrived at the Westbury the previous afternoon, and after checking into his suite had set out to explore the city. Despite the presence of some ugly and incongruous buildings he had been charmed by the streets of Georgian houses that still graced the centre of Dublin. He passed Trinity College now, where according to his guidebook, Oscar Wilde had once been a student, then as he drew nearer his destination he began to consider how he should behave when he finally saw the man he planned to meet.

Formally and in a business-like fashion was how some would handle it, he knew, but at twenty-nine years of age Steve suspected that he would be by far the younger man, and besides, by nature he tended more towards informality. Yet if he were too casual there was the risk of not being taken sufficiently seriously. As it was he had dressed in a well-cut jacket and slacks but with an open-neck button-down shirt. *Smart casual*, as his sister

Gretchen would have characterised it in her usual analytical fashion. He smiled at the thought, then pushed back the thick brown hair that the wind had flopped into his eyes, straightened his rimless glasses, and entered an impressive cut-stone building.

"Good morning, may I help you?" said a stout, middle-aged woman at the reception desk.

"Good morning, I'm looking for Mr McEvoy, please."

"Have you an appointment?"

"No, I'm afraid not –"

"Mr McEvoy's an extremely busy man," said the woman, before Steve could elaborate further. "Extremely busy."

Steve looked at her and had to suppress a wry smile. It seemed that the world over, there was a breed of receptionists and secretaries who savoured the power they felt was theirs by virtue of their association with people in authority. There should be an association, he thought, for personal assistants, doctors' secretaries, and counter clerks whose instincts were to block you or to make you jump through hoops to gain access to what they controlled. "I think he'll want to see me," said Steve.

The woman looked at him as though she had heard this one before.

"And your name is?"

"Steve Johnson."

"Of?"

Steve paused and looked at her, then decided that she

61

wasn't putting on an act. His kidnapping last year had been a pretty high-profile story but clearly this woman didn't follow the news very closely, despite working for a newspaper herself.

"I'm from Media Group International. We've recently acquired the *Clarion*."

"Oh . . ."

Bingo, thought Steve as the woman gaped at him, the wind very obviously taken from her sails.

"I'll – I'll ring Mr McEvoy straight away," she said, reaching for the phone.

"Thank you."

Steve watched the flustered receptionist dialling an internal number, then she spoke in an over-enunciated tone, the kind that he associated with people who were unsuccessfully trying to impress. "Mr McEvoy, reception here. I have a Mr Steve Johnson down here to see you . . . Well, he's from Media Group International . . . Very good, Mr McEvoy. All right . . ."

The woman hung up, then turned to Steve and tried for a professional smile. "Mr McEvoy will be pleased to see you. If you'd like to take the lift over there, his office is on the third floor."

"Thank you for your help," said Steve, unable to resist injecting just a hint of sarcasm into the comment, then he made for the lift and pressed the button. *Interesting response from McEvoy*, he thought. In lots of take-over situations the boss of the acquired company would be eager to make a favourable impression on the new owners. Yet here was an editor who didn't come down three floors to escort one of the family who owned Media Group International up to his office. Full marks for balls, thought Steve, who had never liked the toadying that had inevitably come his way as the boss's son, during the four years he had worked for the company. And besides, he had always believed that newspapers needed independent-minded editors if they were to keep their integrity and thrive in the marketplace.

Of course McEvoy's reaction mightn't necessarily have such a positive spin, he reasoned, as he took the lift up to the third floor. The editor could simply be rude, or deeply aggrieved at the take-over, or engaged in the kind of macho posturing that was meant to suggest strength but that more frequently characterised weakness.

Well, he'd know soon enough, he thought as the lift came to a halt and he stepped out.

"Mr Johnson?"

"Yes."

"Eamon McEvoy."

The man before him was in his late fifties, wirily built with unkempt grey hair and shrewd eyes. His demeanour was friendly, however, and he offered his hand, which Steve shook.

"My office is just down here," said McEvoy, leading the way down a short corridor, then into a medium-sized untidy room. "Please, have a seat."

Steve took a comfortable chair that was opposite the editor's desk. While McEvoy lifted the phone and requested that any calls be held, Steve took in the mound of papers, files, and sub-edited stories that cluttered the man's desk. Obviously not the type of editor who puts a premium on tidiness, Steve thought, but clearly someone with a sense of humour. For on the wall behind the desk was a blown-up poster containing Mayor Daley's infamous saying: *"There's nothing so low as a newspaper."*

Wanting to break the ice, Steve smiled and indicated the poster. "A fan of Mayor Daley, I see . . ."

McEvoy raised an eyebrow in surprise. "I'm impressed. Mayor Daley was a bit before your time."

"I've always been interested in politics," said Steve modestly, but he could sense that, notwithstanding the boss's son handicap, his credibility had gone up a notch.

"Well, if everyone in Media Group International is as informed as yourself we should all get along together."

"I hope so. Though I should stress that I'm not here as part of the Group's first formal contact. The board in New York will want to meet you in person, naturally . . ."

"Naturally . . ."

"But probably not till early next month when the next board meeting takes place."

"Fine."

"I just happened to be coming to Europe and I thought I might combine a trip with becoming familiar with our latest asset."

"Well, I'll be more than happy to show you round the *Clarion*," said McEvoy.

Had he winced slightly, Steve wondered, when the paper had been referred to as an asset? Understandable really – this man had worked here for thirteen years, rising through the ranks from senior sub-editor to assistant editor, to editor. It would be important to proceed sensitively and not appear as a brash new owner flying in and ruthlessly upsetting established and successful structures. Besides which, Steve was still officially on leave of absence, though he had told his father that he was making a visit to Europe and it had been agreed that he would look in on the *Clarion* as part of the trip.

"That would be fine," said Steve now in answer to the older man's offer. "Though I realise that I've come unannounced and you probably have a busy workload. You can show me the place at your convenience."

"That's considerate of you, Mr Johnson."

"Please – call me Steve."

"OK – Steve. By the same token, I'm Eamon – but everyone calls me Mac"

"What do you prefer to be called?"

"Mac is fine. I've been called worse . . ."

"OK, then," said Steve, "Mac it is."

"Anyway," said the editor, "as I say, it's considerate of you, but I'm not so pressurised that I can't show a new colleague the set-up here."

"Good. Actually there was one other thing I wanted to suggest."

"Yes?"

"I've a little time on my hands, so I thought – I thought it might be a good way for me to get a feel for the *Clarion* if I were to accompany one of your reporters on a story. Get a handle on the tone and style of the paper."

"Right . . . "

Steve sensed that despite McEvoy's positive behaviour so far, the older man would be resistant to anything that might be seen as editorial interference. "I wouldn't want to influence in any way what was written, or how the story was pursued. I know the *Clarion* has a fine record – that's why we bought it – but I thought it would be helpful if at least one person from the group saw it from the inside out as it were."

"Sure," answered McEvoy, and Steve wasn't sure if he had convinced him or if the editor was simply shrewd enough to know that despite Steve's polite phrasing, Media Group International now controlled the *Clarion*, and it would be wise for the sitting editor to get off on a good footing. Whatever the reason, Mac now nodded and said, "Yeah, that shouldn't be a problem."

"Great. So is there any good story or investigation I might tag along on?"

"Actually, I might have just the thing," said the editor.

"Yeah?"

"Have you heard of Laura Kennedy?"

"Yes, she wrote the book on the Harrogate assassination bid."

"Right. Just now she's starting on a story that sounds interesting."

"Really?"

"Early stages of something that's a bit of a mystery — might be just what you're looking for."

"And what's her status? *Vis-à-vis* the *Clarion*?"

"Technically she's freelance. But she works for us a lot, so there's a very strong link."

"And you reckon someone of her stature wouldn't mind me tagging along?"

McEvoy paused briefly, then shook his head. "No, I wouldn't think so."

"Well, if that's the case, I'd be eager to meet her."

"Good" said Mac with a smile. "I'm sure she'll be eager to meet you too."

If you had to be buried somewhere, Bishopsquarter was attractively scenic, Laura had decided. It was where Conn Lynch had been laid to rest in a family grave, and from the hillside cemetery Laura could see the deep blue waters of Galway Bay stretching out into the distance, while to the rear of the burial ground green terraces sloped back up the mountain.

It was a beautiful vista and Laura had gone to the cemetery to look at Lynch's grave and to sort out her notes, but right now she was oblivious to her surroundings as she argued with her boss on her mobile. "Baby-sit some millionaire? You must be joking, Mac!"

"It's for the good of the *Clarion*."

"I'm not *Clarion* staff – use someone who is."

"This is the best story we have in hand, Laura."

"It's also real life, not a Hollywood movie."

"Meaning what?"

"We're not characters in *The Front Page*. This isn't some romantic drama where this guy and I start out hating each other and by the end of the film I want to bear his child."

"Let's be reasonable, Laura. I mean, we could have the child adopted . . ."

"I'm serious, Mac."

"OK, OK. Look, he's in the office next door and I need to get back to him with an answer."

"Fine. Just tell him the answer is no, and put him on some other story."

"Come on, kid. Don't do the reverse-prejudice thing."

"Reverse prejudice?"

"Just because he's rich doesn't make him an asshole."

"I didn't say he was."

"You commented on him being a millionaire, but the guy's not a stereotype. You know as well as I do that all poor people aren't noble and dignified – some of them are idiots. Likewise all rich people aren't heartless parasites, some of them are sound."

"Sound, parasitic, rich, poor – I don't want some number-cruncher breathing down my neck!"

"You read about the kidnapping, Laura. I reckon this guy is still putting his life back together. And he seems like a genuinely nice fella – so how about we cut him some slack?"

"Sure. I just don't think I'm the one to take him under my wing, not right now."

"It's important that the *Clarion* doesn't get off to a bad start with these people. I need to facilitate him."

"I understand, Mac, but –"

"I'm asking this as a personal favour."

Laura paused and looked out across the fields that sloped down towards the shoreline of Galway Bay. She owed Mac, and they both knew it. He had gone out on a limb for her in the past, most notably when he had allowed her to follow a hunch, backed by fairly flimsy evidence, but which had enabled her to crack the Harrogate story that had made her name. Now he was calling in the debt and she couldn't in conscience say no to him. "All right then," she replied.

"Thanks, kid. And eh . . . "

"What?"

"Don't hold it against the guy that I twisted your arm, all right?"

"Would I ever, Mac?"

"It falls within the boundaries of the conceivable."

Laura chuckled. "Relax. I'll be gracious. Might even go

so far as to be pleasant."

"Here, steady on."

Laura laughed again, then Mac moved to finalise matters.

"So will I send him down to the Burren?"

"No point. I was planning to leave Clare today."

"Yeah?"

"Yeah, I'm coming up to Dublin."

"Have you found a lead?"

Million-dollar question, thought Laura. Her enquiries of the previous day had uncovered something about Conn Lynch that might point towards a lead, but for the moment she would play her cards close to her chest. "Just coming back to check a few things out," she answered.

"Why don't you drop into the office then, meet Steve Johnson and bring him up to speed."

"Could we leave it till tonight, Mac? I've a couple of things to nail down here before I head back."

"OK. How about the three of us have dinner this evening?"

"All right."

"Cannerys at eight thirty?" suggested Mac.

"Cannerys? Out to impress, are we?"

"Well, if you won't bear his child, one of us has to be accommodating."

Laura laughed. "What can I say?"

"Don't say anything. Just concentrate on being

alluring in the soft glow of candlelight . . ."

"Mac, if even a fragment of your brain is thinking of matchmaking – don't. It's enough that I have to baby-sit this guy. Reading me loud and clear?"

"Sorry, Houston, your signal is breaking up," said Mac in a crackly voice, and Laura had to smile despite herself.

"I'll see you this evening," she said.

"OK, kid. See you then."

Laura hung up, then sat back against the warm stone wall of Bishopsquarter's ruined church, soaking up the early summer sunshine. On the negative side, the call from Mac meant that she was going to have to continue her investigation in the company of Steve Johnson – a millstone she could have done without, despite Mac's assertion that he was a genuinely nice guy. On the positive side though, she had learned something yesterday that had sent a tiny tingle up her spine. It wasn't earth-shattering and it could easily turn out to have no significance, yet she knew from experience that her hunches were usually worth following. So she would lock up the cottage in Kilfenora, travel back to Dublin and make some enquiries, then have dinner with Mac and Steve Johnson. Eager to pursue her story, she put away her mobile, rose from the wall and started briskly for the cemetery gate.

Daniel Trenet savoured the touch of the masseuse. She was a stunning-looking Chinese woman in her late twenties with fine features and long, shiny, jet-black hair. As she leaned over him to massage his shoulders Trenet felt her hair lightly brush against his chest and he smiled to himself, knowing that the woman was doing it deliberately.

Soft oriental music played in the background, the air was scented with jasmine, and Trenet gave himself up to her sensual ministrations. He could have opted simply to have had sex with the woman, but it both entertained and aroused him to begin with a conventional massage that would only gradually develop into a full-blown sexual encounter.

It was the kind of sophisticated service available to those who could afford the fees in Brussels' exclusive Clinique Special. The Clinique, despite its medical-sounding name, was in fact an up-market brothel geared towards meeting the desires of wealthy business people and EU bureaucrats for whom cost wasn't an issue, but for whom the Clinique's policy of absolute discretion was important.

As the chief executive of a profitable arms manufacturing and exporting company, Trenet had never stinted himself in the matter of paying for erotic adventure. Whether skiing in the winter or yachting each summer, he arranged in advance for the Clinique to provide suitably exciting companions to liven up his holidays.

Although now sixty-three years of age he was lean and fit, and still had a greater libido than many men twenty years his junior. Enjoy the pleasures of life as intensely and for as long as possible, was Trenet's credo, one that he recognised as having its roots in his deprived childhood.

Born in 1940, he had grown up in an orphanage in Reims, in northern France, where the wartime austerity had continued in his case until his late teens, when he left his job in the orphanage's sheet-metal plant to serve in the army. With the other conscripts Trenet had been shipped to Algeria to fight for France in a vicious colonial conflict. Many of the troops he served with complained of the heat, the food, the pay and the danger, but Trenet had thrived in Algeria. After a lifetime of winters in an under-heated and draughty orphanage he had embraced the warmth of North Africa. He had also grown to savour the local cuisine, had happily frequented the brothels of Oran and Algiers, and adapted to army life more readily than most of his companions.

Being both tough and athletically built he had emerged as a natural leader, and by the time he had finished his tour of duty he had risen to the rank of sergeant. His superiors had suggested to him a career in the regular army, but Trenet had declined, reckoning that an orphan who had started out as a private soldier was unlikely to be viewed by conservative staff officers as a candidate to be groomed for serious advancement.

For even as a twenty-year-old Trenet had a vision of how his life should be. Never ever again was he going to be poor, or patronised, or cold, or badly dressed. He had tasted freedom in Algeria, known the pleasure of having money in his pockets, had savoured for the first time a sense of pride, generated by the respect shown to him by the men under his command.

He had also emerged unscathed but combat-hardened from a bitterly fought war, so that it had been an obvious step when he had taken up a post with the mercenary force that the breakaway Congolese state of Katanga was then raising. The money on offer was excellent and with Trenet's combat experience and leadership qualities he had immediately been commissioned as an officer.

It was while serving as a mercenary in the Congo that he had met Alain Chavant, the broken-nosed boxer who had become his senior sergeant. Chavant too had come from a poor background, and like Trenet he was determined to have a better life than the impoverished one he had left behind in Antwerp. Chavant couldn't match Trenet for either drive or intelligence, but the tough Belgian sergeant had hitched his star to Trenet's, beginning a mutually beneficial relationship that would last over forty years.

It was Chavant who had used his contacts in Antwerp to fence the diamonds that Trenet and Conn Lynch had acquired during the fall of Kaburi, Chavant who first mentioned to Trenet that Brussels would be in a considerable state of flux, with thousands of Belgian citizens returning to the motherland in the aftermath of Congolese independence. Perfect circumstances for someone who had suddenly acquired a small fortune to make a fresh start. Easy to reinvent yourself without attracting too much attention in the turmoil of countless former colonists having to carve out new lives for themselves.

And so Trenet had used his new-found funds to get into the lucrative field of arms dealing, concentrating at first on Africa, and again Chavant had turned out to have useful contacts with Belgians who had stayed on there after the Belgian withdrawal.

Trenet had sensed from the beginning however that it might be wise to keep his relationship with Chavant at arm's length, and by mutual agreement Chavant never actually worked for Trenet's company, but instead set up his own security firm, using as seed capital his share of the diamond-fencing deal. Trenet always made sure to err on the side of generosity in paying Chavant commission, be it for providing contacts for arms shipment, bribing officials, paying off customs officers, or having the necessary muscle to dissuade rivals from cutting in on the action.

As the sixties gave way to the seventies Trenet found himself in a position where he had the capital to begin manufacturing and bidding for tendering contracts in the specialised fields of armaments and security-related hardware. With Trenet's coffers continuing to swell, his company – International Weapons Supplies – became increasingly respectable, eventually gaining government contracts and exporting weapons components from a plant that employed over three hundred people. Chavant still had his uses however, enabling Trenet to maintain his role of respectable and successful industrialist while Chavant did all necessary palm-greasing. Sometimes too there were labour difficulties or issues of petty crime and all it took was a discreet word from Trenet, and Chavant saw to it that the problems were resolved by what he euphemistically called his "security consultants".

It had all gone better than either of them could have dreamt when they had sweated together in Katanga, yet now Trenet faced a business problem that even Chavant couldn't help him to resolve.

In the early nineties he had invested heavily in research and development on a range of surveillance equipment, and some of the items that had emerged from his laboratory had bordered on state-of-the-art. To further develop and to market the products properly required huge financial backing however, and despite some misgivings Trenet had taken a chance and raised the capital by floating the company on the stock market. It had been a successful move with the new products ultimately proving lucrative, and by retaining a large shareholding Trenet had continued to run the company as he saw fit. Then, gradually but inexorably, the market had gone into a slump and the company shares dropped in value. International Weapons Supplies – or IWS as it was commonly called – was still a successful company, but the drop in share price left the operation open to a takeover bid.

Trenet knew that business was simply business and that he shouldn't take it personally, yet his alpha-male instincts were aroused and he railed against the idea of losing control of the company he had built from nothing. He had used his personal finances to buy up shares to such an extent that he was now in debt to a number of banks. It had been a high-risk strategy, and at times Trenet regretted the stubborn pride that had prevented him from settling for the sensible option of remaining a wealthy man whilst relinquishing control of IWS.

The situation could still be turned around, he knew – if it couldn't the banks would have moved in on him before now – but to boost profits and get the share-price up in the short-to-medium term he badly needed a large NATO contract for side-arm components for which he had tendered. And for the moment that was in the lap of the gods . . .

Right now however he breathed in the heady scent of jasmine and gave himself up to the pleasures of the Clinique Special. It was doubly important, now that his finances were in jeopardy, not to appear in any way financially vulnerable and so he maintained his luxurious lifestyle, of which visits to the Clinique were an important part.

The Chinese masseuse was good, he decided, relaxing him yet tantalising him to just the right degree. He felt her fingers softly kneading the muscles on his thighs, then once again her long black hair lightly brushed his chest as she leaned over him. He felt a stab of desire, but resisted the temptation to reach out for her. Better to remain passive for now, he thought, and to relish each incremental heightening of pleasure at whatever pace the woman imposed on him.

Trenet breathed out deeply, savouring his heightened sense of anticipation, then the soft sound of the oriental music was disturbed by the ringing of a mobile phone. Trenet saw the flash of irritation on the face of the masseuse as he suddenly sat up, and he made a mental note of it. *Not for hirelings to make their feelings known to the clients*, he thought. He would mention it later to the manager of the Clinique, but for now his mind was concentrated on the call and what it might mean.

Normally he disliked mobile phones and wouldn't have allowed himself to be interrupted while taking his pleasure, but today was different. Alain Chavant was meeting someone who could have an influence on the awarding of the NATO contract that IWS so badly needed. Trenet sat on the edge of the massage table, saw from the caller ID that it was indeed Chavant, and answered the phone. "Well?"

Chavant followed Trenet's lead by using no names or greetings and by keeping the conversation oblique. "I met him as planned. He seems well disposed towards us."

"How well?"

"Not as well as if we paid him a consultancy fee . . ."

"How much?" asked Trenet.

"A hundred thousand euro was mentioned."

"What would he offer for that?"

"His enthusiastic support."

"That guarantees nothing."

"In fairness he pointed that out," said Chavant. "He says he can't give a guarantee, too many others have an input. Having said that, his support might just tip the balance."

Trenet considered a moment, then made a decision.

"Offer him twenty now, the balance if he succeeds."

"It's – it's a good bit less than he's asked for," said Chavant.

"It's an opening bid. Secure the best deal you can, rising if need be to forty now, and another full hundred if he delivers. That way he'd end up with forty per cent more than he asked for."

"OK."

"That's the ceiling, understand? Try to do better than that. Try hard, but make sure you hook him."

"I'll do my best."

"Do that. I'm counting on you."

"Right."

Trenet hung up and switched off the phone, aware that the bribe was hard cash he could ill afford to lose, yet also knowing that it was money he couldn't afford *not* to spend. He got back onto the table, beckoned to the Chinese masseuse, and tried to put his business worries on hold. The woman looked at him boldly and approached with a professionally lascivious smile, but Trenet knew that the spark was gone from the encounter now and even as she began to stroke him again his mind was grappling with how to keep control of IWS.

Steve Johnson looked askance at a large canvas on which the painter had etched one tiny purple squiggle. Steve smiled wryly, reminded of John Ciardi's famous remark that modern art was what happens when painters stop looking at women and persuade themselves that they have a better idea. He moved on, deciding that he would view the rest of the exhibits in this part of the gallery, then head back to the hotel to have a light lunch.

With time on his hands before his evening meeting with Mac and Laura Kennedy, he had decided to visit the Municipal Gallery, whose classical paintings had greatly appealed to him. Now however he was wandering around one of the gallery's special exhibitions and he found the art on view here less to his taste. He strolled on, his mind going back to his earlier meeting with the

Clarion's editor. Mac had told him the background to the Conn Lynch story, and Steve was curious to see how a journalist with Laura Kennedy's track record would approach such an assignment. On the face of it, the lead had seemed pretty limited, yet Steve had read the book she had written after breaking the story of the Harrogate assassination bid, and he felt that Mac had been astute in assigning someone with her investigative instincts to a story that might unearth a murder.

Despite his eagerness to meet her, however, he had some reservations. In asking Mac to allow him to observe a story being pursued he hadn't expected to be allocated something with such strongly criminal potential. In reality he knew that he hadn't properly thought matters through, but without having analysed it he had expected perhaps to be assigned to a political story, a major arts feature, maybe something with an American or international element. Instead he had been given a project that involved exploring the possibility of a serious crime. It shouldn't have come as a surprise – a large part of any newspaper's reportage would naturally concern crimes of one sort or another – yet Steve hadn't prepared himself for it.

Although Dr Glasser had agreed with the decision to stop the psychoanalysis, Steve knew that he still had an issue with crime and criminals. Even now he still had nightmares about his kidnappers. They had chained him to a wall, threatened to cut off his little finger for starters if their ransom demands weren't met, and generally broken his spirit in the two weeks in which he had been kept captive. Steve knew that normally two weeks was a short time, yet his captivity had seemed unending, with no certainty available to him, either in terms of how long he would be held, or – more disturbingly – whether he would be released alive. He remembered the terror he had known, the self-loathing he had felt for trying to strike up a relationship with the least aggressive of his captors, the searing but sublimated anger and frustration he had felt at being helpless and knowing he would live or die at the whim of a band of vicious criminals.

Still, maybe now he could strike a small but symbolic blow against crime in general if he helped Laura Kennedy solve her murder mystery. Assuming of course that there had actually been a murder, and the story wouldn't turn out to be a wild-goose chase prompted by the ramblings of a dying man.

Steve reached the end of the modernist display, and he paused, then made his mind up. However feeble an anti-crime gesture it might be, however unlinked to the criminals who had kidnapped him in New York, he would make a point of enthusiastically supporting Laura Kennedy in solving this crime. And if she didn't want his support? If, despite Mac's assurances, she resented his accompanying her? Well, he couldn't force himself on her – all he could do would be to try to persuade her that he wouldn't be a nuisance. Either way though, he would know soon enough.

He walked to the exit door and stepped out of the gallery and into bright sunlight. The clear blue sky and warm May sunshine lifted his spirits and he started back towards his hotel, pleased with how his morning had worked out and looking forward to meeting Mac and Laura Kennedy that evening.

"OK, kid, you've kept us on tenterhooks long enough – what gives with this story?"

Laura laughed, aware that her editor had been champing at the bit to question her, but out of politeness had forced himself to wait until their waiter had taken away the starters.

They were seated in the plush surroundings of Cannerys restaurant, an expense-account establishment off Saint Stephen's Green that Mac had clearly chosen for the benefit of Steve Johnson. The American was smartly dressed in a navy blazer and cream slacks, and Laura thought that he appeared younger and more relaxed-looking than in the newspaper pictures she had seen at the time of his kidnapping.

The conversation so far had been easy and free-flowing, with no-one bringing up the reason for their meeting during the drinks and starters. To Laura's relief, Johnson had been neither the sort of brash young media mogul she disliked, nor had he come across as the somewhat traumatised kidnap victim that Mac had hinted at. In fact she had found the New Yorker to be quite witty, with a nice line in deprecating humour. Which didn't mean that it mightn't still be pretty tiresome, she knew, to have him shadowing her every move as she pursued the Conn Lynch story. Still, it could have been a lot worse, and, from the softly-softly approach that the American had so far adopted, Laura suspected that he was aware enough to realise that perhaps he had been foisted on her by Mac.

Now, however, she faced her editor across the table and repeated his query. "So what gives on the story? Good question . . ."

"Tell me you've some good answers, kid. This place costs a packet."

Laura grinned, pleased to note that Mac's good-humoured bluntness hadn't been inhibited unduly by his role as host to Steve Johnson.

"I've lots of answers, Mac. Whether they'll help solve this mystery – who can say?"

"What have you discovered so far?"

"Quite a bit. My family links really helped."

"You've got family in Clare?" asked Steve.

"Had. My aunt died a couple of years ago, but she'd lived there all her life, knew everything that happened in a radius of fifty miles. I used to go down most summers, so there was a network of contacts I could tap into."

"And what did you find on Conn Lynch?" asked Mac.

"Rags to riches story. Started out without a brass farthing, ended a up a multi-millionaire. Born just outside Ballyvaughan in 1942, died a couple of weeks ago, aged sixty-one."

"Siblings?" asked Mac.

"Two sisters and a brother. Conn was the youngest."

"Were they a local family?"

Laura shook her head at the editor. "No, the father was originally a labourer from Donegal. Met the mother when she was a chambermaid in a hotel in Ennis. They married, rented a small cottage, had four kids before he died young."

"Are any of them still down there?" asked Steve.

"No, they all emigrated to the States donkey's years ago."

"Donkey's years?" queried Steve.

"Back in the late fifties the two sisters, Bridget and Maureen, went to Connecticut. A few years later they were joined by Shay, the older brother, and Mrs Lynch and Conn."

"How many of them are still alive?" asked Mac.

"The two sisters are. Shay died back in sixty-eight."

Immediately Mac's eyebrows went up. "Yeah? Anything suspicious?"

"Nothing linked to Conn. Killed in Vietnam. Joined the Marines and died at Hue during the Tet Offensive." Laura sipped her wine, then continued. "Mrs Lynch died in 1988 in Connecticut."

Again Mac looked at her with interest but Laura shook her head. "Died in hospital of pneumonia, no question of foul play. Conn had her brought home to Ireland – she's buried in Bishopsquarter."

"Bishopsquarter?"

"Cemetery near Ballyvaughan," explained Laura, "where Lynch himself is buried."

Mac nodded as though satisfied. "So when did Lynch return to Ireland from the States?"

"Nineteen sixty-four. Then in nineteen sixty-six he met an American tourist called Gail Rudich. Whirlwind romance, married her three months later."

"In Ireland?" asked Steve.

"No, in Bangor, Maine – her home town. She came to Ireland to live, but things didn't work out."

"*Marry in haste and repent at leisure,*" said Mac with a grin.

"Not that leisurely. A year later she was back in the States and filing for a divorce."

"Wow!"

"Can I ask a question?" said Steve.

"Sure," answered Laura.

"Do you know if his wife was wealthier or poorer than Lynch?"

"Wealthier. Seems she never sought any kind of alimony – and there were no kids. No motive for Lynch to kill her."

"Is she still alive?" asked Mac.

"Yes. She must have been notified of the death by Lynch's relations in Connecticut."

Mac looked at Laura with interest. "How do you know that?"

"On the day of the funeral a bouquet arrived from Bangor, Maine. It's the kind of thing that's noticed in a small community."

"I'll bet," said Mac wryly.

"So with no obvious family leads to follow up – we've the entire span of Lynch's life as a possible timeframe for this crime," said Laura.

"Well, maybe not his entire life," suggested Mac. "Not if he said the murder happened 'when he was younger', as quoted."

"Technically speaking he was younger last year, Mac. Or two years ago, or five years ago. Though I take your point, it was probably some time back. Whatever way you look at it though, there's a huge range of times and places to consider. The trick is narrowing it down to a much smaller range – the ones that seem likeliest to yield something."

"Supposing we were to start with place then?" suggested Steve. "How about checking on unsolved murders in Lynch's neighbourhood over the period he's lived there? Or for that matter, in his neighbourhood when he was living in Connecticut?"

Laura looked at him, encouraged by the example of logical thinking. She had already decided that he didn't fit the category of the wealthy boss's idiot son who had to be indulged, but she had feared that he might be the type of man who traded on good looks and an easy charm rather than mucking in and tackling whatever work had to be done. Now, it seemed he was willing to do some thinking. "Both are in hand," she replied.

"Yeah?" queried Mac.

"I'm checking records here and I've already contacted a research agency I've used before in New York. They're checking the records for the area of Connecticut where the Lynches had their family business."

"On the ball as ever," said Mac with a smile.

"They started a family business when they got to the States?" asked Steve.

Laura nodded. "They'd been dirt poor here in Ireland. The mother used to take in washing after her husband died. So when they got to America they wouldn't have been lacking in energy and ambition. It seems Shay had started up a successful lumber company soon after he got there in the late fifties."

Steve looked thoughtful, and Laura saw him biting his lip.

"What is it?" she asked.

"Nothing much. Just sounds like the brother would have been a bit old for the draft by the late sixties."

This guy was sharper than the Ivy League college boy image suggested. "Fair point," she said. "Thing is, he wasn't drafted. He volunteered. An old guy I inter-

88

viewed in Ballyvaughan told me. He'd been saddened when he'd heard of his death, but proud that he'd volunteered to defend his adopted country."

"Defending his adopted country – in Indo-China?" said Steve.

Again Laura was a little surprised at the political awareness underpinning Steve's comment. "'Defending America' was how the old man in Clare saw it. What the guy's actual motives were we'll never know."

"Did Conn Lynch ever remarry?" asked Mac.

"No," answered Laura. "Though it seems he didn't want for female company."

"Yeah?"

"Bit of a ladies' man, apparently, though he didn't flaunt the fact."

Steve raised an eyebrow. "Cuckolded husband maybe? Jealous boyfriend?"

"It's possible," conceded Laura, "but there'd almost certainly be whispers if there'd been a *crime passionel* – and I got no hint whatsoever."

"What about business rivalry?" suggested Mac. "Presumably over the years he must have made some enemies?"

"I wondered about that too," answered Laura. "It seems he was pretty popular though. Good employer, paid well. I couldn't discover any major feuds with other companies, certainly nothing that ended in the death or disappearance of a rival."

Mac looked thoughtful. "This could be a hard nut to crack. Maybe even uncrackable."

"Possibly," said Laura, "but don't despair yet – I've kept the best wine till last . . . "

"Well, don't keep us hanging!" said Mac.

"It mightn't yield anything, so don't get your hopes up too high. But I found one area of Lynch's life that might be promising."

"Yeah?" said Steve encouragingly.

"In 1958, when he would have been sixteen, Conn Lynch joined the Irish army. Seems he rarely talked about it, most people never even knew he was once a soldier." Laura saw that she had Mac's full attention.

"How long did he serve?" asked the editor.

"Three years."

"Three years in a macho organisation," said Steve musingly. "With scope for bullying, being bullied, making enemies . . ."

"That's still a long way from actually murdering someone," countered Mac.

"Granted," said Steve, "but it is an environment where arms are available. Sounds to me like the most promising area so far."

"There's more," said Laura. "In his final year in the army, his unit saw actual combat."

"Where?" asked Mac.

"In the Congo."

"How come the Irish army were in the Congo?" asked

the American.

"UN duty," answered Mac. "They went out on a peace-keeping mission. Took a fair number of casualties too."

"Of course all of this might have absolutely nothing to do with his death-bed confession," said Laura. "Even if he saw action and killed people – lots of soldiers do that without feeling they've committed murder."

"Even so," said Steve.

"I know," agreed Laura. "I got that tiny little tingle in the spine when I found out about it."

"So what's your next move?" asked Mac.

"We see if anything shows up by way of interesting murders. Either in Connecticut or over in the West. Meanwhile the army connection is our best lead – I want to follow that up tomorrow."

"How will you do that?" asked Steve.

"I found out there's a society for former soldiers who served with the UN. They've a place here in Dublin – sort of a museum at the back of Arbour Hill cemetery."

"I never knew that," said Mac.

Laura smiled. "Amazing what you can discover when you start asking questions." She turned back to the American. "So, I was planning to call on them in the morning. If you'd like to come along . . . ?"

"Sure," he said. "I'd love to."

The summer evening sky had turned a deep blue, and Steve could see the first stars through the large bay windows that allowed the customers a view of Cannerys' fastidiously landscaped back garden. The waiter was taking the dessert order, having just delivered a detailed spiel on the range of desserts available. It was a routine Steve was used to from the States, but as usual he had found it slightly irritating. Why not simply list the choices on a menu, he thought, instead of asking diners to memorise everything? Still, he was a guest tonight, and he had responded politely, not wanting to appear curmudgeonly in front of Mac, and, if he were honest, particularly in front of Laura Kennedy.

Even allowing for the flattering ambience of candle-light she was a good-looking woman with thick, curly brown hair, a slim figure and large blue eyes that flashed when she spoke animatedly.

Steady, boy, he thought, this isn't a date, it's a working dinner. Not that he had actually been doing much dating recently. There were plenty of appealing women in New York, and pretty frequently he picked up the signals from women who found him attractive. Despite occasionally making the effort, however, his heart hadn't been in it recently. He had discussed it with Dr Glasser, who had pointed out that in the aftermath of such a traumatic event as a kidnapping it could be difficult to trust other people. And dating could lead to emotional involvement, which called for trust, which, understandably, he was nervous about giving.

Yet here he was, consciously wanting to make a good impression on Laura Kennedy. He had seen the approval in her expression when they had chatted earlier about travel and he had mentioned that he had worked with the Peace Corps in Senegal. One part of him had felt almost guilty about his time in Africa gaining him brownie points, yet he couldn't but be pleased at Laura seeing that he wasn't simply another spoiled rich kid who lived a life of greedy self-obsession.

Even as he found her attractive, the reflective part of his mind realised that there was an interesting dynamic at play here tonight. In reality Media Services International held all the cards as the new owners of the *Clarion*. Normally in such circumstance those in Mac's position – and to a lesser extent Laura's – would be the ones eager to impress. Yet both these people seemed to have such innate – what was it? Self-belief? Integrity? *Presence*, it would probably have been called, had they been actors. Whatever it was, it was appealing, and Steve found that he wanted to impress them, to let them see that although he was a representative of the new owners, it didn't make him a crass profiteer.

Laura now ordered the mixed fruit crumble with ice cream from the waiter, and Steve found himself noting that she wasn't like some of the women he had dined with in New York, who took the good out of a meal by calorie-counting and abstaining from anything remotely unhealthy.

Mac ordered the even more cholesterol-raising Death by Chocolate, then the waiter left and Mac sat forward, his elbows on the table as he looked at Laura. "So – what does your gut tell you?"

Just for one, surreal moment, Steve thought that the editor was talking about the meal they had eaten, then he realised that the expression was one the journalist had heard from Mac before, as Laura answered reflectively, "There's a story here, is my gut feeling. Though what was overheard could still be the ramblings of a heavily medicated, dying man."

"But your sixth sense tells you it's not?" persisted Mac.

Laura looked across the table and smiled. "You must think we're very superstitious, Steve."

"I think . . . I think instinct shouldn't be underestimated."

"Very diplomatic," answered Laura, but the slightly mocking tone was counterbalanced by the warmth of her smile.

"Besides, Laura's gut feelings have a habit of turning out to be right."

"Here, don't set me up for a fall, Mac. What I was going to add was that even if there is a big story hidden away in Conn Lynch's past, it may be pretty hard to unearth. It may even prove impossible."

"You know what they say, Laura – 'The difficult we do immediately, the impossible takes a little longer'.

Right, Steve?"

"I don't know. Is that editorial policy or something you read in a fortune cookie?"

It was something of a smart-alec retort and no sooner had Steve said it than he hoped he hadn't been too sharp with his reply.

"Touché!" said Laura with a grin, and Mac smiled also, a smile that Steve could see was genuine.

"I read it in a fortune cookie – then made it editorial policy!" Mac responded.

"Sounds reasonable," said Steve with a straight face. The others grinned, and when Steve caught them exchanging a look he sensed that he had somehow passed an unspoken test.

"Joking aside, lads, there is a serious point to be made," said Laura. "We could invest a lot of time and effort on this kind of story and eventually hit a brick wall. Just so you're not disappointed if that happens, Steve."

"I hear what you're saying."

"It's just that when there's a really juicy story buried away – and this could be one of them – sometimes the people who've done the burying win out."

"But only after we've given it a hell of a good try," said Mac.

"Absolutely," agreed Laura. "That's a given."

Steve looked at her as she said it, and even the soft glow of the candlelight couldn't mask the determined set of her jaw. Somehow he knew at that moment that pursuing this story was going to be eventful. "I think we all know where we stand now," he said. "So let's give it our best shot." He raised his glass in a toast. "To the *Clarion* – long may it prosper! And to the mystery of Conn Lynch – may we find out the truth of what happened."

"Well spoken," said Mac, raising his glass.

"I'll drink to that," agreed Laura.

They all clinked glasses, and Steve smiled, pleased that a potentially awkward evening had gone well, and looking forward to the case with more excitement than he had felt in a long time.

CHAPTER 3

"Conn Lynch? No, never met him, never heard of him."

Laura's heart sank a little, even though she knew that the likelihood of Lynch having met the man she was questioning was slim. She was in the Irish United Nations Veterans' Centre at the back of Arbour Hill cemetery where she had been subtly quizzing the curator, a heavily built man in his sixties who still carried himself with a military bearing.

"Thousands of soldiers served in the Congo," continued the man. "You wouldn't know the half of them."

"Sure."

"What's your interest in this Lynch fella?"

"Oh, he was a distant uncle. Just wondered if you'd

97

ever met him."

"No, did two tours in the Congo – but I never ran into your uncle."

Laura saw Steve suppressing a smile and she winked at him. She had told Steve before going in that it might be better not to reveal that they were from a newspaper – some people tended to clam up in front of the press, however innocuous the enquiries. Now that she had met the curator she reckoned that she had chosen the correct strategy, notwithstanding a slight sense of guilt she felt at deceiving the man who had willingly shown them around the premises. It wasn't a museum, as such, more a repository of photos and souvenirs from the various countries where Irish troops had served with the UN. Laura had discovered at the outset that the curator was a retired soldier himself, and she had sensed that he might well close ranks with a former comrade if he felt that a nosy reporter was here to rake up something from the past.

Now she listened as Steve asked the man about a Congolese spear mounted on the wall. He was good with people, she realised, which might come in handy as they went about the difficult task of unearthing Lynch's secret past. At a minimum he would be an inoffensive companion, and provided his accompanying her didn't become claustrophobic, it might actually be fun to have him along.

Certainly he had turned out to be good company at

last night's dinner in Cannerys, and he had shown both cop-on and consideration by courteously refusing Laura's offer to collect him from the Westbury Hotel this morning. The traffic, he knew, would be bumper to bumper coming into the city centre, and he had said that it would be much more sensible for him to walk from his hotel to the Veterans' Centre and save Laura from becoming unnecessarily snarled up in traffic.

The previous evening too she had sensed that in spite of her instructions to the contrary, Mac had tried to engage in a tiny bit of subtle matchmaking. When the evening had ended the editor had contrived to make his farewells and to leave Laura and Steve alone in the afterglow of a pleasant night out. Just for a moment it had almost felt like being on a date, and Laura had suspected that perhaps Steve too had been conscious of it before she had politely shaken hands and said her goodbyes.

The truth was that in other circumstance he would be a rather attractive date. Certainly he was good-looking, he had a strong sense of humour, and he was a good conversationalist who had done some interesting things with his life. In reality though he was one of the new owners of the *Clarion*, and Laura felt that it wasn't a good idea to mix business and pleasure. More fundamentally she knew that apart from all of that, she still wasn't ready for dating again. Even though it was over a year since Declan's untimely death, she still shied away from sexual overtures, however mild. Invariably she ended up comparing the men involved with Declan – a practice that she realised was unfair, but from which she simply couldn't refrain.

Now however it was time to banish such thoughts. There were other lines of enquiry to be followed today and she had probably got all that she was going to get here. The one good thing stemming from this visit was that on arriving early at the Veteran's Centre she had seen a memorial to all the Irish troops who had died on UN service. While awaiting Steve she had listed the details of those who had died in the Congo in the early sixties, reasoning that it might prove a useful reference point.

"One last question," she said now, turning to the curator.

"Yes?"

"I read somewhere about the mercenaries in the Congo. Did the Irish troops have much dealings with them?"

"We were carrying out the UN mandate, the mercenaries were working for the Katangan government. We tried not to cross swords with them any more than we had to."

"But sometimes there were clashes?"

"Sometimes."

"Right. And what about drinking, socialising with them, was there ever any of that?"

"Occasionally. But mostly we kept to ourselves and so did they. Why do you ask?"

"Idle curiosity," answered Laura with a smile. "But listen, we've taken up enough of your time." She offered the man her hand. "Thank you very much for showing us around."

"You're welcome."

"All right, Steve?"

"Yeah."

"OK – let's go then."

Steve watched in surprise as four elderly men played a game of boules on a parcel of land adjacent to the Veterans' Centre. It wasn't a game he would have expected to see being played in the city of Dublin, yet here they were, carefully throwing their boules in the warm May sunshine. He was about to comment to Laura, but she was clearly still in investigative mode and as soon as she stepped out the gate from the Veterans' Centre she looked at him quizzically.

"Well?"

"Interesting old guy," he answered, "pity he never met Lynch in the Congo."

"Yeah. I'm disappointed, to tell you the truth."

"Really?"

Laura grimaced. "It's just that when I discovered Lynch's unit had seen combat I thought 'This could be really interesting'."

"Well, it still could, couldn't it?"

"Only if we can get some detail on it. I thought there'd be far more stuff in the Veterans' Centre. Books about the Congo conflict – that sort of thing."

"There'd probably be books in the public libraries," said Steve.

"I know," said Laura.

Immediately Steve felt that perhaps he had blundered.

"I'm sorry. This is your area of expertise – don't mean to be teaching my granny to suck eggs."

Laura smiled. "That's OK. And look, if we're going to be working together, say whatever comes into your head. I'm not going to take offence if it's something I'd do anyway. Who knows – you might come up with something that wouldn't strike me. So any ideas, however off the wall, let's have them, yeah?"

"Fine."

"And yes, we can check stuff in public libraries – it's just that that kind of thing can be very time-consuming."

"Right."

"I really know my way around the cuttings library in the *Clarion* though. If I plough through that, I might come up with something on Lynch's unit and their time in the Congo."

"Has the *Clarion* a good cuttings library?"

"Yes, pretty good. But we can't afford to spend all our time chasing up the army lead. I also need to follow my enquiries about murders in the Clare/Galway region. Plus later on, when the time difference allows, I want to contact the States, talk to the people I have researching for me there."

"What about the internet? Could be stuff there about the Irish army in the Congo."

Laura nodded. "Could be. I had a bit of a trawl last night when I got home from the restaurant."

Beavering away even after a night out – no wonder Mac rates this woman, thought Steve.

"Really?"

"There wasn't much I could unearth. Though I have to admit I'm not a computer whiz – the internet wouldn't be my strong point."

Steve raised his hand playfully. "Confession time."

"Yeah?"

"Card-carrying computer nerd," he said, and Laura smiled briefly. "If you like I could do some internet checking while you're working your way through the cuttings library."

"Sounds good."

"Now that we have a list of soldiers from Lynch's unit who were killed in the Congo, I could copy it and run the names through a search engine."

"That's a really good idea." said Laura.

"Thanks." Although he tried not to show it too clearly, Steve was pleased, feeling that another small step had been made in moving away from simply being a politely tolerated companion. "Why don't I head back to the hotel?" he suggested. "There's a high-speed ISDN line in my room. I can get cracking with that while you go through the cuttings library. Then maybe after lunch we could meet up, pool any information we find, and chase whatever non-army leads you decide to follow?"

Laura looked at him seriously, and Steve hoped he hadn't sounded too prescriptive.

"You know something, Steve?"

"Yeah?"

"I should have hired you years ago."

Steve laughed. "You couldn't afford me."

"What the hell. I'm seeking a needle in a haystack here – every helping hand is welcome."

"Now I don't know whether I'm being complimented or insulted . . ."

"Complimented."

"Don't tell me – I'll *know* when you're insulting me?"

"Now you have it. So, will we say three o'clock in the *Clarion*?"

Steve was nearly going to say 'It's a date', instead he stopped himself and nodded agreement. "Yeah, three sounds fine . . ."

Daniel Trenet found it hard to mask his impatience as he sat at the head of the boardroom table. The future viability of International Weapons Systems depended on the drop in share price being reversed, and winning the

NATO contract that they were pursuing was critically important in achieving that goal, yet right now there were board members who seemed more concerned about a staff-attitude survey that indicated a drop in job satisfaction among the three hundred workers in the IWS plant.

"Gentlemen!" cried Trenet, his patience snapping. "Can we have done?"

The afternoon sunlight shone in through the tinted glass windows of the top-storey boardroom and Trenet looked down the long teak table at the other members of the board. As chief executive and principal shareholder he held unquestioning sway, although he knew that some of the board members would not mourn his departure if the share price remained depressed and the banks called in his loans.

It was a daunting prospect, and even if such a move didn't actually make him a bankrupt, it would certainly cause a catastrophic dent in his personal finances. Trenet had become used to the comfort and prestige that went with wealth and he was determined to do anything necessary to ensure its retention. Even as it was he didn't like to think too much about old age, but the idea of possibly growing infirm while simultaneously having to cope with sudden poverty was unbearable. Yet here was the board discussing the quality of food in the staff canteen while he was trying to focus on ensuring the long-term viability of the company.

"We've already spent too long on this staff-attitude survey. It's a minor issue."

"It is on the agenda," said Hans Romer.

Trenet felt a stab of irritation, but consciously took a moment before responding. Romer was a cadaverous-looking Dutchman with a wearying regard for correct procedure. He was also the biggest shareholder on the board after Trenet himself. Now Trenet looked Romer in the eye and replied in a controlled tone with a strong underlay of sarcasm. "I'm fully aware that it's on the agenda, Hans. And I think we all realise the crucial importance of not allowing a drop in quality in the wine served in the staff restaurant. It's just that we won't *need* a staff restaurant if we don't have any staff. And we *won't* need any staff if we don't get the order book out of the doldrums."

"Granted," said Romer in his irritatingly precise manner, "but the steps to be taken regarding generating orders are further down the agenda. And we've always prided ourselves on retaining a well-motivated workforce – so the staff-attitude survey was not an insignificant agenda item."

"Which we've now dealt with in more than sufficient detail. I'm taking the next item."

There was a soft tap on the boardroom door, then it opened and Trenet's secretary, Marianne Valerre, came in. She was a plain-faced woman in her late fifties who was somewhat in awe of her boss and she looked decidedly uncomfortable at having to enter during a board meeting.

"Marianne, what is it?" asked Trenet.

"I'm sorry to disturb you, sir, but there's a call for you."

"For goodness sake, I told you to hold all calls!"

"I know, sir, but it was Monsieur Chavant. He was insistent, sir. Said it was a call you'd want to take."

Trenet felt a quickening in his pulses. Perhaps there had been a development with the person they were bribing regarding the NATO contract. "Very well," said Trenet. He turned back to the other board members. "Please excuse me, I'll be back in two minutes." Trenet rose from the head of the table and quickly walked from the boardroom down the corridor to his own suite of rooms. He entered his private office, closed the panelled wooden door and took his place behind a large desk on which there was a state-of-the-art communications console. Trenet pressed a button that would electronically scramble the call, then he lifted the receiver.

"Hello?"

"There's been a development."

Trenet could hear the excitement in Chavant's voice and he felt impatient to hear the other man's news. "What is it?"

"I've just had a call . . ."

"From whom?!" snapped Trenet, irked by Chavant keeping him in suspense.

"From Trojan."

Trenet felt his blood run cold. His gaze out the window took in the landscaped parkland that surrounded the IWS manufacturing plant four floors below him, but his mind took in nothing of the view.

"Daniel?"

Sweet Jesus, he thought, not this, not *now*.

"Daniel?"

"Yes."

"We need to meet."

Trenet's head was still reeling. It must have been, what – fifteen, sixteen years since his warning system had last been activated? And now, just when he was desperately trying to keep control of IWS, the past was back to haunt him again.

"I can come out to the plant if you like."

"No," said Trenet. "My house."

"When?"

"As soon as I finish the board meeting. Say half four."

"OK, see you then."

"Right," said Trenet, then he breathed out slowly and put down the phone.

Laura rubbed her eyes and turned away from the computer screen. She was sitting in a small, dusty office that adjoined the *Clarion's* cuttings library and she stretched now, easing the ache in her shoulders where she had been hunched forward looking at the screen. Some of the *Clarion's* back catalogue had been transferred to computer disk, and some still consisted of original newspapers, chronologically filed and cross-referenced. Either way, trawling through it was tiring work, and she had been at it now for almost four hours with just a short break for a snatched sandwich and cup of coffee.

She had started on the coverage of the Irish Army's mission to the Congo and had tried to zero in on articles relating specifically to Lynch's unit. It had been a difficult task, made all the harder by the fact that the Congo episode had been Ireland's first UN mission, thus making it a novelty on which the newspapers had feasted. There were innumerable articles about the diet the troops would have, their spiritual welfare, the overwhelming equatorial heat and, inevitably, on how the first batch of troops had been equipped with woollen uniforms, notwithstanding their destination. There were articles on the political background, the secession of Katanga, and the death of President Lumumba in addition to a huge number of pieces on the Irish army's military activities. There were touching articles showing the mourning relatives of the Irish troops who had been killed in action, but despite ploughing through these and other articles on the fighting itself, Laura had found no reference to Conn Lynch in any of the pieces that described the action his unit saw. Eventually she had made notes on the dates and times of the relevant fighting, with a view to further library research, then switched her attention to coverage of murders in the Clare/Galway region over the last forty years.

Fortunately most of the back editions of the last twenty years had been transferred to computer disk and she was able to focus on what she wanted more rapidly here. She was surprised at the number of murders there had been over the years, yet once again she drew a blank in terms of anything that suggested any kind of link to Conn Lynch.

Taken in conjunction with the questioning that she had done on the ground in Clare, it was evident that Conn Lynch had led a life of privilege and comfort since returning to Ireland in 1964, but nothing that was known to his workers or neighbours ever seemed to place him on the wrong side of the law, much less involve him in murder. Likewise her research on his divorce suggested a clean break, which he had swiftly put behind him. Certainly it had been noteworthy for a rural Irish person to be divorced back in the sixties – which suggested a decisive and independent streak. But while this might possibly denote the sort of focussed personality capable of murder, she was no nearer to finding anything remotely suspicious in Lynch's background. Nothing odd about the will either – it seemed that he had left a sizeable donation to a charity that specialised in the welfare of orphans, then left the bulk of his estate to his next-of-kin in the States.

Laura pushed her chair away from the desk and leaned

back, her head spinning from all the articles she had tried to assimilate. The cutting library was in the basement of the *Clarion* and the place felt airless and claustrophobic, but Laura was aware that difficult cases such as this one often turned on small, seemingly insignificant leads, and she knew she had to shake off her lethargy and return to her notes.

Just then her mobile rang, and she answered it immediately. "Hello?"

"Hi, Laura. Janet here."

She recognised the softly spoken voice of Janet Taylor, the New-York-based researcher that she had engaged. Behind the gentle middle-aged voice and the pleasant demeanour, she knew from previous experience that Janet had a sharp intellect, an investigative turn of mind and the sort of professional research expertise that relished a challenge. All of which would be required, Laura knew, if they were to get anywhere with Conn Lynch.

"Hi, Janet, any progress?"

"Yes, I'm calling from Dulwich."

Laura felt herself perking up. Dulwich was the small town in Connecticut where Shay Lynch had set up his sawmill, and where Conn Lynch had worked with him for the three years that he had spent in the States in the early sixties. "Well?" she asked.

"Small place. They've only had three homicides in the last fifty years."

111

"Any of them during Lynch's time there?"

"One. The other two were in 1954 and 1989 – long before and long after his time here."

"And the other one?"

"Don't think it's what you want. Elderly guy shot his wife in 1963."

"Yeah?"

"He was seventy-eight. She was seventy-five."

"Right. So Conn Lynch, being twenty-one, was hardly having an affair with her?"

"Hardly," said Janet. "I made some discreet enquiries, and it seems the husband had an alcohol problem."

"And no link to the Lynches – the husband or wife hadn't worked at the sawmill or anything.?"

"No, the couple had a small farm on the outskirts of Dulwich, worked it all their lives."

"Right."

"I'll spread the net now, like you said. Check out homicides in the wider region during the time Conn Lynch lived here."

"Thanks, Janet. Any feedback on what the Lynches were like, whether they were popular in the town?"

"I just got here yesterday, so I'm only starting the local research."

"Fair enough."

"So far though anything I've heard is positive. The two surviving sisters and their families live in the area, so I'll get researching."

112

"Thanks, Janet. And the minute there's anything, anything at all, please give me a call."

"Drawing blanks at your end?"

"'Fraid so," answered Laura.

"Too bad. Anyhow, I'll keep you posted."

"Thanks, Janet. Bye."

"Bye."

Laura hung up, then put down the phone and sat, lost in her thoughts. She knew from another project on which she had engaged Janet that the older woman was a real asset, being a first-class researcher, but also someone who enjoyed a bit of non-academic detective work of the type that Laura had requested. Her fees were fairly stiff, but Laura knew that Mac would authorise payment by the *Clarion*, especially seeing as the new owners of the paper were represented on the story in the person of Steve Johnson.

Thinking of the American, she realised that she would be meeting him soon, and despite all her trawling through the cuttings library she hadn't much to show for her efforts. Back to the grind, she thought, then she pulled her chair close to the desk and returned to work.

Steve had to suppress a wry smile as the receptionist at the *Clarion* fussed over him. Yesterday she had been all smug condescension and "Mr McEvoy's an extremely busy man", now she was so deferential that it was almost embarrassing. Probably frightened that I've flown in to sack half the staff, he thought, as the woman gave him a sickly smile and directed him to the *Clarion's* cuttings library.

"Through the door here, Mr Johnson, down the stairs and first turn left."

"Thank you."

"You're more than welcome."

Steve followed her directions, then knocked on the cuttings-library door and entered. He saw Laura Kennedy sitting at a PC with sheets of notes and several back copies of the *Clarion* spread out before her.

She pushed her wavy brown hair from her eyes, swivelled round in her chair and smiled. "Hi."

"Hi," answered Steve, and despite the fact that this was a business meeting, he couldn't help but admire again the way Laura's eyes softened whenever she smiled. "Any progress?" he said, sitting on a chair opposite her.

"Not much. Got a call from my researcher in the States. Only one murder in Dulwich in the time that Lynch was there."

"Yeah?"

"Seventy-eight-year-old farmer killed his seventy-five-year-old wife."

"Hardly a connection to Lynch then."

"No, but Janet is working her way around Dulwich. She'll broaden the scope of her enquiries and keep us posted."

"Fair enough," said Steve. "Any luck with the

Clare/Galway stuff?"

"Nothing ringing any bells yet."

"And the Congo?"

Laura grimaced. "Loads of articles, good few references to Lynch's unit. Zilch on Lynch himself though, and nothing that – nothing that sounded dodgy. Nothing with even a hint of foul play about it."

"Right."

"When I've time I'll visit the public library – see what books they have on the conflict. Meanwhile how was your internet search?"

"A bit surprising. Not a huge amount online about the Irish in the Congo."

"No?"

"No, a fair bit less than I'd expected. I went through what there was with a fine-tooth comb. Ran the names of the guys from Lynch's unit who'd been killed – nothing. No references anywhere to Lynch, no whiff of anything that sounded irregular."

"Sounds like a dead end for now," said Laura.

"Not quite," answered Steve, unable to keep the satisfaction from his voice.

Immediately Laura picked up on his tone. "You found something?"

Steve nodded, savouring Laura's intense interest for a fraction of a second before expanding. "I was just about to give up when I had a brain wave. It was the term *Belgian Congo* that did it. I mean most people simply refer to it as the Congo, but the word *Belgian* set me thinking."

"How do you mean?"

"Well, the Belgians were a colonial power, so they wouldn't have conducted their business out there in some Congolese language."

"So?"

"So the working language would have been French. Which means that the newspapers would also have been published in French. I'm pretty fluent in it from when I worked in Senegal, so I went back online, using French language search engines this time."

"And you found something?"

"Nothing on the names of the dead guys from Lynch's unit – but then you'd hardly expect that in a Belgian-published newspaper. Loads of stuff though on other aspects of the Congo. Photographs, drawings, articles, newspaper editorials. Again though, none of it any use to us. And then . . . then I found this photograph. It was taken in Elisabethville and it showed two nuns in a Jeep waving farewell to a group of soldiers. The caption said the nuns had been rescued by a mixed force of mercenaries and Irish UN troops after the town of Kaburi was overrun."

"And Lynch was in the photo?"

Unable to resist a flourish, Steve took a sheet of paper from his pocket and handed it to Laura, who quickly unfolded it. "Downloaded from the internet and maybe

116

not a great picture to begin with – but the guy on the right looks to me like a younger version of Conn Lynch."

As part of her research Laura had unearthed a number of photographs of Lynch, and now she studied Steve's internet picture intently, then nodded excitedly. "I think you're right. It's hard to be certain, but it could well be him."

"Notice anything else?" said Steve. He knew it was childish to reveal information in a tension-building way, yet once again he couldn't resist the attraction of having Laura hanging on his every word.

"What?"

"The photograph had been used to illustrate a newspaper article," said Steve, "hence the date. When you gave me the names of the guys from Lynch's unit who were killed, you gave me the date for each death." He indicated the downloaded picture. "This photo was taken one day after the death of . . ." Steve consulted his list, "a Lieutenant Fintan Barrett."

"Right . . ."

"Assuming the guy in the photo is actually Lynch, it's the first time that we've got him at the scene of violent death. And we have the town of Kaburi being overrun – who knows what might have happened in that kind of chaos. I mean, I've heard stories about American troops out in Vietnam."

"What kind of stories?"

"Stories of grudges being settled, officers who were

117

hated being shot in the back, civilians being murdered in disputes over drugs, or women, or smuggling. In the upheaval of war, normal morality can go out the window. And if our photo guy is actually Lynch, then here we have our man in that kind of situation. There has to be at least a fair chance that if ever he was party to murder, this would be a likely time and place."

Laura nodded in agreement. "This is really good work, Steve."

"Thanks," he said, pleased by the obvious admiration in her tone, and hoping that she would be equally taken with the rest of what he had done. "I . . . eh. . . . I went a bit further actually . . ."

"Sorry, just before we get into that – did you read the actual article?"

"No, it wasn't posted online – just the photograph."

"And you weren't able to locate it with any of the search engines?"

"No. But like I said, I went a bit further."

"Yeah?"

"I contacted directory enquiries and got on to the offices of the newspaper."

"In the Congo?"

"No, it was a Belgian publication, *La Vérité*. Their offices are in Brussels. It turns out that both the photographer and the journalist who did the article and the picture are long since dead."

"Pity," said Laura.

"Well, I suppose it was over forty years ago. The good news though is that I got on to *La Vérité*'s library department. The edition of the paper containing that article is on file."

"Excellent! Can they e-mail it to us?"

"Already asked," said Steve with a grin.

"And they have?"

"'Fraid not. Their back editions from the sixties aren't on computer disk or micro-film – it's simply original copies of the paper."

"So what then? Can they photocopy the page and fax it to us for a fee?"

"Tried that. No dice, they don't do it. The man I spoke to – a Monsieur Gilbert – he sounded like an old guy. Pleasant and helpful, but he wasn't about to break the rules for us."

"We've got to see the contents of that article."

"We can," said Steve. "Or rather, you can."

"How do you mean?"

"I told him I was a researcher working for an Irish journalist who's doing a book on the Congo."

"And?"

For the first time in the conversation Steve felt a little nervous. "Tell me if I've overstepped the mark here, but I've . . . well, I've made an appointment for you. If you visit their offices on Thursday morning, he'll give you access to their library."

Laura's raised an eyebrow in surprise, and Steve sensed

that he had in fact overplayed his hand in going from observer and assistant to playmaker.

"You've made an appointment for me, in Brussels, for Thursday?"

"Well, yeah. Look, if you feel I shouldn't have –"

"What's wrong with tomorrow?" asked Laura with a grin.

"So . . . you don't mind that I went ahead?"

"Not in the least. It's the best lead we've had by a mile."

Steve felt relief that he hadn't caused offence and admiration also for Laura's innate confidence, whereby she was comfortable to take assistance from an amateur if she felt it would prove useful. "Good," he said. "Though of course it may still lead nowhere."

"Sure," replied Laura, then she flashed him a grin. "But don't say that in front of Mac, or he mightn't authorise flying to Brussels!"

"OK."

"Besides, we'll still keep all the other enquiries going."

"Right."

"And joking aside, why lose a day? Could we not go to Brussels tomorrow?"

"I asked. But the librarian is going to a funeral and he said Thursday was the earliest that was convenient. I didn't want to push it – we might be glad of his co-operation."

"Right," said Laura.

"So will I ring him back and confirm the appointment?

"Absolutely. And Steve?"

"Yes?"

"Nice one."

Daniel Trenet sat in the conservatory at the back of his home, warmed by the late afternoon sunlight that reflected on the waters of the ornamental pond that was the centrepiece of his lawn. The house itself was an imposing redbrick mansion in Tervuren, an up-market suburb of Brussels, and Trenet had furnished it lavishly but in good taste. Even the conservatory in which he now sat with a glass of whiskey in hand had been fitted out by a landscape gardener, and its collection of African plants and shrubs was one of the few sentimental gestures that Trenet allowed himself by way of remembrance of his past life in the Congo.

He poured a second whiskey and handed it to Alain Chavant, who sat opposite him in a matching wicker armchair. At sixty-four Chavant was only one year older than Trenet, but whereas Trenet swam, skied and played golf, Chavant had given up on sports and had allowed himself to go to seed. Trenet's former sergeant had once been a heavily muscled middleweight boxer – his crooked nose being testimony to his days in the ring – but the muscle had turned to flab, and years of good living had made him at least twenty kilos overweight. By contrast Trenet had kept his athletic build, and with his neatly coiffured grey hair and year-round tan he looked considerably younger than the other man.

Now he drank from his whiskey glass, then put it aside and looked at Chavant. "OK, tell me exactly what happened."

"About three o'clock this afternoon the phone rang. The caller wanted to speak to Monsieur Durand. I was taken aback – it's been so long."

"Sixteen years," said Trenet.

"Is that what it's been? Anyway when he asked for Durand I knew it had to be Trojan, so I answered as Durand and got the details."

"Which are?"

"There was a phone call to *La Vérité* around lunch-time. The caller was a researcher, said he was working for a journalist based in Dublin. He was interested in the article about the fall of Kaburi and wanted to know if it could be e-mailed to him."

"Shit!" said Trenet with venom. "Shit!"

"I know," said Chavant sympathetically.

"You don't know!" snapped Trenet. "You've no idea how delicate things are in IWS. This is the worst possible time for prying journalists stirring things up." Trenet breathed deeply, then appeared to calm down. He raised his hand in a gesture of apology. "I'm sorry, Alain. It's just I could really do without this right now."

"It mightn't be that bad. Apparently the journalist is writing a book about the Congo – it's not like she's specifically writing a piece about the fall of Kaburi."

"So what's been arranged?"

"They were told the article couldn't be e-mailed or faxed," said Chavant. "So she's coming over to see it in the library in *La Vérité*."

"When?"

"She has an appointment for Thursday morning at ten o'clock."

"Right . . . " Trenet stroked his chin as he considered the implications of what he had heard.

Trojan was a codeword they had given to the librarian in *La Vérité*. Many years previously the man's cousin had served in the army with Chavant, and back in the sixties when the present librarian had first been appointed, Chavant had arranged the payment of a small fee to have an entry made on the reference card for the edition of *La Vérité* containing the article on the fall of Kaburi. As a contact point he had given one of the phone numbers used by his security firm, plus the name Monsieur Durand, knowing that if any such call ever came to his switchboard it would be from the librarian.

For a cover story Chavant had told the librarian that he knew a retired officer, a former Captain Durand, who had served at Kaburi. If anyone made enquiries in future about the article in *La Vérité* Monsieur Durand was to be notified – being keen, as he was, to make contact with anyone who had a link with or interest in Kaburi. Another small fee would be paid to the librarian any time this happened, but the whole thing had seemed to Chavant to be a convoluted arrangement. He had argued against the notion, saying that if Trenet felt that he needed to take action then surely the simplest thing would be to ensure the disappearance of that day's edition of the paper from the archives. Trenet however had overruled him, saying that to offer a bribe to make the paper disappear would only draw attention, whereas the idea of the nostalgic colonial officer was far more credible in a nation that had just recently lost its valuable African colony. Although careful not to challenge Trenet directly, Chavant had made clear that he thought the idea of using the article as a sort of early warning system was patently unnecessary. At the time of the fall of Kaburi there had been chaos in the Congo, and Chavant had never seriously worried that they would be pursued one day regarding the Union Minière diamonds that had gone missing.

Trenet had nonetheless insisted on putting the arrangement in place, and it was only in retrospect that his foresight had been seen to have value. While the rescue of the nuns and the loss of some Union Minière diamonds were of some interest, there were, as Chavant had said, countless other incidents taking place in the Congo around the same period. Trenet's vision however was to foresee that his future career would turn out to be highly successful, thus giving the story a future significance. Diamonds vanishing during civil upheaval was one thing; diamonds vanishing and a penniless young soldier who was present at the time acquiring the capital to start up a business that grew enormously – that was a different matter. And one that had to be kept from the press at all costs.

As it happened they had received only four calls from Trojan in over thirty years. One had related to the family of one of the rescued nuns wanting to get a copy of the article, one had been regarding a student who was doing a project on the role of missionaries in the Congo, and one – the only worrying one until now – had been from a journalist. The journalist had been checked out by Chavant's security people, but it had turned out that the man was writing a series of articles about mercenaries in general at the time of the Congo conflict. Trenet had told Chavant to arrange to meet the man and Chavant had provided the journalist with lots of colourful material, while making sure to gloss over events at Kaburi as a minor and not very interesting side-show. In truth the fall of Kaburi hadn't actually been of great significance and government forces had retaken it from the Balubas later the following day – which probably explained why none of the Belgian papers other than *La Vérité* carried a story specifically relating to the fall of the town. Nevertheless Trenet had always been at pains to make sure that what happened in the past remained buried there.

As his profile as a successful industrialist had risen he

had cultivated the persona of a businessman who found enquiries about his personal life to be tiresome. The fact that he was living in Belgium rather than his native France meant that he tended not to run into former inmates from the orphanage in Reims, and in the rare interviews that were sometimes unavoidable he simply said, truthfully, that his family in France had been killed during the war and that he had settled in Belgium as a young man. So far it had invariably worked, yet at the back of his mind there was always the fear that the past could come back to haunt him.

Of course, even the most nosy and mud-raking journalist couldn't *prove* that he had killed Lieutenant Barrett and taken the diamonds. The problem however was that it wasn't a matter of proof. Trenet had worked hard to create a niche for himself and he thoroughly enjoyed his status as a successful businessman – but he knew how precarious such a position could be. The tabloid press would relish the idea of bringing down a respectable industrialist, and even unproven allegations about how he had amassed his initial capital and about the death of Lieutenant Barrett could fatally undermine Trenet's social standing. Worse, it could be enough to tip the balance against him in winning the vital NATO contract that IWS so desperately needed.

This was going to take careful handling, he knew, and he breathed out, calming himself, then turned back to Chavant. "Who is the journalist?"

"Her name is Laura Kennedy."

"And the newspaper?"

"It's a Dublin paper apparently. *The Sunday Clarion*."

"Tabloid or broadsheet?"

Chavant shrugged his shoulders. "No idea. There hasn't been time to start checking things out."

"We need to get onto this straightaway. Check out the paper. Find out what you can about this Laura Kennedy."

"Right."

"Do we know in what hotel she'll be staying in Brussels?"

"No, but we have the mobile number of the researcher who made the appointment for her."

"Should be able to find out from him," said Trenet.

"That's if she's staying overnight in Brussels – she could be flying in and out the same day."

"Let's hope not. If we're to know what's going on we need access to plant a bug."

"Right."

"This is absolutely top priority, Alain. Let me emphasise that."

"I understand."

"I want the very best man you have on this case."

Chavant sipped his whiskey and looked thoughtful. "I think Ricardo Perez would be our best bet."

"What's he like?"

"He's good. Really good. Spanish guy in his early

forties, he's been based in Belgium about fifteen years now."

"Can he be absolutely depended on to keep his mouth shut?"

"Absolutely. No loose talk with Ricardo – ever."

"And if it's a thing that . . . that action is called for?"

"Lethal when he needs to be."

"Yeah?"

"Former legionnaire. He's smart, he's highly effective, and he keeps his trap shut – you'd like him."

"OK, let's get him on the case. Straight away."

Chavant knocked back his whiskey, then lowered the glass. "Consider it done," he said.

Despite the heat of the late afternoon sun, Ricardo Perez buttoned his jacket, not wanting the silenced Glock pistol in his shoulder holster to be visible. He slipped on a pair of sunglasses, knowing that the tinted Polaroid lenses would make it harder to identify him, then he crossed the street and made for the entrance to the Flamingo Club.

It was a quarter to five, a time Perez had chosen as being late enough in the afternoon for the place to be open, but too early for there to be many customers about. He entered the bar, its interior softly lit, and paused a moment to adjust his eyes after the bright sunlight. The Flamingo was one of Antwerp's larger clubs, with a long bar and plenty of tables spaced around

128

a dance floor, behind which there was a raised stage. Later in the evening when it was functioning as a nightclub he knew it would be crowded and noisy, but for the moment there was just a small scattering of people nursing drinks at the bar.

Perfect, thought Perez, no security staff to contend with. Not that he would have had difficulty with the kind of oafs he had seen manning the door when he had checked out the place the previous night. Still though, better to keep the rough stuff for the man he was seeking.

He crossed to the bar, keeping a good distance between himself and the other drinkers, then beckoned to the barman. He was a small, stocky man, and he lowered a glass that he was polishing before moving a little slowly to Perez. "Monsieur, what can I get you?" he said, his manner deferential.

"Nothing, thank you. I need to talk to Monsieur Leclerc, is he here?"

The barman's eyes flicked for a second to a door at the end of the dance floor, then he answered a trifle warily. "He's in his office, but . . . is he expecting you, monsieur?"

"No, but he'll want to see me. I plan to hire the entire club for a private function. Through here, isn't it?" said Perez making for the door.

"Yes, but —"

"It's fine. I'll make my own way," said Perez over his

shoulder as he strode confidently to the door. Once through it, he saw a stairwell and he ascended quickly, wanting to take Leclerc unawares if possible before the barman might ring to say that someone was seeking him. He took the steps two at a time and swiftly arrived at the next floor, on which there was a narrow corridor. Off one side of the corridor were a number of dressing-rooms, and on the other side there was a door marked *Jean Leclerc, Manager*. He tapped on the door perfunct-orily, opened it and stepped into the room, then immedi-ately closed it behind him.

Sitting behind a desk was a swarthy man of about forty-five. He was handsome, if a little overweight, with dark hair greying at the temples, and he looked up at Perez with a mixture of surprise and irritation.

"Monsieur Leclerc, I presume?" said Perez.

"Yes. Who the hell are you?"

"Someone who wants to conduct important business with you."

Leclerc rose and started round the desk. "You can't just come barging in here."

Perez raised a hand in appeasement. "Not barging in. I told your barman I'd see myself up – that I was interested in renting the entire club for a private function. Can we sit down and talk terms?" As he had expected, Perez saw that the prospect of financial gain had piqued Leclerc's interest, and the man hesitated, then indicated a chair on the other side of the desk, before returning and lowering his bulk back into the chair he had vacated.

Perez looked at the other man, weighing him up. Leclerc was big, and he looked moderately fit, but Perez knew straight away that sorting out the nightclub manager wasn't going to be a challenge.

Although he himself was only a little taller than average, Perez had the well-muscled body of an athlete and he still weighed only about a kilo more than when he had been a paratrooper in the French Foreign Legion. It had been an elite unit that had one of the toughest selection courses of any army in the world, but Perez had positively excelled in the gruelling training.

He had been born in 1960 in Port Boo, on the Spanish side of the border with France, and by the time he had left school in the late seventies he had already decided that life in a small tourist town wasn't his destiny. He had watched his elder brother, Hernando, settling into a job as a waiter, getting engaged to his girlfriend, then saving for an apartment, and the mind-numbing predictability of his brother's future had heightened Perez' determination to embark on a more exciting life. He knew that the Spanish army in which he was scheduled to do national service was unlikely to provide the kind of adventure he sought, and so he had crossed the border into France, gone to the recruitment centre at Castelnaudary and joined the Foreign Legion.

For the next ten years he had served in the legion, and had spent time in Corsica, Beirut and Chad. Since his discharge in 1987 he had based himself in Brussels, and through contacts he had built up he had subsequently worked as a mercenary in Cambodia, Somalia and Bosnia. He had seen mayhem and slaughter, been party to death and destruction, so that now there were very few things that could frighten him.

Certainly the man before him now was no threat, a self-important nightclub manager whose idea of appearing impressive was to fill the walls of his office with photographs of himself taken with third-rate celebrities. Perez sat forward and looked him in the eye. "I wonder could I ask that we don't be disturbed and that your calls are held – we've important business to discuss?"

He could sense that being orchestrated like this irked the other man, but once again Leclerc hesitated, then acceded to the request. He dialled an internal number, gave a couple of terse instructions and turned back to Perez.

"So, you want to hire the entire club?"

"Actually, that was a lie."

"What?"

"I wanted to talk with no interruptions – thought your greed might overcome your reservations."

"Who the fuck do you think you are?!"

"Who I am doesn't matter," answered Perez calmly. "What matters is that you're going to do what I say."

"Like hell I am!" Leclerc rose angrily, and Perez could

see that this guy had a short temper all right. But while he might have some connections with local muscle as an established nightclub owner, he wasn't personally tough, Perez could tell, and this was a personal matter, so there wouldn't be a problem.

Leclerc made to round the desk, but without rising from his chair Perez withdrew the silenced Glock and pointed it at the other man.

"Sit down and shut up," said Perez, his voice low but threatening.

Leclerc stopped, obviously shocked, but he didn't obey Perez' order to sit.

"If you're not sitting behind your desk in ten seconds I'll blow your ankle off. Clock's ticking . . ."

Leclerc hesitated briefly, then returned and sat in his chair with as much dignity as he could muster.

"That's better."

"What the hell is this about?"

"It's about that temper of yours."

"What?"

"You really need to control it. And I'm here to give you a lesson."

"Look, I don't know —"

"Shut your mouth and listen!" said Perez, aiming the Glock at the other man's face.

Leclerc raised his hands in a gesture of appeasement.

"OK, OK . . ."

"I've never liked guys who beat women. And that's

what you are, isn't it, tough guy? A wife-beater?"

Leclerc didn't reply, and Perez could see him trying to control his anger. "Just one problem, tough guy. Someone found out. And they reckoned that like all bullies, you needed to be taught a lesson."

"That bitch can't keep her trap shut!"

"Your wife has no idea that I'm here," said Perez. "Doesn't even know I exist. And she never will, if you know what's good for you." It was true, Perez had been hired by an uncle from Leclerc's wife's wealthy family, but the deal was that the wife must never know there had been intervention, and Leclerc mustn't know who it was that had arranged it.

"So, here's what we'll do," said Perez. "Place both your hands well forward on the desk, then push back your chair so your arms are outstretched along it. Do it!"

Leclerc complied reluctantly and, keeping the gun trained on him, Perez rose and crossed behind him.

"I can pay you," said the man nervously. "Whatever someone's paid you, I can pay you more. Tell me who sent you here, and I'll pay more again."

Perez looked thoughtful. "That's generous of you," he said as he positioned himself behind Leclerc.

"Just tell me who put you up to this and –"

"Keep your hands on the desk!" snapped Perez as the other man began to move. "Push back the chair and keep your arms out stiff!"

Shocked at the change in tone, Leclerc did as ordered,

and Perez moved quickly now, deciding that it was time to end this. He slipped the safety catch onto the Glock, then pivoting on his heel he swung round with the weapon grasped in both hands and brought the butt down with all his might onto Leclerc's outstretched left arm. He heard the crack as the arm broke, then he stifled Leclerc's cry of agony by covering the nightclub manager's mouth with his left hand as he pulled him backwards in the chair.

Perez pushed the Glock into the traumatised man's forehead with his other hand and ignored the muffled but agonised cries. "Take the pain and pull yourself together. I'm going to ease my hand away from your mouth in a minute. If you cry out for help I'll shoot you, believe me. If you understand that, nod now." He loosened his grip slightly, and despite the agony that he must have been in, Leclerc nodded.

"OK, here's the deal," said Perez. "Lay so much as a finger on your wife again and I'll be back – and you'll be in a wheelchair for the rest of your life. Got that?"

Again Leclerc nodded.

"And you never, *ever* ask her anything about any of this. No one's ever to know what happened here, no questions are to be asked, no enquiries of any sort made. If I get the faintest hint that you've been asking about me, I'll regard that as a hostile act – and today will be like a picnic in comparison to what happens then. Understood?"

Leclerc nodded once more.

"Do I need to hit your broken arm to remind you I'm serious?"

Leclerc shook his head frantically.

"Good. Just remember everything I said – you wouldn't like life in a wheelchair. Now I'm going to take my hand away from your mouth. I don't want to hear any screams but feel free to whimper quietly until the ambulance comes. Oh and don't ring for the ambulance or anything else until two minutes after I leave. Then you can explain to them about tripping and smashing your arm against your desk."

Perez eased his hand from the man's mouth, and he cried out softly in pain.

"A word of advice, pal," said Perez with a crooked grin. "Next time you feel angry at home – kick the cat." He crossed to the door, looked back once at the white-faced Leclerc, then he slipped the Glock back into his holster and walked out of the room.

CHAPTER 4

Laura drank a strong coffee, hoping that the caffeine would kick in and shake off her early morning lethargy. The seemingly endless tannoy announcements rang tinnily in her head as she sat with Steve at the departure gate in Dublin airport, awaiting her flight to Brussels.

"This is the last and final boarding call on flight RA 257 to Stansted . . . " proclaimed a nasal voice over the tannoy, and Steve turned to her, a wry smile on his lips.

"The last *and final* call?" he said.

"Moronic, isn't it? What do they think 'last' means?"

"Typical case of 'I have the microphone'."

"'*I have the microphone*'?" said Laura.

"When people who have a moment in the limelight want to . . . *build up their part*, I think actors call it. It's about savouring extra attention – even if it means tacking on meaningless words when you've already made the point."

"Right."

"I heard a reporter on the radio this morning saying that a protest march had been 'peaceful – *and non-violent.*'

"Just so we wouldn't think it was peaceful *and* violent," said Laura with a grin.

"Right."

"I tell you, Mac would crucify a reporter who wrote something like that. He's down like a ton of bricks on any kind of tautology."

"You admire him a lot, don't you?"

"Yeah, he's a terrific editor. I hope . . . maybe it's not my place to say this, Steve, but I hope he's kept on as editor." She looked at the American, wondering if perhaps he would take offence at being canvassed, albeit spontaneously, but he showed no signs of being put out.

"The reality, Laura, is that the board of MGI will make the final decision on who's editor of the *Clarion*."

"Right."

"But my own opinion – for what it's worth – is that Mac seems exactly as you say, an excellent editor."

Laura was relieved to hear Steve's endorsement, but slightly worried at his questioning the weight his opinion would carry. *Was he just being modest?* She needed to know, concerned as she was for Mac's future, and she looked at him quizzically. "You say for what your opinion is worth. But aren't you a board member, and – well, doesn't your family own MGI?"

"Yes to both questions. But I'm the least senior family member on the board."

"Yeah?"

"My dad's the CEO, my Uncle Richard is president in charge of television, my sister Gretchen's a vice-president – so I'm the most junior family member on the board."

"Is your mother on the board?"

"No. She's heavily involved in charities. That takes up most of her time."

"Right."

"I know," said Steve, pulling a face. "It's a real cliché. Rich trophy wife collects charitable causes with the other Ladies Who Lunch."

"You're the one said that, not me."

"I know. But in fairness she has a good heart, and she really does do a lot of good."

"OK," said Laura with a straight face, "we won't hang her from a lamppost, come the revolution."

Steve grinned, and she found herself warming to him further, liking him for feeling the need to defend his mother.

"So your sister Gretchen who's a vice-president – is she much older than you?"

"Three years older. Well, three years *chronologically* –

about twenty years older in most respects."

"And no other brothers or sisters?"

"No, classic WASP family."

"So what's Gretchen vice-president of?"

"Magazine publishing. She's very high-powered, very focussed – she was always going to be a vice-president in her twenties."

"Right . . ." Laura longed to probe the conflict of world views that she suspected existed between Steve and his sister, but she felt that she had already questioned him as much as good manners would allow.

Now he looked at her and smiled. "Obviously you're too polite to ask – so I'll tell you."

"Tell me what?"

"Why I'm not a vice-president."

"You don't have to explain yourself, Steve. I mean –"

"It's OK, I've no hang-up about it. Truth is, I was off swanning around with the Peace Corps for two years when Gretchen was busting a gut, working her way up the ladder. And she did work her way up. She didn't just get landed her job as the boss's daughter."

Laura knew that Steve was being disingenuous in describing the work he had done in Senegal as swanning around, but she didn't challenge him, wanting to see where this conversation would go. "I dare say," she said non-committally.

"When I got back to the States I went into our TV production company for a few years, but then after the kidnapping I took a long sabbatical, and I'm still on it. So you see, I haven't exactly been a company man."

"Maybe that's to your credit."

"You don't like company men?"

"Not in the usual sense of the phrase. I like loyalty, but . . ."

"But to people, not businesses?"

"I suppose. Though there's nothing wrong with the right kind of loyalty. I mean, without wanting to canonise Mac, but I really admire his loyalty to the *Clarion*. He's worked on it since 1989 and he's fought tooth and nail to keep high standards and increase circulation."

"Tough goals to achieve."

"He's a tough guy. Tough editor too – he put me through a few hoops before funding this trip to Brussels."

"Yeah, I get the feeling that . . . well, that in his heart of hearts he thinks it's a wild-goose chase."

Laura knew that Steve was right, and she suspected that had the American not been so keen on following up the mystery she would have had to work even harder to persuade Mac to fund what was, unquestionably, a speculative trip to Belgium. As it was she had won the editor over by reminding him that the most spectacular stories could sometimes arise from hunches and slims leads that were followed up relentlessly. Her big break in covering the Harrogate assassination bid – which the *Clarion* had syndicated all round the world – had come from just such a slender lead, and reminding Mac of this, she had persuaded him to send her to Brussels at the *Clarion's* expense.

To his credit Steve had insisted from the very beginning that all costs incurred by him should be scrupulously separated from Laura's expense account, and so it was that they now found themselves travelling on separately paid-for flights to check out the article in *La Vérité*.

"Of course it may actually *be* a wild-goose chase," said Laura.

"But?"

"But none of our other enquiries on Conn Lynch have thrown up anything. And this Congo story . . ."

"What?"

"I don't know. I don't want to get our hopes up. But something . . . call it intuition, call it a hunch – but something tells me this lead's worth following."

"You know what?"

"What?"

Steve smiled and raised his coffee cup in a toast. "I'll drink to that."

Daniel Trenet looked appraisingly at the man sitting opposite him. They were in the study of the house in Tervuren, and while Trenet knew that the Spaniard he was about to interview was forty-three years of age, the lean, muscular man who returned his gaze looked younger. *Tough without looking thuggish*, Trenet thought approvingly. There was something else too, a sense of alertness about this Ricardo Perez even as he sat, that suggested that the former legionnaire would be an impressive operator.

Despite Chavant having arranged the meeting for first thing in the morning, Trenet had opted not to offer the Spaniard breakfast, or any other form of refreshment, wanting as he did to keep matters as business-like as possible. For the same reason he had chosen to hold the meeting in his study rather than in the more informal surroundings of the conservatory where he had been briefed by Chavant the previous afternoon.

Trenet sat now behind his large mahogany desk, pleased with his first impression of Perez as a man who looked like being effective.

"So," he said, "Monsieur Chavant recommends you highly."

"We've worked well together in the past."

"So I gather. Monsieur Chavant made the point that you can tread lightly and be discreet – but also take firm action when required."

"Different circumstances call for different responses."

His French was perfect, Trenet noticed, with just a hint of his Spanish origins in his accent. "The circumstances in this case are unusually delicate," he said. "I want you to investigate someone, but it's essential that they're not aware of it."

143

"Fine."

"Chavant will provide state-of-the-art surveillance equipment."

"Good. And the subject?"

"Her name is Laura Kennedy. She's an Irish journalist with a newspaper called *The Sunday Clarion*."

"Laura Kennedy, *Sunday Clarion*."

"Memorise it, please, I don't want anything written down."

"Understood."

"It seems she made a bit of a name for herself a couple of years back. Wrote a book about an attempted assassination at the EU ministers' conference in Harrogate."

"I see. Presumably there's something you don't want her writing about?"

"In common with many business people I don't like snooping journalists. Miss Kennedy has a research assistant called Johnson, Stephen Johnson. He rang *La Vérité* yesterday, seeking access to an article in a back edition of the paper. He's made an appointment for her to attend the *Vérité* cuttings library tomorrow morning at ten o'clock."

"May I ask what the article is about?"

Trenet hesitated instinctively, but he knew he couldn't expect Perez to be effective if he was working too much in the dark. "It's about the fall of a town called Kaburi. This was during the fighting in the Congo, back in the sixties."

Perez raised an eyebrow. "That's going back quite a way. Do you know what her goal is?"

"That's what I want you to find out. Ideally before she goes near the newspaper office. She may or may not be travelling with this Stephen Johnson. This is his mobile number . . ." Trenet handed over a slip of paper. "You'll need to devise some cover story and ring him to discover their plans, as soon as we finish talking here."

"OK."

"I want to know what their agenda is, what prompted them to seek the information they seek, what they plan to do if they find it, whether they're reporting back to Dublin as they go. The only way all that will emerge is if they don't know they're under surveillance – so you'll need to be skilful."

"Can you tell me how you discovered their activities in the first place?" asked Perez.

"From a source in *La Vérité*."

"Any idea what might have led them to the article to begin with?"

"No," said Trenet, shaking his head, "that's another of the things I want you to discover." In truth Trenet did have a notion, though it was one he didn't want to entertain too much. For Laura Kennedy was Irish, and so too had Conn Lynch been Irish. Trenet had told himself that it was probably coincidental that the one person who was a witness to the killing of Lieutenant Barrett and the taking of the diamonds was of the same nationality as this journalist. And yet there was a niggling doubt. To decide that potential links were coincidental *could* be burying one's head in the sand, but Trenet had reasoned there was no point fretting now about whether Conn Lynch had let something slip after all this time. Either way though it was information Trenet didn't want to share with Perez, and so he now continued briefing the younger man.

"This is my mobile-phone number," he said, passing over a sheet of paper. "Memorise it please and then destroy it – there must never, *ever* be any links between you and me. Understood?"

"Sure. Don't worry," said Perez reassuringly. "I'll take care of everything."

This guy is a little too sure of himself, thought Trenet. *Better let him know who's in charge.* "Actually you won't take care of everything. What you'll do is *report* everything – to me. Every few hours. More often if there are significant developments."

The Spaniard shrugged. "As you wish."

"Just so we're clear."

"And if this journalist starts uncovering things that don't concern her?"

"That's something I'd have to decide on – if the situation arose."

"I can provide as gentle or as harsh a response as is needed," said Perez meaningfully.

"So Chavant told me," said Trenet.

"Just so we're clear on that too," said the Spaniard, a hint of a smile playing on his lips.

Despite sensing that Perez was probably a very good choice for the job, Trenet found the man's self-assurance a little bit irritating, and although he knew it was petty of him, he found himself looking forward to the next item on his mental agenda. "There's one other thing . . ."

"Yes?"

"If even a whisper regarding any of this were to get out, I'd be highly displeased. And believe me, you don't want to feel my displeasure."

Perez's expression hardened and he looked Trenet in the eye. "Are you threatening me?"

Trenet held his gaze. "You shouldn't have to ask that question."

"I *am* asking."

"Then I'll answer. Yes, of course I'm threatening you. Don't let your *machismo* blind you. If you're as sophisticated an operator as Chavant says you are, you should expect to be warned on a job like this. You should also realise the power and influence I wield, and the potential muscle at my disposal. You may be tough and resourceful, and clearly you have balls, but in the unfortunate event of a conflict between us . . . " Trenet shrugged, "there could only be one ending. So . . . we've said what has to be said. It need never be referred to again."

Perez didn't reply, and Trenet could see that he was

147

still resentful of being threatened. Satisfied that he had made his point, Trenet decided to relent a little, and he raised his hand in a gesture of conciliation. "Forgive me, but such distasteful points have to be made at the beginning. In the interests of clarity. All right?"

Perez hesitated a moment, then nodded. "All right."

"So, we're agreed on what's required?"

"Very well. Except there's the matter of fees."

"Chavant will arrange all of that," said Trenet. "There'll be generous fees and expenses. I always pay well, so whatever he normally pays you, you'll get extra for this job."

"OK."

"Good. Well, I think that's everything for now. I suggest you ring the researcher as soon as possible."

Perez took out his mobile phone. "Why don't I do it right now?"

Trenet allowed himself a small smile, sensing that Perez was going to work out well. "Yes," he agreed. "Now sounds good . . . "

Steve tried to curb his impatience as the voice over the tannoy announced that the flight to Brussels would be delayed by thirty minutes. It wasn't going to affect their appointment at *La Vérité*, which wasn't until the following morning, but he still found it irritating that airlines could be so cavalier and unapologetic. "Must be a great business to be in," he said.

"Sorry?" answered Laura.

"Aviation. What other industry would think it OK to keep clients waiting half an hour without an apology?"

"Not too many, right enough. Still – look on the bright side," said Laura.

"There's a bright side?"

"Yeah, they didn't say the delay was due to the 'late arrival of the incoming aircraft'," said Laura with a smile. "I mean, it's like saying that there's no food in the restaurant because the cupboard is bare. 'The reason your flight will be late, folks, is because the plane is late' – 'Ah well, that's OK then!'"

Steve laughed. "I hadn't really thought about it like that, but yeah, it is a kind of surreal excuse." Just then his mobile rang. "Sorry, excuse me a sec," he said, then rose and moved away a little to answer the phone. "Hello?"

"Hello, is that Mr Johnson?" said a man's voice.

"Yes, this is Steve Johnson."

"Good morning, Mr Johnson. I hope I'm not calling you too early." The man's English was heavily accented but fluent.

"That's OK, I'm up and about. Who's this, please?"

"*La Vérité*. I'm just calling about the appointment tomorrow morning."

The caller wasn't the older man that Steve had spoken to yesterday and he felt a stab of anxiety. "I hope it's still on. I'm in the airport now with Ms Kennedy – we're flying to Brussels this morning."

"You're coming with her?"

"To Brussels, but not to the actual appointment. The appointment is still OK?"

"Yes, the appointment is fine. I was just ringing to confirm it and give you directions."

"Great. Well, thank you very much."

"No problem. What hotel are you staying in?"

"Eh, the Novotel."

"Is that the Novotel at the Grasmarkt or the Novotel at St Katelijne?"

"I'm not sure. Just give me a second and I'll check." Steve quickly unzipped the pouch in which he kept his passport, tickets and hotel voucher, then he quickly looked at the hotel address and returned to the phone. "Sorry about that – it's the one at St Katelijne."

"Fine," said the man, "so you'll be arriving there today?"

"Yes."

"OK, well when you come out of the hotel tomorrow morning turn right, then left into Rue St Catherine de Marche. It's a narrow street that takes you up towards the Grand Place."

"Rue St Catherine de Marche, all right."

"Keep going and you'll cross Rue des Halles, then you reach a major road – Boulevard Anspach, OK?"

"OK. Maybe I should write this down?"

"No, you're nearly there now. Just turn right onto

Boulevard Anspach, keep going past the big Bourse building on the opposite side, and another couple of hundred metres up the road you'll see *La Vérité* on your right."

"So onto St Catherine de Marche, cross Rue des Halles, keep going till Anspach, then turn right for several hundred metres?"

"Exactly. *Bon voyage, monsieur.*"

"Thank you." Before he could ask any further questions the other man hung up, surprising Steve by the slightly abrupt ending of the conversation. Still, it had been nice of the newspaper to ring back with directions to the offices. He switched off the phone and rejoined Laura. "That was *La Vérité*. All systems go for tomorrow, even have directions from the hotel to their offices."

"Great," said Laura. "I presume you didn't hear the announcement when you were talking on the mobile?"

"No, what?"

"Brussels flight delayed another three hours."

"Ah no."

"Yeah. Late arrival of incoming aircraft . . ."

Steve looked at her, and Laura burst out laughing.

"Sorry," she said, raising her hand apologetically. "Couldn't resist . . ."

In spite of being the victim of the joke Steve found himself smiling back.

"You should have seen your face," said Laura.

"OK, you got me – hook, line and sinker."

151

She smiled at him warmly, and he thought that being the butt-end of a mild joke was a small price to pay for the company of such an attractive woman. And they would be spending the next two days together seeking to unravel an intriguing mystery. All in all it had been a good idea to follow his whim, leave New York, and show up at the offices of *The Sunday Clarion*.

Ricardo Perez gave his most practised smile to the receptionist in the Novotel as he put down his suitcase. "Good morning," he said, "how are you?"

"Fine, thank you."

The receptionist was in her late twenties, but plain-looking, and Perez reckoned that she wasn't the type who would get attention from most male guests. "Lovely morning," he said, maintaining eye contact.

"Yes, isn't it?"

She's interested, he thought, sensing that the woman would be co-operative if he persisted with a bit of subtle flirtation. Despite turning forty a couple of years previously, his hair was still jet black, and with his sallow good looks and athletic body he knew that most women found him attractive. It was something he often used to his advantage when he was on a job, and for his plan to succeed today he knew was going to need assistance from the hotel staff. "I'd like to book a room, please," he said.

"Certainly, sir. How many nights will you be staying with us?"

"Probably just one. Though possibly longer, depending on how business goes." *Put yourself in her hands*, he thought. *Make her feel important.* "Is that OK with you, bookings-wise?"

"Yes, I'm sure we'll be able to look after you," she answered with a hint of perkiness.

Good, he thought, *when they start trying to flirt back you know you have them.*

"I feel like I'm in good hands already," he said seductively, and the woman gave a half-embarrassed, half-delighted smile, then turned her gaze towards the computer console on which bookings were entered.

"Would you prefer smoking or non-smoking?"

"Which would you say?"

She looked at him appraisingly, hesitated a moment, then as though emboldened, suddenly spoke. "You look like you'd be athletic. I'd say non-smoking."

Perez smiled. "Thank you for the compliment. And yes, I don't smoke. So normally you'd be right."

"Normally?"

"Yes, but you see today could be different. It depends . . . well, it depends if you can help me."

"Help you? Well, if I possibly can . . ."

"The thing is, I'm supposed to meet up with some old business friends here. I was hoping you might be able to put me in the room beside theirs – but I don't know if they've booked smoking or non-smoking."

"What are the names?"

153

"Stephen Johnson and Laura Kennedy."

The woman tapped some keys, then turned back to Perez. "Non-smoking. They're in two adjoining rooms on the fourth floor."

"Any chance of putting me in the room next door?"

"No problem, we're not full at the moment."

"Great," said Perez, flashing the woman a smile. "And thanks for looking after me."

"A pleasure. If there's anything we can do to make you more comfortable . . . "

"I may take you up on that!" said Perez with a playful laugh as he handed over his Visa card .

"Feel free to," said the woman, clearly emboldened by the direction in which Perez had driven the conversation. Then, when he didn't take it any further she lapsed back somewhat into receptionist mode as she quoted him the rates. "I can give you a superior room on one side of them, or a standard room on the other side."

What the hell, he thought. Daniel Trenet was dripping in money so there shouldn't be any problem with expenses. "Superior, please."

"Fine."

Perez completed the formalities of checking in. Although he had extracted the information he needed about Kennedy and Johnson, he remained charming and flirtatious with the receptionist, knowing it would still be important to keep her onside.

"Right, then, your key," said the woman, handing it

over. "I'll call a porter for your luggage."

"No need."

"No?"

"No, thanks all the same – but I can manage."

"Sure?"

"Positive."

"Athletic to the end, eh?"

Perez smiled. "Something like that. Oh, one last thing?"

"Yes?"

The receptionist looked at him with what he thought was a hopeful air. *She probably thinks I'm going to ask her to meet me for drink*, he thought. He'd need to tread cautiously, he realised, so that she didn't stop being co-operative through disappointment. "My friends next door – any idea what time they're checking in?"

"One second . . ."

Perez thought he detected a just a hint of disappointment in the woman's tone, but she was professional enough not to let it show clearly. "Between eleven and twelve, it says here."

Plenty of time to do what was required before they arrived. "That's fine," said Perez. "Would you do me one last favour?" he said, looking her in the eyes and trying for his most appealing expression.

"If I can."

"Don't tell them I'm here. I'd like to surprise them. Maybe knock on the door as room service and arrive in with a bottle of champagne. OK?"

"Sure."

"Thanks for everything – look forward to seeing you over my stay."

"You're welcome," said the woman, warming again to the compliment.

"Bye," said Perez, then he took his luggage and made for the lifts. One was open. He stepped inside and pressed the button for the fourth floor, pleased with how things had gone.

It had been an interesting twenty-four hours, what with travelling the previous day to Antwerp to sort out the nightclub owner, and then finding a message on his mobile telling him to contact Alain Chavant as a matter of urgency. He had done some work before for the former army sergeant when Chavant wanted problems solved that he didn't wish to have dealt with by the staff of his security company. He had never before been hired by a toff like Trenet, however, and the meeting of this morning had left him with mixed feelings. On the one hand Trenet had authorised Chavant to pay generous fees and expenses, but the arms manufacturer's officer-in-command style had irked Perez, as had the man's attitude in threatening him about keeping his mouth shut. Perez had found it offensive, both as a professional who never blabbed about his work, but also in terms of the *machismo* to which Trenet had referred.

Still, it sounded like an interesting case. And there was obviously something important that Trenet was

pretty anxious not to have revealed, as was evident by
Chavant being on hand with a suitcase containing a full
range of state-of-the-art surveillance devices for Perez to
choose from, as soon as the meeting in Trenet's study
had ended.

Perez had stopped off fleetingly in his apartment on
the way to the Novotel and packed some clothes into
the other suitcase that he now carried, then made
some calls on his car phone. He was confident that the
bug-planting and eavesdropping were tasks he could
handle alone, but for outdoor surveillance he knew he
needed to hire some additional bodies. It was all in hand
now, however, and as he stepped out of the lift and
started down the hotel corridor he felt pleased at how
much he had set in train in a short space of time.

He entered his room, closed the door behind him
and placed his luggage on the bed. The room was
spacious, with windows along two of the walls, but
Perez kept the curtains closed and instead turned on the
lights. He removed his jacket, then took the Glock from
his shoulder holster and slipped it under the pillow on
the bed. He wondered which of his subjects would be in
the room adjoining his. Maybe Johnson *and* Kennedy if
he was lucky and they were sleeping together but
booking separate rooms for the benefit of her newspaper.
Failing that, he hoped it would be the woman who was
next door, she being the journalist and therefore the
more important of the two. Either way he had to find

out what they were up to, and he had already decided on what his first moves would be.

He crossed the room to where a safety chart showed a diagram of the rooms on his floor and the emergency exits, and he studied the layout of the rooms, calculating where his bedroom wall shared a boundary with the bedroom next door. He returned to the bed and opened the suitcase containing the surveillance equipment. He took out a compact battery-powered drill and a highly sensitive listening device encased in narrow plastic tubing, which could be fed through a small hole bored through the party wall.

He glanced at his watch. Two minutes to ten. Plenty of time before his targets arrived from the airport. He briefly flicked on the switch of the drill to make sure it was working properly, then switched it off again. One more thing to check, he thought, then he went to the phone on his bedside locker and lifted the headset. He glanced at the instructions, found the prefix for ringing another room, and dialled the two rooms allocated to Johnson and Kennedy, just in case chambermaids were making up the beds or cleaning the rooms. In neither case did anyone answer the phone however, and Perez smiled in satisfaction. Then he put down the phone, took up the drill and the listening device and made for the party wall.

The train sped from the airport towards Brussels, and Laura watched the suburbs flashing past the carriage window. After the late take-off from Dublin the pilot had made up some lost time, and Laura and Steve had passed quickly through Brussels airport and boarded the train for the city centre. Although the appointment at *La Vérité* wasn't until tomorrow, Laura instinctively hated delays, and she was pleased that they were now running only about twenty minutes behind schedule.

Less pleasing however was the call to Galway that she had just finished on her mobile, with nothing significant emerging there from the ongoing checks on the life of Conn Lynch. She was drawing blanks in the research at the American end too and she fervently hoped that tomorrow's visit to the cuttings library wouldn't end in disappointment also.

But what if it *did* turn out to be a complete dead end? Well, she'd just have to return to Dublin and acknowledge that Mac had been right, and that the trip to Belgium had perhaps been more speculative than she had admitted. She would then do what there hadn't been time for before leaving, which was to make a thorough check in the Dublin libraries on any books written about the Irish army in the Congo. She would also persist with her enquiries in Clare and Galway, and allow Janet to do the same in Dulwich, Connecticut.

And yet . . . for all that she extolled the virtue of persistence in the face of setbacks, she knew that she –

and probably even more so Steve – would be disappointed if the journey to Brussels were in vain.

She glanced over at him now as he sat watching each succeeding view unfolding on the journey to the city centre. He was an interesting man, no question about it. After they had finished in the *Clarion's* cuttings library the previous night, they had gone for a pizza locally. Laura wasn't sure if it was appropriate to go for dinner with him a second night in a row, yet she had felt it would be inhospitable to leave a visitor all alone.

And so she had compromised, suggesting a quick pizza, followed by an early night – an approach that seemed reasonable bearing in mind their seven o'clock check-in at the airport the next morning. As it turned out she had enjoyed his company, and in the one-to-one conversation that had ensued he had opened up more than on the previous night in Cannerys. Although he didn't state it bluntly, it was obvious that his family was seriously wealthy, and that Steve had enjoyed a privileged childhood, divided between what sounded like a palatial apartment in Manhattan and summers spent in the family's summerhouse in the Hamptons. He had amusingly told of how his father was, as he termed it, "a lessons man", who felt that every blue-blooded American child should be taught a wide range of social and sporting skills. And so Steve and Gretchen had been sent for French lessons, piano lessons, tennis lessons, golf lessons, swimming lessons, singing lessons, dance lessons, painting lessons, art-appreciation lessons. The list had seemed endless, and Steve had told with self-deprecating humour an entertaining story about how his father had once tried to get a local sculptor of note to teach a teenage Steve the glories of classical sculpture. It had ended in disaster, with the man suing the family after Steve accidentally knocked the artist's work-in-progress off his workbench, smashing it to smithereens.

Laura had laughed with delight at the story and had enjoyed the American's company, the only awkward moment in the evening coming when she had touched on his kidnapping. He had responded courteously, but she had sensed immediately that it was still a sensitive topic for him, and so she had brought the conversation back to less contentious matters. She remembered reading the previous year how it was rumoured that the family had paid a large ransom to get him released, although the Johnson family's lawyers had denied this. Assuming that the ransom had been paid however – and Laura reckoned that it probably had – it must be awful for him, she thought, knowing that there was always the possibility of someone else trying to abduct him at some point in the future. Although it wasn't usual for kidnap victims to be kidnapped twice, it was nonetheless a possibility with such a wealthy family.

She knew from their conversations that Steve had changed homes, moving from a chic East-side condo to a loft apartment in the more bohemian Greenwich Village area, but his movements must still have been traceable, and although he had made passing reference to improved levels of self-defence, she reckoned that he might be burdened both by what had actually happened to him and by the possibility of a recurrence.

"You seem miles away," he said now, interrupting Laura's musings.

"Just . . . just day-dreaming . . "

"Of this story turning into a scoop?"

"Something like that," she answered, then realised that the train was slowing down. She looked up the track towards the station that they were approaching. "Brussels Central," she said. "This is us."

"Good," he said, rising and gathering their travel bags from the overhead rack. "So . . . Brussels – and the moment of truth. Fingers crossed."

Laura looked at him and nodded. "Yeah, fingers crossed . . . "

Daniel Trenet angrily crumpled the letter that had come in the morning post, then threw it in the bin. He was seated behind the desk in his lavishly appointed office on the top floor of the IWS plant, and he cursed softly, then tried to gather his thoughts. He had arrived late to the office after briefing Ricardo Perez and subsequently attending a tedious but necessary meeting with the managing director of one of their principal suppliers.

With her usual efficiency Marianne, his secretary, had date-stamped and laid out his post on the large executive desk at which he now sat. The offending letter was from a senior manager in the merchant bankers with whom Trenet had the largest of his loans, and though phrased reasonably courteously, there was no doubt that the bank was now pressurising him on the subject of repayment.

Bastards, he thought. When he didn't need them they had lavished him with offers of funding, and now when he actually needed financiers they were getting cold feet. Still, no point wasting energy on anger. Instead he had to give the bank the impression that soon all would be well again regarding cash flow in IWS. Meanwhile, if it really became necessary, he had one useful card to play in keeping this particular banker off his back. It need only be alluded to, but Trenet could remind the man of the short luxury cruise on a chartered yacht that IWS had arranged a couple of years previously, as part of the launch of their new range of surveillance equipment. The merchant banker – a married man – had been more than happy to enjoy the services of the high-class call-girls that Trenet had engaged via the Clinique Speciale. It would of course be blackmail, however obliquely the point was made, but if the worse came to the worse it would very likely buy some precious time.

Life was ironic, Trenet thought. The galling thing was that they actually deserved the NATO contract that they were desperately pursuing, whereas in the past he knew they had sometimes outmanoeuvred competitors whose products and prices should have won them the commissions. Still, in the end he had only himself to blame for the position in which he found himself. It was his pride that had made retaining control of IWS an overriding cause, and he knew that if he had been less macho he could have sold his shares for a fortune and allowed a take-over bid to go ahead. Instead of clinging to control by borrowing so heavily, he could be relaxing now, yet even as he thought it he knew that such a response wasn't in his nature. Besides, he felt much too vigorous to retire yet, and if he had to fight the bank, and the conservatives on his board like Hans Romer, then so be it. Thinking of Romer he wondered, not for the first time, if the punctilious little Dutchman was grooming himself to be a replacement Chairman of the Board. *Over my dead body*, thought Trenet, then his direct line rang, interrupting his musings.

"Yes."

"Calling with an update."

Trenet recognised Perez's voice, but as per instructions, the Spaniard had refrained from using names.

"So, what's happening?"

"Our friends have arrived. She's in the room next door to me. Equipment's in place."

"Good."

"Saw them in the lobby, gave a detailed description to my support team."

"Excellent. And at the risk of repeating myself – it's important these people never suspect a presence."

"I've made that clear to my assistants. The subjects are staying in separate rooms, but they're meeting up in about fifteen minutes."

"Any idea of their plans?"

"A quick lunch, then a trip to the African museum out in Tervuren."

Were they simply interested in matters African as background to journalism on the Congo, or were they pursuing a specific enquiry? "I take it you'll be in attendance?" said Trenet.

"My team will. I need to go next door – prepare for tomorrow's appointment. Thought I'd pay a visit while they're visiting the museum."

Trenet knew that Perez would want to conceal high-quality miniature bugs, probably in the unpacked clothes of this Laura Kennedy, so as to find out what was said tomorrow at the office of *La Vérité*. "Right," he said. "And keep me updated. If they say anything remotely significant, I want to hear about it. If they go someplace else after the museum I want to know about it."

"Sure. My people can follow them on foot, by scooter, by tram – whatever. Any place they go, you'll hear about it."

"Good. Call me again when there's anything."

"Will do."

Trenet hung up, then sat for a moment, lost in his

thoughts. He could really have done without snooping journalists just when he was trying to secure the future for IWS by winning the NATO contract. Still, you couldn't choose convenient times to fight your battles. As his company sergeant used to say in the barracks in Algiers, the very day you're hit with a dose of the clap – expect the enemy to attack. Besides, even if Kennedy and Johnson *were* the enemy they hadn't attacked yet. And if Perez did his job properly there was a good chance of finding out their plans – and stopping them in their tracks, if need be. Satisfied that there was nothing further he could do for now, Trenet breathed out deeply, consciously put the journalist and her researcher from his mind, and went back to his correspondence.

"They've boarded the tram – I'm about to follow."

"Good," said Perez, pleased to have one of his surveillance team confirm that Laura Kennedy and Steve Johnson were safely dispatched to the museum in the suburbs. It left the way clear for him to seek access to Kennedy's room. "And remember," he added, "really discreet surveillance – keep your distance."

"Sure."

"Keep me posted if they do anything unusual, or if they make for somewhere else after the museum."

"OK."

Perez hung up, put the mobile back into his pocket and rose from his hotel bed. He had eaten a room-service lunch while Kennedy and Johnson had had their lunch in the bar, and now he planned to use the lunch-tray with its used crockery as part of his ploy to get into the room next door. He placed his room key in his trousers pocket, then put on his jacket and slipped the miniature listening device into the jacket pocket. Despite the bug being really small, Chavant had assured him that it was absolutely state-of-the-art, and that notwithstanding the tiny batteries it was capable of transmissions of high quality. He took the silenced Glock from under the pillow and placed it in his shoulder holster, then he buttoned his jacket, picked up the tray and made for the door.

As soon as Kennedy and Johnson had left the hotel Perez had checked out the corridors of the fourth floor, reasoning that the chambermaids would probably still be making up rooms. To his relief they had been down the corridor and around the corner, and he was anxious to go there now before they finished their task. First however he carefully placed the used tray on the ground, adjacent to the room occupied by Laura Kennedy. He glanced around, confirming that there was nobody about to see what he had done. Good, he thought, then he walked briskly down the corridor and turned the corner. He continued on to where the chambermaids' trolley was pushed to the side of the corridor opposite an open bedroom. He looked into the room and saw two women changing the sheets on the bed. Here goes, he thought, then he tapped politely on the opened door and stepped into the vestibule.

Remember – you're the nice guy, sorry to be a nuisance and to disturb two busy workers. "Excuse me?" he said with a contrived tentativeness.

The women looked up. The younger one was in her late teens and was dark-skinned and had large, frightened-looking brown eyes. The older woman was in her forties with dyed blonde hair and a more confident air about her. *Definitely the one to make his pitch to.*

Perez gave a sort of apologetic smile, while catching the older woman's eye. "I'm sorry to disturb you," he said, "but I was hoping you could help me."

"Yes?"

"I've done something really silly. It's embarrassing." *He definitely had her interest now.*

"Oh?"

"I was putting a room-service tray in the corridor outside my door, and, well –"

"You let the door close behind you."

"Yes. I suppose . . . I suppose I'm not the first?"

"You're not the first."

"Any chance you could let me back in – save me going all the way back down to reception?" He tried for a little-boy-lost look, gazing into the woman's eyes as though they were the only two people in the world.

She didn't respond in any way to the sexual element of his charm offensive but nodded in a business-like manner and reached for her master-key. "OK – where's your room?"

"Down the corridor to the left."

"Right. Let's get you back in. You carry on, Farrah," she said to the teenager, then she strode ahead without waiting for Perez.

He followed in her wake, slightly taken aback at how impervious she had been to his charms, but satisfied nevertheless that his ploy had worked.

They reached the door, and the woman opened it. "Now . . ."

"Thank you very much." Perez slipped her a two-euro coin, and the woman accepted it without demur, offered a muttered thank-you in return, then made her way back down the corridor.

Perez stepped into the room, and closed the door after him, breathing a sigh of relief. First things first, he thought, as he made for the party wall and got down on his knees. He looked for the corner just above the skirting board, and there, right enough, just about visible to someone looking, was the nose of the tubular listening device that he had inserted through the partition wall. There was a small amount of dust where the drilling had displaced a tiny portion of plaster, and Perez blew hard on it, scattering the dust. A professional who was looking for a device would have found it, he knew. But Laura Kennedy wasn't a professional. She was a journalist who had no idea she was being monitored, and so he reckoned that there shouldn't be a problem.

He rose from his knees and looked about the room, then glanced into the bathroom. There was the faintest aroma of perfume, and the cosmetics in the bathroom indicated clearly that this was a woman's room. No difficulties there though, he reasoned: the matronly chambermaid who had let him in would have made up the room before Laura Kennedy had arrived, and by the time the room was made up again tomorrow they would all have departed the hotel and there would be no evidence that Perez had gained entry to someone else's room.

He looked around, noting that the journalist was neat in her habits, then he crossed to the wardrobe and opened it. Her clothes had been unpacked and were on hangers, and he studied them, gauging what he thought she would wear to the office of La Vérité tomorrow. There was a well-cut, light woollen suit in grey, and he reckoned that this would be her outfit. Stylish but business-like, it was by far and away the most likely contender. He took the jacket off its hanger and turned up the collar, then reached into his pocket, taking out a tiny microphone and transmitter. Although the jacket material was light, the device was sufficiently thin not to be felt under the collar once the material was folded back down, and utilising minuscule pieces of Velcro on either end of the device, Perez attached it to the garment.

He turned the collar back down and observed his

handiwork. There was no sign of the bug visible through the woollen material, yet Chavant had assured him that such was the sophistication of the device that it would still provide high quality transmissions over short distances. Satisfied that the bug was highly unlikely to be found by Laura Kennedy – after all who looked under the collars of their suits? – he replaced the jacket on its hanger.

He closed the wardrobe, then looked about the room to ensure that there was nothing he had disturbed and that all doors were as Laura Kennedy had left them. Satisfied that nothing was amiss, he made to leave, then suddenly stopped in his tracks. *Someone was unlocking the door from the corridor.* Perez instantly spun about and lunged round the corner of the vestibule out of sight. He had moved as quietly as possible while still reacting at speed, and even as he responded to the peril of his position his brain was evaluating the situation, and he reckoned that the carpet had probably absorbed any slight sounds he might have made.

He swung open the door to the bathroom, stepped in and pulled the door as far over as he could without having to snap it closed. His heart was pounding, but he knew that under pressure he could still review options and make decisions at speed, something he had always been capable of when he went into action.

His first thought was that maybe Kennedy had come back unexpectedly – in which case there was a problem, as she would undoubtedly enter the bathroom sooner or later. Even as he thought it though he knew it wasn't a likely scenario. The journalist had stepped onto a suburban-bound tram, and even if she got off again immediately she could hardly have returned to the hotel this fast. Or without Perez being notified by the people he had tailing her. *So who was it then?*

He waited in the darkened bathroom, his eye to the crack in the door as the person entered the bedroom. Just supposing that somehow it was Kennedy – could he pretend to be a member of the hotel staff? Checking a fault in the plumbing, say? The main light-switch for the bathroom was outside the door but he could flick on the light over the sink. Though it might strike her as odd that a staff member would be checking a fault with the main light switched off.

Just then he saw a shape passing across his field of vision. Keeping the door open only a fraction, he followed the passing of the intruder and saw that it was a chambermaid. Although the woman had her back to him and was dressed in the standard hotel uniform he could tell from her build that it wasn't either of the women he had approached when pretending to be locked out of his room. Should he just brazen it out now? He could step out into the bedroom as though he were the occupant and had been using the bathroom, shutting the door quickly behind him, at the same time putting his hand to the light-switch as if he were just turning it off. Except that this housemaid might have been on the corridor when Laura Kennedy had moved into the room. And even if she hadn't, his instincts were to show himself to as few people as possible. But supposing he risked flicking on the light above the hand-basin and staying in the bathroom – and the woman discovered him there? Could he sit on the toilet and perhaps embarrass and fluster her? Decide now, he thought. Either step out, or chance it and stay.

He went with his instincts and stayed put with the lights out. The woman turned around. She was pretty and petite and she looked across the room. Perez froze, then he realised that she wasn't looking directly at the bathroom door. She adjusted her hair, and Perez realised that there must be a mirror on the wall to the side of the door and that she was checking her hair from across the room.

The woman turned away and Perez realised then what her task was. She had placed a tray on the table, and from the tray she took out spare packets of biscuits and miniature containers of milk, which she placed beside the room's tea and coffee-making equipment. Her job completed, she took up the tray and started across the room. Instead of making for the corridor however she headed in the direction of the bathroom. Although now an atheist, Perez's childhood Catholicism kicked in as he prayed she wouldn't decide to use the bathroom while she was here.

He moved fractionally to the side and slipped the Glock from its holster. If she came in he would try to knock her out with the gun before she could see his face. But then there would be an enquiry, even if she couldn't identify her assailant. And it would emerge that a man had gained access from the other chambermaids. A man who was checked into the room next door – *Jesus, it didn't bear thinking about.* Unless he killed her with the silenced gun. He had killed men while in the Legion, it wasn't such a big deal. And it would mean that she couldn't tell any story about an attacker – but on the other hand the hotel would then be crawling with cops, and Kennedy might well be freaked and decide to check out.

He stood, gun in hand, holding his breath and waiting in case she opened the bathroom door. Instead she just stood outside the door and Perez suspected that she was fixing her hair again but this time closer to the mirror. *Vain bitch!* He waited for what seemed like an age, but which in reality was probably only about ten seconds, then he heard a movement as she made for the hall and the next thing the bedroom door was firmly closed.

Perez breathed an enormous sigh of relief and stepped out into the bedroom again. *Time to get out of here.* He looked around once more to confirm that everything was as he had found it, then he made for the door to the corridor. He opened the door a little and peered out very carefully. There was no sign of anyone in the corridor and he quickly exited the room, pulling the door closed after him. He swiftly covered the few yards to his own door, then used his key and let himself in.

Once more he breathed out in relief, knowing that he had had a close call, yet also knowing that it had been one of those things that couldn't be legislated for. Besides he hadn't been caught and both his bugs were now in place, so despite the scare things had been pretty successful so far.

He made for the drinks cabinet, deciding that he would have a whiskey to celebrate, then he stopped. Better to check in first with Trenet, he thought. The man was fussy and demanding but he was also paying well. No harm to ring him then with a bit of good news. And although Perez had squared up to the arms manufacturer when Trenet had threatened him, the reality was that the older man was powerful and well-connected so there was nothing shameful in staying on the right side of him while this operation unfolded.

And who knew what might emerge? Clearly Trenet had something in his past that he didn't want people in general to know about. Perez could identify with that – he himself had been discharged from the Legion after a fracas in a bar in Chad in which he had stabbed two locals, but he never referred to it, always simply said that he had served in the Legion for ten years.

Somehow though he reckoned that Trenet's secret might be more interesting. And interesting things could sometimes be profitable to know about. Meanwhile he would call Trenet and keep him sweet. Then he would have a whiskey and await developments with Kennedy and Johnson. All in all it was shaping up to be an interesting day.

"Anything about this place strike you as odd?" asked Steve.

He was seated with Laura in the café of the Musée Royal de l'Afrique Centrale, and they were sipping coffees after trekking around the museum's various exhibits.

"I suppose the café's a bit small for the size of the place – and the number of people who'd probably visit the park in summer."

The museum was an imposing classical building and it housed a wide range of Congolese artefacts in a beautiful park on the outskirts of Brussels, but Steve hadn't been referring to the architecture or the location. "I was thinking more of the message being projected," he said.

"How do you mean?" asked Laura.

"Well, the Belgians occupied the Congo for eighty years. Ran a place that was – what, about seventy times the size of Belgium?"

"Something like that."

"And the museum here is full of artwork, carvings, masks, spears. They've got displays on wildlife, natural resources – all sorts of stuff. But it's like it exists in a vacuum, politically speaking."

"They're a bit coy about their colonial past, right enough."

"I suppose it would be naive to expect them to give us chapter and verse on how they acquired the Congo and treated the people there. But a bit more historical context, a bit of acceptance of past evils wouldn't go amiss."

Laura looked at him and smiled. "You're something of an idealist, aren't you?"

"Am I?"

"It's not a complaint – it's a compliment."

Steve could see that although Laura had made the comment lightly enough, she still meant it, and he couldn't help but feel pleased. "Thank you."

"It's just that . . . well, you're dealing with human nature," said Laura, "even in a museum. The Belgians didn't exactly cover themselves in glory in the Congo. So it's understandable that they gloss over the parts that make them look bad. *Wrong* maybe, but predictable."

"I suppose. I just thought after all this time they'd be more willing to face up to what actually happened in the Congo. I mean they've been gone out of it over forty years."

"I know. Eternity in some ways – but probably a vivid enough memory still to lots of people here."

"So it seems."

Just then Laura's mobile rang, and she asked Steve to

excuse her as she took the call. He listened to her questioning Janet, the researcher who was checking out the village of Dulwich in Connecticut, to which the Lynch family had emigrated. He could tell from Laura's tone that nothing dramatic was emerging, and he allowed his mind to wander as he looked at the other visitors in the café.

He amused himself by trying to guess the nationality of each one. *Japanese. American. Scandinavian probably. Italian.* As he studied them one by one he saw a ginger-haired woman whose face looked familiar. For a moment he couldn't place her, then he remembered. He had seen her boarding their tram just before it had left Brussels. Presumably she too had been travelling all the way out to the suburbs to visit the museum, although funnily enough, he hadn't seen her at any stage while he and Laura had been viewing the exhibits. *Scottish* or *Irish* – or was that leaping to conclusions just because the woman had ginger hair? Before he could give it any further thought Laura finished her call and turned to him.

"No luck in Connecticut?" he said.

Laura shook her head. "Zilch. Janet is a first-class researcher – and she has a really good feel for people. If she can't find anything remotely suspicious . . . maybe there's nothing to find."

"Did she get any additional information?"

"Lots. But the bottom line is that the Lynches didn't

seem to make any enemies. Shay was really popular until he was killed in Vietnam, and Conn was well-liked in the couple of years he spent there."

"Right."

"She's staying there a bit longer and checking homicides in the wider Connecticut region."

"Good."

"Yes, but . . ." Laura grimaced.

"You're not hopeful?"

"No. My instincts tell me there's nothing there."

"Well . . . let's hope tomorrow at the newspaper proves more fruitful."

"Don't fancy going back to Mac with my tail between my legs," said Laura with a wry grin. "So yeah – let's hope so . . ."

Trenet slipped off his Chinese silk dressing-gown and sat on the edge of his king-size four-poster bed. It was eleven at night and he had had a wearying day, but he knew that sleep wouldn't come easily. He had spent the latter part of the evening in the Clinique Speciale, but had been unable to savour fully the pleasures afforded him there. Normally he slept well after his evenings in the up-market brothel, but tonight his head was still buzzing with the complications arising from the arrival in Brussels of Laura Kennedy and Stephen Johnson.

The one encouraging thing was that Ricardo Perez seemed to be a thorough professional and, as instructed, had kept Trenet posted on all developments. Already Perez had bugged Kennedy's room and planted a listening device in the business suit she was presumably going to wear for her visit to the office of *La Vérité* tomorrow. In addition the journalist and her researcher had been discreetly tailed all afternoon and evening. Nothing particularly significant had emerged so far, either from the bugging or the surveillance, with the two subjects returning to their hotel after visiting the museum. After washing and changing they had gone for dinner in one of the tourist restaurants in the quaint, narrow streets of the Sacré d'Ilses, then had a coffee in a pavement café in the Grand Place.

It had all seemed innocuous and predictable – exactly the sort of thing done by countless visitors to Brussels, and although Perez had reported that they weren't acting like lovers in public, Trenet had hoped nonetheless that they might retire to Kennedy's bugged bedroom.

Instead they had gone to their separate rooms shortly after ten, and Kennedy had made a call on her mobile. According to Perez she had spoken to someone called Mac, whom she had apparently tried to contact earlier. From the tenor of the conversation, Perez had reckoned that Mac was probably her editor – a suggestion that tied in with his research on *The Sunday Clarion*, whose editor was listed as Eamon McEvoy, 'Mc' as he knew being an abbreviation of 'Mac'. The woman had told Mac that she was hoping for the best at *La Vérité* tomorrow, as she had had no joy either with Clare or the States.

Trenet reasoned that 'no joy' was slang for not making progress, but where did the United States come into enquiries about the Congo? And who was Clare? There was no way of knowing as yet, and Trenet consoled himself that prior to her visiting the newspaper, it didn't sound like the journalist was specifically focussing on Kaburi.

But if she were simply writing about the Congo why was she reporting back a lack of progress in the US? There were more questions than answers, Trenet knew, and until he had further information it would be impossible to figure out what was going on. His fervent hope was that Laura Kennedy would just visit *La Vérité* and write something for publication in Ireland that would have no bearing on Trenet's own delicately balanced situation.

In truth he felt that there must surely be a fair chance that his worries would come to naught, and that the Trojan warning and the engagement of Perez would simply be sensible precautions that would turn out not to require further action.

What if that weren't the case though? Supposing Kennedy's visit wasn't so innocuous and she began asking the wrong kind of questions? In his heart of hearts he already knew the answer, though he was reluctant to dwell on it too much. Yet if it really became necessary, a journalist who was making too much trouble could be stopped. By persuasion if possible, but also by force if need be. Admittedly there would be a huge hue and cry if a journalist were – for argument's sake – to vanish suddenly, and it was a daunting problem that he didn't want to have to face. But then his company was fighting for survival and that was daunting too.

He found his mind starting to go in circles once more and he consciously forced himself to stop. Chances were things would work out OK, but if it came to it and Laura Kennedy had to be dealt with, then she would be, journalist or not. Satisfied at having made a decision, he climbed into his bed, lay back upon his eiderdown pillows and switched off the lights.

CHAPTER 5

"My cholesterol is just about to go off the radar screen!" said Laura as she tucked into her cooked breakfast in the dining-room of the Novotel.

"Does cholesterol show up on radar?" asked Steve with a straight face.

Laura smiled. "OK – bit of a mangled metaphor, but you know what I mean."

"Sure. That's the problem with buffet breakfasts. You don't eat the food because you're hungry, you eat it because – well, because it's there. Sort of an Everest vibe?"

Laura smiled again. "Right. Talking of cholesterol –
here's one for you. What animal's meat contains no
cholesterol?"

"Is this a trick question?"

"Absolutely not. Well?"

Steve shook his head. "Haven't a clue."

"Sure, have a guess."

"The Lesser Spotted Gibbon?"

"Close, but no cigar."

"So what is it?" asked Steve.

"The kangaroo."

"Really?"

Laura adopted an Australian accent. "Bonzer, mate.
Chuck a bit of 'roo steak on the barbie. Filling tucker, no
cholesterol, Bob's your Uncle . . . "

Steve laughed. "Are you always this good-humoured in
the mornings?"

Laura shrugged. "I fluctuate between cheerful and
Antichrist, I suppose, this morning. I'm . . . well, I'm
kind of excited that we're finally going to see this
article."

"Me too. Though it's you who'll actually see it. I'd love
to come along, but we probably shouldn't try to change
the arrangement now."

"No. No, I suppose not," said Laura philosophically,
then she returned to her breakfast.

Despite her initial misgivings about being accompanied by the American, she couldn't deny to herself that

she had grown to like having him along. Last night they
had gone out to dinner, and it had turned out to be an
excellent evening. The meal with Steve and Mac in
Cannerys had been pleasant, admittedly, and the quick
pizza they had had in Dublin the night before their flight
had been agreeable, but last night had been different,
with both of them more relaxed with each other than
they had been previously.

He was a good-looking guy and on the one or two
occasions when he had been mildly flirtatious, Laura had
found herself responding in kind.

It had easily been the most enjoyable dinner she had
had with a man since Declan had died, and to her
surprise she had even found herself talking about her loss
at one stage. Steve had been a sympathetic listener, and
it had struck her that perhaps having undergone the
trauma of a kidnapping had made him sensitive to
trauma in other people's lives. At any rate she had talked
more than she had planned about her personal life, then
in turn she had queried him a little about his ordeal.

She had been impressed that he hadn't tried to be all
macho and to play down its effects upon him, instead
admitting that his kidnappers had been abusive and that
he had been in fear for his life while chained to a cellar
wall. Obviously it had been a life-altering experience,
but despite the honesty of his response Laura could sense
that the topic was one he was uncomfortable with, and,
notwithstanding her curiosity, she hadn't pressed him

too much on it. Having moved on from such momentous matters they had chatted easily about other areas of their lives, and about music, the cinema, travel and a myriad of other things.

It had been like a date without actually *being* a date, and now as she finished reflecting on it she polished off the end of her breakfast and pushed her plate aside.

"Ready to rock and roll?" asked Steve.

"Just. You know, now that the moment's come, I'm kind of excited, but . . . "

"What?"

"I'm a bit nervous. I just hope it'll have been worth coming all this way."

"Even if the trip doesn't throw up anything, it was worth a try."

"If it doesn't throw up anything, Mac will have my guts for garters!"

"Somehow I doubt that."

"Anyway can you give me ten minutes to do myself up, and then we can check out and head off?"

"Sure. Though eh . . ."

"What?"

"You look pretty well done up already to me."

Although he wasn't making an issue of it, Laura was aware that Steve was complimenting her directly on her looks, and for a second she wasn't sure how to respond. "Why thank you, kind sir," she answered playfully to cover the slight awkwardness she felt, then she glanced at her watch. "Say half nine in the lobby?"

"Sure."

"OK. And then, like you say – time to rock and roll."

"Good news," said Perez softly into his mobile.

"Yes?"

"The subject is wearing the suit, as anticipated. And the device is operational, I can hear every word she says."

"Excellent."

"Got to go now. I'll ring later."

"Do that."

"OK."

Perez hung up, pleased to have been able to report to Trenet that his bugging of Laura Kennedy was successful. He sat discreetly tucked away in a corner of the Novotel's lobby, yet he could clearly see the journalist and her colleague preparing to leave the hotel. Although he had been fairly confident that the woman would wear the suit under whose collar he had placed the bug, nevertheless he had been unable to relax until this morning when she had entered the dining-room for breakfast. She hadn't worn the jacket at that stage, having come down for breakfast in a blouse and trousers, but even from behind a newspaper at the far side of the dining-room Perez could tell that the trousers matched the suit jacket in which the device had been placed.

187

Now, via a miniature receiver and earpiece, he could hear Kennedy and Johnson discussing their route to the office of *La Vérité*, having left their luggage at the Novotel. Perez stayed put in the lobby, reading his newspaper once again, and knowing that his surveillance team would pick up the two subjects who were now leaving the hotel. He waited a couple of minutes until the journalist and her researcher had travelled down the street and rounded the corner into Rue St Catherine de Marche, then he casually folded his newspaper and rose to go. The tiny transmitter in the bug that he had planted sent an excellent signal, but only over a moderate distance, and he wanted to err on the side of caution in being well within range to hear everything that was said. Right now Kennedy and Johnson were simply chatting about how nice the morning was, but soon the Irishwoman would be visiting *La Vérité*. At that point Perez hoped to discover if she were genuinely doing background research for a piece on the Congo or whether she was interested in Trenet's secret – whatever that might be.

Eager to have the mystery solved, Perez crossed the lobby, stepped out of the hotel and started after her.

"Well, the parting of the ways," said Steve.

"Yeah."

They had reached the offices of *La Vérité*, and although Steve had spoken lightly about parting while

Laura met the librarian, he *was* actually sorry that the moment had come to split up.

"Why don't we meet up at the Grand Place?" suggested Laura. "Say at last night's café?"

"What time?"

"How about eleven? An hour will probably be ample for what I have to do, but if I'm going to be later I'll call you. OK?"

"Well . . . as OK as any man would be, cut adrift in Brussels . . . " said Steve with a mock woebegone air.

Laura smiled, then indicated the sunlit boulevard that stretched away behind them. "Footloose and fancy-free in the heart of Europe – be a tourist."

"Can't visit a museum in under an hour."

"Shopping then. Souvenirs for your family."

"Souvenirs of Brussels?"

"Yeah. Get them a life-size model of the Mannequin Pis – for the mantelpiece."

Steve smiled. "Don't think so, somehow . . . "

"Belgian chocolates then, Jacques Brel's *Greatest Hits*, a vat of Pils beer . . . "

"Is this what the Irish call slagging?"

Laura grinned. "You're learning."

"Just so I know."

"Listen, I'd love to stay here on the pavement and engage in light banter, but eh . . . "

"Yeah – time to do what we came for."

"I'm slightly nervous, now that the moment

189

has come."

"Well, if your instincts are as good as Mac says, this is where we might unearth something."

"Fingers crossed," said Laura.

"Absolutely."

"Wish me luck."

"Good luck."

"See you in an hour."

"It's a date."

Steve watched as Laura made for the entrance to the newspaper, then she turned around at the door, gave him a thumbs-up sign and entered the building.

Perez watched the first of the tails falling unobtrusively in behind Johnson as the American crossed Avenue Anspach. In reality there seemed little likelihood that Johnson would do anything other than kill time for an hour, as had been discussed in the bugged conversation. Nevertheless there was an outside chance that Laura Kennedy might have discovered the bug and that all subsequent conversations might have been stage-managed. Perez thought it was extremely unlikely – the bug was tiny, and the conversation between the American and the Irishwoman had seemed entirely natural and unselfconscious – but it was better to cover every eventuality, and so he had arranged for the tails to earmark Johnson, while he himself stayed on the trail of Laura Kennedy.

He listened carefully after the journalist entered the *Vérité* building, and he heard her stating at reception that she had an appointment with Monsieur Gilbert, and the receptionist asking her to wait while she contacted the librarian. Perez had kept well behind the couple as they had walked to the newspaper's head office, but now he wanted to get as near to his subject as possible, knowing that there would be no risk of Kennedy seeing him once she entered the newspaper's cuttings library.

He wondered once more what game the Irishwoman and the American were playing. Listening in on their conversations, he had discovered that Johnson wasn't actually a research assistant but in fact one of the new owners of *The Sunday Clarion*. For some reason the man seemed to be making a field trip with the journalist, a fact that Perez had reported back to Trenet. So why had he claimed to be a researcher when initially contacting *La Vérité*? And what had the checks that Kennedy had instigated in the US got to do with the article she claimed to be writing on the Congo? Trenet had given him no clue when he had reported it all to him, simply reiterating that Perez should follow the couple's every move, but without alerting them to the fact that they were under surveillance.

With any luck though he might discover what was going on when Kennedy got the back edition of the paper containing the article on the fall of Kaburi. Eager to get to the heart of the matter, Perez entered a large café that was next door to the newspaper office. He went through into the quieter rear of the café, took a table in the corner, adjusted the volume on his receiving device, and settled down to listen.

Laura rose expectantly as a small man with thinning grey hair entered the reception area and approached her. "Monsieur Gilbert?"

He nodded and extended his hand. "*Bonjour, madame.*"

Laura shook hands and spoke in French, in which she was moderately fluent, though without Steve's colloquial ease. "Laura Kennedy. Thank you for letting me see the archives."

"My pleasure. This way, please." He returned to the side door through which he had entered reception, opened it with a pass key and ushered Laura through.

The man appeared to be in his mid-sixties and was slightly shabbily dressed, and Laura thought that if this were a movie he would be perfectly cast as the diligent but mildly otherworldly librarian.

They passed down a long corridor that flanked a series of offices and approached another door marked Bibliothèque. Gilbert had said nothing further by way of conversation, and Laura felt that she had better make some of the running. "Thanks for the directions," she said. Gilbert looked slightly confused and she added, "I had no trouble getting here."

"*Bien*," he said, nodding in response, then he opened the door and again ushered her through. "Our cuttings library," he said, indicating a large room with seemingly endless rows of filing cabinets running from floor to ceiling. There were numerous tables with opened back editions of *La Vérité* upon them, and Laura could sense from the little Belgian's tone of voice that he was proud of his private domain of dusty old newspapers.

Laura reckoned that if *La Vérité* had begun computerising its more recent editions then it must have been done by someone else in another part of the building – Gilbert was clearly a librarian of the old school. Yet in spite of her awareness of the advantages of technology the unashamed old-fashionedness of the cuttings-room appealed to the romantic in Laura.

"Excellent," she said, nodding her approval, then she turned to Gilbert. "You have the details of the edition I wanted?"

"A copy is already set aside for you, *madame*," he answered, indicating a table and chair in a corner of the room. "Page five for the article."

Laura could see that a slightly yellow-looking copy of *La Vérité* had been laid out on the table and now that the moment was finally at hand she felt her pulses beginning to race. "Thank you, *monsieur*."

"I'll leave you to study it. If you wish to photocopy the page, that can be done for a small fee."

"Fine."

"You can call me whenever you're ready. I'll be in my office." Gilbert indicated a Spartan-looking room with large but grimy windows that had been partitioned off from the main library.

"Thank you."

Gilbert nodded, then went to his office, and Laura paused a moment, knowing that a lot rode on the contents of this forty-two-year-old newspaper. For a moment she was almost afraid to go and open it, knowing that if it shed no light on Conn Lynch's story she would have to return to Mac in ignomiply, then she dismissed her reservations and made for the table. She sat down, took a notepad from her bag and opened the paper. It smelt slightly musty, an aroma she actually found attractive in old documents, and taking care not to crease it unduly, she turned over the leaves to page five. *"Dramatic Rescue at Kaburi"* read the headline, topping an article that ran for several column inches and which was illustrated by the photograph that Steve had downloaded from the web. The downloaded print that he had made had come from an amateur article for which, presumably, someone's home copy of this picture had been scanned, for the original picture printed here in the newspaper was a good deal clearer. Both the article and the photograph had separate credits, as she knew they would have, and she couldn't help thinking again what a pity it was that both the photographer and journalist involved were now dead.

Still, the article itself was sizeable enough to contain a good deal of detail, and with a mixture of nervousness and excitement Laura started on it. She read it all the way through without pausing or making any notes, then she breathed out deeply and stared into space. *Good news and bad news*, she thought.

The article described how the town of Kaburi had been overrun by marauding Baluba tribesmen and how a mixed unit of Gendarme Nationale – for which she knew to read mercenaries – and Irish UN troops had effected the rescue of two trapped Belgian nuns. It also made reference to the killing of Monsieur Gaston Picard, the local Union Minière manager, a bachelor whose life seemed to have centred around the company with whom he had served for over forty years in the Congo. Both Monsieur Picard's home and offices had been looted according to the article, with rare artefacts stolen from the house, and valuable company property stolen from the office.

Glowing reference was made to Lieutenant Fintan Barrett, a UN officer from County Mayo in Ireland, whose body was recovered the following day when government forces retook Kaburi and the surrounding region.

It was obvious to Laura that the photograph had been taken prior to the article being written – the lack of names in its caption and the opportunistic nature of the picture suggested a hastily captured moment, whereas the article went on to describe how the nuns subsequently had been safely reunited with colleagues in a Sacred Heart convent in another part of Elisabethville.

So the photographer hadn't managed to get the names of any of the four men in the photograph, which was a pity, but which Laura already knew to be the case before coming to Brussels. The bad news was that the article didn't name them either. Lieutenant Barrett's body had presumably been returned to Elisabethville, which would explain how the journalist had such detail on him, but the rest of the men in the photograph must either have been dispersed by then or been unwilling to provide personal details for publication.

The good news however was that both the nuns had been named – a Mother Benedict, whose family name was Thullier and who was originally from Ghent, and a Sister Sophie, whose family, the Ducrats, were well-to-do brewers from Liège.

Laura made notes regarding the nuns, then read the article through once more, unable to suppress a tiny tingle that ran up her spine at the thought of finally placing Conn Lynch in a situation where looting, chaos and actual killing had clearly taken place.

She looked at the photograph again, this time concentrating on the nuns. Mother Benedict looked to be in her sixties, so the chances were strong that she was dead by now. Sister Sophie however appeared to be only in her mid-twenties, which meant there was a good chance that she would still be alive. And if she were alive and living back in Belgium now – as seemed likely – it might well be possible to track her down and get her eye-witness account of what had happened and who exactly had been involved.

Pleased now that she had followed her hunch and come to Brussels, she carefully folded back the page for photocopying, rose from the table and crossed to the office of Monsieur Gilbert.

Daniel Trenet sipped distractedly at his coffee, his mind focussed on the document before him. Normally he took at least a half-hour break at lunch-time, but today he had told his secretary, Marianne, that he wasn't to be disturbed and to have sandwiches and coffee brought to his office.

In fact he didn't have much appetite just now, but he had forced himself to eat the chicken sandwiches, knowing that he needed to muster all the energy he could. He looked at the draft of the document on which he was working and read through what he had written. It was a reply to the letter from his merchant bankers that he had angrily thrown into the bin yesterday. Originally he had planned not to respond until he had to, but on reflection he had decided instead to take the initiative. Maybe it was the fact that he couldn't personally deal with the problem of Laura Kennedy and Steve Johnson that made him want to be hands-on and proactive with the bank, but whatever the reason it was still important that he buy time regarding his loans.

Evaluating the tone that he had struck so far in his letter, he nodded in approval. He had played down the scale of the financial problems that he was facing and had confidently asserted that he would accelerate repayments on his loans when the new NATO contract was landed. Although he was moderately confident that the contract could be landed – provided he allowed no scandalous accusations about his past to emerge – he had made it sound in the letter as though there was no doubt whatsoever but that the deal would go to IWS.

He had then made reference to the cruise on which the merchant banker had behaved injudiciously, recalling what fun it had all been, and he had followed that with a pointed enquiry about the man's family, and his hope that all was well with them.

To a third party reading the letter it might sound innocuous, but the banker would unquestionably grasp the underlying threat. Trenet decided that he would finish up with a low-key repetition of the fact that he simply needed a little more time to weather a short-term slow-down before repaying the loans.

His mind made up on how to finish the letter, Trenet was beginning to write again when his direct line rang.

He leaned forward and clicked on a switch that would scramble the line, then took the call. "Yes?"

"I said I'd ring when there was news," said Perez.

"Well?"

"It's not good. Johnson's been on to the Sacred Heart order of nuns. He's discovered that the younger nun is still alive."

"*Merde!*" cried Trenet in frustration. "*Merde!*" He breathed out deeply and tried to pull himself together. He knew from an earlier call that Perez had listened in on Kennedy's conversations, both in the cuttings library, and more importantly later on when she had briefed Steve Johnson at a café. He knew too that Johnson wasn't in fact a researcher, but while he didn't know exactly why the American was tagging along on the story, his presence had actually worked out well, in that Kennedy had a partner with whom to discuss matters during the bugged conversations. The worrying thing however had been the emergence of the fact that they weren't interested in simply writing an article on the Congo, but instead were clearly after a story on the late Conn Lynch.

But what the hell had happened with the Irishman? For forty years the events at Kaburi had presumably been successfully assigned to Lynch's past – so why were questions being asked now? Trenet's fear that these people might start querying the circumstances surrounding the deaths of Monsieur Picard and Lieutenant Barrett was being realised, but he had hoped that the trail might be completely cold by now. Clearly however this was not the case.

"So what's the story with the nun?" he asked.

"They've traced her through the Sacred Heart order. Seems she's a social worker these days."

"Yeah?"

"Her name is Sister Sophie Ducrat."

Sister Sophie. Trenet remembered her. *Pretty, big brown eyes, terrified but determined to be brave* . . . The good thing was that they had had very little one-to-one contact during the chaos at Kaburi. Trenet had had all sorts of problems to overcome at the time and they had never been introduced, so there was a good chance she wouldn't have known his name, even back then.

"Where's she based now?" he asked.

"In a convent outside Bruges."

"Have they made contact with her?"

"Not in person. She works out in the community. When they rang the convent they were told she wasn't expected back till about seven thirty or eight this evening – they're hoping to see her then."

"Right . . ."

"Assuming she agrees to see them, I can get close to the convent. The equipment is pretty good – I can report back what's said provided our friend wears the jacket."

"She should," said Trenet. "If she's meeting a nun she'll want to dress respectably."

"Right."

"Where are the subjects now?"

"In a hired car. They're on the road to Bruges."

"And where are you?"

"Following behind them. So – what do you want me to do?"

Trenet thought a moment. No point doing anything too radical just yet, he decided. "OK, stay on them, but discreetly. Keep listening to everything that's said and notify me if anything emerges."

"Will do."

"The meeting is critical. If they get to see the nun, it's vital we know what's said."

"Understood."

"If our friend doesn't wear the jacket to the meeting you'll have to find out what happened some other way – no doubt they'll talk about it in the car, or back in the hotel, or even to this editor guy back in *The Sunday Clarion*."

"Right."

"But first priority is to hear it live at the meeting."

"Absolutely."

"Right then, call if anything happens, and call me the minute the meeting ends. OK?"

"OK, I'm on it."

The line went dead and Trenet hung up, but he sat unmoving behind his large mahogany desk, disturbed by what he had heard, and aware of just how much hinged on the memory of Sister Sophie Ducrat.

"Too many tourists," said Steve as he regarded the hundreds of visitors milling about the picturesque main square in Bruges.

"And what exactly are *we*?" asked Laura with a smile as they made their way across the sunlit plaza towards the towering edifice of the old Belfry.

"I know," conceded Steve. "Adding two more to the numbers. But we're not really tourists."

"We weren't tourists this morning in Brussels. We won't be tourists when we visit the convent this evening. This afternoon, Steve – we're tourists."

"More *visitors*, than tourists."

"There's a difference?"

"Visitors make their own way around. Organise their own accommodation, decide for themselves where to have their meals."

"Usually in the same hotels and restaurants as all the other tourists."

"Sometimes. But they don't pour out of air-conditioned coaches with the intention of 'doing' Bruges in one hour. They don't do the 'get the photos, get the souvenirs, get a meal, get a night's sleep, get on the coach and "do" somewhere else the next day' routine."

Laura laughed. "You make it sound like a nightmare."

"It is a nightmare."

"For some of the tourists it's probably the holiday of a

lifetime."

"I suppose. Look, call me a travel snob if you like . . ."

"OK. You're a travel snob."

Steve gave a wry grin. "Maybe. But I just feel it's – I don't know. *Disrespectful* is the word that comes to mind. You're not really seeing the place you visit, you're not absorbing any of the local culture, you're just consuming a sort of product."

"You're right," said Laura. "But let's be honest. Part of the problem is that we'd all really like to have beautiful, picturesque places to ourselves, so *we* could savour them – and not have to share them with loads of other people."

"Hey, leave a guy his illusions, OK?"

"Making you feel guilty?"

"That's the problem with having a rich mother who votes Democrat – everything makes you feel guilty!"

Laura laughed, then playfully squeezed his shoulder in mock sympathy and said: "Poor little rich boy!"

Steve smiled back, then they negotiated their way through the crowds and headed in the direction of Bruges's famous Vismarkt. Steve had read in his guide book about the boats that left from the quays to cruise the little canals that criss-crossed the perfectly preserved heart of the old town, and they had said that they might go for a short cruise.

The narrow winding streets made for a romantic setting, and as he strolled along with Laura by his side he couldn't help but feel chuffed at the admiring glances that she drew from other men. He told himself that he wasn't her partner and that just because others assumed that they were a couple didn't make it so, and yet he couldn't shake off what he knew to be a juvenile pride in having such an attractive woman by his side.

They had checked into a medium-priced hotel about half an hour earlier, after Laura had rung the *Clarion* offices from the car as they drove from Brussels. Laura had brought Mac up to date on developments, and the editor had agreed that it was worth an overnight stay in Bruges if it meant an opportunity to meet Sister Sophie. He had, however, stressed to Laura the undesirability of incurring further expense by retaining the researcher in Dulwich, Connecticut, now that the focus of their efforts had shifted much more promisingly to Belgium.

Steve had been impressed by the editor's instinctive grasp of the balance between running a tight ship yet also allowing a journalist the leeway to follow wherever a story might lead. He had been struck too by Laura's pragmatism in agreeing to give up on costly research that she would nonetheless have preferred to continue with a little longer, with the journalist recognising that Mac had to channel limited resources where they were most likely to provide results.

Laura had agreed to update Mac after they visited the convent that evening, and Steve had actually been pleased that the nun wouldn't be back until half seven or eight, thus giving himself and Laura a legitimate reason to spend a few hours in Bruges.

To break up the journey they had stopped for an hour in Ghent, and had had a coffee and done a little shopping. Steve had bought a pair of fashion slacks and also some shirts and underwear – not having had Laura's foresight in bringing extra clothes in case their stay needed to be extended. The whole ambience since Laura had rung Mac had been holiday-like and relaxing and it was with some reluctance that Steve had reminded himself that they were still investigating the possibility that someone had actually been murdered.

"Vismarkt quay ahoy," said Laura now as they crossed a narrow hump-back bridge that spanned the sparkling waters of Bruges's Groene Rei.

"So it is."

"Looks lovely."

"Yeah."

"So. Me, you and boatloads of camera-toting tourists – what do you say?"

"What more could a man ask for?" said Steve with a grin, then he stepped forward to buy their tickets, deciding to be a tourist, and to enjoy their time out before the meeting with Sister Sophie Ducrat.

Ricardo Perez knew that his next move was a calculated risk and he sat at the table in his hotel bedroom thinking how best to minimise his exposure. He believed in taking calculated risks, however, and it was thoroughness of preparation rather than fear that fuelled his desire to weigh up every eventuality before going into action. His training back in the Foreign Legion had been intensive, and he had learnt how important it was to be able to judge when to proceed with caution and when to act boldly. And the best option now, he knew, was to act boldly.

Earlier in the day he had made a significant decision when he had chosen to work solo in following his subjects as they had left Brussels. He could have transferred his surveillance team from the capital to Bruges but had decided that to do so would be to make the operation more cumbersome than was necessary. Had he felt that Kennedy and Johnson had any inkling that they were under observation he would have continued using the surveillance team rather than following them single-handedly. It was clear however from the naturalness of the bugged conversations and the lack of any precautions against tailing that the journalist and her American sidekick were oblivious to the notion that they might be under surveillance.

And so he had stopped in Ghent when the subjects had done so. He had reported back to Trenet on how they had had coffee there and done a little shopping – with Johnson buying some articles of clothing. The arms manufacturer had quizzed Perez on precisely what had been bought, and had interpreted the purchase of socks and underwear as discouraging, a sign that Johnson was preparing to extend his stay in Belgium. Perez couldn't argue with the older man's reasoning, though he found himself slightly irked by Trenet's irritable tone – as though he, Perez, were in some way responsible for the American's behaviour. He had also reported that while travelling in the car Kennedy had rung her editor, the man called Mac. The news here had been more mixed. Firstly it had emerged that Conn Lynch had prompted the newspaper's enquiries with some sort of cryptic, death-bed confession. It had also emerged that the research they had been carrying out on Conn Lynch's life in America was being dropped, the better to concentrate on matters in Belgium. The good news however was that the editor was the only other person on the *Clarion* who was in on their investigations – the editor stating that it was best to remain discreet about a story that was sensitive, yet still fairly tenuous.

Trenet had sounded slightly relieved at this information and had ordered Perez to stay alert and to report back immediately there were any further developments. Perez had responded with an edge to his tone that he would have done so in any case, but Trenet didn't seem concerned about the younger man's feelings and had simply replied with a terse "Good," then hung up.

The man's demeanour irritated Perez, reminding him of officers he had served under in the Legion. Although flattered to have been entrusted with such an important mission, Perez wished that Alain Chavant had remained his contact point. The broken-nosed former sergeant had long since left behind his working-class origins, but Perez nonetheless found him easier to relate to, and he much preferred Chavant's macho bonhomie to Trenet's aloof commanding-officer persona.

Still, there was no point wasting energy over something that couldn't be altered, and there were enough real issues to be handled without worrying about Trenet's manner. Chief among the challenges facing Perez had been the question of accommodation. From the bugged conversation in the car he knew which hotel his subjects had opted to check into in Bruges. The problem was that if he were to stay in the same premises there was the risk that his face might strike them as familiar. It was a slight risk, he knew, bearing in mind how low a profile he had kept while staying in the Novotel, and how confident he was that they were unaware of his subsequent surveillance. Nevertheless it wasn't good field practice to get too close to one's subjects. On the other hand Perez knew that notwithstanding Trenet's confidence that Laura Kennedy would wear her jacket while meeting the nun this evening, there was a risk that she wouldn't – in which case he wouldn't be able to hear live the critical conversation with Sister Sophie. He wanted to have a fall-back position and in the end he had chosen to stay in the same hotel, having first allowed Kennedy and

Johnson time to check in before approaching himself.

He had rationalised that if he were to avoid the dining-room by using room service, and if he kept to the back stairs rather than using the lift, he should be able to avoid bumping into his subjects, while still being able to listen in on some of their conversations.

Using the same spiel as he had employed in the Novotel, he had sought to obtain an adjacent room to those occupied by the Irishwoman and the American, but this time both the adjacent rooms were already taken. Instead he had had to settle for the next room down, and it was here that he now sat fine-tuning his plan to gain illicit access.

He knew that Kennedy and Johnson had gone out to do some sightseeing and he reckoned that with a town as picturesque as Bruges they should be gone for at least an hour. Which should be plenty of time, all going well.

He rose from the bed, took a towel from the bathroom and made his way to the French windows that opened out onto his balcony. He was on the fourth floor, which was the top storey, and he stepped out into the sunshine, then glanced casually around. It was twenty past four in the afternoon, a good time, he reckoned. Most tourists should still be out sightseeing, with few residents either in their rooms or out on their balconies. His theory was borne out by a complete absence of guests on all of the balconies and he leaned over the rail and looked down, but again there was nobody in sight. His room was at the rear of the hotel and a belt of tall trees at the boundary wall of the hotel grounds largely shielded him from being seen from the rear of the nearest building, which looked like another hotel. *Largely shielded, but not entirely,* he thought, but then no plan was entirely risk-free, and gaining entry from the rear would be much easier than trying to pick the deadlocked bedroom door from the corridor.

If there had been any housekeeping staff in evidence on his floor he might have tried the ruse he had used to gain access to the journalist's room back in Brussels, but presumably by now all the rooms had been made up as there had been no staff around.

Right, time to act, he thought, then he unrolled the bathroom towel that he had carried out with him. Just in case anyone might be watching him he shook the towel vigorously, as though shaking it free of sand. He flicked his wrists several times, then in an apparent misjudgement the towel flew from his grip and landed on the balcony two rooms along from Perez. He paused a moment as he reckoned an embarrassed guest might do, then he glanced around once more. Still there seemed to be no one about and in one swift movement he vaulted over the dividing rail between his balcony and the room next door. He knew there was nobody in the room just now, having knocked on the door to check just a moment previously, and he quickly vaulted the next dividing wall to take him onto the balcony of the first of the two rooms occupied by his subjects. Lest anyone might be watching he reclaimed his towel in an embarrassed manner, then he surreptitiously scanned the horizon in all directions. There was no-one in sight anywhere. He quickly reached into his pocket and withdrew a small set of lock picks. He knew from examining the door of his own room that the balcony door had a much simpler lock than the deadlock on the main bedroom door, and less than thirty seconds after inserting the pick he had the door open and stepped into the room.

He closed the balcony door after him, pocketed the picks, wiped the door-handle clean of prints with the bath towel, then looked around. Although he reasoned that there was little likelihood of Kennedy and Johnson coming back unexpectedly, nevertheless his pulses were racing and he moved immediately to do what he had come for. It was an identical room to his own, and he swiftly made his way to the wardrobe and reached out to open the door. He hoped that this was Johnson's room and that he wouldn't have to repeat his break-in technique from the next balcony.

He opened the wardrobe door. *Bingo*, he thought, *men's clothes*. He saw the new beige trousers that the American had bought in Ghent and he took from his pocket another miniature bug which he carefully velcroed inside the turn-up of the trousers. This way he reckoned that even if Kennedy chose not to wear her jacket for the meeting with the nun there was a fairly good chance that the American would wear his smart new trousers and that Perez could hear the crucial conversation.

He shook the trousers to make sure the tiny bug was sufficiently secure not to fall out, then he replaced the trousers exactly as they had been on the hanger. Pleased with his work, he closed the wardrobe again. He wiped the handle with the bath towel, then moved across the room to the bedroom door. He knew that the chances were slim of anyone being out in the corridor just as he emerged from the wrong room, but nevertheless his heart was pounding. He took a deep breath, used the towel to depress the handle of the lock, then stepped out into the corridor. To his relief it was empty, and he strode along the carpeted corridor, quickly removed his key and stepped back into the safety of his own room.

Laura waited nervously in the convent parlour. She knew that a lot rode on her meeting with the Belgian nun, and while she was pleased that she and Steve had been courteously received and told that Sister Sophie would be with them shortly, nevertheless she was anxious about the outcome of the meeting. The room in which they waited was simply furnished, its plain cream walls featuring religious pictures and a large wooden crucifix, but it had comfortable armchairs, a big airy window overlooking the convent orchard and a highly polished wooden floor.

The evening sunlight warmed the room, and Laura breathed in the scent of polish from the floor.

"Beeswax," she said. "Whenever I smell it I'm seven years old again."

Steve looked at her quizzically. "Yeah?"

"You know the way smells can really bring you back?"

"Sure."

"Beeswax always brings me back to the convent where I went to school."

"Were you a boarder?"

"No – it was enough being a day pupil."

"Bad memories?"

Laura shrugged. "Bad and good. The smell of polish always reminds me of Mother Georgina."

"Let me guess. Mother Georgina doesn't conjure up the good times?"

Laura smiled. "Her idea of moral development was to tell a class of eight-year-olds what eternity in hell would be like."

"Dare I ask?"

"Eternity would be like if a bird flew down onto a beach once every million years. And every million years this bird took away one single grain of sand. Think how long it would take to empty the beach? And imagine yourself burning in the roaring flames of hell for all that time."

"Charming."

"Catholic guilt and repression – you can't beat it!"

"I'll take your word for it."

"You're not Catholic then?"

Steve shook his head. "Nominal Baptist. Our family goes to church at Easter, Christmas and Thanksgiving. The rest of the year's given over to making money – America's real religion."

"Cynic."

"Even worse – rich cynic. But you said there were good memories too?"

Laura nodded. "There was a Sister Mary – she was really nice. The way you felt a nun ought to be. And she'd a great sense of fun. I remember one day Mother Georgina came into our class and Sister Mary had us all walking in a circle, with each girl impersonating the animal of her choice."

"What happened?"

Laura smiled at the memory. "Proceedings came to an abrupt halt. I'd say Sister Mary got an earful afterwards."

Steve grinned. "So, million-dollar question."

"Yeah?"

"What was your animal?"

"A monkey – what else?!"

Just then the door opened, and Laura rose on seeing a slim woman in her sixties entering the room. She wasn't dressed in a conventional nun's uniform but wore understated civilian clothes with a cross around her neck. Her hair was grey and her face somewhat lined, but Laura could see that she must once have been very pretty, and she had large, expressive brown eyes.

"Sister, thank you for meeting us." Laura spoke in French as she extended her hand. "I'm Laura Kennedy."

"How do you do?" said the nun, shaking Laura's hand with a surprisingly firm grip.

"This is my colleague, Steve Johnson."

"Mr Johnson."

"Sister," answered Steve, who had risen to shake hands.

"Please, have a seat," suggested Sister Sophie, "and if you wish we can speak in English."

Laura knew that for delicate probing English would be much easier, and she reckoned that if Sister Sophie was suggesting it, then presumably she must be pretty fluent.

"Thank you, Sister, that would certainly be easier for me."

"Then English it is," said the nun with a smile. "Can I offer you some refreshments?"

"I'm OK, thank you," said Steve.

"Thanks all the same, Sister, but we ate in the hotel."

"Fine," answered the older woman, then as though having extended the necessary courtesies, she turned to them, joined her hands and spoke more seriously. "So. I'm told that you are journalists who wish to write about the Congo?"

Laura sensed that Steve was going to point out that he

wasn't strictly speaking a journalist and she quickly answered first, not wanting to get bogged down on side issues. "That's right, Sister. And I'd like you to know how grateful we are that you've agreed to meet us. I hope it's not too much of an intrusion."

"Not at all."

"Specifically, we're interested in writing about the fall of Kaburi. We read the article in *La Vérité* that featured your photograph and we hoped . . . well, we hoped you might be kind enough to share some of your impressions with us."

"I see."

"I know it was a difficult time and . . . well, I hope it's not too hard – too traumatic to talk about it . . ."

"It was, of course, a difficult time, but . . . " The woman gave an eloquent Gallic shrug. "I've since discovered that refusing to talk about difficulties does not make the difficulty go away."

"Indeed," said Steve.

"Sure," agreed Laura, relieved. She recalled the phone call to the convent and being told that Sister Sophie worked in the community as a counsellor – certainly this encouraging attitude seemed to tie in with such an occupation.

"For a long time I preferred not to think too much about the Congo," the nun continued. "When we were repatriated to Belgium I choose not to read the newspaper articles – it was all too painful."

"I can imagine," said Laura.

"Now though . . . I've accepted what happened – it's history."

Laura nodded. "And talking of history, can I ask you a little about your own background, how you came to be in the Congo?"

"I left school at seventeen and joined the order – I presume it's through the order that you tracked me down?"

"Yes," answered Laura. "Though it was actually Steve who did that."

"The article in *La Vérité* mentioned the Sacred Heart order, so that gave me a starting point," explained the American. He looked at the nun and grinned engagingly. "I hope it doesn't feel too much like you've been stalked or something?"

"Not at all," she said.

Laura smiled to herself, struck by how Steve's good looks and easy charm could be a winning combination, even with a nun, then Sister Sophie turned back to her and continued her explanation.

"Anyway, as you know, the Congo at that time was a Belgian colony, so nuns from Belgian convents went out there to work."

"How long did you spend there?"

"Just under three years. I helped Mother Benedict run the dispensary in Kaburi for what turned out to be my final year in Africa."

217

"I presume from her age in the *Vérité* photograph that Mother Benedict has passed on?" said Steve.

"Yes, she died in Brussels, back in the seventies. Is that significant?"

"Just want to be sure to have our facts right for the article," he answered.

"And this article – I presume it's the Irish connection that interests you?"

"That's right, Sister. Though naturally we also want to write about the mercenaries who were at Kaburi. Can you remember any of them?"

"Of course. After all, they saved my life."

Laura felt a shiver of excitement but tried to give no outward sign of it. She had feared that Sister Sophie might be a reluctant interviewee, or the type of person who lived in the here and now, attaching little importance to the past, but it seemed that this woman was both co-operative and still mindful of what had happened on those eventful days over forty years ago.

"Can you remember the men's names, Sister?" she asked.

"Some of them."

"Great. You see they never included names in the caption that went with the picture in *La Vérité*, so we've been in the dark a bit."

Sister Sophie nodded. "I understand."

"You say you remember some of the men's names. Can I ask you which ones?" said Laura, taking out the photograph from her folder and placing it before the older woman.

Sister Sophie looked at the picture for a moment without speaking. There was a hint of wistfulness in her expression and Laura realised that it was probably a very long time since she had looked at this picture of her younger self and her rescuers. Despite being eager to pursue her enquiries regarding Conn Lynch, Laura hadn't the heart to disturb the other woman's reverie and she waited until Sophie herself chose to return to the present.

"This man here on the right was called Vince," said the nun eventually, pointing to a tall rangy man in battledress. "He was a Rhodesian."

"Any idea of his second name?"

"I'm afraid not. It was a war zone, everything was chaotic, we weren't being formally introduced."

Laura nodded in understanding.

"The man beside him in the picture was called Dutchie. I don't think that was his proper name, I think it was – what is the word?"

"A nickname?" suggested Steve.

"Yes, a nickname."

"Dutchie is usually the nickname for someone called Holland. Did you ever hear him called Holland, Sister?"

The older woman considered. "Possibly . . . possibly by his officer. But I definitely heard him called Dutchie."

"Any idea of his nationality?"

"British. I remember Vince joking with him that he wasn't in the British army any more."

"Right." Although Laura was eager to get to the topic of the Irish troops her journalistic instincts were sufficiently ingrained for her to seek details on all aspects of the story, and so she now looked at the nun quizzically. "When you say British, do you reckon he was English, Scottish, Welsh?"

Sister Sophie looked thoughtful. "From his accent, I think English."

"You could tell from his accent?"

"Not for certain, but to me it sounded English. Also he was the most friendly, the most talkative, and once I heard him saying to Vince that when he finished soldiering he'd like to retire to Devon and run his own trawler. Devon is in England, I think, yes?"

"It is indeed," replied Laura, jotting down some quick notes. "So, we have Vince from Rhodesia, and Dutchie, probably from England. What about this man?" She was fairly convinced that the figure she was pointing at was a younger version of Conn Lynch, but she wanted to hear the Belgian woman confirm it.

"He was the junior of the two Irish soldiers."

"Do you remember his name?"

Sister Sophie looked into space, and Laura bit back her impatience, forcing herself to give the older woman all the time she needed.

"I'm sorry, said the nun. "I can't recall."

Laura felt a stab of disappointment. "Right . . . "

"It's so long ago, and we never really spoke much."

"Sure," said Laura. "The thing is, we think his name was Conn Lynch. Does that sound familiar?"

Once more the nun looked thoughtful. "It sounds . . . the name Lynch sounds vaguely familiar."

"Yes?"

"As I say it was many years ago, but now I think about it, it sounds . . . it sounds familiar, yes."

"Right," said Laura, keeping the excitement from her voice even as she was conscious of Steve raising an eyebrow at the apparent confirmation.

"You say you think his name *was* Conn Lynch?" said the nun. "He's no longer alive?"

"I'm afraid not. And his family emigrated to America so we don't have relatives in Ireland to check with."

"I see. Well, I can tell you his officer was Lieutenant Barrett," continued the nun. " I remember Lieutenant Barrett, God rest his soul."

"He was killed in action," said Laura, knowing this to be the case but wanting Sophie to elaborate.

"After we got away in the Jeeps, he died going to rescue Monsieur Picard."

"With the other Irish soldier?"

"Yes. Mother Benedict and I left with Vince and Dutchie when some other mercenaries got through in a couple of Jeeps. The Irish troops and the commander of the mercenaries stayed behind to give us – I'm not sure what the phrase is in English. Eh . . . shooting to make the enemy stay occupied . . . "

"Covering fire," said Steve.

"Yes. Covering fire. He stayed back with the Irish soldiers to give us covering fire and to rescue Monsieur Picard. It was very brave."

"It certainly sounds like it," agreed Laura.

"Unfortunately Monsieur Picard was killed by the Balubas. We learnt about it later, in Elisabethville."

"Right."

"Kaburi, of course, was looted, and we heard that all of Monsieur Picard's personal effects were stolen from his body."

"Sounds awful," said Laura.

"It could have been worse. At least he wasn't mutilated. Dreadful things happened at that time you know, dreadful things . . . "

Laura could see that the nun was recalling horrors that were probably long suppressed and she felt a stab of guilt.

"I'm sorry, Sister. I can see how this may be painful."

"My pain is nothing compared to what others suffered," answered the nun quietly.

Laura decided it was time to move matters on and she pointed to the last man in the photograph. "Do you have a name for this man?"

Sister Sophie looked at the picture once more, then shook her head. "Again I can't remember. You must realise the tribesmen were chanting, firing spears and arrows at us, there was chaos all around. So we were never introduced. I just know he was the commander of the mercenaries, a Lieutenant in the Gendarmerie Nationale."

"A Belgian?"

"Belgian or French – a native speaker for certain. But he had good English."

"And he went to the Union Minière office with Lynch and Barrett, and only he and Lynch came back alive?"

"Yes."

"If we could get a name, and he's still alive, it would be really good to talk to him," said Laura.

"I'm sorry, I can't give you a name. Maybe it would be in some kind of army records."

"I've already tried internet searches, " said Steve, "but the Republic of Katanga was a breakaway state and the political situation was incredibly turbulent. Not really a situation where you'd expect records to be kept. And the mercenaries scattered to the four winds when Katanga ceased to exist as a state."

"There is one possibility," said Sister Sophie. "It depends really on how important it is to contact the lieutenant."

"Very important," answered Laura. "It's wonderful that you're prepared to give us background detail about what happened in Kaburi, but this lieutenant was the one who was actually there when Barrett was killed. For our readers it's the Irish dimension that would be interesting. So anything that might help us find this man and throw some light on all that happened . . ."

"I understand," said the Belgian woman. "The only clue I can offer you is a location."

"A location?"

"Not for the lieutenant, you understand. I've no idea what happened him. But I know where you might find Vince – and he might know."

"Vince – the Rhodesian?"

"Yes. Though, of course, today it's called Zimbabwe. Rhodesia was the colonial name . . ."

"Right," said Laura not wanting to get into the nomenclature of African countries but eager to hear how Sister Sophie would know Vince's whereabouts after all these years. "So, where is he, Sister?"

"I don't actually have an address . . . "

"So, what do you have?"

"Knowledge of where he was the summer before last. You see I work as a counsellor out in the community, and one of my colleagues does a lot of work with underprivileged children. Each year she takes groups of them away on adventure holidays. The summer before last she took a group to the south of Spain. While they were on a mini-safari in the mountains above Fuengirola she got chatting to the man whose company was providing some of the Jeeps. His African background emerged, she mentioned that I had served in the Congo, and eventually they made the connection to Kaburi. The man turned out to be Vince."

"Amazing," said Laura.

"Perhaps," said Sister Sophie with a shrug. "Perhaps not. In over forty years of people constantly meeting other people, it seems reasonable that occasionally paths might cross."

"So did you make contact with each other?" asked Steve.

"No. He just passed on his best wishes to me, via my colleague. She didn't know the name of his company or where he operated from – she had enough to do watching out for her group of children, and he was just a man she chatted to on a day trip."

"Right," said Laura.

"But if it was important enough you might be able to find him. It was only the summer before last, so his company might well be operating still in the region."

"It might indeed," said Steve.

"Thanks, Sister, that's great," said Laura. "Just to go back to Conn Lynch for a moment. Can I ask you – how did he strike you?"

"Strike me?"

"How did he appear to you? I mean, I know there was lots going on, and it was all pretty traumatic, but . . . from what you saw of him, how did he appear to you – what sort of a person did he seem to be?"

Sister Sophie thought for a moment then looked at

Laura. "Strong, I would say."

"Yes?"

"Less afraid than his officer, I think."

"Barrett was afraid?"

"Everyone was afraid of falling into the hands of the Balubas."

"But Lynch seemed to you . . . braver than his commanding officer?"

"All of them were brave. They defended us and they tried to save Monsieur Picard, so you couldn't say that any of them lacked courage."

"Sure. But Lynch appeared the stronger of the two?"

"I thought so."

"How did that show itself?"

"The leader of the mercenaries decided to stay behind while his men evacuated us in the Jeeps. When he told the two Irishmen that he needed them to provide covering fire and then to help in getting Monsieur Picard out, Lynch took it better than his officer."

"Barrett objected?" asked Laura, fascinated.

"He did at first, yes, but the mercenary commander overruled his objections."

"So what happened?"

"The mercenary said that he was in command – which in fact he was. Anyway Lieutenant Barrett went along with him finally."

"And was there conflict between Barrett and Lynch?"

Sophie considered a moment. "Not about staying

226

behind. Like I said, Lynch seemed to accept that more readily."

"Was there conflict about something else?" asked Steve.

"Not that I saw . . . but . . . "

"But what, Sister?" prompted Laura gently.

"But there seemed more – more strain between Barrett and Lynch than between the mercenary commander and his men."

"What sort of strain?" asked Laura.

"I haven't thought about it since then," answered the nun, "and at the time I was too terrified to weigh up all the nuances."

"But you got some kind of impression," persisted Laura.

"Well, the mercenaries had a *rapport* with their commanding officer. He was clearly in charge, but there was a *rapport*. There was definitely none of that between Lynch and Barrett."

"Did you sense they might have disliked each other?" asked Steve.

The Belgian nun considered a moment, then nodded. "Possibly."

Laura glanced at Steve, and Sister Sophie intercepted it.

"Is there something . . . did something happen that you're looking into?" she asked.

This woman was sharper than she looked, thought Laura, but she decided there was no point burdening the nun with the details of Lynch's death-bed confession, or with the so-far unproven theories that herself and Steve had been exploring.

"No. No, I just want to capture the dynamics of the situation as accurately as possible."

The older woman hesitated a moment, then seemed to accept the reply. "Right. I think though that's probably all I can tell you about either of the Irish soldiers. We were only thrown together for a short time."

"I understand," said Laura. "And I'm really grateful, Sister. You've been very helpful . . ."

CHAPTER 6

The evening sun was dipping in the sky and bathing the countryside in warm golden light as Steve drove the rental car back towards the hotel in Bruges. Out of courtesy they had stayed chatting with Sister Sophie and had enquired about her own experiences in the Congo, and her subsequent career as a counsellor. Steve had known however that Laura was as excited as he was by the information regarding Lynch and Barrett, and both of them had been eager to discuss its ramifications in private.

The first significant point had been the nun's admission that the name Lynch rang a bell when linked to the soldier in the *Vérité* photograph. There had been little doubt in Steve's mind that the man in the picture was Conn Lynch, but as far as he was concerned it was now confirmed.

More importantly there was the fascinating matter of a strain between Lynch and Barrett that was evident to a third party – on the very day on which Barrett was to die. It was of huge potential significance, and while Steve knew Lynch might simply have disliked his commanding officer and been party to murder at some other juncture in his life, nevertheless the combination of a war situation, a disliked CO, and a patrol from which Lynch returned but Barrett didn't, seemed to Steve to cry out for investigation. Add in the offices of a diamond-mining company being looted on the same day – perhaps by Balubas, but also perhaps by Lynch's rescue unit – and the stage could certainly have been set for murder.

Whatever had actually happened back in Kaburi, both he and Laura were energised by the possibilities, and Laura was now on the phone to Mac, explaining why it was important for her to visit the south of Spain. He heard Mac asking with what he knew was mock incredulity if Laura was suggesting that the *Clarion* should pay for her to take a jaunt to the Costa del Sol. Laura pointed out that the former Rhodesian soldier was the only link she had to the mystery commanding officer of the mercenaries – and thus her only link to the one person who could still be alive of the trio that had left on the fateful trip to the Union Minière office.

The editor had previously complimented them on having successfully tracked down Sister Sophie and now he agreed without further argument to Laura taking the search to Spain. Laura thanked him, then on finishing the conversation she turned to Steve.

"So – take a bow," she said.

"For what?"

"For finding Sister Sophie and getting us on the trail of this Vince guy."

"You'd have found Sister Sophie yourself anyway."

"Hey, when you get a compliment in this business – take it!"

Steve smiled. "OK, compliment taken."

"The next thing now is to get to Fuengirola, post haste."

"Probably the quickest thing would be to fly to Malaga."

"You're very well up on European geography."

"Not really. It's just my sister went on a European vacation last year. She went golfing on the Costa del Sol and they flew into Malaga."

"Anyway, you're right. It's too far to drive, so a flight's our best bet."

"Too late to get away tonight, I'd say, but if we pursue it as soon as we get back we should be able to get an early flight in the morning."

"Let's get the first flight there is," said Laura. "I feel we're on a bit of a roll right now – let's go with it, OK?"

Steve looked at Laura's eager face, softly lit by the fading rays of evening sunshine and he smiled. "You know something?"

"What?"

"Wild horses wouldn't stop me now . . . "

Beads of sweat stood out on Trenet's brow as he rhythmically lifted and lowered the barbells on his weight machine. He had built a fully equipped gymnasium in the basement of his house, and he regarded the effort involved in remaining in shape as a worthwhile investment, the dividend from which was being fitter than most men twenty years his junior. Lately though he had begun to feel all of his sixty-two years, what with cash flow problems with IWS and now the additional pressure of an investigative journalist poking her nose into matters that he didn't want investigated.

He picked up the pace on his workout, knowing that hard physical effort was a good antidote to stress. He had settled into a demanding but satisfying rhythm when his mobile rang. It was a security enhanced mobile with a built-in scrambler, and he had specifically earmarked it for his dealings with Perez, his natural caution dictating that his normal number should never show up on any phone records of calls that the Spaniard had made. Quickly lowering the weights and mopping his brow with a towel, Trenet took up the mobile and answered it. "Well?"

"They've visited the convent. I got it all live."

"And?"

"They've just checked back in with the editor, *en route* to their hotel."

"Did our subject in the convent name names?"

"She more or less confirmed the ID of the first Irish soldier and positively confirmed the ID of the Irish officer."

Trenet waited for Perez to elaborate but the other man didn't. *Don't have me drag the information out of you,* thought Trenet, but he wouldn't give the Spaniard the satisfaction of knowing how worried he was and he forced himself not to sound anxious. "And the mercenaries?" he asked, his tone unflustered.

"Named one of the privates, gave a nickname for the other – didn't know the name of the CO."

Trenet breathed out quietly, but inwardly he felt a huge surge of relief. *Maybe everything was going to be fine after all,* he thought.

"But there's a problem," said Perez.

Trenet felt a sinking feeling in the pit of his stomach, allied to a flash of irrational anger at the other man for dashing his hopes "What?" he snapped.

"Through a chance encounter a colleague of the nun once ran into the first mercenary. He was running a Jeep-hiring service in the south of Spain."

"When was this?"

"The year before last."

"Damn!" *Why couldn't this stupid cow of a journalist butt out and mind her own business?*

"He may not still be there," said Perez. "And even if he is, they have no address – just the fact that he'd been operating somewhere in the Fuengirola region."

"If they found the nun, they can find him!"

"Possibly – if he's still in business. Holiday companies like that though, they come and go . . . "

"If he's there though, and they find him, he'll shoot his mouth off." *And then they'd ask who his commander was, and then they'd come tracking down Daniel Trenet . . .* He tried to think of what the sequence of events would be, and he found he could envisage it with frightening ease. They'd come to Brussels and say that they wanted a quiet chat about the deaths of Picard and Barrett, and they'd ask about missing diamonds and slowly but surely they would unravel the cocoon that Trenet had protectively woven for himself over the past forty years. *And it had to be now, just when he absolutely couldn't afford any scandal with the NATO contract in the balance.*

"What do you want me to do?" asked Perez.

Don't panic. This is a critical decision – take your time. "I need to consider," he answered as calmly as he could. "Stay on them and I'll call you back."

"Will do."

Trenet hung up and suddenly the effort of staying calm and in control was too much. His frustration at the journalist's intrusion just when he could least afford it boiled over and he lashed out, sweeping a jug of water off the table beside the weights machine and onto the floor tiles. It landed with a loud smash, the glass shattering and the water spilling in all directions. He sat there ignoring the broken glass and the spreading pool of water, and having vented his temper he began to calm down. He needed to consider his options carefully, yet part of him already knew what he needed to do. No, he told himself, nothing is automatic. Think it all through like a chess problem. Figure it out as many moves ahead as possible. And when that process was complete – and not before – then go into action . . .

Laura strolled the quaint cobbled street of Bruges, the atmosphere even more enchanting now that night had fallen. The occasional horse-drawn carriage bearing visitors clip-clopped by, but the hordes of tourists who had come close to overrunning the town during the afternoon were far less in evidence now.

Despite her eagerness to get to the south of Spain, Laura had been unable to get a flight to Malaga until the next morning, and recognising that there was nothing she could do to get there any sooner, she had accepted Steve's suggestion that they might as well enjoy their time in what was said to be the prettiest town in Belgium. They walked together now over the hump-backed canal bridge leading to the entrance to the Begjinhof, a nunnery that provided a haven of tranquillity in the heart of the medieval town.

"Founded in 1245, by Margaret of Constantinople,"

said Steve.

"Yeah? Where did you uncover that nugget?"

"History class – back in high school."

"You're kidding me?"

Steve grinned. "Yeah, I am. Read about it in the hotel."

Laura smiled, then they strolled past the convent entrance and along a path that flanked a small man-made lake. They shared a companionable silence, and Laura was struck by how she had come to be so relaxed in this man's company in the space of just a few days. He was an interesting character, more complex than she had at first expected, and his flashes of wit and frequently self-deprecating humour didn't always shield the fact that this was a man whose kidnapping the previous year had left him marked. Nonetheless for the vast majority of the time he was entertaining company, and for someone who was clearly very wealthy he seemed to Laura to have a surprisingly well developed social conscience. He was good with people too, as had emerged in his skilful handling of the initial contact with the Sacred Heart order, and also with his demeanour during the meeting with Sister Sophie.

And he was good-looking. Let's not kid ourselves that looks count for nothing, she thought wryly. She recalled her initial rejection of Mac's suggestion that she let the American accompany her, and her comment that this wasn't a movie, by the end of which two people who'd disliked each other at first sight would have fallen in love. In reality it certainly hadn't worked out like that. There had been no dislike, and she wasn't now in love. And yet . . . if she were honest, she'd have to admit that she felt herself becoming somewhat attracted to him. Of course, finding someone attractive and doing something about it were two very different things. And mixing business with pleasure wasn't a good idea, especially when there was such a potentially important story in the pipeline. And there was still Declan . . .

They reached the end of the lakeside walk and without speaking they both turned back to look in the direction in which they had come. They could see the hump-back bridge near the Begjinhof and the spill of yellow light from the cafés reflected on the placid surface of the lake. It was a balmy evening with the scent of nightstock in the air, and Laura breathed in deeply.

"Beautiful, isn't it?" said Steve.

"Gorgeous."

"Glad now we came for a walk?"

"Absolutely."

"Me too."

Neither of them said anything for a moment, then Laura looked across the waters and saw a couple leaning against a lamp standard and kissing languorously. Steve followed her gaze and took in the couple, then turned back to Laura and smiled. Not quite sure how to respond she smiled back, then for want of something to say she asked "Did you read up on here as well?"

"Yes."

"And?"

"It's called the Minnewater."

"Minnewater?"

"Also known as the Lake of Love."

"Really?"

"Yeah."

Laura was suddenly conscious of Steve's proximity and of the fact that they were standing together in the shadows, with the old town of Bruges providing a strikingly romantic backdrop. "I . . . I can see why . . . " she said.

"Yes . . . "

Steve looked at her, neither of them speaking, and she felt her pulses quickening, sensing that he might reach out and kiss her. Part of her wanted him to, while another part of her knew that if he did, a line would have been crossed and things couldn't be the same between them again. Time seemed to freeze as they stood close together, still with no words spoken, then they were distracted by a sudden splash nearby.

Laura spun around, and after a moment identified the source of the sound. "Waterhen, " she said, turning back to Steve.

"Gave me a start," he said.

"Yeah, me too." said Laura, recognising as soon as they began discussing the waterfowl that the moment

238

between them had passed. Steve must have sensed it too, she reckoned – or maybe the distraction had caused him to lose his nerve – but either way she knew he wasn't going to try to kiss her now.

"Maybe . . . maybe we should head back?" he said.

"Yeah. Yeah, early start in the morning . . . "

They turned and began to walk back along the path, and Laura found her mind racing. All her instincts told her that they had nearly kissed. It would have been her first really romantic kiss since Declan had died and to her surprise she found that part of her was disappointed that it hadn't happened. *But did she really want that? And all that it might lead to?* She wasn't sure that she was ready yet for a serious relationship – and she sensed that with Steve it wouldn't be a fling, but would be serious or nothing. But did she want that right now? And if she didn't or wasn't sure, then she reckoned that she ought to revert quickly into business-colleague mode until she *was* sure.

"I'm really looking forward to getting to Malaga tomorrow," she said. "If we can find this Vince character, things could get pretty interesting,"

"Sure could. Fingers crossed . . . "

"Absolutely," answered Laura. She felt that she had spoken with conviction, and Steve seemed to accept the return to business affairs, but for the first time since committing herself to the trail of Conn Lynch she knew that the task hadn't got her undivided attention.

"We've got to assume a worst case scenario," said Trenet. He was seated in his softly lit conservatory with Alain Chavant, having summoned the security consultant to the house shortly after the telephone call from Perez. This time there had been no small talk or refreshments, and Trenet had got straight to the heart of the matter.

Chavant eased his bulk forward in his wicker chair and looked at Trenet quizzically. "So what is the worst case?"

"Kennedy and Johnson tracking down Vince and Dutchie."

"Even if they succeed in doing that –"

"They can't succeed – we can't let them."

"How can you stop them?"

"By taking action," said Trenet.

"What sort of action?"

Trenet simply looked at the other man, and Chavant raised an eyebrow. "Jesus, Daniel . . . you're not seriously suggesting taking out a journalist? You can't – there'd be such a stink."

"That's not what I was suggesting."

"Well, what then?"

"I was thinking in terms of Vince and Dutchie."

"What?! Christ, Daniel – they were our comrades!"

Trenet felt a flash of irritation but he controlled it and instead opted for cold logic. "Drop the sentimental crap, Alain. We can't afford it. The fact of the matter is we can't have them talk to a journalist."

"Who says they would though?"

"Who says they wouldn't? Vince always talked too much when he was drunk."

"If we got to him first though, and told him to keep his trap shut?"

"Then he'd know we were worried about something and he might try to exploit it. More likely he'd swear himself to silence, but then spill his guts out to the first person who bought him a bottle of whiskey. Either way it's a risk we can't take – he needs to have an accident."

"Before anything's decided, let's think this through. I mean, what's the worst that can happen here?"

"That's pretty fucking obvious," snapped Trenet. "One of them gives my name to the journalist, a can of worms is opened, I get linked to what went on and it's headline time in the papers."

"They can't actually prove anything."

"They don't need proof. Once there's a scandal in the offing I can kiss goodbye to the NATO contract. And if that happens I'm finished – it means I'll lose the company I built up from scratch."

"Yeah?"

"Yeah."

"I didn't realise things were so tight."

"I have huge borrowings. They can only be met if we land the NATO contract."

Chavant nodded. "I can see why you'd fear the worst. On the other hand though –"

"There's no other hand!" interjected Trenet. "And it's not just me who should fear the worst."

"What's that supposed to mean?"

"If I go down over this, I won't be alone."

"That sounds like a threat," said Chavant softly.

"Of course, it's a threat. And it doesn't come from me. It comes from this journalist talking to Vince or Dutchie. She's a muck-raker, an investigative journalist. Do you seriously think that if she gets my name she won't keep digging? That she won't eventually hear about missing diamonds? Who fenced those diamonds, Alain? Who started a security company with the proceeds? Who's been linked to me for over forty years – having served with me in the Congo?"

Trenet could see his overweight former sergeant digesting what had been said and he knew that his words had hit home. "We're both in danger here, Alain, and we have to act together to deal with it."

"Yeah . . . it's just . . . "

"What?"

"If someone has to cop it I wish it could be the journalist. Not men we served with."

"The journalist is too high risk. You said it yourself."

"I know, but –"

"But nothing, for Christ's sake! What the hell's happened to you, Alain. You used to be able to do what had to be done – no matter what."

"Not with our own guys."

"With whoever it had to be done with. You tortured suspects in Algeria. Why? Because it was a filthy war and we needed the information to win. *You did what had to be done.* We both did, all our lives – that's why we're successful."

"Maybe . . ."

"There's no maybe about it. It's the law of the jungle. We shot enemy wounded; we made prisoners talk; we did what had to be done. Don't even think about going soft now – it's a luxury we can't afford."

Chavant looked uncomfortable, but after a moment he nodded reluctantly. "You're right. We do what has to be done. But there's still a couple of problems."

"Such as?"

"A: we don't know where Dutchie is – assuming he's still alive."

"According to the nun he wanted to retire to Devon. Make some discreet enquiries. You have contacts, so use them. Say you want to contact several former mercenaries. Make Dutchie one of three or four former comrades whose addresses you'd like to have – cover your trail."

"That brings me to B."

"Well?"

"However carefully I cover the trail won't this journalist be extremely suspicious if Vince has a fatal accident and then she tracks down Dutchie – and he has too?"

243

"She may not find either of them," said Trenet. "We don't know yet if Vince is still in Spain. Even if he is though, and assuming we have to deal with him, we don't move immediately on Dutchie."

"We just try to locate him?"

"Exactly. Then we monitor how things are progressing. If she can't locate Dutchie – and she may not, she doesn't have our contacts – then there's no need for us to intervene. And remember every day she's on this case it's costing the newspaper money. So if she has delays – or better yet hits a brick wall – they'll be frustrated. And if the story hits a dead-end the newspaper won't be long about telling her to drop it and come home. In which case we don't have to act regarding Dutchie."

"Assuming we find him, you wouldn't think of just telling him to stay mum? I mean he was never a drinker like Vince. He'd be far better at being discreet."

"He wasn't a drunk in 1961. Who knows what he's like now? And there's still the matter of alerting him that we're worried. For all we know he might be down on his luck. He might have pressing debts. I'm not giving someone the chance to try and blackmail me."

"Right . . . "

"Don't misunderstand. If at all possible we take no action on Dutchie. But if we have to waste Vince, and then Kennedy's about to track down Dutchie, we have to act."

"It could look dead suspicious if Dutchie died only a

few days after Vince."

"Who said anything about dying? He could just go missing – thousands of people do every year."

"But he would be dead?" pressed Chavant.

"Yes, but without a body there'd no evidence of foul play. Chances are it won't come to that, but if it does we'll cover every angle. OK?"

"Yeah . . . OK."

"Which brings me to our friend, Perez. So far I've been pretty impressed by him, but you're the one who really knows him. So, million dollar question."

"Yeah?"

"If it comes to it, can we absolutely count on him to handle two hits? No questions asked about the whys and wherefores, no evidence left to suggest a murder?"

For the first time during the meeting Trenet was pleasantly surprised when Chavant immediately nodded assent. "No problem there. He's smart and he's lethal."

"How lethal?"

"Extremely. He was discharged from the Legion after a brawl in Chad. Three guys insulted him in a bar and he got into a fight – and stabbed two of them to death. He saw plenty of action too in the Balkans. I know someone who was there, said he revelled in the combat – no hang-ups about killing."

"Good."

"So you'll send him to Fuengirola?"

Trenet nodded. "I've already recalled him to Brussels.

He's on his way right now – I want to brief him face to face, then he needs to get to Spain as far ahead of Kennedy and Johnson as possible."

"Right."

"Meanwhile your priority is to find Dutchie without arousing any suspicion."

"OK."

Trenet looked at his watch. "It's only twenty past ten. Head back to your office and start making calls tonight. Ring me at once if there's anything."

"Will do."

"And, Alain?"

"Yes?"

"No more sentiment. From now on it's us versus them. And the loser can't be us. Clear?"

"Clear."

"All right," said Trenet. "Let yourself out."

Chavant rose and crossed to the door, then looked round to nod farewell, but Trenet had already turned away and was sitting back in his wicker armchair, lost in his thoughts.

Steve undressed in his hotel bedroom but his mind was elsewhere as he began to sort out clothes for tomorrow. He hung on a hanger the new slacks that he had worn tonight, satisfied that the beige trousers would also go with the cream shirt that he had chosen for the next morning's flight to Malaga.

It had been a busy and eventful day, and he was tired now, but his mind was racing. He thought back yet again to the scene by the Minnewater, still unsure what he would have done if they hadn't been distracted by the sudden splash-landing of the waterhen. The mood and the setting had been conducive to romance, and he had certainly been tempted to kiss Laura. Part of him was disappointed that he hadn't, while another part of him was relieved, being unsure how she might have responded. Supposing a kiss would have been unwelcome, causing her to rebuff him? Their relationship was at a stage where they had genuinely been enjoying each other's company, but he knew that a budding friendship could be killed dead by one wrong move.

Or supposing she had responded? She was a really desirable woman, and he wanted her and would have been flattered by a response, but he also knew that such an action could have significant consequences. He hadn't had a proper relationship with a woman since his kidnapping ordeal the previous year. Assuming she *did* find him sexually attractive – which might be assuming too much – but if she did, was he ready now to enter a relationship?

He wasn't sure if it would even be fair on a potential partner to risk involvement when he was still in the process of trying to put the kidnap trauma behind him. It was all hypothetical for now anyway with the moment having passed, yet try as he might he couldn't decide what Laura's attitude would have been had he actually kissed her. Certainly there had been a sudden awkwardness with both of them self-consciously aware of the other as they had walked back along the shore of the lake. He had recognised that Laura had instinctively retreated to safe territory by going into work mode and, following her lead, he had chatted about their plans for travelling to the south of Spain.

By the time they reached the hotel they had appeared to have put their awkwardness behind them, yet neither of them had suggested a nightcap in the bar. Laura had mentioned an early start in the morning, and he had agreed that it was important they be at their best next day, whereupon they had retired to their respective rooms.

In truth he felt that it *would* be important to be on top of their game in pursuing the Conn Lynch story. It was satisfying to have made so much progress since coming to Belgium and he was pleased with his own role in tracking down Sister Sophie, and with the first-hand information that she had given them. It would be exciting tomorrow to go to Fuengirola and try to track down Vince – and thus the mystery officer who had led the mercenaries. His problem was that while excited by pursuing the story, he was excited also by Laura Kennedy – and he wasn't sure what he should do about it.

Tired with mulling things over, he opted for what he normally did when unsure about something, which was to sleep on it. He used the bathroom, brushed his teeth, got into bed and turned out the light. Tomorrow would be interesting whatever way it worked out, and wanting to face it refreshed, he forced himself to put Laura from his mind, turned over and tried to get to sleep.

Ricardo Perez listened to the roar of the aircraft's engine as he settled back comfortably in the leather upholstery of his seat. He knew that the pilot was building up the revs prior to take-off, and he closed his eyes, hoping to get some sleep while they were in the air. It was a quarter to one now and it had taken him this long to get to the airport from Trenet's house and to charter a private flight to Malaga. Trenet had given him the name of an air-transport company that operated on a twenty-four hour basis, and by paying a pretty steep fee Perez had managed to hire a small commuter jet to take him speedily to the south of Spain.

He knew that it would be essential to get there as much ahead of Kennedy and Johnson as possible and by flying through the night he reckoned that it should give him a head start of seven or eight hours. It wasn't much, particularly if he had to try and arrange a death that would look like an accident – a point he had stressed to Trenet.

"Don't tell me the reasons that justify failure," the older man had said.

"I'm simply pointing out the reality of the situation,"

249

Perez had countered.

"I know. But every mission has difficulties. Admittedly this one has lots. The challenge is to accept that whatever the problems, you'll overcome them."

"I never said I wouldn't."

"Good. So let's not waste precious time arguing about how difficult your task is. I'm taking it as a given that a man like you is up to any challenge that arises in the field. I want you to take it as a given that no matter what problems arise you'll regard it as essential to overcome them. Agreed?"

Perez hesitated only briefly, then nodded. "Agreed."

"Right, well, any further time spent here is wasted time, so –"

"No."

"Sorry?"

"It's not wasted time if it's spent on something important," said Perez.

"We've discussed the important points. What else is there?"

"My fee."

"That's already been agreed."

"That was before we decided on two possible hits. If I locate either or both of the subjects and if I have to waste them, you can't seriously suggest that I don't get extra payment."

"What are you suggesting?"

"Say forty K a hit."

Trenet immediately shook his head. "Way too much."

Perez indicated the luxurious surroundings of Trenet's conservatory. "You're not a poor man – and we are talking about homicide here."

"I know what we're talking about!" snapped the industrialist. "There's a budget for this operation – and it's not open-ended."

"All right then," said Perez, "let's say forty for the first guy, and thirty if I have to do the second. How's that?"

Trenet considered a moment. "Fifty for both of them. Thirty if you only have to do one."

Perez looked the older man in the eye. "If you want this done on the cheap you could get a street thug who'll do it for half the price. If you want it done professionally, if you want it to look like an accident, and if you want it to happen in the very short time-frame before this journalist arrives on the scene, then you shouldn't take this approach."

Trenet sat unmoving, then held his hand up in a gesture of appeasement. "OK, we won't fall out over it. What would you say to sixty for both of them?"

Perez thought a moment. "Thirty-five for the first guy – another twenty-five if I've to do the second?"

"Done."

"OK."

That had been two hours previously, and now that Perez had made the necessary preparations and was on the runway he was anxious to be away. He kept his eyes closed and allowed his mind to drift, and he found himself thinking about how a millionaire like Trenet had haggled over the cost of the hit. *Thirty-five thousand euro for a man's life. Probably less than Trenet spent on one of his luxurious holiday cruises.*

Not that Perez was particularly shocked. Growing up poor in the back streets of Port Boo had made him cynical and he had heard it said that rich people could sometimes be surprisingly tight when it came to spending their money. And as for the idea that a price shouldn't be put on human life, he had long ago dismissed such a view as naïve. Back in his early days in the Legion Perez had seen very clearly that far from being sacred, life in the real world was decidedly cheap. Even as he had grown up in Port Boo with priests and nuns sounding off about the sanctity of human life, Perez had realised that society paid only lip service to the notion. Later he had decided that whatever about its bullshit in other areas, at least the military wasn't hypocritical about life, and the taking of it. Their credo was every man for himself, kill or be killed, and its blunt honesty appealed to Perez. And so it was that despite having no animosity for the former Rhodesian mercenary he knew that when the time came he would kill him unflinchingly. He wouldn't actually savour it, but neither would he have any qualms, and he would pocket his thirty-five thousand euro without feeling guilty.

He heard the whine of the engines rise to a crescendo

now, and he opened his eyes and watched as the aeroplane accelerated down the runway, then rose smoothly into the night sky. He looked out the window, watching as the lights of Brussels stretched out below him. He took in the panorama of twinkling lights for a moment, then he sat back in his seat, closed his eyes, and prepared to sleep as the jet carried him southwards to Spain.

The bazooka hit the fuel tank of the first lorry and turned the vehicle into a ball of fire. The sheet of flame singed Trenet's eyebrows, and he frantically vaulted out over the rear-board of the second lorry.

He hadn't had the nightmare in a long time, but now he twisted and turned in the throes of the dream, the imagery as vivid as when the actual events had happened in Algeria, implanting themselves forever in the brain of a nineteen-year-old conscript.

Thrashing about in sweat-soaked sleep, he saw again the blazing vehicle light up the night sky and cast a harsh flickering light on the scene of the ambush. Mixed in with the agonised screams of the men on fire in the first lorry Trenet could hear the deafening retort of heavy machine-gun fire and he knew that this time the members of his two-vehicle patrol were significantly outnumbered and out-gunned by the FLN guerrillas. The Algerians were fighting a bitter war of independence with the French, and with atrocities occurring on both sides, Trenet knew better than to consider surrendering, even as he saw both the lorries being thoroughly raked by gunfire. The moment he hit the ground he began returning fire but he knew at once that the situation was grim. The French troops had been returning from a patrol in a sparsely populated region of the Atlas mountains and had been taken by surprise by what was clearly a well co-ordinated attack by a large band of guerrillas.

Even as he rolled for cover behind a series of boulders at the edge of the road a rain of machine-gun fire poured in his direction and he had to fight hard to dampen his fear. Several of his comrades had also escaped from the second lorry, which had driven into a ditch as its driver attempted to avoid the burning first vehicle, and they too were starting to return fire at the Algerians.

It was a hopeless predicament, Trenet realised, for once the heavy machine guns finished raking the vehicles they would be turned on any of the French troops still returning fire. The only chance of survival was not to give your position away with gun flashes and to make a run for it in the darkness. He realised that their lieutenant had almost certainly died in the first lorry and he had seen their sergeant being hit by gunfire as he had tried to exit from the second vehicle. The chain of command was broken, and he knew that if his panic-stricken comrades continued to return fire with small arms they would be wiped out in the next minute or so.

"Stop firing!" he shouted. "Stop firing and scatter. Scatter now. Scatter!" he roared. Without waiting any further he rolled away from the boulder behind which he had been sheltering, then jumped to his feet and ran, crouching low as the Algerians sprayed machine-gun fire in his direction. The French small-arms fire had stopped, and as he began to sprint he realised that his comrades must have heeded his cry. In the moonlight he saw a figure bursting out through the bushes to his left and he swung his submachine gun around. Just in time he stopped himself from firing as he recognised the terrified face of Henri Lebrun. Lebrun was an eighteen-year-old conscript from Marseilles, an earnest young man who got a ribbing from his comrades for his devout Catholicism and his lack of sexual experience.

"Scatter, Henri! Scatter!" Trenet whispered urgently knowing that the more the escaping men ran in different directions the better their chances of evading FLN pursuers. Trenet knew that even if their radio operator had been killed – which was quite likely – reinforcements would be sent out when the convoy failed to return to base and radio calls weren't returned. And having secured their victory, the FLN would be unlikely to linger too long, which meant that there was a fair chance of surviving if they eluded their enemy for now. If . . .

Even as he thought it, Trenet heard the Algerians racing to pursue them on foot. The guerrillas were shrieking and whooping, knowing that their quarry were outnumbered and fleeing for their lives. Trenet considered stopping to fire a burst in an attempt to slow his pursuers but he knew that the flashes from his weapon would provide an excellent target in the darkness and instead he concentrated on running fast. Despite the call to scatter, Lebrun was running in the same direction, a little behind and to the left of Trenet. The man was clearly terrified, occasionally giving vent to tiny whimperings as he ran. Trenet too was frightened, fearing what the FLN might do to him if he was captured, but he tried to channel all his energy into running flat out and gradually he began to pull ahead of Lebrun.

The pursuers were still shrieking but Trenet reckoned that the gap between himself and Lebrun and the Algerians had widened a little. The guerrillas must have thought so too, for while up to now they had been content to shout and scream as they gave chase, now they let loose a heavy burst of machine-gun fire. Instinctively Trenet ducked, even as he kept running, then he heard a scream of pain from Lebrun. The man stumbled, then fell, crying out the first oath that Trenet had ever heard him swear.

For a second Trenet stopped and looked around. In the soft moonlight he could see the shocked face of the wounded man as he clutched the shattered remnants of his right leg. Trenet was loath to leave a fallen comrade to the mercy of the FLN, but he was far too heavily outnumbered to stop and fight, and if he tried to carry Lebrun he knew they would be swiftly overtaken by their pursuers. Seeing the fallen Frenchman, the guerrillas unleashed a roar of excitement, and the primal nature of their screams triggered an instinctive reaction from Trenet. He sprinted away, straining every fibre of his being to accelerate away from the Algerians. Even as he zigzagged in anticipation of more machine-gun fire he felt a sense of horror at having abandoned Lebrun, yet he knew that to have stayed behind would have been suicidal.

To his surprise there was no burst of gunfire in his direction, and hearing further hysterical cries of triumph, he realised that the FLN had reached the fallen Lebrun. He reasoned that his pursuers must be distracted for the moment with the excitement of having captured an enemy alive and he tried to marshal his thoughts to take advantage of the opportunity. Up ahead he saw the faint outline of what looked like a ditch and on reaching it he jumped down into it and lay still. He could still hear the cries of the guerrillas who had caught Lebrun, mixed in with screams of pain from the wounded Frenchman, who was obviously being mistreated by his captors. Although Trenet's heart went out to his comrade, the survivor in him couldn't but be pleased to note the absence of a more significant sound: the pounding feet of his pursuers had stopped, and he reckoned that for the moment they were more interested in an incapacitated Frenchman than in one who was fleeing. Still, at any minute they might come after him again, and he decided not to linger in the ditch. He was just about to climb out on the far side when the night sky was suddenly lit up by a flare. There was immediate gunfire and Trenet instantly dropped down into the ditch again. If he had moved ten seconds earlier he would have been exposed on the open terrain that he had seen stretching away along the side of the mountain. Fortunately the ditch was quite deep, probably a channel for the flash floods that occasionally swept down from the hills, and he risked a careful glance over its edge as the flare began to lose its power and to fall from the sky.

He saw a large group of guerrillas gathered around the fallen Lebrun who was no longer being beaten but who was trying unsuccessfully to pull back from a man who was holding something up to his face. Trenet dropped back down below the lip of the ditch and tried to decide on his next move. The flare was a major worry, and the immediate gunfire that had followed its illumination suggested that others fleeing for their lives might well have been caught out in the open. All of Trenet's instincts were to climb from the far side of the ditch and run for his life but he knew that if he did and another flare were fired he would be a perfectly illuminated target on the open mountainside. There was an alternative, but he knew that taking it might stretch his nerves to breaking point. Before the flare had gone out he had seen a culvert about ten metres away, through which the ditch ran. If he crawled into that he might well avoid detection, even in the light of further flares. But it meant lying like a rat in a trap, less than fifty metres from the group of FLN gathered around Lebrun. Another flare suddenly shot up into the sky and Trenet began crawling to the culvert, his mind made up. He moved as silently as possible, taking care not to alert the Algerians to his presence, then he reached the culvert and crawled right in, flattening himself against the rough concrete wall to minimise the silhouette he might present to any searcher.

He had just settled himself when he heard a scream from Lebrun, then he heard a hard voice speaking French with an Algerian accent. "That's for starters," said the man, "to show you how we deal with French pigs!"

Trenet felt sick to his stomach, suspecting that the object he had seen held before Lebrun's face must have been a knife, which was now being used on the wounded Frenchman. The next ten minutes were the worst of Trenet's life as the interrogator questioned Lebrun about his unit, their objectives, who their commander was, who their informers were and a host of other questions to which the young conscript couldn't have known the answers. Trenet reckoned that the man asking the question wanted to torture the wounded soldier, and was enjoying the screams of agony from the helpless prisoner who had answered the queries about his unit, but been unable to satisfy his captor beyond that.

Each scream of pain cut Trenet to the quick and part of him wanted to run from the culvert and spray the assembled FLN with his submachine gun. Except that while he might put Lebrun out of his agony it would mean certain death for himself, given the number of enemy troops at hand. And maybe an excruciating torture session for him too, if he wasn't killed outright.

And so he had waited as the screams and the questions went on and on. He stayed crouching in the culvert, sickened by what was happening to his abandoned comrade, while simultaneously terrified that he too might be discovered. Eventually the FLN had decided that they had lingered for long enough, and almost as suddenly as the initial assault had come, the guerrillas regrouped and disappeared down the mountain side.

When he was sure they were definitely gone, Trenet emerged from the culvert and went to where Lebrun lay slumped and unmoving in moonlight. He knew the man would be dead and he had steeled himself for the worst, yet nothing could have prepared him for the sight he saw on rolling Lebrun onto his back. The Frenchman had been horribly mutilated, and Trenet spun around, retching violently. The image of what had been done to Lebrun seared into his brain, so that his stomach heaved in a series of convulsions. He continued until he was dry-retching, as though it would in some way cleanse him of what he had seen.

It was the heaving, as usual, that woke Trenet now

from the nightmare, and he bolted upright in bed, bathed in sweat and unsure for a moment of his surroundings. He breathed out shallowly, aware now that it was 2003 and not 1959 in the Atlas mountains, but the dream had been so vivid that he could still feel a trembling in his limbs.

He pulled back the blankets and, sitting on the side of the bed, turned on the lamp upon his bedside locker, then took a drink of water from the glass he habitually left beside the lamp. It was a long time since he had had the dream so badly as tonight, yet even as he breathed deeply to steady himself he knew, deep down, what had brought it on. For years he had been haunted by the notion of having abandoned a comrade, even though he knew, rationally, that he wasn't a coward – a fact that had been established on numerous occasions, both in Algeria and subsequently in the Congo. Nonetheless he had never felt right about what had happened to Lebrun. Notwithstanding the fact that he was grossly outnumbered and that going to the other man's defence would have cost him his life, Trenet had never been able to rationalise matters completely or banish a residue of shame about that most serious of military failings – betraying a comrade.

And now there were echoes of that betrayal in what he had planned for Vince and Dutchie. It was a different situation in many ways, yet he knew that the dream had been brought on by the underlying notion of betrayed comradeship and abandonment for personal gain.

So what should he do? Call off Perez and take his chances with the journalists? Everything about Laura Kennedy so far had suggested someone who wouldn't be easily dissuaded from digging up unpalatable truths. So was he to let his loyalty to comrades of forty years previously contribute to his possible ruination? For there was no doubt in his mind that if Kennedy printed a damaging story of what had happened at Kaburi he could forget about the NATO contract. Was he prepared to pay that price, losing control of IWS, having to sell off possibly all his shares to clear his bank loans? And then what? The gutter press hounding him, the loss of his status, the loss of his company, the loss of the comfort and luxury that were the only things that would make old age bearable. Was he prepared to end his days in a down-market nursing home with awful food, smelly toilets and staff who would patronise him at best, and order him around like a fool at worst?

And yet . . . No, he thought suddenly, *and yet nothing!* People had never sacrificed themselves for him, not when he was an orphan, not when he was building up IWS, not now, not ever. He had always had to look out for himself – it was the way of the world and he couldn't afford to indulge in guilt or sentimentality at this stage of his life. He hoped that Vince and Dutchie wouldn't be traceable, and that no action would be required against them, but he also knew that if action was required he had to be decisive and take it. It would be a pity, but the law of the jungle dictated the survival of the fittest and he couldn't afford to ignore that reality just because he had had a bad dream.

He sat on the side of the bed for a moment, the cold sweat in which he had awoken drying on his skin, then he told himself that he needed to be fit and alert over the next few days and that he should dismiss all of this and try to get back to sleep. He reached out and opened the drawer of his bedside locker, removed two sleeping pills and took them with the glass of water, then got back into bed. He still felt a little shaken by the vividness of the nightmare, but he told himself that he had never before had the dream twice in one night and there was no reason why he should start now. Bolstered by the thought, he reached over, switched off the light and lay down to sleep.

CHAPTER 7

Laura strode towards the exit doors of the arrivals area in Malaga airport, hoping that her luck would change. It had been one of those days where no calamity occurred but where a string of minor setbacks had frustrated her.

Firstly there had been a slight residual awkwardness with Steve when they had come down to breakfast, and she had sensed that the moment of halted intimacy at the Lake of Love had registered with both of them more than they had been willing to acknowledge. Neither of them had made reference to it however, and after a while they seemed to regain their ease with one another.

They had made good time driving from Bruges to Brussels airport where they had left their rented car and booked another for Malaga, but on entering Departures they had found that their flight was delayed. Originally it was meant to be for forty minutes, but in the end it turned out to be an hour and a half. Killing time in the airport bar, Laura had been jostled by a drunken football supporter and had spilled half of her glass of red wine over Steve's new beige slacks. He had downplayed the incident and gone off to change in the gents', but Laura couldn't help but feel it was going to be one of those days.

She had rung Mac to let him know that there had been no further developments from the enquiries that she had set in train, both in Clare/Galway and in the US, and although Mac's wry comments had sounded no more sardonic than usual, she was still left feeling under increasing pressure to come up with something tangible on reaching the south of Spain.

Normally when travelling at the *Clarion's* expense she would stay in good quality rather than luxurious accommodation, but Steve had booked them rooms in the Byblos Hotel – in which his discriminating sister Gretchen had stayed the previous summer. Laura knew it would be over the budget allowed for company expenses, but Steve had insisted on looking after the balance between what the *Clarion* would pay and what the Byblos actually charged. He had argued that since arriving in Dublin he had been shown exemplary hospitality and that it was only fair that he should be allowed to reciprocate at least once. Eventually she had agreed to let the balance of the cost be his treat. It had seemed a reasonable – indeed a generous – action on his part, and yet Laura couldn't help but regard it as another slightly discomforting experience on a day when nothing seemed to be going smoothly. She knew it was silly to regard it as placing her under a compliment, yet a tiny part of her mind couldn't entirely shake off the notion of being, however briefly, the kept woman of a wealthy man.

"Well, the Costa del Sol," said Steve, breaking her reverie as the reached the exit door of the terminal.

"Right."

"Fingers crossed, Laura."

"Yeah," she said, telling herself it was time to dismiss her reservations and to become positive again. "Yeah, fingers crossed . . ."

Perez finished a scan with his binoculars, then lowered the glasses from his eyes and sat back against the bough of a tree as the Spanish sun beat down from a clear blue sky. He had parked his rented car well out of sight along a mountain track, then proceeded on foot to the heavily wooded hillside from which he could observe the long drive leading from the road to Vince Douglas's remote cottage.

He had sat unmovingly waiting for his quarry, and the long wait under the blazing sun reminded him of his time in the Legion. The NCOs who had trained him had emphasised the importance of waiting alertly when on a mission. He had learnt to be patient, to wait, unmoving but observant, for hours on end. He had learned to ignore boredom, to ignore sleepiness, simply to blend into a landscape – and then suddenly to spring into violent action when the unsuspecting enemy showed himself.

It was a lesson that he had found valuable in the years since he had left the Legion, yet he couldn't draw solace from it today. Instead he found anxiety impinging on him and eating into the energy that he wanted to conserve for his mission. It was a problem of timing, he knew, but knowing that he couldn't control the timing of other people's movements didn't lessen his frustration that his head start on Kennedy and Johnson was being eroded with each passing hour.

It was four o'clock in the afternoon now, which meant that he had had the hillside cottage staked out for six hours. That sort of waiting in itself didn't faze him, but he recalled Kennedy stating that the flight from Brussels to Malaga was scheduled for eleven that morning. Which meant that Kennedy and the American would have arrived at the Costa del Sol by now. Even allowing for the time it would have taken to gather their baggage, rent a car and drive to their hotel, they might well have begun their enquiries into the whereabouts of Vince Douglas. And if things had gone well for them it mightn't take long to discover the whereabouts of this cottage, and to make their way here, just as he had done.

He had arrived at Malaga in the middle of the night, then driven in a hired car to the Byblos hotel, wanting once again to be based in close proximity to Johnson and Kennedy when they arrived later on. He had quickly checked in and allowed himself two hours' sleep, then he had showered, had breakfast and studied a hotel brochure that advertised day trips departing from the general area of Mijas and Fuengirola. He had scanned down through those companies that did Jeep safaris up into the mountains, and his attention had immediately been taken by a company called Salisbury Tours. He knew from his time in Africa that Salisbury had been the capital of the former Rhodesia, although the city was now called Harare. With Vince Douglas being Rhodesian-born and reared, it seemed like too much of a coincidence for the company not to be his, and on driving down into Fuengirola to the address given in the brochure, Perez had been proven to be right.

"Good morning," he had said cheerily in English on entering the small office of Salisbury Tours and approaching the counter.

"Good morning, sir," answered a rugged-looking man of about thirty who was sitting at a desk doing paper-work. The office had just opened and there were no other customers present, just one other staff member. He was another slightly unkempt-looking man of about the same age who was packing provisions, presumably for one of their safari trips. The two men had been talking

269

in colloquial Spanish as Perez entered, and he quickly took in his surroundings, but could see no sign of Vince Douglas. Unabashed by the owner's absence, Perez went into the routine he had planned on his drive from the Byblos to Fuengirola.

"I'm with a Turkish trade delegation that's visiting Marbella," he said. "I'm interested in getting prices for Jeep excursions, and I was told I could get a good deal from Vince Douglas."

"We can give you good deal, but Vince . . . well, Vince won't be in today."

"He's not working at all?"

"No, sir."

"Except on Maria!" muttered the second employee in Spanish as he hoisted the safari equipment onto his shoulder, nodded to his colleague and Perez, and made for the door.

Perez had adopted the phoney Turkish persona as a matter of fieldcraft and now he was glad that it had paid an additional bonus, with the two employees unaware that he too was Spanish and could understand anything that was said.

So there was a Maria – presumably Vince's girlfriend. He hoped that her presence wouldn't become a complicating factor. Before he could ponder it any further the first employee – who had smothered a smile at his colleague's snide remark – went into sales mode.

"Our rates are the best in the area. You won't beat us

for price. How many are in your party?"

"Probably about ten," answered Perez.

"And have you any special trip in mind – half day, full day, we can fix it to suit?"

"We haven't decided yet. Maybe you could organise some brochures and price lists for me?"

"The brochures are all on the counter there. If you hold on one minute I'll get you a price list with all the different trips – we have new ones in the back."

"Take your time," said Perez, then as soon as the man went into the rear of the shop he quickly leaned over the counter to read the heading on an invoice that he had noticed. It was addressed to Vincent Douglas and was a charge for water rates. Presumably Douglas used his travel company to pay his personal expenses, but the thing that interested Perez was the address on the top of the invoice. He quickly memorised the details, then gave the impression of perusing the brochures as the assistant came back with the price list.

"Now sir, I think you'll find these prices are good. And we are happy to help you with any queries."

"Thank you, you've already been very helpful," said Perez with a smile, then he nodded to the man and walked out of the shop.

That had been almost seven hours ago, and having consulted a detailed local map, Perez had found his way to the region of Vince Douglas's cottage, parked his own car up the mountain trail and called to the cottage.

There had been no vehicle in evidence and no reply to his knocking, and he had assumed that Vince must be in Maria's house, if what had been said in the travel shop had been accurate.

He had seen that there was good cover on the opposite hillside and he had settled down there to wait, hoping that Maria lived locally and that Vince would return home within a reasonable time. But would he come home at all tonight? And even if he did, what would happen if Kennedy and Johnson located the cottage and decided that they too would await his return? He tried to tell himself it was unlikely, and that in such a situation they would return to their hotel and try again later. Besides, worrying about these things would do nothing to prevent them happening, and so he tried to regain his former mental state of being alert without being fretful.

Moving slowly so as not to give his position away in the unlikely event that anyone else might be around, he unscrewed the top from his water bottle and took several deep slugs. The water was tepid by now but he knew it was important not to become dehydrated in the harsh summer sunshine. He was screwing the cap back on when he heard the faint droning of an engine. The sound became louder, and he realised that a vehicle must be ascending the hill toward the cottage. Immediately he put down the water and took up his binoculars. He prayed that it wouldn't be Kennedy and Johnson, barging in on the scene before he had a chance to deal with Vince, then something about the sound he was hearing struck him. It wasn't one engine, but two. He kept the glasses trained on the drive and then, sure enough, he saw two somewhat battered-looking Jeeps driving in convoy towards the cottage. They reached the tarmacadamed area in front of the cottage and the door of the leading Jeep opened.

Perez took care not to let the sun reflect on his binoculars as he swivelled to follow those alighting from the vehicles. From the driver's side came an overweight but curvaceous woman with long black hair. *Maria*, he thought, then he moved the glasses to focus on her passenger. He was a big man in his early sixties with thick, unkempt grey hair. He looked heavily tanned but had the fleshy appearance of an athlete gone a little to seed. *Vince Douglas, no doubt about it.*

Perez felt a quickening of his pulse now that he had finally seen his quarry and even as he wondered about the presence of second vehicle he got his answer. Vince was moving unsteadily with the shambling uneasy step of a drunk and Maria quickly kissed him on the cheek, then gave a cheery wave and retreated to the other vehicle which was being driven by a youth with long bleached-blond hair. *Perfect* thought, Perez, suddenly understanding. *He's had too much to drink so she drove his Jeep home. Which would leave the field wide open the moment the second Jeep left.*

Perez watched Vince wave in farewell, then the

woman got into the second Jeep, the youth gunned the engine and they drove off. Perez waited until the sound of the vehicle was fading down the valley, then he took another slug of water, stowed his binoculars in their case and started towards the cottage.

"Bingo!" said Steve, pointing at the screen of his laptop. "Twenty-nine Hollands listed, with phone numbers, in the Torquay area." He had his lightweight laptop propped on his knee and had been using it to gain internet access via his mobile phone as they made the car journey from Malaga airport to their hotel.

During the flight from Brussels it had struck him that it would be wise to plan ahead a little, just in case Vince Douglas should prove untraceable. And so as soon as they had left the confines of Malaga airport, he had begun searching for a website from which it was possible to download telephone directory listings in Devon.

"Good work," said Laura.

"Thanks."

"Though let's hope we don't need it."

"Sure," agreed Steve. He knew that it should be much simpler to seek out one individual on the Costa del Sol, where they now were, than to have to travel on to Devon in the hope of locating a former soldier once known as Dutchie Holland. Still, it was no harm to think a few steps ahead, just in case, and he was pleased at having negotiated the Web to find the listing of

Hollands in the Torquay region.

"Of course he may not live in Torquay any more," said Laura. "Or his number could be ex-directory. He could even be dead."

"Absolutely. And I'm not going to even think about working through this list unless we draw a blank with Vince Douglas. But at least if that happens, we've got a plan B."

"*Bí ullamh* is our motto," she said.

"Sorry?"

"Scout's motto in Irish. *Be prepared.*" She glanced over at him and grinned. "Bet you were a Boy Scout."

Steve smiled. "Coyote Patrol. My clove hitches were much admired."

"I'll take your word for it."

"Were you a Girl Guide?"

"Bluebell Patrol. My bowlines were the talk of the campfire."

Steve smiled again, pleased that they had regained their rapport after this morning's slight awkwardness in the wake of their stroll at the Lake of Love.

"OK – Byblos Hotel," said Laura, indicating a roadside sign.

"Great."

She slowed and turned off the road on reaching the hotel entrance, then drove up the driveway. "Wow, nice-looking place!"

"Yeah," agreed Steve. "But then if my pernickety sister

275

enjoyed a hotel – it must be good."

"Pity our stay will be short – I could get used to a place like this."

Steve looked at her playfully. "Maybe it will take us a while to locate Vince Douglas."

Laura grinned but shook her head. "Mac wants progress on this yesterday. And so do I. So pleasant as the surroundings are – we need to get out looking for Mr Douglas. OK?"

Steve nodded. "Sure . . . "

Perez took a moment to gather himself together, then he reached out and rang the bell on the front door of the cottage. He had read once that salesmen were taught not to stand straight on when calling door to door – apparently it looked less threatening if you offered more of a side profile – and so he stood sideways to the door as he waited for the older man to answer the bell.

He heard no sound of anyone coming however, and after a moment he rang again, hoping that Douglas wouldn't have fallen into a drunken stupor in the few minutes it had taken to get from the observation point on the hillside to the door of the cottage. Although Douglas had looked to have drink taken, he hadn't appeared drunk to the point of being incapacitated, and Perez had counted on him being capable of opening the hall door to a caller.

Almost as soon as he had rung for the second time he

heard a sound from within the cottage and his spirits soared as he made out the sound of footsteps approaching the door. Suddenly the door opened and Douglas was standing before him, blinking a little against the harshness of the sunlight.

Close up, Perez could see that Douglas had light blue eyes that were now somewhat bloodshot. His face was tanned but craggy, and the former mercenary looked bigger than he had appeared from a distance. Still blinking against the sunlight, he seemed to fill the door-frame as he looked quizzically at his visitor.

"Yeah?"

Perez noted that the man pronounced the word in a similar way to South Africans he had served with in the Legion. He smiled by way of reply and looked the older man in the eye. "Vince? Vince Douglas?"

"Who's asking?"

"My name is Ernesto Suarez. An old friend of yours sent me."

"Don't have old friends."

Although the man's speech was slightly slurred, Perez nonetheless sensed a degree of alertness in Douglas, and he reckoned that he might well be the type of drinker who could consume significant quantities of alcohol and yet still function reasonably effectively.

"Dutchie sent me. Dutchie Holland."

"Dutchie . . . ?"

The man looked reflective and Perez could visualise

277

him processing such an unexpected link to his past. *No harm to jog his memory a little.*

"He hasn't forgotten Kaburi," said Perez, "and I'm sure you haven't either."

"No . . ." he answered after a moment. Again the man looked reflective, then he turned a surprisingly alert gaze on Perez. "What's any of that got to do with you?"

"Dutchie is my uncle."

"Yeah?"

"Yes. If you can spare me a few minutes, I'd love to have a chat."

The older man didn't answer immediately and Perez unobtrusively bunched his right fist. He had to question the man before Kennedy and Johnson arrived on the scene, and if Douglas didn't allow him into the cottage voluntarily he would fell him with a blow and enter that way.

"Old Dutchie is your uncle?"

"That's right."

Douglas shook his head disbelievingly, then grinned. "Best come in then . . ." He stepped aside and gestured with his hand. "This calls for a drink . . ."

Trenet pored over the papers spread before him on his desk. He was in his office on the top floor of the IWS building and late afternoon sunshine flooded the room, but Trenet was barely aware of his surroundings. He studied intently the loan statements spread before him, calculating which ones were most pressing, and estimating what would be the minimum repayment needed to ease the pressure in each case. He reached for his calculator, and began working out a sliding scale of share price valuations and dividends, based on how much the stock could rise were they to land the NATO contract. He was about halfway through the calculations when his phone rang, and seeing Chavant's name on the caller ID, he switched his phone into electronic scrambling mode, then answered the call.

"Yes?"

"Said I'd keep you posted."

"Well?"

"I've been using the excuse of a possible reunion, and I've lumped our friend's name in with those of some other mercenaries."

"And?"

"Made some progress. I spoke to someone who used to have occasional contact with our man."

"Used to?"

"The last contact was five or six years ago. At that stage he was working in a school in Torquay."

"In a school?"

"As a janitor."

"Right. Did you get an address or phone number?"

"I'm working on that," said Chavant. "The guy I spoke to couldn't find an address or phone number but he knew someone else who might have one, and he's trying to contact him. He'll ring me back as soon as he does."

"OK, keep me posted."

"I'll ring you the minute he rings me."

"Right. And listen –"

"Yes?"

"Good work."

"Thank you. Let's hope . . . well, let's hope none of this is needed."

"Let's hope not. I'll talk to you."

Trenet hung up, then considered the implications of the call. On the one hand Chavant's contact sounded promising. Chavant's own attitude however was disappointing. Trenet felt that his former sergeant had gone soft – physically that had been the case for quite a few years – but now it appeared that he was losing his mental toughness as well, worrying about former comrades when there were far bigger things at stake. It was something that might need addressing, Trenet thought, but for now though it seemed Chavant was on course to track down Dutchie Holland. And, with Perez having located Vince Douglas's cottage in Spain, matters were as much in hand as could be hoped for. *And when the time was right, whatever had to be done, would be done . . .*

Trenet paused a moment, considering the twists of fate that had brought him to this point, then he dismissed them as the inevitable complications that arose in the founding, development and protection of a profitable business empire.

Talking of which . . . He looked at the calculations that he had been making regarding the IWS stock, then he breathed out, consciously put his other concerns from his mind and went back to work on the figures.

Laura felt her heart beginning to race as she and Steve traversed the narrow streets of Fuengirola en route to the premises of Salisbury Tours. The concierge back at the Byblos Hotel had given them accurate directions, and they had found a parking space for the rented car, then continued on foot in the hot afternoon sunshine.

For a day that had started badly – what with the residue of awkwardness between herself and Steve, the postponed flight and the spilled drink – things now appeared to be picking up.

Steve's choice of the Byblos as their base had turned out to be an excellent one, with the hotel even more luxurious than Laura had expected. She had been impressed also by his expertise with the internet and the way that he had obtained the list of telephone numbers and addresses for the Hollands in the Torquay region. The information looked like being of academic interest now that they had found Vince Douglas's location, but Laura felt that Steve had shown commendable initiative nonetheless in seeking the whereabouts of Dutchie Holland.

They crossed another narrow street now to walk in the shade, and Laura felt her excitement mounting as they spotted the offices of Salisbury Tours.

"Let's hope it was worth the journey," said Steve.

"Yeah," said Laura, then they arrived at the office and she reached out to open the door. To her surprise the office door was locked. Through its glass panel she could see that the lights were off in the interior.

"What the hell?" said Steve. "Hardly the siesta, all the other shops have reopened."

"It's not the siesta," said Laura, disappointedly. "Look at this." She indicated a handwritten note that had been stuck to the inside of the glass door. The top part was written in Spanish, and below was what she assumed to be its English translation: *Sorry for your inconvenience, we are opening again tomorrow morning at 0900.*

Laura looked at her watch. "Just gone half-four. They should be open for another three hours at least."

"Something must have cropped up," said Steve.

"Like what?"

"Who knows? Maybe an unscheduled group showed up, asked for a safari up into the hills."

"So they close the office?"

"Maybe there's a very limited staff – it doesn't look very fancy. Could be Vince Douglas needs the money. Perhaps he felt a definite booking was better than manning the desk but possibly earning nothing in the process."

"*Sorry for your inconvenience, we are opening again tomorrow morning at 0900,*" read Laura aloud. "Doesn't sound like it was written by someone whose first language was English."

"Granted. Maybe he was out with another group and one of his staff wrote this. Whatever the reason, looks like we'll get no joy here till tomorrow."

"I'd really like to be able to report to Mac with something tonight."

Steve shrugged. "Well, there is progress to report. I mean we've established that this outfit is run by Vince Douglas. OK, so it's a hiccup that he's not here and the office is closed, but one way or the other we should be face to face with him tomorrow."

"Yeah," said Laura. "Thing is . . . I really want to be face to face with him tonight."

"Right . . ."

"We've had enough delays, Steve – I want to press on now."

"Fine by me. So what's our next move?"

"We could go back to the Byblos and talk to the concierge. He seemed to know a fair bit about Vince Douglas and Salisbury Tours. He might be able to get us a mobile number – or even an address."

Steve looked at her appraisingly. "You've really got the bit between your teeth, haven't you?"

"Yeah," agreed Laura. "Don't you?"

"Must be infectious, because yeah, I do too. Back to the Byblos then?"

"Yeah. Let's go . . ."

"So, old Dutchie told you to look me up?" said Douglas as he and Perez sipped their drinks in the living-room of the cottage.

"Yes."

The room was sparsely furnished, with no photographs and few pictures on the walls, but it was clean and tidy. *The home of an unsentimental man with a military background*, thought Perez.

"How did he know where I was?" asked Douglas.

"One of his friends was out here on holiday. He'd gone on one of your Jeep trips and mentioned to Dutchie that they were run by a Rhodesian guy called Vince."

"Yeah?"

Perez nodded. "The age matched, the description matched, the name, the nationality – he thought that it must be you."

"Right. And you're Dutchie's nephew?"

"Yes."

"But you're what – Spanish, Portuguese?"

"Spanish."

"So how are you his nephew?"

"My father was Spanish. He met and married my mother, Dutchie's sister, in Barcelona."

Perez watched the older man's face carefully, to see how he would respond. He had been slightly thrown by the way that Douglas could still ask perceptive questions, despite that fact he had been drinking heavily earlier in the day. Now though, Perez had to risk being caught in a lie – for all he knew Dutchie could have been an only child – but not to have answered such a straightforward question would have appeared suspicious. He had to hope that Dutchie actually had a sister, or that Douglas wouldn't have known the family details of a man he had served with over forty years previously.

"Fair enough," said Douglas. "Pity he didn't come with you, would have been nice to meet up again."

"He eh – he has a problem with his hip."

"Arthritis?"

"Yes."

"It's a bugger . . . "

"Yes, he finds travelling uncomfortable."

"Ought to get the hip replacement," said Douglas decisively. "Run-of-the-mill operation nowadays. Loads of blokes get it."

"He's – he's considering that."

"Good on him."

"Meanwhile though he's planning a book –"

"A book?" said Douglas, raising an eyebrow.

"Yes. That's the main reason why I called on you. You see I'm a journalist, and I'm ghost-writing it with him."

"Yeah? What's the book about?"

"The adventures of the mercenaries in the Congo. Especially during the fall of Kaburi."

"Kaburi . . . that was a rum bloody show . . ."

"Yes. I was hoping we could talk about it. We want to

285

be sure that Dutchie has remembered everything correctly."

"Not a problem."

"Good. Though there is . . . there is one thing that could be a problem," said Perez.

"What?"

"There's a rival publisher bringing out a similar book. We're trying to get ours finished first."

Douglas looked up quizzically. "Another book on the Congo – coming out at the same time?"

"Yes."

"After all these years?"

"Maybe it's that the people who were there are retiring now," Perez improvised. "That they've time to write their memoirs."

"We're not all out to pasture yet, you know," said Douglas challengingly.

I bet this guy was an aggressive bastard in his day, thought Perez but instead he smiled, partly to win Douglas over, but also with relief that Douglas seemed to have been distracted from the coincidence of two books on the same subject being published over forty years later.

"You're certainly far from out to pasture, Mr Douglas. You look pretty fit."

"Swim every day," said the older man boastfully. "Always have. Anyone who does that stays in shape."

"Absolutely," agreed Perez. "Anyway like I said, we want to get our book out before the other publisher,"

"Right."

Now, thought Perez, *slip in the crucial question as though it's incidental.* "Talking of which, you haven't by any chance been approached by our rivals? Rung up by journalists?"

Douglas shook his head. "Nah. Haven't spoken to a journalist since Elisabethville in '61."

"Good," said Perez, "that's good." *Excellent in fact.* It confirmed that he was still ahead of Kennedy and Johnson. Which meant that now he could safely dispose of Douglas before they ever got to him.

"Listen, if we're going to talk chapter and verse on Kaburi and all that, I need to wake myself up," said Douglas.

"Yes?"

"Why don't I put on a pot of coffee, and then we can get down to business."

"Fine," said Perez, suppressing a smile. "I look forward to it . . . "

"What way are we going to play this?" asked Steve as he killed the engine of their rented car in the parking lot of the Byblos hotel.

"How do you mean?" asked Laura.

"Well, when we asked the concierge about Salisbury Tours, he was doing his job in directing us to the Fuengirola office. He was pleasant and helpful, sure, but he was just doing his normal job."

287

"And what we're asking for now is a bit more?"

"Well, if we're asking for a person's mobile or home address, yeah, he mightn't be so eager to oblige."

"OK . . ." said Laura, "Suppose we tell him the Salisbury office was closed unexpectedly. If he has a mobile number for Vince Douglas it would be perfectly reasonable to provide it in the circumstances."

"Supposing he hasn't a phone number but knows where Douglas lives – why can't we wait till the office opens tomorrow morning?"

"Because we're busy people, and we've private business to conduct with Mr Douglas. That's all the concierge needs to know. Well, that and the fact that we'll be tipping generously."

Steve smiled. "You're good at this kind of thing, aren't you?"

"All part of the job. Tracking down the stuff people don't want you to discover is often what makes a story worth telling."

"Right."

"OK, let's go to it."

They opened the doors of the car and stepped from its air-conditioned interior out into the late afternoon heat. Steve could feel the sudden warmth of the sun on his shoulders and the sweet smell of bougainvillaea was in the air as they walked briskly towards the hotel.

The short blast of heat ended suddenly when they entered the air-conditioned lobby, and Steve was pleased to see that the same concierge that they had spoken to earlier was still on duty. He was a suave-looking man in his late forties and he smiled a professional smile as he saw them approaching.

"Good afternoon, sir. madam . . ."

"Hi," said Steve.

"You found the Salisbury office all right?"

"We found the office," answered Laura, "but it wasn't all right."

"Oh?" said the concierge in surprise. "There was a problem?"

"Yes, they'd closed unexpectedly."

"Ah . . ."

Steve was taken aback at the concierge's lack of surprise and he realised that Laura had picked up on it also when she looked quizzically at the man.

"This happens a lot?" she asked.

"Sometimes. It's – it's a small company. They run nice tours but they can be a little – a little disorganised at times."

"We need to conduct some business with Mr Douglas," said Steve. "Would you have a mobile number for him, by any chance?"

The concierge shook his head sadly. "No, sir, I'm afraid not."

"We wanted a quick word with him tonight if possible," said Laura. "Any idea where he lives?"

The man hesitated, and Steve considered offering a

tip, then thought better of it. It was an up-market hotel after all, and a blunt offer of cash for information would feel more like a bribe than a tip. Better to hold out the prospect of a good tip on departure – in gratitude for friendly co-operation.

"We'd be very grateful if you could oblige us," he said, weighing the words sufficiently to hint at future reward but without explicitly reducing matters to a commercial transaction.

"Well . . . if you really want to see him tonight . . . you might get him at home."

"You know where he lives then?" said Laura.

"He has a cottage in the hills. Maybe a fifteen minutes' drive from here. But eh . . ."

"Yes?" prompted Steve.

"Sometimes he's not – he's not always ready to receive visitors."

Steve's mind raced. Was the concierge warning that Douglas was a drunk? A drug addict? Someone who held orgies in his remote cottage?

"A little bit fond of the bottle sometimes?" said Laura.

The concierge nodded. "I don't wish to speak badly of Mr Douglas . . . "

"Of course not," said Laura. "We understand."

"Absolutely," agreed Steve, "but we'll take our chances in calling, if you can show us on the map where he lives."

"Very good, sir," said the concierge, then he indicated the route they should take on a large-scale map of the area that he spread out on his desk.

"Thank you very much," said Steve when he had memorised the route, "much appreciated."

"You're welcome, sir."

They said their goodbyes to the concierge, then headed back across the lobby towards the entrance. Laura looked at Steve and smilingly winked. "Well played."

"Thanks," he answered, pleased at her approval. "So, straight up to the cottage?"

"Absolutely. Time to talk to Mr Douglas . . ."

CHAPTER 8

Trenet pushed aside the share-price valuations on which he had been working and leaned back in his leather upholstered swivel-chair. He had calculated the minimum loan repayments that he would have to make to keep the banks satisfied, and the earnings required from his stocks and shares, but whatever way he did his calculations the numbers didn't add up, and there was no getting away from the fact that landing the NATO contract was vital.

He breathed out slowly and deeply, knowing that getting agitated wasn't going to solve his problems. Perhaps he'd visit the Clinique Speciale later tonight, he thought. A break might do him good. He had heard about a new girl, a former acrobat from Bulgaria, whose services were said to be impressive. Then again maybe something physically demanding mightn't be appropriate. The business with Perez and the prying journalist was stressful, and he didn't want to engage the new Bulgarian woman only to find that his sexual performance was undermined by stress. Maybe a return visit to the masseuse would be a better option, he thought, with its less demanding combination of relaxation and arousal. He thought back to his last visit, and just as he began to recall its pleasures the phone on his desk rang.

He answered the scrambled line immediately, recognising Chavant's name once again on the caller display.

"Well?"

"Good news. I've heard back from my contact who was making the enquiries."

"And?"

"Got the phone number and address in Torquay."

"Excellent. Let's have it."

Chavant gave the details and Trenet jotted them down on a slip of paper which he folded and placed in his jacket pocket.

"Good work," said Trenet.

"Thank you. Though like I said, this information is six years old, so we can't be certain he's still there."

"Still a pretty good lead."

"Absolutely. Though eh . . ."

"What?"

"Well . . . let's just hope –"

"That it's not needed," interjected Trenet. "I know. But if it *is*, we've got something to go on now."

"Yes . . . Any further word from Spain?"

"No, not yet."

"Right . . ."

"I want to keep the line open for when there is," said Trenet.

"Of course. Well, we'll – we'll talk whenever there are developments then."

"Yes. And well done again."

"Thanks. Bye."

"Bye." Trenet hung up, then gazed reflectively from his penthouse office. The upper foliage of a mature oak-tree shimmered gold and green in the late afternoon sunshine but Trenet only half took it in, his mind focussing instead on the developments with Perez and Chavant. The Spaniard had called earlier to say that Vince Douglas was still running the tour company on the Costa del Sol and that he, Perez, had located his home, a remote cottage in the hills above Fuengirola. Perez had been lying in wait for Douglas to return home when he had made the call, but Trenet reckoned that the Spaniard had sounded calm and in control, despite what was planned for the former mercenary.

Trenet had hoped that it wouldn't come to this, that Douglas's company wouldn't have been operating still, and that the Rhodesian would have been untraceable.

The fact that he was traceable by Perez however meant that he would also be traceable by Kennedy and Johnson, and so it was essential that Douglas have an accident before the journalist made contact. A pity, but such was the way of the world. And with any luck another dead-end should be enough to persuade the *Clarion* newspaper not to waste further time and effort on a story that was yielding nothing. Just in case they persisted however and in the event that they got onto the trail of Dutchie Holland also, he now had an address and telephone number that Perez could utilise if it became necessary for the Englishman to go missing.

Trenet remained gazing out the window, thinking things over. In reality, though, he knew that matters were out of his hands until Perez had dealt with Vince Douglas and until it became clear what the Irish journalist chose to do at that stage. He looked at his watch. Five o'clock. He hoped that Douglas would return home soon – before Kennedy and Johnson discovered the location of the cottage. Still, no point worrying over things he couldn't influence – it was Perez' mission now and the former legionnaire would have to play it by ear. Knowing there was nothing more he could do about it, Trenet pulled his chair closer to his desk, went back to work, and waited for the phone to ring again.

"So . . . Dutchie Holland's bringing out a book," said Vince Douglas shaking his head, "who'd ever have thought it?"

"I think it could do pretty well," lied Perez easily. "It was a fascinating time, back in the Congo."

"Waste of bloody time in the end, of course. The *kaffirs* screwed up the Congo when they took over, just like in Rhodesia and South Africa."

"Right," agreed Perez.

He had come to realise that the former mercenary was both racist and reactionary but he had led the older man to believe that he was sympathetic to his politics as they had sipped strong black coffee over the last three quarters of an hour. There was no doubting that Douglas was a tough old bird, and when the discussion had moved on from the Congo, he had told hair-raising stories of his adventures in the Rhodesian Army. After returning to Salisbury in 1962 he had served for eighteen years in the army, rising to the rank of major, but the latter years of his service coincided with a bitter guerrilla war against insurgents who eventually triumphed against the white-run regime and founded the state of Zimbabwe. Like lots of other whites he had then relocated with his wife and children to South Africa, only to leave that country also when apartheid ended and Nelson Mandela's ANC began to govern the country. At that stage his son and daughter had grown up and Douglas had been divorced for six years, and so he had moved alone to Europe, living in London for a year before making his final move to the south of Spain.

It had sounded to Perez like a life marred by political inflexibility, hard drinking and marital strife, yet Douglas struck him as being far from stupid. He had a certain street-wise air about him, and flashes of insight had been evident as they spoke, despite the fact that he had had a good deal to drink during the course of the day.

"So this book," said Douglas now. "Does Dutchie talk it into a tape recorder, or is it interviews . . . or what?"

"Usually he writes it all out, after we've decided what scenes to break it down into," Perez improvised. "Then we discuss what he's written before I edit it."

"Really?"

"Most of the time, that's how we do it," explained Perez.

"Right . . . and . . . and how about you? What newspaper do you write for?"

"No single one, I'm freelance," answered Perez, sorry now that he had started this, even though he knew that the journalistic ploy had been necessary in order to quiz Douglas about an approach from other journalists.

"Based in London, are you?"

"Yes."

"And which of the London papers would you write for?"

"Eh . . . sometimes *The Times*," said Perez, racking his brain for the names of other well- known English newspapers. "Occasionally . . . occasionally the *Express*. I do a lot of stuff for the *Mail* . . . "

"The *Mail*? You'd know my old mate Hoppy then."

"Hoppy?"

"Jack Wallace, the soccer correspondent. Former Para, lost two toes, has a funny walk. He's the guy who always sings 'My Old Man's a Dustman' at the Christmas party – you must know him."

"Yes – but just to say hello to. Our paths wouldn't cross very much."

"Hell of a character, was Hoppy . . ." said Douglas reflectively, "hell of a character . . ."

"Absolutely," agreed Perez.

"And when is the book due to be published?"

"In the autumn. We're just tidying up the last few things now."

"I'd love to see it when it comes out," said Douglas.

"No problem. We'll post you a signed copy."

"Great," said Douglas. "I'll give you my card. The address is on that."

"Fine."

Douglas hoisted himself from the sofa on which he had been sitting, crossed to a light pine desk and opened the drawer. "Should have some here," he said, sitting down and rooting in the drawer.

"Good."

"No," said Douglas, "*not good*. I don't have any business cards – but I have this . . ."

Perez looked up, then stopped dead. Douglas was sitting in the swivel-chair behind the desk, a Browning

Hi-Power pistol in his hand. His outstretched right arm was supported by his left, and the gun was aimed squarely at Perez' chest.

Perez was shocked, but he had the presence of mind not to make any sudden moves. He was familiar with the Browning Hi-Power and knew that it had a magazine capacity of thirteen 9 by 19mm rounds. It was a lethal weapon, and Vince Douglas looked like a man who knew how to use it.

"Now," said Douglas, keeping the gun trained on Perez, "just who the fuck are you?"

"I told you I'm –"

"You told me a pile of shit!" interjected Douglas. "There's no journalist called Hoppy at the *Mail* – I made that up!"

Perez swallowed hard, knowing he had made a bad mistake in underestimating this opponent. It was obvious that despite being a lush Douglas had a sharp mind, even when sobering up, and he should have been more careful in handling him. He was going to have to lie inventively now, and he looked at Douglas and tried for a wry grin. "If you'd just let me explain –," he started.

"Spare me the bullshit," said Douglas.

"Please, I –"

"No! Enough of the lies. Want to know where you went wrong?"

"Look –"

" I'll tell you where you went wrong, mate. You didn't know enough about Dutchie. Because Dutchie Holland was never going to write a book. He might have talked one into a recorder or told his story to a journalist, but he was never going to write one. Know why? The bloke was semi-illiterate. Last guy on the planet to try and write a book."

Perez said nothing as he frantically tried to think how best to explain his way out of his predicament.

"So the question now, mate, is very simple. What the hell's your game?"

"You're right," said Perez, raising his hands in appeasement. "I have lied to you. I'm sorry. In fairness, there was a good reason. If you could lower the gun, I'd like to explain."

"I've a better idea. Explain anyway. And if I don't like what I hear, maybe I'll blow your fucking face away."

Perez knew that Douglas had killed plenty of times in Africa, and sensed the older man would still be perfectly capable of violent action, especially if he got any hint that Perez had come here to kill him. This was going to take extremely delicate handling. "OK then," he said. "It started . . . it all started with the death of Conn Lynch . . . "

"Next turn on the left," said Steve, studying the map. "Maybe a mile, mile and a half from here."

"Fine," answered Laura without taking her eyes off the

road that curved up into the hills. She had the car's air-conditioning on and felt pleasantly cool despite the heat haze that shimmered above the surface of the tarmac road. Far below her she could see Fuengirola and the sparkling blue waters of the Mediterranean and she found herself pondering the twists of fate that found her travelling with Steve in search of a former Rhodesian mercenary. Who would have thought that a man dying in a Galway hospital would have uncovered a trail that led back forty years to the Congo? Or that she would find herself accompanied by a wealthy representative of the new American owners of the *Clarion* as she tried to piece together what had occurred? She recalled the original phone call from Mac and how strongly she had resisted the notion of having Steve Johnson foisted upon her.

A lot had happened since then, she thought wryly, her mind harking back to the intimacy that seemed to have suddenly overtaken herself and Steve in Bruges.

Several times since then she had found herself wondering what would have happened had they kissed, as they so nearly had. It would have been her first seriously romantic moment since the death of Declan, and she was still unsure how she would react to physical intimacy with another man. In addition to which, continuing to work together would have been difficult if they had gone ahead and things had turned out badly. On the positive side they both seemed to have overcome the awkwardness that the incident had created, and as today had progressed they had regained their ease in each other's company. And yet . . . behind the relaxed rapport, Laura still sensed that Steve was interested in her as more than a colleague. And there was no denying that she in turn found him a handsome, witty and engaging travelling companion.

"Penny for them," said Steve, and Laura realised that she had been engrossed in her thoughts.

"Just thinking . . . well, how strange life can be."

"In what way?"

"A week ago you were in America, and I was in Clare. Now here we are, driving around the Costa del Sol."

"Yeah . . . " Steve smiled and indicated the sunlit countryside and the sparkling sea. "Lousy job, but someone's got to do it!"

"Absolutely," she said grinning back at him.

After a moment he looked more serious. "So . . . what's your instinct now – regarding this Vince Douglas?"

Laura considered a moment before replying. "I hope he's in the cottage when we get there. I mean, I can't be sure, but . . . well, I sense he's going to be significant."

"Right."

"You feel it too?"

Steve nodded. "Yeah. Now that we're getting near, I'm getting a touch of that tingle-up-the-spine feeling."

"Well, we'll know soon enough."

"That we will. OK – this must be our turn coming up."

"Great," said Laura, then she indicated, slowed down

and swung onto the track that would take them to Vince Douglas's cottage.

"You remember Conn Lynch – the Irish soldier from Kaburi?" asked Perez.

"Yes – what's he to do with anything?" replied Douglas, the gun still trained unerringly at the younger man's chest.

"Lynch died in Ireland about ten days ago."

"So?"

Despite the fact that Douglas clearly wanted to get to the heart of the matter, Perez spoke at a moderate pace, anxious to buy himself as much time as possible. As long as they were talking he reckoned he could come up with the kind of details that would back an innocuous story. "When he was dying, Lynch made a comment about committing murder," he said. "Somehow the *Clarion*, a newspaper in Ireland, heard about this and they began asking questions."

"They think he committed this murder in the Congo?"

"They weren't sure, so they've been asking a lot of questions."

"Which someone doesn't want answered."

"Why cause problems over things that happened half a lifetime ago? It's pointless now."

"No, it's not," contradicted Douglas. "If it was point-less, you wouldn't have come here lying through your teeth."

"Look, I'm sorry about that, I really am."

"You're sorry because you're looking down the barrel of a Browning."

"No, I really am sorry. But I was afraid you might have spoken to the people from the *Clarion*, and that you mightn't want to say so."

"You think Vince Douglas is a snitch?"

"No, I'm not saying that, Mr Douglas."

"Sounds like it to me."

"I wasn't suggesting that at all. But these journalists, they'd do anything for a story – twist things, put words into your mouth. I really needed to find out if they'd contacted you, that's all."

"Why? You weren't even born at the time of Kaburi – what's it to you?"

"Well, I've . . . I've been engaged to try and find out what's going on."

"Engaged?"

Perez paused briefly, then tried for a tone of man-to-man sincerity. "Look, I'll be honest with you. I'm a private investigator."

"So there *was* a murder needs hushing up."

"No. But my client doesn't want damaging rumours, stories in the paper, all that stuff."

"I'll bet he doesn't. I presume it's Lieutenant Trenet you're working for?"

Perez instinctively hesitated about confirming his client's identity and he saw a flash of irritation on the other man's face.

"Don't have me to ask you things twice," said Douglas threateningly.

"I'm trying to be straight with you, but I also –"

"Is it Trenet who sent you?!" snapped Douglas.

"Yes," answered Perez, feeling that there was no point antagonising a volatile former mercenary who had drink taken and was brandishing a gun. "Yes, it was Trenet."

"Stands to reason," said Douglas, his temper flash gone as suddenly as it had come. "He's the one got back from Kaburi with this Lynch bloke. The local Union Minière manager and Lynch's officer never made it, so I reckon one of those was the one murdered – maybe both of them."

"They were killed in action. It wasn't murder."

"That was Trenet's line at the time," said Douglas, "and he was always pretty convincing."

"He still is convincing, but he's afraid of being damaged if the wrong spin is put on this."

"Must be some kind of a big shot, is he?"

"He's a very successful business man, yes."

"Back in France?"

"No, he's living in Belgium now," answered Perez, deciding it would be best to keep his lies as close as possible to the truth.

"And he's scared enough to hire a private detective over something that happened forty years ago. Doesn't sound like an innocent man to me."

"You can be innocent and still have difficulties. Appearances are important in business. So even a hint of murder would hang over him, cause him problems."

"Sounds like he's had no problems since 1961. So why is there a problem now – unless Conn Lynch was telling the truth?"

"Two reasons," said Perez, sipping coffee from his mug. Despite Douglas still having the gun pointed at him, Perez could sense that the immediate threat had passed and that the older man had relaxed slightly while listening to the answers to his questions. "The first reason is that Lynch had gone into politics in Ireland," lied Perez. "So he made a fair number of enemies who'd like to blacken his name – and wouldn't care if they hurt someone like Trenet while doing it. The second reason . . ." Perez' voice trailed off and he looked quizzically at the doorway behind Douglas.

The Rhodesian glanced around, and the second he did so Perez flung the coffee mug hard, catching his opponent in the face. Simultaneously he kicked vigorously at the edge of the light pine desk, forcing it upwards into the air between himself and Douglas.

Taken by surprise, the older man cried out in pain when the mug smashed into his face but despite the coffee getting into his eyes he swung back around, the pistol still in his hand. The upended desk forced him back in the swivel-chair however, and Perez was on him in an instant, having sprung forward immediately after kicking the desk. He grabbed the Rhodesian's gun-hand and forced it upwards, then buried his knee in his opponent's solar plexus. Douglas doubled up in pain and Perez quickly wrenched his gun-hand down, banging it against the side of the overturned desk. Douglas cried out and dropped the weapon. Perez immediately kicked the gun away across the room, then swung around and aimed a karate chop at the older man's ribs. To his surprise the Rhodesian blocked the blow, knocking Perez off balance. Douglas followed up with a pile-driver of a punch from his left fist, aimed at Perez' head. The Spaniard pulled to the side by reflex so that the blow only half caught him. Nonetheless it hurt, and Perez knew that if his opponent hadn't been handicapped by the blow to his solar plexus, and had landed the punch properly, the fight might be over now. *Served him right too for underestimating an opponent. Time to end it now though*, he thought as he moved in on his quarry. Douglas was rising from the chair and Perez feinted as though aiming a blow at his head. Douglas again went to block it, but as he did so Perez swung around at speed and landed a vicious kick to the Rhodesian's groin. The older man screamed and collapsed to his knees, and as he did Perez moved in fast and felled him with a right hook to the chin. Douglas sank to the floor, and Perez swiftly moved across the room and retrieved the Browning. He slipped the gun into his pocket then went to his briefcase and withdrew a number of cheap women's headscarves that he had bought in a street market in Fuengirola.

He crossed the room and replaced the swivel-chair in an upright position, then grabbed the prone form of Douglas, lifted him from the floor and flopped him down into the chair. Moving quickly, he tied each of the Rhodesian's hands to an arm of the chair using the scarves, then he bound each of his feet to a chair leg.

By this time the Rhodesian was starting to come to, and Perez slapped his face to speed him back to consciousness. "Not a bad effort," he said as the former mercenary came to and focussed his cold blue eyes on Perez in an angry stare.

Douglas made to move but Perez shook his head. "Don't bother struggling, you're securely bound. Yeah . . . not a bad effort for an old guy. But only *not bad*. And the thing is, you *are* still an old guy and way out of practice, otherwise you'd never have made your big mistake, would you?

Douglas said nothing, and Perez smiled. "You see, you *never, ever* leave a suspect with something in his hands. Especially something like a mug – that can hold a hot liquid." Perez shook his head. "Very amateurish."

"What the hell is it you want?" said Douglas.

"What we want is your silence. But you're a drinker with a big mouth. And that's the thing – silence and having a big mouth – they don't go well together . . . "

"I'd say that must be it," said Steve indicating a cottage in the distance.

Laura looked up from behind the steering wheel and out across the valley to where a small cottage was perched on the opposite hillside. "You reckon?"

"Well, unless the map is wrong. But the track doesn't seem to lead anywhere else."

"Fair enough," said Laura, returning her gaze to the road and concentrating on avoiding the potholes in its dusty surface.

Steve felt his heart beginning to beat a little faster now that the moment of reckoning was approaching. He hoped for Laura's sake that Vince Douglas would be here and that he would be able to provide them with the name of the mercenary commander at Kaburi. He knew how much she wanted to crack the Conn Lynch story, and he really wanted her to succeed, knowing that she had gone out on a limb in persuading Mac to fund a speculative trip to Spain.

Like Laura, he too felt that the key to the mystery was likely to be held by the French officer who had returned from the bush with Lynch after the fall of Kaburi. Of course the man might be dead by now, or he might be unwilling to meet them, or Vince Douglas might even refuse to reveal his name. There were all sorts of imponderables, he knew, and yet as they drew nearer to the cottage he couldn't help but feel that they were on the brink of something significant.

"Steve!"

His musings were interrupted by Laura who indicated with a nod to look ahead. He looked once more in the direction of the cottage and saw a parked Jeep that had been shielded from view until now by a dense patch of foliage. "Bingo!" he cried. "Looks like our man is at home."

"I hope so," said Laura with a smile. "We've come a hell of a long way."

"We have," agreed Steve. "But something tells me it'll be worth it . . ."

Perez felt pleased with himself, but made the effort not to sound self-satisfied when he rang Trenet on the mobile. The industrialist had answered on the second ring and Perez couldn't help but savour the altered dynamics whereby the arrogant Frenchman was the anxious one and he, Perez, was the person controlling the situation.

"Subject located," said Perez, deciding to keep things cryptic.

"Yes?"

"Located and questioned. Nothing has been revealed to the press."

"Excellent. That's – that's very good news," said Trenet, the relief evident in his voice.

"Yes."

"And you're quite sure about that?"

311

"I just said it, didn't I?"

"Yes, But I –"

"But nothing. Everything is in hand. I'll keep you posted." Perez hung up. This bastard Trenet was far too used to being top dog, he reckoned – do no harm to show him that his fate was in the hands of the man on the ground – and that he ought to be a bit more respectful in his manner. Perez switched off the mobile in case Trenet tried to call him back, then his mind tuned in to a sound that had begun to impinge on his subconscious during the brief phone call.

"Sweet Jesus!" he said, recognising the sound now as that of a car engine approaching.

He ran to the window and looked out, careful not to show himself. Coming up the drive was a dark blue Seat Ibiza with a woman behind the wheel and a man in the passenger seat. He saw them for just a couple of seconds, and the sunshine made him blink, but nonetheless he recognised them. *Johnson and Kennedy.* There wasn't any doubt.

He had to get Douglas and the chair to which he was bound out of the line of sight of any of the windows, he realised, there being every chance that a nosy journalist would look in if her knock wasn't answered. He started back towards Douglas but before he could stop him the Rhodesian shouted at the top of his voice. "Help! Help! Hel–"

Perez reached him in time to clamp his hand over the

older man's mouth, choking off the third cry. Even as his left hand covered the man's mouth, Perez punched his captive hard in the ribs. "Shut your fucking mouth!" he hissed. He grabbed the chair and dragged Douglas back out of the room and into a windowless passage between the two back bedrooms. He slipped his free hand into his pocket and withdrew a flick-knife that he had bought in Fuengirola. He pressed the button, releasing the blade, and threateningly held the shining weapon up for Douglas to see. His mind was calculating now and he reckoned that there was a good chance that the Rhodesian's cries wouldn't have been heard. They had, after all, been made from inside the cottage while Kennedy and Johnson were still approaching in the car. And it was still very hot outside, which meant that they probably had the car windows shut and the air-conditioning going. So what with engine noise, the sound of the air conditioning and the cries coming from inside a building, he reasoned that his prisoner shouldn't have been heard.

He tightened his grip on Douglas's mouth and jerked his head back, placing the knife blade right up against his exposed neck. "One sound. Just one sound out of you – and I'll slit you from ear to ear. Got that?"

Douglas's eyes were bulging as his head was contorted backwards but he managed to give a tiny nod of assent.

"Good," said Perez. "And make no mistake. One wrong move – and it's your last . . ."

Laura slowed the car to a halt, then cut the engine and climbed out. She was hit by a wave of heat, the sudden rise in temperature almost like a blow after travelling with the car's air-conditioning switched to high. Steve stepped out also, and as he closed the door of the car Laura looked around. The house was quite small – probably the home of a modest farmer or a shepherd originally – but its garden was a riot of colour, and the location was certainly scenic, even if it was a long way off the beaten track. The house itself looked reasonably well-maintained but its exterior was devoid of any touches of ornamentation, and Laura could well believe it to be the home of a single man who drank more than was good for him. Casually parked at an angle to the front door was a slightly battered-looking Jeep that she assumed Douglas must hold for his private use when not ferrying tourists in it for Salisbury Tours.

"Well, here goes," she said as Steve came around the front of their car and they made for the hall door. She could feel her heart starting to race, then they reached the door and she paused a moment to gather herself together.

There was no bell in evidence, but a heavy metal knocker was attached to the door, and Laura reached out and lifted it, knocking twice. As she waited for an answer Steve smiled and indicated his crossed fingers, and Laura smiled back and gave him the thumbs-up sign.

She strained her ears, hoping to hear the sound of

Vince Douglas coming to the door, and she readied herself to try and sound pleasant and undemanding, knowing how much first impressions mattered in a situation like this. She waited expectantly, but no sound carried from within the house and after a moment she felt a tiny stab of anxiety. She told herself not to panic, after all the Jeep was here, so the chances of Douglas being inside seemed high. She waited a bit longer, then knocked again. Once more she strained her ears, but still there was neither an answer nor any sound of life within the house. "This isn't great," she said, turning to Steve.

"Maybe he's had a fair bit to drink. Could be sleeping it off."

"Then we've a choice. We can try to wake him and risk getting off on a bad footing. Or we can leave it and hope to get him at a more opportune time."

"So what do you think?" asked Steve.

"Well, we have come all this way . . . sometimes on a story you have to be a little bit brass-necked."

"So we try to rouse the dead?"

Laura nodded. "Yeah. Yeah – let's go for it."

A louder series of knocks sounded on the front door and Perez kept the knife taut against Douglas's throat and his hand firmly pressed against the older man's mouth. For his plan to work Perez knew that it was critical to get Kennedy and Johnson to leave. Any sound from Douglas could scupper everything, and so it was vital that he discourage the Rhodesian from being tempted to resist. To reinforce his point he tightened his grip on his prisoner's mouth and pulled his head further back, exposing his throat even further to the blade of the flick-knife.

His victim was sweating now and Perez reckoned that he had got his message across, yet there could be no relaxing until the callers outside decided to leave. *If they decided to leave* . . . He dreaded to think of them staying outside, forcing him to remain in his present awkward position, but for now there was nothing he could do except keep Douglas quiet and hope that the unwanted visitors would go.

He stood immobile in the passageway, one hand still firmly clamped to Douglas's mouth and the other holding the knife, and he could smell a mixture of garlic and brandy from the Rhodesian.

An even louder series of knocks sounded now, and Perez felt a flash of anger at the callers. Why the hell couldn't they take no for an answer? *Because the Jeep is outside, and they reckon Douglas is probably here.* Still, if they got no reply then eventually they would probably assume that Douglas had gone out in someone else's vehicle.

Just then Perez saw shadows cast across the living-room and he realised that the callers must be looking in the window, with the sun backlighting them and casting their shadows. There were light net curtains on the windows which would restrict what they could see, and even looking in at an acute angle wouldn't afford them a proper view of the passageway, yet Perez felt at risk. He knew it wasn't entirely logical, but even with Douglas forced into silent immobility he still felt very much exposed. Suddenly the shadows moved away and Perez breathed out in relief. He didn't relax his grip on Douglas, however, and no sooner had he breathed out than a fresh worry struck him. Supposing they went round to the back door – and it was unlocked? He was about ten feet away from the back door – too far to reach without noisily hauling Douglas along in the chair – and he could see an old-fashioned handle and lock unit on the door. Would Douglas customarily leave the rear entrance to the cottage unlocked? Quite possibly, Perez reasoned, especially in a location so off the beaten track. And if it wasn't locked, would Kennedy and Johnson be sufficiently nosy and intrusive to let themselves in? It was possible; journalists weren't generally renowned for their reticence.

He quickly tried to weigh up his options. If they let themselves in, there could be no explaining away the circumstances. He would have to take decisive action, even though Trenet had instructed him not to act against the journalist. But then Trenet had hardly envisaged a scenario like this. Before he could think about it any further he heard the sound of people approaching the back door.

"Will I give it a try?" said a woman's voice, and Perez

prayed that the back door was locked.

"Why not. Might as well be hung for a sheep as a lamb," answered her companion.

Perez increased the pressure of his grip on Douglas and held his breath, awaiting Kennedy's next move. "What the hell," he heard her say, and he swallowed hard, feeling beads of sweat forming on his forehead.

There was a sudden knocking on the back door. Perez stayed stock still, his hand still firmly clamped across his captive's mouth and the flick-knife pressing threateningly against his exposed neck. Perez held his breath, knowing that if Kennedy was going to try the back door handle it would be now, on getting no response to the knocking.

"What do you think?" he heard her saying from the far side of the door.

"Pity to come all this way and miss him," answered the American.

"Yeah . . . "

Perez steeled himself, praying she wouldn't try the door handle – or that it would be locked if she did.

"We could always wait here," said Johnson. "If he's in a deep sleep he might wake up in a while. Or if he's out somewhere he might arrive back."

"Don't really fancy waiting around," said Kennedy.

Please, thought Perez, *don't let her be so impatient that she tries to gain entry.*

"So what do you want to do?" asked Johnson.

"Well, the thing is . . . we know now where he is. Instead of waiting round in the heat, why not go back to the hotel, unpack our stuff, maybe have a swim, then drive back here in a couple of hours?"

"Sounds good to me," said Johnson.

"OK then, let's get out of the sun."

Perez listened to them going and he breathed out slowly, but kept up his firm grip on Douglas. After a moment he heard the engine of the car starting up, then he listened as the vehicle moved off and started back down the valley. When he was certain that they were well out of range he removed his hand from Douglas's mouth and simultaneously sheathed the flick-knife.

The Rhodesian was breathing heavily and he looked angrily at Perez. "Just what the hell is your game?"

Without hesitation Perez swung round and slapped the other man hard in the face, rocking him backwards in the chair. "I ask the questions here. And try shouting for help like that again and I'll slit your throat."

Perez could see that despite being bound to the chair the older man was more angry than frightened, and not wanting to waste energy arguing with him he quickly went back into the living-room, took another scarf from his bag and placed it over Douglas's mouth and was tightening it as a gag before the Rhodesian could protest. He left his prisoner gagged and bound in the passageway, then returned alone to the living-room, sat down at the table and looked at his watch. Five thirty. Plenty of time to think things out. And then, once darkness fell, he would put the next part of his plan into action.

CHAPTER 9

Laura watched admiringly as the golden rays of the setting sun sparkled on the surface of the cut-glass decanter on her table. She was sharing a meal with Steve in the plush surroundings of the Byblos's Narlhac Restaurant and the luxurious ambience, discreet service and fine food and wine had combined to make her feel a heightened sense of wellbeing.

Earlier she had come back with Steve from the abortive trip to Douglas's cottage and they had quickly unpacked, then met at the pool for a swim. It was the first time they had seen each other in swimming gear and she was struck by Steve's lean and lightly muscular physique. Several times too she noticed him glancing at her as they lounged by the side of the pool and she was aware that her bikini showed off her slim but curvaceous body to good effect. Though neither of them alluded to it in any way, there had been a definite sexual frisson between them, causing a stirring of excitement that Laura couldn't deny.

When they had finished swimming, they had changed and driven once more to Douglas's cottage, but despite the presence of the Jeep they still had no response to their knocking. Returning to the Byblos, they had gone to the concierge and explained their lack of success. The man hadn't seemed unduly surprised, and without actually saying so, had intimated that sleeping heavily after a drinking bout was not unusual for the Rhodesian. He had suggested that they try again reasonably early the next morning, it being Douglas's habit to go for a swim most mornings, and they had reluctantly decided to follow this advice and to accept that their subject wasn't likely to be in a fit state for an interview tonight.

With the business part of their reason for being together out of the way until the morning, Laura found that the element of sexual attraction that had been evident at the pool had heightened during dinner. They had both dressed up in their best clothes and she had caught the whiff of expensive aftershave from Steve, while she herself had taken more effort than usual in applying her make-up.

To begin with their conversation had centred on Vince Douglas and the prospects of cracking the story for the *Clarion*, but after a while they had left the story in abeyance, and the conversation had turned more personal. For the first time since the death of Declan, Laura had felt no sense of disloyalty in acknowledging to herself an interest in another man, and she had found herself speaking frankly about the sense of loss she had felt and how difficult it had been for her to resume anything like a normal life after her bereavement. She knew it wasn't the kind of thing one normally discussed on a date – and there was no denying that this meal felt like a date – yet on some instinctive level she recognised that if matters were to progress with Steve she needed to – what? Exorcise the ghost of Declan? No, she thought, she would never forget Declan. It was more a case of acknowledging her love for one man while accepting that the person to whom she was doing so, might, in time, also be someone to whom she could grow close. Part of her was inclined to scoff at the notion and to say that she was losing the run of herself, and that they were simply two people having dinner together, yet she sensed that what was happening was more than that. And Steve had responded with an empathy and understated sympathy so patently genuine that the intimacy between them had heightened as the meal went on.

He had an interesting mixture of qualities, she thought. He was clearly sensitive, but wasn't in any way wimpish. And without seeming arrogant he had a quiet confidence in most of the things he did. She felt entirely comfortable with him at this stage, despite the personal nature of the revelations she had made. She watched him now as he sipped his wine and tilted his head to one side in a gesture she had come to associate with him.

"So," he said. "last week was your first time back to County Clare alone?"

"Not to Clare. But it was my first trip back to the holiday home in Kilfenora."

"Right."

"I'm glad I went though. I mean, it was sad, of course, but . . . well, it would have been more sad to have sold off the cottage because I couldn't face going back. It's such a lovely spot, it means so much to me . . . and I've so many memories there going right back to my childhood."

"Sure."

"So despite a few weepy moments, it was actually good to be there."

"And then Mac rang you and hauled you back from your holidays."

"Didn't really *haul* me back. I could have said no."

"You could have said no to having me tag along too."

Laura looked at him and smiled. "To tell you the truth, I did at first."

"Yeah?"

"Then Mac persuaded me – as is his wont . . . "

Steve grinned in return. "Good old Mac."

"Yeah."

He continued to look at Laura and his smile slowly faded. "Joking aside, Laura, I'm . . . well, I'm really glad he persuaded you."

"Me too."

"Yeah?"

Laura nodded. "Yeah."

Steve looked at her, then he reached out and squeezed her hand. "Good . . . "

It was the first overtly physical gesture to pass between them, and instinctively Laura squeezed back, and as he left his hand covering hers she was surprised at just how right it felt.

Perez turned to his captive and began to undo the gag as the red orb of the sun dipped behind the hills. "Time for some more whiskey," he said, reaching for the bottle and glass on the table beside the bound Rhodesian.

"Stuff you!" said Douglas, the venom evident in his voice despite his speech being somewhat slurred.

"Let's not do this the hard way," said Perez, then he poured out a full tumbler of the whiskey and held it up to the other man's mouth.

In the hours since Kennedy and Johnson had called he had forced over half the contents of the whiskey bottle on his prisoner, reckoning that his captive would be less of a threat when the time came to leave if he was disoriented by having his system awash with alcohol. Also Perez wanted it to be established that Douglas had been drinking heavily – that way, subsequent police investigation would be unlikely to consider foul play, opting instead for a fatal drunken accident.

"No more whiskey," said Douglas, shaking his head. "It'll . . . it'll make me sick . . ."

"Don't waste my time with stupid lies," said Perez. "I've known plenty of alcoholics – this won't make you sick."

"It will . . . I've had –"

"Just fucking drink it! Drink it, or I'll use the knife!"

When Perez had first ordered Douglas to drink he had refused, and it was only when Perez had placed the blade of the flick-knife under the Rhodesian's eyes and threatened to carve his face into strips that the older man had reluctantly complied. Now he looked sullenly at Perez, but the Spaniard knew that having caved in already to the threat of mutilation, his victim was unlikely suddenly to find the courage to resist now.

"Don't make me slash your cheek open to prove I'm serious. Just drink the whiskey – now!"

Douglas flashed him a look of searing hatred, but there was fear in his eyes also, and Perez saw that the older man knew a genuine threat when he heard one. He pushed the glass against his captive's lips, and the Rhodesian began to drink, eventually swallowing all of the whiskey in the glass.

"That's better," said Perez, placing the glass back on the table.

"What's . . . what's the point of this?" asked Douglas in a slurred querulous tone.

Perez didn't deign to answer but instead quickly replaced the gag, muffling the older man's words of protest. It was better this way, better to keep a distance from his victim and to spare himself from listening to the Rhodesian and having to engage with him. The one concession he had made to the older man's dignity had been to allow him to use the bathroom – albeit at gunpoint – but otherwise Perez knew it was better to depersonalise matters and not relate to his victim on a one-to-one basis.

He took up the whiskey bottle and deliberately spilt some on the floor – wanting to leave signs of alcoholic consumption to be found later on – then he crossed to a rocking chair in the corner and sat down. He looked out at the hills, silhouetted now by the setting sun, and he figured he would give it another half an hour. No, say three-quarters of an hour, so it would be completely dark – and then he would put his plan into action and deal with Vince Douglas.

"You know what I'd really like?" said Laura.

"What?" asked Steve, looking at her across their candlelit dinner table in the Byblos.

"I'd like you to tell me about the kidnapping."

Steve swallowed, a little taken aback by the request, and he realised that Laura had picked up at once on his unease, for she immediately squeezed his hand sympathetically.

"Look, I know it's a painful subject. But I'm not being nosy, it's just . . . well, anytime it's come up I've felt you back off. I don't want it to be . . . something that's always there between us. Something that can't be spoken of, you know?"

"Yeah . . . I know." And he did know. Laura was telling the simple truth; he did shy away from any such discussion, not just with Laura but with anyone who alluded to the subject of the kidnapping. But tonight she had opened up to him, discussing her grief after Declan's death, and he had been flattered by her doing so. It had heightened the atmosphere of intimacy that had already existed between them and had spurred him to reach out and take her hand for the first time. Then when she had squeezed his hand in return he had felt a thrill – the kind of thrill that he hadn't experienced from such a simple action since he had been a teenager. So now it seemed only right that he should be forthcoming in return. Yet he hesitated, not having taken this step with anyone other than his psychiatrist, Dr Glasser.

Laura looked at him and he could see concern in her eyes.

"Look . . . if you really don't feel comfortable talking about it . . . " she said.

"No. I mean, I *am* uncomfortable but . . . it's right you should know."

"I don't want you to feel you *owe* it to me, because . . . well, because I told you about my situation."

"No, that's not it. I'm just . . . I suppose I'm a bit nervous. I haven't really spoken about it to anyone except to the doctors. But if I'm going to talk about it, then I'd like . . . well, I'd like the first person to be you."

"Thanks, Steve. "

He looked at her, her eyes seeming to sparkle in the candlelight, and he bit his lip, uncertain how to start, despite her clearly supportive interest. "I'm . . . I'm not sure where to begin. It's such a . . . such a big subject."

"Begin wherever seems right."

"Yeah . . . " He breathed out, then forced himself to begin speaking. " I suppose . . . I suppose I should begin at the beginning . . . the day of the kidnapping."

"OK."

"I'd finished work about six. Left the office and was making my way on foot to my apartment." He grimaced. "Looking back, I made it easy on my kidnappers – walked home the same way most nights, didn't change my routine."

"Right."

"The company had security people, and they'd said about taking more precautions, but I thought, 'No, I don't want to live like that'. Which was stupid really, because if your family are rich, then behaving as if they're not, as if you're just an ordinary guy working for a living – it's a kind of indulgence. So . . . I was punished for my indulgence."

"What happened?" asked Laura.

"They planned it perfectly. A block from my apartment there's a short cut I often took, through a service alley. And on the day there were these three guys in overalls beside a van in the alleyway. They were doing something to a ventilation duct, I didn't give them a second glance. Then *wham*, as I walked by, one of them hit me on the head. When I started to come to I was bumping around in the back of the van with my hands and feet tied and a sack over my face. My head was throbbing, and the sack made me feel really claustrophobic so . . . I started to scream."

"And they hit you?" asked Laura, the concern evident in the eyes.

"They didn't need to. When I tried to scream I discovered I was gagged under the sack. That made me even more claustrophobic, and I must have thrashed around because the next thing I knew someone kicked me hard in the ribs and told me if I moved a muscle for the rest of the ride he'd break my arm with a crowbar."

"God . . ."

"Yeah. So they took me to a place, I reckon it was some kind of warehouse – not that I ever saw it, what with the blindfold and sack. Anyway they took me there and locked me in a room. Whenever one of them was coming into the room they'd bang on the door and I had to put the sack over my head. The first time they did it I wasn't quick enough, so they beat me, to show me who was in charge. After that, even though I hated the sack I always put it on the second they banged on the door. They put a heavy chain around my ankle and attached that to the foot of a camp bed. And that was it. A bare room, no books, no newspapers, no radio – it was like solitary confinement."

"And how long did they keep you there?"

"Six days. It felt like an eternity. I mean it wasn't like I knew it was going to *be* six days, I'd no idea how long it might go on. And then towards the end, when they weren't happy with the way the ransom negotiations were going, I thought it might end at any moment . . . with a bullet in my brain."

"They threatened that?"

"They threatened worse."

"Yeah?"

"They threatened to carve me into pieces and send my parents the pieces, bit by bit, if the ransom wasn't paid."

"Jesus!"

"I know – what sort of an animal would put parents through the mill like that? I suppose I was lucky that that part remained a threat."

"Right."

"And that's the awful thing, really . . . "

"How do you mean?" asked Laura.

"The fact that you become *grateful* – that their worst threats aren't carried through. Have you heard of

331

Stockholm Syndrome?"

"Yes. Where kidnap victims end up identifying with their kidnappers, right?"

Steve nodded. "Classically it happens when someone threatens to kill you, is capable of doing it, but then doesn't."

"Right."

"The threatened person also has to be isolated, unable to escape, and the threatening person has to be perceived as showing some degree of kindness to the victim."

"Did that happen to you?"

Again Steve nodded. "Most of it. Certainly one of the kidnappers was less vicious than the others. Sometimes he'd even indulge in minor acts of kindness. You've no idea how important that is to the victim. So . . . like lots of kidnap victims, I went into appeasement mode . . . "

"Yeah?"

"In order to increase the chances of surviving, victims avoid reacting honestly to the treatment meted out to them. They deny their anger. They deny their terror. They adopt behaviour they feel will please their captors – so they're dependent, docile, lacking in initiative. They become highly attuned to pleasure or displeasure responses in their captors. They're grateful for being allowed to live, pathetically grateful for even minor acts of kindness. I discovered later these are all classical reactions, survival strategies that people resort to. The thing is . . . even though I learned that none of this is uncommon, I still felt . . ."

Laura looked at him sympathetically and Steve found he had to turn away from her gaze.

"What, Steve?"

"I felt disgusted with myself."

"Why?"

"For not being stronger. For trying to curry favour, for sucking up to those bastards, for pretending everything was fine, and the situation was reasonable and that I could see things from their perspective."

"You did what you had to in order to survive, Steve."

"I know. But it really wrecked my self-esteem. All that helplessness and humiliation. All the self-loathing – it took months of therapy before I could get my head around it. Before I could deal with all that suppressed anger."

"And have you dealt with it now?"

"As best I can. Hasn't been easy . . . "

"No . . ."

"At this stage they're not likely to catch the guys who did it. I've . . . well, I've pretty well accepted that now."

"Right."

"And I used to have fairly bad nightmares, and they've eased a good bit, so that's progress too. But I still have issues of anger when it comes to criminals – I doubt if that's ever going to go away. Not even sure if I want it to."

"How do you mean?"

Steve grimaced. "It's complicated. On the one hand I know anger can be a very destructive emotion. On the other hand though, anger's given me a focus. Helped me regain my self- esteem."

"Yeah?"

"Yeah. You see I hate what the kidnappers did to me, not just in mistreating me, but even more in what they turned me into. I was – I was such a hapless victim, so passive and pathetic – I was desperate to make them like me so they'd be less likely to kill me."

"That's entirely understandable, Steve."

"I know, I know. But it's still . . . it's still so *degrading* – to feel you tried to win the approval of people you knew in your heart were scum."

Laura squeezed his hand sympathetically. "I think you're being really hard on yourself."

Steve looked at her. The sincerity of her concern was touching and he liked the way she had taken his hand but now that he had started he wanted to tell her the whole truth. "On a rational level, Laura, I can see that, you know? But on an emotional level . . . the whole thing was much harder to come to terms with. Eventually though I found the answer – it was to use the anger constructively. If I couldn't *not* feel anger, then I wanted the anger to be an energy working for me. So I decided to use it in gaining the one thing I completely lost as a kidnap victim – control."

"Anger gives you control?"

"Not normally, but in this case it did. Because I was so angry I swore that I was never again going to be a victim. Never again going to be bullied or frightened or threatened by anyone. If anyone ever tries to kidnap me again, or mug me, or assault me I won't be a passive victim. I'll be fighting back. Making that decision, Laura, and then – then taking all the steps I did to follow it up – it gave me back a sense of myself. Gave me back a sense of control. It was a real turning point."

"Right. And these steps you say you took . . . ?"

"My family are wealthy – that's why I was kidnapped in the first place. So I thought, if I'm going to suffer the downside of wealth, I'm entitled to use its upside. So I did. I hired a guy called John Popovic. Ex FBI. He'd served with an elite unit they have called the HRT."

"HRT?"

Despite the seriousness of the conversation Steve smiled. "Nothing to do with Hormone Replacement Therapy."

"Somehow I didn't think so."

"It stands for Hostage Rescue Team. Those guys were trained to the nth degree. Weaponry, marksmanship, unarmed combat, surveillance, forcible entry, criminal psychology, you name it. John Popovic worked with me one-to-one. And when I say we worked, I mean intensively. In the gym, on the firing range, on the streets, in my home."

"Sounds like a huge commitment."

Steve nodded. "It was exhausting and it cost a small fortune, but by the end of it I felt . . . I don't know, it was like the strength it gave me somehow balanced out the weakness I'd shown during the kidnap. And the one thing I could really cling to was the knowledge that if ever anyone tried it again – and with all the publicity there's always a chance someone else might try another kidnapping – well, this time I'd be no hapless victim. I wouldn't be currying favour, or trying to please my captors. I'd be resisting with all the force at my disposal right from the start."

"Mightn't that be dangerous too though?"

"Maybe. But it's a price I'm willing to pay. And knowing that, it's . . . well, it's given me back my sanity. Does that make sense?"

Laura squeezed his hand again, then spoke softly. "Yes, it makes sense."

"I've never told all of this to anyone before."

"Not even your family?"

"Not family, or friends or . . ."

"Lovers?"

Steve shook his head. "I haven't felt close enough to anyone. Not till now . . . "

"Oh Steve . . ."

He squeezed her hand, then looked at her face in the soft candlelight, uncertain how she would respond.

She hesitated a moment, then taking his hand

in hers she raised it up, leaned forward and gently kissed it.

Perez looked at his watch then rose from the sofa. It was half past ten now and dark outside the cottage – time to go. He crossed to the chair where Douglas sat bound and gagged, then stopped just short of his prisoner. He had forced more whiskey on the Rhodesian about twenty minutes previously, wanting to keep him groggy but capable of walking for what lay ahead. The next phase of his plan was going to be tricky. Even in his inebriated state the former mercenary wasn't a man to be underestimated, as had been proven when he had nearly landed a haymaker of a punch earlier, and Perez knew he would have to stay alert and rigidly maintain the upper hand so that Douglas wouldn't be tempted to try anything.

Perez had found a loaded Smith and Wesson while searching the Rhodesian's bedroom, and while the flick-knife had served its purpose well when he had needed to intimidate the older man, nevertheless a gun would be more convenient for covering the prisoner during the operation that Perez had planned.

He kept the pistol trained on Douglas now, then bent down and undid the scarves binding his ankles to the legs of the chair. Standing behind his captive, he shoved the barrel of the gun into the back of the other man's neck. "Don't even think of trying anything. Understood?" The Rhodesian nodded, then Perez undid the gag. The former mercenary breathed out noisily, then Perez used his left hand to undo the scarves binding his captive's arms to the chair. He kept the gun pressed firmly against the other man's neck as Douglas tentatively moved his arms and massaged where the scarves had bitten into his wrists.

"Stand up. We're leaving now," ordered Perez.

Douglas made no move to rise but turned to look at his captor. "Leaving? Where for?"

Perez felt a stab of irritation. Although the other man's speech was somewhat slurred he didn't appear as affected by the whiskey as Perez had expected. And despite his status as a prisoner he was presuming to ask questions. *Time to make clear the true dynamics of the situation.* Perez moved round to the front of the chair, the gun still trained on Douglas, then without warning he lunged forward and punched the older man in the stomach.

Douglas cried out as he doubled up in pain, and Perez grabbed him by the hair, yanking his head back and placing the gun at his temple. "Don't ever question an order I give you! You do what you're told, when you're told, or I promise you, you'll be sorry. Got that?!"

Despite the pain he must have been in Douglas seemed to have sufficient awareness to know what self-preservation required. "Yes," he muttered, "yes . . ."

"Good. So put your hands in your pockets and make your way slowly outside to the Jeep. Do it!"

Without further prompting Douglas rose unsteadily

and made his way towards the door, and Perez realised that in fact the whiskey had had a significant effect on the older man. Or could it possibly be an act? Maybe a guy like Douglas who was experienced both as a drinker and a soldier might be pretending to be more shaky than he actually was. Either way Perez knew that he needed to keep the Smith and Wesson carefully trained on his prisoner while staying well back out of kicking distance.

"I can't . . . I can't open the door . . . with my hands in my pockets," said Douglas.

"Take your left hand out, open the door, then put it back in your pocket and step outside."

The Rhodesian did as instructed and Perez followed him, switching off the lights and locking the front door with a set of keys he had found earlier on a table just inside the door.

The evening air was still warm and carried the scent of jasmine, but the last rays of daylight were gone now. Perez could see his prisoner and the nearby Jeep in the soft yellow glow of the porch light, and just on the off-chance that someone might conceivably be walking in the nearby hills he kept the pistol discreetly down by his side.

"Into the Jeep!" he ordered. "Passenger door."

Douglas still moved shakily, but he obeyed the command and opened the door of the vehicle, then climbed in awkwardly. Still keeping the gun down by his side, Perez crossed round to the driver's side and climbed in also. "Face to the side and put your hands behind your back! Do it!"

Once again the Rhodesian obeyed, and Perez slipped the pistol into his pocket, then quickly rebound his prisoner's hands behind his back.

He was pleased at how things were going, reasoning that anyone seeing them emerging from the cottage wouldn't have observed a jailer and his prisoner, but would simply have seen Douglas and another man getting into the Jeep. And inside the vehicle it was too dark for anyone to see the Rhodesian being rebound. So far, so good, thought Perez as he placed the key in the ignition and switched on the engine.

"Where are we going?" asked Douglas.

"You've got to meet someone."

"Who?"

"You'll see," answered Perez, then he put the Jeep into gear and started down the bumpy track.

Steve could feel his heart pounding as he walked hand in hand with Laura through the grounds of the Byblos Hotel. A crescent moon had come out from behind a bank of cloud and it cast a faint ivory light on the lawns and shrubbery. In the distance Steve could see the moonlight reflected on the ocean, and he turned to Laura. "Beautiful, isn't it?"

"Gorgeous," she answered.

His pulses had been racing ever since she had kissed

his hand a few minutes previously, and he had suggested that they go for a walk, then had quickly signed the bill for their meal. On stepping outside he had turned to her and held out his hand and Laura had slipped her hand into his and walked closely beside him as they headed away from the hotel building. He had felt a tangible sense of intimacy between them after the revelations that they had each made, and neither of them had spoken until now, as though both of them were reluctant to do anything that might alter the atmosphere.

The sight of the moonlight reflecting on the waters of the Mediterranean had been too captivating not to refer to however and with the sweet smell of bougainvillaea hanging in the air Steve found the atmosphere almost overwhelmingly romantic. He thought back to the night in Bruges and the sudden intimacy that they had shared at the Lake of Love, only for each of them subsequently to feel awkward about it. This time however he was much more sure of his feelings and the signals from Laura made him hope that she might be as attracted to him as he was to her. Yet supposing she wasn't? Supposing he was reading too much into her behaviour?

They walked on through the grounds, the ocean lightly shimmering below them in the soft moonlight, and Steve knew that the pounding in his heart was partly fuelled by fear that he might be over-optimistic in his reading of the signs, and that he might spoil everything if he tried to force the pace. They continued on their way through the sweet-smelling grounds, then, on reaching a bower of Mexican Apple Blossom, Steve slowed to a halt. He turned to Laura, unsure what to say, but knowing that something was required. She returned his gaze without speaking and suddenly he knew instinctively that this encounter wouldn't end as the night at the Lake of Love had.

They continued to gaze at each other, neither of them speaking, then Steve reached out and gently touched her face. She responded by drawing nearer, then in an instant they were in each other's arms. Laura raised her lips to his and they kissed passionately. Steve could smell her perfume and when she kissed him with her tongue he tasted the faint flavour of the wine they had been drinking. He felt her fingers entwined in his hair as they clung together, then eventually she broke off the kiss but stayed in his arms and gazed up at him again. The warmth of her body through the light material of the dress and the touch of her breasts against his chest aroused him even further. He lowered his lips to hers once more and again they kissed passionately, then moving his lips to her neck, he covered her skin with soft kisses and heard her groan with pleasure. Lowering his mouth, he kissed her breasts and she groaned again, then suddenly her fingers were at his shirt and she quickly undid the buttons and ran her hands over his chest.

"Oh God, Laura . . ."

"Yes?"

"I want you so much . . ."

"I want you too . . ."

It was all he needed to hear. Reaching out, he enclosed her tightly in his arms, then without another word they sank to the ground, unheeding of all discomfort as they frantically began to make love.

Perez rounded a sharp bend then pulled in off the road and killed the lights of the Jeep. He was at a broad grassy verge overlooking a gorge that he had identified earlier, and he had turned off the road while there was no other traffic about. Guided by faint moonlight, he drove on slowly until a small belt of trees shielded him from the road and the probing headlights of any passing cars. Satisfied that he would be unobserved now, he switched off the ignition and applied the handbrake.

Douglas was still bound hand and foot in the passenger seat and now he turned to his captor. "Who . . . who are you bringing me to meet?" he asked.

Your Maker, thought Perez, but instead he answered brusquely "You'll see." He took the Smith and Wesson from his pocket and trained it on the Rhodesian, then with his other hand he took out the flick-knife. Keeping the gun aimed at Douglas's chest he leaned down and slit the bonds around his ankles. "Now face away and hold out your wrists," he ordered.

The older man complied, and Perez again used the knife, this time freeing the Rhodesian's hands from behind his back before slipping the flick-knife back into his pocket.

"I feel really sick," said Douglas.

"Tough."

"The whiskey . . . I think I'm going to puke . . ."

"No!"

"I can't . . . I can't keep it down! Can I open the door? Please?!"

"Open it then. But just lean out – don't even think of running."

Douglas quickly pulled on the door handle and pushed open the door of the Jeep. He leaned over the side and made a horrible hawking noise but didn't actually get sick.

Perez kept the gun trained on him, but in truth he reckoned that the older man was in no fit state to attempt an escape. He watched as the former mercenary fell back against the seat, closed his eyes and clasped his stomach.

"Christ!" cried Douglas. "Oh Christ . . ."

Perez was a little surprised, thinking that a drinker like Douglas would have been able to hold his drink, notwithstanding the large quantity of whiskey that had been forced upon him. Perhaps the punch to the stomach had triggered this, he thought, then Douglas made the hawking sound again and Perez felt a stab of disgust. The older man leaned further out of the Jeep, presumably to avoid getting sick on the vehicle, and

Perez willed him to finish, so that he could get on with things.

Suddenly however the Rhodesian launched himself backwards, taking Perez unawares. He felt a searing pain in his ribs as Douglas jabbed back viciously with his elbow, then twisted around in the seat, forcing Perez' gun-hand up into the air. He grasped Perez' wrist so that the gun couldn't be swivelled down, then launched a ferocious head-butt.

The initial assault had surprised Perez and his ribs ached badly but he had fast reflexes and he just managed to avoid Douglas's thrusting forehead. The head-butt would have shattered his nose had it landed, but the sheer ferocity of it had unbalanced Douglas, and Perez moved quickly to take advantage. With his gun-hand still being clasped by Douglas, Perez used his left hand to unleash a karate chop at Douglas's neck.

The Rhodesian was clearly a born street-fighter however and even in his drink-sodden state he instinctively rolled away so that Perez only caught him a glancing blow. The former mercenary gave no indication of any pain and was still succeeding in holding Perez' gun-hand aloft. The older man was also surprisingly strong, and in the cramped compartment of the Jeep Perez couldn't gain the leverage to aim the weapon down at him. Instead he threw a vicious punch at Douglas. This time the Rhodesian wasn't quick enough to roll with the blow and the uppercut connected solidly with his chin. His head snapped backwards and then smacked hard against the frame of the door. Immediately Perez felt his opponent's grip loosening on his gun-hand as Douglas slumped unconscious onto the passenger seat.

A small trickle of blood came from his head where it had banged against the door. No problem, thought Perez, it would be consistent with Douglas's other injuries. Talking of which. . . . Perez slipped the Smith and Wesson into his pocket, then reached out his left hand and grabbed Douglas by the hair. He pulled his head upwards, then placed his right hand on the back of his victim's neck and with one swift movement smashed Douglas's neck against the steering wheel, severing his windpipe.

He allowed the former mercenary's inert form to slump back down onto the passenger seat, then immediately checked for a pulse, even though he was pretty sure that it had been a clean kill. Still, better to be absolutely certain. He checked for a few moments, then satisfied that Douglas was dead, opened the driver's door and climbed out. He went around the Jeep and closed the passenger door that Douglas had opened, then returned to the driver's side. He reached in and used a handkerchief to wipe his fingerprints from the steering wheel, before doing the same with the door handle, handbrake and indicator column. When he was satisfied that no print could have been left he reached over and took hold of the front of the dead man's shirt, then hauled

346

him across into the driver's side of the Jeep. He sat Douglas up in the seat and placed his feet on the controls, then he used the dead man's hands to place fingerprints on all of the areas that he had just cleared of his own prints.

He gathered up the cut scarves that he had used to bind Douglas, then looked round the Jeep to make sure that there was nothing that he was overlooking. He could think of nothing further that he hadn't dealt with and so he slipped the handkerchief around his fingers and let off the handbrake. The car was largely still on the level and only rolled slightly forward. He stepped back, again using the handkerchief to close the driver's door before opening it out and wrapping it around both his hands. He walked quickly to the rear of the Jeep, then placed his handkerchief-enshrouded hands on the rear of the vehicle and began to push.

The Jeep moved forward easily on the grassy wasteland and began to pick up speed. Perez ran with it for several yards, then he stopped and watched as it disappeared over the edge and tumbled down into the gorge. He listened as the vehicle smashed against trees and boulders on its way down, then he was rewarded with a sudden flash of light as the fuel tank exploded, turning the Jeep into a fireball that eventually came to rest on the bottom of the gorge about one hundred feet below.

Excellent, he thought, even less evidence now. He had reckoned that with Douglas's reputation there would be little suspicion of foul play and that it would very likely be decided that he had driven off the road after having too much to drink. He had reasoned that if the time of death was established at a post mortem then Douglas's blood levels would be shown to be sky high and that the broken neck and the cut head would seem like logical results of driving over a ravine with no seat-belt on. Now however it was academic – nothing of the former soldier was going to be retrieved from the fireball down below. Pleased with a job professionally done, Perez turned away and set off into the night.

Laura could feel the warmth of Steve's breath on her neck as they lay together naked on her bed. In the months after Declan's death she had sometimes wondered what it would be like to make love again with another man, and she had worried that being with a new partner might be fumbling and awkward, or, almost worse, exciting and therefore probably guilt-inducing. As it turned out her fears had been unfounded, and making love had simply felt like the right thing at the right time. After the passionate lovemaking in the grounds of the Byblos, she and Steve had tidied themselves up as best they could, then headed back to the hotel. It had seemed like the most natural thing in the world that they should go to her room, and Laura had experienced no regrets for what had happened but instead had felt a surge of emotional wellbeing.

They had drunk a couple of glasses of chilled wine from the minibar, then kissed lingeringly. The kissing had turned to caressing, and with less urgency this time but with more savoured pleasure, they had made love again. Eventually they had both been sated and Laura had lain in Steve's arms, drowsily content as she listened to his even breathing and to the droning sound of crickets outside in the moonlit grounds.

Steve had been all she could have asked for in a lover – ardent, yet sensitive and skilful – and although she had decided simply to go with the flow and let tonight unfold as it would, she couldn't help but wonder a little where they would go from here. Although neither of them had made any declarations she sensed once again that a relationship between them wouldn't be a casual thing. At least she hoped not. He was, after all, handsome, and bright, and amusing and rich – and so was never likely to want for other partners. At the same time she sensed that perhaps he in turn was smitten with her, in which case who knew what the future might hold for them? For now, though, Laura was happy simply to lie in his arms, glad that for once she had broken her normal rule of not getting romantically involved with those with whom she worked. She turned a little to look at him, and he opened his eyes. They were an attractive shade of grey and they softened as he smiled at her.

"You were dozing," she said.

"Guilty as charged." He looked at her and raised an

eyebrow. "*But . . .* "

"Yeah?"

"The sight of a beautiful woman, hair cascading across her breasts – that's enough to *awaken* me."

"Steve . . . " said Laura in mock protest, then she felt his arms encircle her as he rolled onto his back and gently pulled her towards him. "What are you on, monkey glands?"

"Yeah – old family recipe," he answered with a grin.

Laura smiled back, then he reached up and kissed her. The warmth of his mouth and the taste of his tongue suddenly rekindled her desire, and she kissed him back passionately, then lowered herself down onto him, eager to make love once more.

Trenet started when the phone in his study finally rang, even though he had been awaiting the call from Perez for the previous six hours. He had been angry at the Spaniard for the abrupt way in which he had ended their previous conversation and when he had tried to call back he had found that Perez' mobile was switched off. Clearly the former legionnaire had been making a point, underlining the fact that he was the one who would make the operational decisions, including when he would report back to Trenet.

It was an unsatisfactory attitude, the sort that Trenet wouldn't normally tolerate in a subordinate. On the other hand this wasn't a normal situation, and Trenet knew that the price of dealing with someone like Perez might mean some indulging of the other man's machismo. It was now eleven forty-five however, and even allowing for the fact that Perez had presumably been busy in pursuing matters with Vince Douglas, a wait of over six hours before reporting in smacked of insubordination.

Trenet confirmed from the caller recognition on his telephone console that it was indeed Perez, and he made a conscious effort to keep his anger in check until he found out the state of play regarding the Rhodesian. He sat forward in his swivel-chair but allowed the phone to ring several more times, not wanting to give Perez the satisfaction of appearing to be anxiously awaiting his call, then he picked up the scrambled phone. "Yes?" he said, dispensing with any form of greeting.

"Thought you'd like to know – your friend has had an accident," said Perez.

"Yes?"

"Yeah."

"How bad an accident?"

"Fatal. He'd been drinking very heavily and drove his car into a ravine – turned into a fireball. No question of surviving."

"I see." Trenet felt a flood of mixed emotions. Partly he was impressed by the speed and decisiveness of Perez' action, certainly he was enormously relieved to have Vince Douglas out of the equation, yet also there was a

351

touch of guilt at having had to betray a former comrade. Additionally there was the underlying irritation of Perez' lack of proper respect, something that Trenet's pride compelled him to deal with. Yet it had to be done diplomatically, bearing in mind that Perez was, unquestionably, an effective operative in the field. "I have to say your work has been excellent, really excellent," said Trenet.

"Thank you."

"But I do want to be kept more informed."

"I have been keeping you informed."

"Six hours is a long time to be incommunicado. Please stay in touch more, OK?"

"Fine," answered Perez airily.

Trenet picked up on the other man's tone and recognised that the Spaniard was adopting a sort of magnanimity-in-victory stance, as though it were beneath his dignity to argue the point and he was indulging Trenet. Although it sounded polite, it was an irritating response, but Trenet knew that it was wiser to let it go. "What's the position on our other two friends?" he asked instead.

"Interesting developments there . . . "

"Yes?"

"They've put off calling to their subject until tomorrow morning. Meanwhile – well, you can probably guess the rest."

"I'm not paying you so I can guess. What's happened."

"They've become lovers. They're both in her room now."

"Interesting . . . "

"Could be. For the moment though they're not talking about the case. Otherwise engaged . . . "

"Right."

"I'll continue to monitor them, but probably there'll be nothing of interest till the morning."

"The most important thing is going to be hearing what their plans are when they find out about our friend," said Trenet. "That's got to be your top priority."

"Naturally."

"So please, keep me posted if there's anything before then, and immediately they respond to the news they're going to get."

"Right, I'll be in touch," answered Perez, then he hung up.

Trenet lowered the phone and sat gazing unseeingly across his study. There was no denying that Perez had turned up trumps, particularly in engineering a death for Douglas that shouldn't arouse any suspicions. Which left Kennedy and Johnson and the *Clarion* story. Trenet knew from the bugged conversations that the newspaper's editor was already less than convinced about the value of the trip to Spain in pursuit of a nebulous story. With any luck he reckoned that the *Clarion* would regard Kennedy's line of enquiry as having now reached a dead end, and that they wouldn't approve additional expenses in trying to pursue the matter further.

Of course, nothing was certain, and he couldn't relax until Laura Kennedy turned her attention to some other story, but still, things had gone well this evening. He knew that tonight he ought to sleep more soundly than since the whole business had begun, yet despite his relief a tiny part of him felt guilty. It was the lingering military notion of honour, he knew, a sense that comrades in arms don't betray each other, whatever the cost. But then Douglas was no longer a comrade, he told himself, and hadn't been for over forty years. And in truth it had been a stark choice between the disastrous consequences of allowing Douglas to talk to the journalist, and authorising what Perez had done. If there had been some in-between course that could have guaranteed Douglas's silence he would have considered it, but it hadn't been a case that lent itself to half measures. Besides which, Trenet had long since regarded half measures in any endeavour as dangerous.

The foolishness of not going for broke had been brought home to him years previously when he was a ten-year-old in the orphanage in Reims. He remembered how a smaller boy had snapped one day and taken on the orphanage bully. Fuelled by a sense of outrage, the younger boy had stunned the bully with a couple of swift punches, then shouted at him that he'd kill him if he ever laid a finger on him again. Even as a ten-year-old, Trenet's instincts had told him it was a mistake, and that the younger boy should have pressed his advantage when the bully was stunned and given him the kind of hiding that would have shattered his air of invincibility. Instead the bully had been given the time to recover, and being bigger and stronger than his attacker, he then went on the give the smaller boy a vicious beating.

The lesson, imprinted on Trenet's mind, had stood him in good stead for the rest of his life, and now he told himself that his present situation was a classic case, where, feelings of decency and honour notwith-standing, ruthless, decisive action had been necessary. And if the law of the jungle decreed survival of the fittest, it also decreed that the survivors didn't weaken themselves by fretting about those who didn't survive.

Renewed in his resolve, he put Vince Douglas from his mind, rose from the desk and crossed the room. He took out a decanter and poured himself a glass of Napoleon brandy. It was a vintage year, bought when his finances had been buoyant, and he savoured the bouquet, then slowly sipped the brandy as he looked round his opulently furnished study. This was the life he had fought to attain, and this was the kind of life he intended to go on living, and nobody – not board members like Hans Romar with his accountant's tunnel vision, or drunkards like Vince Douglas, or nosy journal-ists like Laura Kennedy – nobody was going to take it away from him. Buoyed in his determination, he finished the drink, turned on his heel and headed off to bed.

Chapter 10

Steve carefully studied the sheet of paper on the table before him, then made handwritten notes beside several of the names listed, lowered his pen and stretched languidly. The early morning light streamed in through the window of Laura's hotel room, and looking out across the landscaped grounds of the Byblos Hotel, he could see a clear blue sky. It was going to be another beautiful day.

Clad only in his boxers he had gone to the furthest corner of Laura's spacious bedroom and sat at the window there, not wanting to wake her by turning on a light or opening a curtain near where she slept. Seeing her form stretched out in the large double bed, he thought back to the previous night and the passionate lovemaking that they had enjoyed. Even now a part of him couldn't believe that things had turned out as they had. He had been aware for some time that he had been increasingly attracted to the Irishwoman, but for her to have returned his feelings as wholeheartedly as she had had been more than he would have dared to hope.

It had been one of those magical nights where everything just seemed to fall into place. Apart from the physical thrill of lovemaking with a woman as beautiful and passionate as Laura, there had also been a sense of connection, a feeling that their being together felt overwhelmingly right. Surprised by his own forwardness, he had actually said as much to Laura, and to his delight she too had admitted to feeling the same.

He looked fondly at her now, her brown hair a mass of tossed curls on the pillow and he thought how striking she looked, even when asleep. Just then the alarm on her mobile went off and she stirred in the bed, then reached out and switched off the phone. Steve felt a welling of affection for her and he gathered up his list and crossed the room to where she was beginning to sit up in the bed. "Morning," he said.

"Hi," she answered with a warm smile.

If there had been any question of a slight awkwardness, a morning-after-the-night-before atmosphere, Steve knew as soon as she smiled that things between them would be OK. "Sleep well?" he asked.

"Yes. You?"

"Fine."

"So . . . what were you doing up?" asked Laura, having

noticed the sheet of paper in Steve's hand.

"Just woke up early. Thought I'd go through the list of Hollands in the Torquay area, see if I could whittle it down a bit. Probably be academic once we meet Vince Douglas, but seeing as I'd downloaded it, thought I might have a look at it."

"As distinct from sharing my bed. That's romantic …"

She said it with a straight face, but Steve knew that she was joking and he drew nearer the bed. "Well, if it's romance you want … " He reached out and kissed her tenderly, then lowered himself onto the bed

Guessing his intentions, Laura laughed but rolled out of his reach. "Don't even think about it!"

"All I'm doing –"

"I know what you're doing! We have to shower, have breakfast and get out to Vince Douglas for eight thirty!"

"Fine. Just – just *use* me, and then cast me aside …" he said with mock stoicism.

"You forgot to say 'like a squeezed-out lemon'."

"Sorry?"

"'Cast aside like a squeezed-out lemon', I think, is the full phrase."

Steve smiled, pleased that they were confident enough in their intimacy to be able to joke.

"OK then, cast me aside like a squeezed-out lemon!"

"No better woman. But first, how about you ring for room service?" said Laura, rolling out of the far side of the bed and slipping on a hotel dressing-gown.

359

"Your wish is my command."

"And while you're doing it, sure I might as well have a look at your phone list."

"Be my guest," replied Steve. He placed the list on the bed for Laura, then moved to the bedside telephone and lifted the receiver. "Continental breakfast?"

"Sure," answered Laura, her attention already on the telephone list.

Steve dialled the number for room service and was pleased at how swiftly his call was answered and his order taken. If the room-service operator thought there was anything irregular in the occupants of two adjoining rooms both taking their breakfast in one of the rooms he gave no indication of the fact, and Steve finished the call, then turned back to Laura.

"Well?"

"Narrowed from twenty-nine to fifteen, that's not bad."

"Well, eleven of the twenty-nine were women, so obviously I discounted them."

"Plus three of the men."

"Yeah, one is a doctor, one a retired major, one had the letters QC after his name – I presume that stands for a Queen's Counsel?"

"Yes, it does."

"It's not impossible, I suppose, but it's not all that likely that a former mercenary would take a degree in Law. Likewise Medicine."

360

"I agree," said Laura. "Not sure about the retired officer though."

"A major's a fairly senior rank. And Dutchie Holland was a private in the Congo. Even if he gave up being a mercenary and rejoined the British army, the chances of him rising through the ranks to that extent must be pretty slim."

Laura nodded. "Yeah, you're probably right. Good work, Steve."

"Thanks. Hopefully though Vince Douglas will tell us what we want to know, and we won't need to go down this road."

"Absolutely. Especially since Holland could be ex-directory, or living in Scotland or whatever. Still, if we draw a blank, at least we have something to fall back on."

"Right. And talking of falling back . . ." Steve slipped his arms around Laura's waist and fell back onto the bed with his arms around her.

"Steve!" she cried laughingly. "The room service will be arriving!"

"Ten minutes, the guy said."

"Ten minutes?"

"Ten whole minutes."

Laura lay back on the mattress, looked him in the eye and smiled. "Well, then – what are you waiting for?"

Perez was getting concerned about the listening devices. Although they were absolutely cutting-edge in terms of technology and miniaturisation, their inbuilt transmitters began to fade after several days, and he had noticed a deterioration in the strength of the signal that he was receiving.

Last night he had picked up on the unmistakable sound of lovemaking from Kennedy's room and he reasoned that she must have left the jacket with the device under its collar draped over a chair or somewhere else nearby. At some stage before this morning however he reckoned that she must have put the jacket away in a closet, because on arising Perez had tried listening in again but could only pick up muffled sounds. The bugs would still be serviceable for a couple of days more but as their transmitting power weakened Perez knew that he would have to get increasingly closer to his subjects to hear their conversations.

Right now he was travelling in his rented car, tailing Kennedy and Johnson as they drove up to the hills for their planned early-morning rendezvous with Vince Douglas. Perez kept well behind them, feeling that at this stage it was more important not to be noticed than to hear what was being said inside their car. Later when they discovered that the Rhodesian was dead he would have to ensure that he was close enough to pick up a good signal, but for now he was content simply to tail them from a distance.

Back at the hotel he had noticed that Johnson wasn't wearing the beige pants in whose turn-up he had planted one of the miniature devices, and he had been relieved to see that Laura Kennedy had carried her bugged good jacket over her shoulder, presumably to don when she called to Douglas's house.

He drove through the sunlit Spanish countryside, pleased at how things were going and hopeful that by lunch-time at the latest he would be able to make a definitive report back to Trenet. He had rung the industrialist earlier this morning, just to keep him satisfied, but if he could report that Kennedy's fruitless journey all the way to the Costa del Sol had caused the *Clarion* to pull the plug on underwriting such a nebulous story – and he reckoned there was a fair chance that it would – then he knew that the older man would be enormously relieved. And who could say where that might lead? A wealthy man with a guilty secret might be persuaded to pay a significant bonus for a difficult job well done. Still, that was for later, for now he needed to stay on the case of Kennedy and Johnson.

He followed the course of the road as it rose up into the hills, then recognised that he was approaching the area where he had forced Douglas off the road and down into the gorge. He slowed down as he came to a wide bend, then on rounding it he saw that traffic was backed up ahead and that Johnson and Kennedy's car, along with several others, was stopped. Partly blocking the road was a large crane manned by yellow-hatted workmen, and Perez realised that they must have been engaged by the police to retrieve the wreckage of Douglas's Jeep. He slowed right down, and even though he couldn't see the remains of the Jeep, a thin pall of smoke still arose from the gorge. He brought his car to a halt, uneasily aware of his two subjects in the car directly in front of him, and also conscious of two uniformed police officers, one of whom was diverting traffic around the caterpillared wheels of the huge crane where it partly blocked the road.

Damn! he thought. It wasn't good field practice to get this close to subjects. He also felt uncomfortable about coming to the attention of the police – however fleetingly – while on a mission. He turned his face away from the nearest policeman, and lowered his head, ostensibly to retune the car radio, but in reality so that Kennedy and Johnson wouldn't see him in their rear-view mirror. Then he fiddled with the radio as he waited anxiously for the traffic to clear.

Curious to find out what was happening, Laura wound down the passenger window. An ambulance was pulled in on the grass verge, and in addition to policemen and workers operating the crane there were various other people gathered by the side of the road.

Laura could see one of the policemen directing a contraflow around the base of the crane, and while awaiting the turn of the traffic on her side of the road to start moving again, she spoke to his colleague, who was standing nearby.

"What happened?"

"A Jeep went down into. . . " His English was heavily accented, and he didn't know the word for gorge, so he indicated.

"The gorge."

"Yes."

"God. Any survivors?" Laura asked, the journalist in her kicking in from force of habit.

"Sorry?" replied the police officer.

"Did anyone survive the accident – come out alive?"

"No."

"Really? So how many died?"

"Excuse me," answered the man somewhat abruptly, then he turned away and sauntered over to join his colleague.

Probably thinks I'm being ghoulish, thought Laura, then her attention was taken by a florid-faced man of about sixty who had been standing with the group by the side of the road, and who now lowered his head to speak in the car window.

"One dead," he said in an unmistakably English accent. Laura recognised from past experience that he was one of those people who thrived on the edges of other people's tragedy, and who liked to make themselves part of the drama by sharing the inside track on what had occurred.

"Yeah?" she responded. "Do you know what happened?

"Looks like he just drove straight off the road and down into the gorge."

"God, what a way to die!"

"Yeah. Though I reckon it would have been over quick enough – seems the engine exploded."

"Really?"

"Complete fireball." The man looked reflective. "Poor Vince, probably bought it before he knew what was happening . . ."

Laura felt her skin coming out in goosebumps. "Vince? It wasn't . . . it wasn't Vince Douglas?"

The man nodded grimly. "'Fraid so. Did you know him?"

Laura's head was reeling but she managed to stutter an answer. "No, not . . . not really. I –I knew of him . . ."

"Who didn't? Kept a few of the bars out here in profit, did old Vince."

"I can't . . . I can't believe this," said Laura.

"None of us can. Happened last night, they reckon. Probably had a few too many – as was his wont – then went off the road in the dark."

"Right."

"Oops – moving again," said the man.

Laura looked and she saw that the traffic on her side of the road was now beginning to edge around the base of the crane.

"Thanks," she said to the Englishman. "Thank you."

He nodded, then stepped back as Steve slipped the car into gear and started forward.

Laura turned and shook her head. "Unbelievable," she said.

"Yeah."

"Better make a U-turn."

"What?"

"Turn around. No point going to the cottage, let's go back to the hotel."

"OK."

Stunned by the news of Douglas's untimely death, Laura gazed vacantly out the window as Steve quickly turned the car round and headed back towards the Byblos. Lost in her thoughts, she didn't notice as another car from the line behind them also did a U-turn and started back in the same direction.

Perez could tell that his subjects were in shock and he hoped that it would have dulled their powers of observation. Normally he wouldn't have dreamed of risking attention by doing a three-point-turn in view of the people he was tailing, but this time he had felt there was no option but to take the chance. It was essential that he stay within range of the listening device now that they had learned of the demise of Vince Douglas and were likely to discuss where it left them regarding the newspaper story. He had followed them back to the

Byblos Hotel, staying closer to their car than he would normally have done as he strained to hear every word they said.

The short journey to the Byblos had been taken up with Johnson and Kennedy speculating about the freak stroke of bad luck that saw their interview subject dying just when they were on the brink of locating him. So far they had expressed no suspicion regarding the man dying just before he might have provided the information that they sought. – though of course that might come on reflection. Perez hoped not; he hoped that they would simply report back to the *Clarion*, and that the matter would be taken out of their hands with their editor recalling them to Dublin.

Meanwhile he sat in his hotel room with the earpiece from his miniature receiver pressed firmly into place. The sound quality had gone a little fuzzy, and he reasoned that Kennedy must have put down the jacket containing the bug somewhere in the bedroom that was just about close enough to pick up what she was saying, but far enough away from her to diminish the strength of what was being recorded. Straining hard not to miss anything, Perez sat on the edge of his own bed and listened intently, knowing that this was when it would be decided whether or not to drop the story.

"God, it's just so bizarre," said Laura.

Steve nodded. "Freakish timing." He took two

brandies from the minibar at the other side of his bedroom and indicated them to Laura. "I think we need something for the shock."

"Yeah. I'll have a little soda water in mine."

"OK." Steve poured the drinks, then brought them over to where Laura sat on the side of the bed. "So what do you think?"

Laura sipped her drink then shook her head. "I think this is just the weirdest thing ever."

"Isn't it?"

"And I know it's awful to be callous, and a man has died an' all, but . . . well, it's such a setback to the story, after coming all this way."

"There's still the Torquay angle," said Steve. "We can switch our search to there and try and find if Dutchie Holland is still in the region."

"Selling that to Mac might take a bit of doing."

"Maybe. But I'd say he'll moan a bit but ultimately back your hunch – provided you feel strongly enough about following it."

"Quitting's not my style."

"Well, we could probably get a flight this morning from Malaga to the UK. Be in Torquay by this evening."

"Right."

Just then there was a knock on the bedroom door, and Steve went to answer it.

"Your laundry, sir," said a housemaid in heavily accented English.

"Thank you," replied Steve.

The housemaid stepped into the room carrying the pressed beige slacks from which the wine-stain had been removed. She placed them down on the end of the bed then turned to Steve.

"This falls out," said the woman, handing him a tiny device. "From here," she said, indicating the turn-up of the trousers.

Steve looked in amazement at the miniature electronic component.

"Is OK?" asked the housemaid.

"Yes . . . yes . . . thank you," answered Steve. He quickly handed the woman a tip, and she gave him a smiling *gracias*, then crossed the room and closed the bedroom door behind her.

Steve leaned back against the wall. "Jesus Christ!" he muttered.

"What?"

He closed his eyes, unable to believe what he was seeing, yet there could be no doubt. John Popovic, his ex-FBI trainer had discussed surveillance equipment and listening devices, and there was no question but that the device in his hand was a miniature bug.

"Steve?"

"In there," he said, indicating the bathroom.

"Sorry?"

"In there!" He indicated again and strode towards the bathroom, leaving the door open behind him that Laura might follow.

"What's going on?" she asked, stepping across the threshold and looking at him quizzically.

"You'll see," he answered. Before Laura could speak again he raised both hands to stop her dead, then placed a finger on his lips to indicate silence. He quickly inserted the plug into the bath and turned the cold tap on full. The pressure was good, and a torrent of water cascaded loudly into the bath. Steve raised a hand and silently indicated for Laura to cross the spacious room to where he stood at the rim of the bath.

She hesitated briefly then came and stood beside him. Despite the loud noise of the running water he leaned close and whispered in her ear. "We've been bugged – that's what the device was."

"What?!"

"Keep your voice down, just in case there's other stuff planted."

"Christ," said Laura, the shock evident on her face. "Who'd . . .who'd do this?"

"Someone who's worried about the story we're on? I only bought the trousers on the way to Bruges – so it's been planted since then."

"Jesus, this is unreal!"

Steve's mind was still racing, but he tried to think clearly. "We've got to check all our other stuff," he said. He indicated the water cascading into the bath. "And this is the one place where we can talk without fear of being overheard. "Let's get all our clothes and our other things in here and check through them."

Laura nodded. "Right . . . but then what?"

"Then we can decide our next move. But first we need to find any other bugs. OK?"

"Yeah."

"All right then, let's do it."

The bath was full now, but the tap still spewed forth its liquid torrent, the level being maintained as the water escaped via the overflow hole. Laura had checked her laptop, her mobile phone, all of her toiletries and her clothes, but only one more bug had shown up, carefully concealed under the collar of her jacket, while Steve had found nothing further. Laura felt the same sense of outrage that she had sometimes heard burglary victims describing, but even the violation of her privacy seemed like a side issue compared to the thought that whoever had been tracking them – presumably with a view to quashing the story – might have been involved in the death of Vince Douglas.

It was a frightening thought and, notwithstanding the noise of the water, she kept her voice low as she asked Steve the question that couldn't be avoided. "Do you think we're in danger here?"

"I've been wondering about that," he answered reflectively, "but I wouldn't say we are."

"Why so?"

"We'd no idea we were being targeted, so we weren't taking precautions. If they'd wanted to take us out they could surely have done it before now."

"You really think so?"

"Yeah. And besides, killing a journalist would stir up a real hornet's nest."

"Yeah, that's what I like to tell myself," said Laura. "But Vince Douglas dying just before we got to speak to him – it's a hell of a coincidence."

"Sure is."

"So, do you reckon he was killed – and the thing made to look like an accident?"

Steve paused a moment, then grimaced. "I wish I didn't feel this way, but yeah, I think it's certainly possible."

"Then we really need to alert the guy in Torquay. I mean if these people are leaving journalists alone but removing the sources for our story, then we've got to warn Dutchie Holland that he could be in danger."

"Right. Trouble is, we don't know which name he is on our list – or if he's even on the list."

"We should just go to Torquay," said Laura. "We can try ringing the people on the list en route. We might get lucky and find he's one of them, but the priority should be to get there fast and launch a proper search."

"Privately or via the police?"

"Privately," she answered. "Time is of the essence here. I don't want to waste it sitting in some police station trying to convince a cynic of a detective to drop everything else and try and find Dutchie Holland. Especially when we haven't a shred of evidence that's not circumstantial. Once we find Holland and warn him, *then* we can go to the police."

"Right."

Another thought had struck Laura and she looked at Steve quizzically. "So . . . do you reckon the people who planted the bugs know now that we're onto them?"

He nodded. "Has to be a fair chance they do. I mean your jacket was lying on the bed when the housemaid brought in my trousers. If the conversation with the maid was picked up, then they must know that *we* know."

"All the more reason to move quickly then," said Laura.

"True."

"I'm not going to waste time arguing with Mac about whether it's safe, or whether it's worth going to Torquay in person. I'll type up the story so far and e-mail it to him, then ring him from England when there's something to report."

"I don't think that's such a great idea."

"Don't worry, Steve. I know Mac of old. If he's presented with a *fait accompli* he'll accept it – provided there's a big story to come."

"That's not what I meant."

"Well, what do you mean?"

"I know you're not going to like this, Laura, but please, just listen to my suggestion and try to view it objectively."

"OK. What is it?"

"That we split up to throw our pursuers off the scent. I mean, we have to presume that if they've bugged our clothes then they'll also have us under observation, right?"

"Right."

"But they won't be expecting us to part suddenly. And they may not have enough people here in Spain to cover us both. So if we go our separate ways at Malaga airport we could take them by surprise."

Laura looked thoughtful. "I'm trying to think what exactly that would achieve."

"An opportunity for one of us to shake off a tail. Both of us if we play it cleverly."

Laura could see that he might have a point, yet she couldn't help but feel a tiny stab of disappointment at Steve's willingness for them to separate. "Right . . . "

"Look, I know we've come all this way together. And . . . well, especially after last night – I really want to be with you. But that's even more of a reason why we need to be serious about safety."

"*Safety*? I thought you felt they'd have done it by now if they were going to act against us?"

"Probably – but that's just a guess. We don't know how desperate they might become. Maybe they *would* consider taking out a journalist if the stakes became high enough, who knows? The thing is we shouldn't put all our eggs in one basket. If we're far apart but in telephone contact, it makes it more risky for them to harm one of us – knowing the other one can spill the beans."

"So what, you go to ground in Ireland, and I keep you posted on how I'm doing in Torquay?"

She saw him take a deep breath, then he looked her in the eye and shook his head. "I think it would be better the other way around."

The sheer unexpectedness of it stopped Laura in her tracks, then she found her voice. "You've got to be joking!"

"No, I'm dead serious. And I know it probably seems outrageous –"

"Damn right! I'm the journalist here, Steve. This is *my* story."

"Absolutely. And if it was about journalism there'd be no argument. But it's not just about journalism any more."

"Isn't it?"

"You know it's not, Laura. If our suspicions are right it may well be about murder."

"It's still a story – and I want to be the one to tell it."

"You will. If I go to Torquay it's for two things only. One, to warn Dutchie Holland; and two, to get the name of his former commander. Once I've alerted Holland and rung you with the name, my part's over.

You then write the story as you see fit. And we can report our suspicions to the police once Holland's been alerted and you have the name. It's still completely your story, Laura."

"Is it?"

"Of course, it is. Look, the laptop means you can work from anywhere. If you shake off any tail, you could go safely to ground – stay in your cottage in the Burren, rather than back in Dublin – and then move on the story the minute I ring with a name."

"There's just one problem, isn't there?"

"What's that?"

"I'd be letting you fight my battles for me."

"Laura –"

"No. I know you mean well, Steve, but I'm not – I'm not the damsel-in-distress type, you know?"

"I know you're not. And I swear to God, Laura, this isn't a sexist thing."

"Then why don't you go to the cottage in Clare? We'll still have the safety of having our eggs in two baskets, but I'll be doing my own dirty work."

"That's just it though. It might *be* dirty work."

"So?"

"You're a journalist, Laura. A damn good one, but a journalist is what you are. And maybe that isn't enough if the people we're up against did what we suspect they did with Vince Douglas."

"I've taken my chances in the past."

"I know that, Laura. I'm not questioning your bravery for a second. But the thing is, I'd never, *ever* forgive myself if anything were to happen to you. It's like . . . I've just found you – and I couldn't bear to lose you now."

In spite of the circumstances, Laura felt herself moved by his sincerity. "Steve . . . you're not going to lose me."

"Please let me ensure that, Laura. *Please*. Look, you've trained in journalism and you've become really good at it. *I've* trained in what may be needed here – and believe me I trained until I was good at it too."

"Good at what?"

"Self-preservation. I told you that after the kidnapping I got this guy Popovic to train me. He really did. Escape and evasion techniques. How to spot and lose a tail. Unarmed combat. Weapons handling. Marksmanship. All sorts of stuff. If push comes to shove, I'm far better equipped for the kind of situations that might arise."

"Even so, Steve . . ."

"It makes sense, Laura. You know it does."

"It just . . . it doesn't feel right asking you to be the one to take the risks."

"You're not asking me. *I'm* asking you. You'd be doing me a favour."

"A *favour*?"

"It's hard . . . it's hard talking about this but . . . well, my self-esteem was shattered by the kidnapping. I told you – I hated myself for being putty in the hands of my kidnappers. That's why I trained with John Popovic. So I could fight back. So I'd never be cowed again by criminals. This is a chance, Laura. This is a chance for me to . . . to settle an account. Please let me. I really want to do it. I *need* to do it."

Laura looked away, her emotions in turmoil.

"For both our sakes, Laura, please – let me go to Torquay."

Laura stared at the water that still cascaded noisily into the bath, then she slowly turned around and faced him. "OK then, if you're absolutely certain."

"I am."

"All right then," she said reluctantly. "We'll do it your way."

CHAPTER 11

Trenet answered the phone on the second ring, knowing from the caller recognition that it was Perez reporting in. At ten to nine on a Saturday morning there were few IWS employees in the building, and Trenet had gone in early to work in the office, knowing that he would only have been restless at home while awaiting the call from Perez. As it was he had found it difficult to concentrate on the monthly accounts spread out before him on his large mahogany desk, and he turned away from it now as he sat back in his leather swivel-chair and took the scrambled call.

"Good morning," he said.

"Morning," answered Perez.

"What's happening?"

"Two developments, neither of them great . . ."

Trenet felt a stab of irritation, irked as usual by the way

Perez always seemed to release information piecemeal instead of reporting all salient paints at once. "Let's have them," he said .

"First off, they've discovered the listening devices."

"Damn!" said Trenet, knowing that tactically this was a big loss of advantage. "How did they discover them?"

"Our friend had his trousers cleaned in the hotel. If they'd been dry-cleaned the bug might never have been found. There was a wine stain though, and the trousers were hand-washed – so the device was found in the turn-up."

"*Merde!*" said Trenet.

"Yeah, because he knew what it was, and now they're freaked."

"Right. So they went through their stuff and found the other one?"

"'Fraid so, it's been dead ever since."

"That's really a pity."

"Yes, normally they mightn't have discovered them for weeks. Just bad luck that the woman doing the hand-washing saw the device and –"

"And now they know they've been bugged," Trenet cut him short.

"Yes. Nobody's fault, just one of those things," said Perez.

Trenet consciously tried to suppress his irritation at the other man's philosophical tone. "What's the other problem?" he snapped.

382

"They've discovered that their first subject is dead."

"Are they suspicious?"

"They sounded more shocked than suspicious. Though, of course, when they think more about the timing they may become suspicious, especially now they know they've been bugged."

"Right . . . "

"That's not all though."

"Well?"

"Just before I lost contact I overheard them talking about their next move – they were discussing going to Torquay."

"Christ . . ."

"And they were talking about getting there by tonight."

"Fuck!"

"I know. But on the positive side they don't have any idea where the subject lives. It could take them a fair while to find him."

"Yeah . . . "

"So – what do you want me to do?"

"Where are you now?"

"In a corner of the hotel lobby."

"Have the others checked out yet?"

"No."

"Good," said Trenet, his mind racing as he figured out how best to proceed.

"So?"

"You've got to get there first. You have the address, so you'll have a head start."

"We don't know for certain that he's still at the address."

"How many things in life are certain?!" snapped Trenet "He's *probably* at the address. Check British directory enquiries and see if a Mr Holland is still at the address. If he is, fine, and if he's not you've a good starting point for finding his new address. Either way you should have a decent head start on the others."

"You want me to . . . take action then?"

"Yes."

"Won't our friend be really suspicious if her next subject also has an accident?"

"He won't have an accident. He just won't show up. Eventually he'll be reported as another missing person. People vanish all the time, probably hundreds every year in somewhere like the UK. Understood?"

"Understood. Though I still think it could make her suspicious if he can't be found."

"Even if she is suspicious, she'll have reached a dead end. With both men unavailable there's no link left to Kaburi. Brick wall, end of story. Time for the newspaper to stop wasting money and assign her to something more productive."

"If you say so."

"I do."

"OK then."

"You need to get moving straight away," said Trenet.

"Before I do, there's something needs saying."

"What?"

"This case has become very awkward. To stay on top of things – on your behalf – I've taken risks I wouldn't normally take. And now you want another really tricky job pulled off against the clock. I take it you'll make this all worth my while?"

Trenet wasn't sure if this was just a bit of commercial bargaining or if there was a hint of blackmail in the other man's pitch. Either way he didn't like the stance that Perez was taking, yet he knew that he needed him.

"Don't haggle with me now," he said, keeping most of the anger from his voice. "We don't have time to waste."

"We have enough time to agree that what you want is more than was originally expected," said Perez in his maddeningly reasonable tone. "I think a bonus for the extra risks that have arisen would be –"

"All right, you'll get a bonus! Look, I promise, you'll be generously looked after, OK?"

"Fine."

"Just do it then. Right away. All right?"

"I'm on my way."

"And keep me posted."

"Will do."

Trenet heard the line going dead, then he slowly lowered his own phone and hung up. He thought of Laura Kennedy and her obstinate pursuit of a forty-year-old story. Why couldn't she mind her own damn business and let the past remain in the past? *Because she's a snooping bitch of a journalist.* Because they *thrive* on stuff like this. Well, she wouldn't thrive at Daniel Trenet's expense, he thought. Others had tried and paid the price, and he wasn't going to allow Laura Kennedy to be the first to succeed. Strengthened in his resolve, he forced himself to put the matter in abeyance, then he swung his swivel-chair nearer to his desk, reached out for the monthly accounts and tried to focus on business.

Steve felt the heat of the Spanish sun beating down on his shoulders as he crouched by the side of the car and checked the bodywork of the rented vehicle for homing devices. His security consultant, John Popovic, had shown him what to look for back in New York, and had suggested that he check his car at least once a week. Admittedly the existence of a homing device would now be academic seeing as they were simply driving to the airport, but he was curious to know if they had been shadowed since their arrival in Malaga by someone using such a device.

Finding nothing, Steve rose from where he had been kneeling in the carpark of the Byblos Hotel and got into the vehicle. "All clear," he said to Laura. "They must have been tracking us with just the bugs."

"Right."

The engine had been left running so that the car inte-

PURSUIT

rior was pleasantly cool from the air-conditioning, and
Steve sat back comfortably in the driver's seat, relieved
to be in out of the heat. "OK, he said, "let's get to the
airport."

Laura nodded in agreement, and he put the car into
gear and pulled out of the parking bay. He watched carefully in the rear-view mirror as they drove through the
hotel grounds towards the exit. "No sign of a tail," he said.

"Good," answered Laura, then she took out her mobile
phone and switched it on.

They had debated whether or not it was safe to use the
phone while driving to the airport. On the one hand
they might be lucky enough to hit the jackpot with one
of the names on Steve's downloaded list of Hollands in
the Torquay area, in which case they could warn him
straight away of the danger he could be in, and also seek
the name of his former commander in Kaburi. If on the
other hand the car interior were bugged then their
actions would be evident to whoever it was who was
trying to bury the story – assuming that that was what
was involved in the bugging and in the suspicious death
of Vince Douglas.

After some consideration they had decided to search
the car carefully and if nothing was found then to use
the mobile. That way they could make for the airport
without losing time on what were, unquestionably,
speculative phone calls.

In the event a thorough search of the vehicle's interior

had revealed no bug of any kind, and Laura now held her mobile at the ready and took out the list of Hollands. "So, how do you ring someone to warn him his life might be in danger – without sounding like a crackpot?"

"With difficulty," answered Steve wryly, "but I'm sure you'll find the right words."

"Thank you so much."

"Besides, the warning only comes into play if one of the guys on the list is actually Dutchie Holland."

"Yeah . . . " Laura twisted round in the passenger seat and looked behind her as they drove towards the airport.

"Still no sign of a tail," said Steve, "I've been watching carefully."

"OK then," answered Laura consulting the sheet of names, "time to start working through the list . . . "

Perez had positioned himself carefully so that he could sip his coffee while unobtrusively watching the doors of the departures hall in Malaga airport. He had paid for a ticket on the next flight to the UK – the eleven forty-five to London – and had already checked in and collected his boarding pass.

He was waiting now to confirm the arrival of Kennedy and Johnson, whom he presumed would also have booked seats on the eleven forty-five flight. He didn't want to bring himself to their attention in any way, but nonetheless he felt that good field practice dictated he establish the opposition's intended movements as early as possible.

Meanwhile he had started thinking about how to proceed on arrival in Torquay. He'd have to move fast, even allowing for the fact that he had a head start over Johnson and Kennedy in possessing Holland's last known address. Even if Holland was still living there however – which couldn't be taken for granted – he would have to assume that the time available to snatch his subject was tight, and that Kennedy and Johnson might be lucky and quickly discover where the former mercenary lived.

He hoped against hope that Holland wouldn't have moved, and that he could therefore locate him without having to make contact with neighbours or workmates who might later recall a stranger making enquiries. And then there was the question of dealing with Holland, disposing of the body so that it wouldn't be found, and trying to set up a scenario to suggest that Holland was alive but had simply walked out on his old life – as a certain number of people did each year.

It was going to be a challenge, no doubt about it, yet Perez relished the adrenaline surge that came with bold planning and lethal action. Still keeping an eye on the entrance doors of the departure hall, he sipped his coffee absent-mindedly and put his mind to finding a workable plan.

Laura looked at her reflection in the window of the shuttle van from which she had alighted outside Malaga airport. Using the window as a mirror, she could see no sign of anyone tailing her, or of anyone behaving in any way suspiciously, and she turned to Steve as he gathered his travelling bag. "All clear, as far as I can see."

"Likewise," he answered, then he gave a tip to the van driver who had taken them to the terminal from the car-hire depot at which they had returned their car.

En route from the Byblos Hotel to the airport Steve had several times employed the evasion techniques taught him by John Popovic and they were moderately confident that no one had tailed them. Of course there could be any number of people waiting at the airport to pick up their trail again, Laura realised, yet it had boosted her confidence to see how coolly Steve had employed the methods that he had learned from his ex-FBI tutor.

They gathered their bags, and Laura was glad that they were travelling light, with just hand luggage, as they made their way through the hot Spanish sunshine to the entrance to the departures building.

Once inside the busy building Laura felt the welcome coolness of air-conditioning, then Steve checked the monitor for the London flight and they made their way to the appropriate desk. There were quite a few people in line to check in, and Laura and Steve joined the queue.

They had chatted with ostensible casualness as they

made their way through the terminal, but each had surreptitiously watched to see if anyone was following them. So far Laura had seen nothing untoward and she raised an eyebrow enquiringly to Steve who shook his head to indicate that he too had seen nothing suspicious.

The queue shuffled towards the check-in desk and Laura pushed her bag forward with her foot. She stood with her hands in her pockets, nervously fingering the wad of dollars that Steve had given her as part of their plan. It was almost time to enact it now, she knew, and she could feel herself getting nervous as the moment drew near.

The queue shuffled forward again and Steve turned to her. "I think it's time," he said softly

Laura looked at him, her heart thumping, and she ached to reach out and hug him, to kiss him lingeringly and say goodbye properly, but she knew that she couldn't. Their whole plan was predicated on misleading anyone observing them, and she could hardly engage in a soulful farewell – or any kind of farewell – if she were supposedly just going to the toilets. Instead she looked him in the eye and unobtrusively squeezed his arm.

"Be careful," he said softly.

"You too." She swallowed hard, then let go his arm. She looked around as though establishing where the toilets were, then turned back to Steve. "I want to head over to the loo. Back in a few minutes," she said.

"OK."

She nodded casually, then picked up her bag and walked as nonchalantly as she could towards the public toilets.

Perez couldn't put his finger on it, yet something struck him as not quite right. He had kept well behind his subjects as they crossed the busy terminal to the check-in desk, and they had joined the London queue, as he expected.

Once they had taken their places in the queue he had drawn nearer, then found a place to sit where he could sip his coffee and appear to read his newspaper while in fact keeping a discreet eye on them. Their behaviour had seemed unflustered and they had chatted in an apparently casual manner, although Perez thought that he detected them glancing about a little more than most of the other people in the queue.

That made sense of course, for having discovered the bugs it would be logical for them to assume that they might be under visual surveillance as well, especially now that the listening devices were no longer operational. *So what was it that stuck a wrong note?* Whatever it was, it seemed to hover just on the edge of his consciousness but when he tried to pin it down it eluded him.

OK then, approach it analytically, he thought. They seemed to be alert to their surroundings, which made sense. But they also seemed pretty calm for two people who had discovered that their private conversations of the past few days had been bugged – to say nothing of their subject meeting an untimely death.

Maybe they were *too* calm, Perez thought, maybe that was what had been striking a slightly false note in his subconscious. Yet Laura Kennedy was a seasoned journalist who wouldn't be easily intimidated. Her book about an abortive terrorist attack on the Harrogate Conference Centre a couple of years previously had been an acclaimed bestseller, but more importantly it had been the work of a woman whose life had been at risk from the principal terrorist involved, and who had nonetheless pressed on with her pursuit of the story. In which case appearing calm despite having been bugged mightn't be out of character, Perez thought as he sipped his coffee.

So what *was* it about the scene that had niggled slightly? He tried again to analyse it, but the more he did the further away it seemed to retreat. Eventually he stopped trying, reasoning that it was better to leave his mind blank and hope that whatever it was would rise to the surface unbidden. It wasn't an entirely satisfactory response, but it was all he could think of for now, and so he settled back behind his newspaper, surreptitiously watching Johnson, and waiting to see what would happen.

Steve looked around him, his gaze apparently casual as he watched out for anyone who might in turn be watching him. He took in fellow queue-members, but they mostly looked like returning holidaymakers, and the occasional business travellers that he saw looked convincingly like business people rather than anyone who might be on his trail. He remembered John Popovic's tips on what to look out for in terms of being followed, and he specifically watched out for people reading books, papers and magazines, and for people who busied themselves with food and drink. He knew that these activities were potential covers for those who wanted to loiter and so he carefully observed anyone he could see engaged in such pursuits. There weren't actually that many, he realised, which made sense what with the bulk of the shops and cafés being on the far side of the departure gates. He saw a blonde-haired woman about twenty yards away who was absent-mindedly sipping bottled water while facing in the direction of his queue. A little further away in the other direction there was a Latin-looking man in his thirties wearing lightly tinted sunglasses who was sitting with a newspaper in one hand and cup of coffee in another. The only other person nearby that fitted the seeking-something-to-do-while-loitering profile was a woman in her sixties. She was dressed all in black and looked like a Spaniard and she seemed to be engrossed in a magazine that she held away from her as though she were long-sighted.

Steve watched all of them carefully, but none of them seemed to be observing him, though, of course, it would make sense that anyone doing so should only do it occasionally and with discretion. Steve told himself not to get paranoid about who might be watching him and instead he decided that it was time now to put the next part of his plan into action. He took his mobile from his pocket, then quickly punched in a sequence of numbers. The call was answered almost immediately.

"Hi, it's Steve Johnson. I'm here now."

"Fine," the man's voice was deep, with a Spanish accent, and he sounded in his thirties or forties. "Where will I meet you?"

"I'm at the check-in desk for the London flight."

"OK, see you in a minute, then."

"OK."

Steve hung up, then resumed his scanning of those who might be observing him. It would be interesting to see what happened when the Spaniard arrived, because if anyone *was* tailing Steve, then there might be an opportunity shortly to force the unknown observer to show his or her hand. None of the three people he had earmarked earlier seemed to be paying him any attention however, and after a couple of moments Steve's attention was diverted by the approach of a handsome, sallow-skinned man with dark hair, greying at the temples. The man looked to be in his mid-forties and was carrying a light briefcase. More significantly, he was dressed in a pilot's uniform, and as he drew nearer to the queue for the London flight, Steve picked up his travel bag and stepped forward.

"Captain Valdez?"

"Mr Johnson?"

The two men smiled and shook hands.

"If you'd like to follow me," said the Spaniard.

"Sure," answered Steve, lifting his travel bag and walking alongside the other man.

He had decided back at the Byblos that with time of the essence it made sense to gain even a short head start on the scheduled airlines, by chartering one of the smaller private jets that could be hired by anyone willing to pay for the privilege. *What the hell*, he had decided, no point being rich if you couldn't occasionally use it to tactical advantage. And with the phone calls to Torquay that Laura had made en route to the airport having failed to locate a Dutchie Holland, his decision to speed up his journey to England in the security of a private aircraft now seemed like a particularly good move.

"We've got a place on the apron, not too far away," said Valdez, "and I asked for the earliest possible take-off slot."

"Excellent," answered Steve.

"So, I just have to clear you through security, then we can board the plane."

"Great."

Steve deliberately kept to a moderate pace, and he

glanced around him as they walked towards the departure gates. A good number of the passengers who had been in the London-bound queue were staring after him – understandably enough, he thought, considering that he had suddenly left the queue and gone off with a uniformed pilot. Of more interest to Steve though was the trio of people that he had earlier been observing. The Spanish woman dressed in black was still standing reading her magazine at arm's length and awaiting whoever it was she seemed to be waiting for. She hadn't given him a second glance as he walked past her, and glancing backwards now, Steve noticed the blonde-haired woman was no longer sipping her water, but was placing the bottle back in her travelling bag. As soon as she did so she hoisted the bag up, then set out in the opposite direction to that in which Steve and Valdez were going. Which left the Latin guy. Steve knew that if he stared back at him also it would be obvious to the man that he was suspicious of him – provided, of course that the guy wasn't simply a normal passenger. But if he *was* a tail, it would be better, Steve thought, not to give the game away by revealing that he knew who his tail was. Accordingly he resisted the temptation to look back and walked on for a while, then suddenly stopped.

"Sorry, Captain, just one second –"

"No problem," answered the Spaniard as Steve lowered his travelling bag to the ground, then went through it, ostensibly seeking to locate his passport.

"Ah, here we are."

He rose again, his pulses racing. The Latin guy had left his original spot and had travelled in the same direction as Steve. Now however he was also stopped as he disposed of his coffee cup in a litter-bin. It could, of course, be a coincidence, but John Popovic had trained Steve to look with suspicion on coincidence.

"OK?" asked Valdez.

"Yes, fine," answered Steve, then they continued on their way. He waited until they had gone another fifteen or twenty yards, then glance backwards briefly. *Bingo*, he thought. The Latin guy was moving once again, following in the general direction that Steve and Valdez had taken.

Steve felt his heartbeat accelerating, part of him uneasy at the idea of being stalked yet the greater part of him excited at the idea of both evading the enemy and forcing him to show himself by virtue of the private-aircraft move. Pleased with his tactics, he walked a little more briskly now as he and Valdez made for the Departures area.

Perez cursed himself for underestimating his opponent. It had never occurred to him that Johnson would join the London queue by way of a ruse. Now he realised that he should have been more on guard, knowing that Kennedy and Johnson had been alerted by the discovery of the bugs. The arrival of the uniformed pilot had taken Perez completely by surprise, however, and he felt angry at having the initiative wrested from him by an amateur. Plus he had had no option but to expose himself somewhat when Johnson had set out across the concourse with the other man. Johnson might even have spotted him when he had suddenly stopped and rooted in the travelling bag, ostensibly to remove a passport but perhaps in reality to watch out for tails. It had been imperative however to find out where they were heading, and reluctantly he had gone out on a limb and followed them until it became obvious that they were going to go in through the Departures area to clear security.

Now however Perez was in a quandary. By showing his own boarding pass he could follow them at a discreet distance through security and into Departures. But then what? How could he find out any details on a private flight? And what was the significance of their going without Kennedy? And suddenly it hit him. He knew now what had struck him as slightly odd when the Irishwoman had gone to the toilets.

She'd taken her travelling bag with her. Hoisted it up casually as though it were the most natural thing in the world to bring to the bathroom. But most women going to the bathroom would have left their travelling bag with their partner and just taken a handbag. So why hadn't it rung warning bells instead of leaving him with a feeling of something nigglingly wrong? *Because he had underestimated them on that too. He simply hadn't credited them enough with tactical savvy.* It was a mistake he wouldn't make again, but for now he needed to do some quick thinking, and he lowered his own travel bag, sat down on a bench and tried to marshal his thoughts.

Was Kennedy taking a separate flight in an attempt to shake off the surveillance that they now clearly suspected themselves to be under? Or was she planning somehow to link up surreptitiously with Johnson and the pilot and travel on the private flight? Perez hadn't seen her leaving the ladies' toilets prior to the uniformed man arriving at the London-bound queue, but supposing she had left while Perez had been distracted by Johnson and the pilot? Or supposing she had joined the queue for some other flight? No, that didn't seem likely; if she wanted to get to Dutchie Holland, then she'd want to take the next UK flight – which was the eleven forty-five to London. But then again they had stopped doing what seemed likely and were now obviously engaging in diversionary tactics. And if he were to go through security and into the departures lounge he wouldn't be able to leave there until his flight was called. Could that be what they wanted?

He wasn't sure, but he knew that a rash decision now could have serious tactical consequences. Better to take a few minutes to mull things over before making his next move, he decided, and he sat back on the bench, closed his eyes and tried to analyse all that had happened.

Laura waited anxiously inside her cubicle in the airport's ladies' toilets, then she glanced once more at her watch. Ten-fifty, time to go. She had spent almost forty minutes in the toilets, timing things so that she wouldn't arrive at the check-in desk for her flight to Ireland until the last minute. It had been part of the plan that she and Steve had devised to try and shake off anyone tailing them, and as she came out of the cubicle now she crossed to the mirror and observed herself.

In spite of her nerves she felt a slight touch of ridiculousness as she took in her altered appearance. Changing her look was another part of their plan to confuse anyone seeking to follow them, yet she couldn't entirely shake off the notion of dressing up, as she had sometimes done for fancy dress or theme parties.

Her thick curling brown hair was gathered up and covered by a folded headscarf, she wore a large pair of sunglasses, and her smart skirt and jacket had been replaced by a T-shirt and a multicoloured, sarong-type summer skirt worn with a pair of thick-heeled sandals. The overall effect was a sort of half-baked ethnic look that Laura would never have countenanced normally, but it did make her look decidedly different from the woman who had entered the toilets over half an hour previously. And in truth she had been limited in what she had been able to acquire – the small number of outfits that she had in her carrier bag presumably being familiar by now to anyone who had been tailing Steve and her over the last few days. Which was why she had forced herself to over-come her embarrassment and to approach a group of Englishwomen who visited the toilets.

Her plan had been to offer a generous cash payment in dollars to persuade them to swap clothes, and to trade her travel bag for some other type of hand luggage. The Englishwomen however had been in high spirits – Laura suspected that they had been drinking before travelling to the airport – and when they had heard Laura's story that she wanted to evade private detectives hired by an over-possessive Spanish husband whom she wished to divorce, they had entered wholeheartedly into the arrangement. Despite their protests that no payment was necessary for a few cheap articles of clothing and a carrier bag, Laura had insisted that they take a hundred dollars and have a drink on her.

This gesture had won the holidaymakers over completely, and when Laura had emphasised how impor-tant it was to keep mum about the whole affair until they got home – for who knew how many watchers might be observing or listening in the terminal? – the Englishwomen had happily sworn themselves to secrecy.

Now though was the moment of truth, when Laura would have to step out in full public view. She took a deep breath, then made for the door to the toilets, her spare clothes and her other possessions in a Marks & Spencer's carrier bag. She stepped out into the terminal and started towards the check-in desk for the Dublin flight. She told herself that however ridiculous she felt in her improvised outfit, to most people she would be just another traveller in a busy airport – a fair number of whose passengers were dressed in dubious fashion. She glanced around her as casually as she could but nobody seemed to be paying her any particular attention.

Steve had rung her on her mobile while she had been in the ladies' and had described a Latin-looking guy in jeans and a blue shirt whom he felt might have been tailing him, but despite watching out carefully, Laura could see no one who matched that description. Maybe this was going to work after all, she thought.

She reached the check-in desk, at which there was no queue, produced her passport and quoted the reference number from her telephone booking to a heavily made-up woman who regarded her unsmilingly. "We're just about to close the flight. Have you luggage to check in?"

Laura shook her head. "No, I've just hand luggage."

"Good." The woman opened Laura's passport, then looked at her.

Laura made no offer to remove the sunglasses and with her hair up under the scarf she knew that she looked a good deal different from her passport photo. Then again so did lots of people. *'If you look like your passport photo you're too ill to travel'* was a line she had heard some-where, but now she reckoned that the desk clerk was about to ask her to remove her sunglasses. The woman glanced from Laura back down to the passport, then she checked that the name matched that on the ticket and handed Laura a boarding card.

"Please go straight to security and on to the boarding gate. Your flight will be called in the next few minutes."

"Thank you," said Laura, then she gathered her bag and set off for the departure gates.

Perez walked briskly towards the security check. He felt more in control now that he had had time to respond to the ruses that Kennedy and Johnson had employed. At first he had been taken aback to have lost both his subjects, but he had refused to panic and had carefully thought matters through. The critical thing, he had decided, was not that Johnson had surprised him by chartering a private plane, nor indeed was it critically important whether Kennedy was taking a different route to throw off pursuers or secretly rejoining Johnson – no, the crucial consideration was getting first to Dutchie Holland.

Even if Johnson's earlier flight gave him a short head start, he lacked the vital piece of information that Perez had, namely an address for Holland. Perez had rung directory enquiries in the UK and had confirmed that a Mr Alfred Holland was still listed at the address that Trenet had obtained. It was good news and bad news. Good in that it confirmed precisely where Perez needed to go in Torquay. Bad in that Holland *was* actually listed in the British telephone book. Having said that, Perez knew that Johnson and Kennedy didn't know his address or first name, so that ringing directory enquiries wouldn't enable them to pin down which of the many Hollands in the Torquay region was the one they wanted.

Of course, they could try to ring every male Holland who was listed, and hope that one of them was actually Dutchie Holland, and hope also that he would be at home on a Saturday morning. And if by chance they hit the jackpot, and if Holland was prepared to give the information they wanted regarding his former commanding officer to a stranger over the phone, then the game was up. But there were a lot of ifs in that scenario, and on balance Perez felt he had a good chance of getting to his man first.

The other encouraging thing was that he had just out-thought Kennedy. At first he had wondered if she had separated from the American merely as a diversionary tactic, with the intention of somehow linking up on the private flight that Johnson had chartered. Now however Perez knew that this was not the case. Having made his phone call to the UK directory enquiries number, he had put his mind to considering the journalist's behaviour, and acting on a hunch, he had struck gold.

He had reasoned that if she were linking up with Johnson on the flight then worrying about her where-abouts in the meantime was pointless. If, however, she was making for another destination then that was a different matter. Although why she, as the journalist, would allow the American to pursue the story in Torquay was a mystery. Nonetheless if she were perhaps spooked after discovering the bugging devices – and perhaps more significantly by the death of Vince Douglas – then maybe she was going to ground while the American sought out the information she wanted from Dutchie Holland. They had just become lovers; it was quite plausible that he might want to impress her with some heroics if they felt that the pursuit of the story had become dangerous.

Whatever the reason though the obvious place for her to lie low was Ireland. Once he had decided that, the rest had been easy. Being a native Spanish speaker had stood to Perez, who had gone to the check-in desk that was handling the next flight to Dublin. The desk clerk had been wary at first, despite Perez' best efforts at being charming. He had made up a story about needing to know if a business rival was travelling on the flight, and when the clerk had replied that she couldn't reveal the passengers' list he had smiled, told her he didn't want her to name any names. Instead he just wanted confirmation if a Laura Kennedy was on the flight. A simple yes or no. A tiny piece of information that was nevertheless valuable to a businessman and for which he would be happy to pay her – say one hundred euro?

That had done the trick, the clerk had suddenly become co-operative, and Perez had thanked her, then walked away. Now that he knew where Kennedy was headed there was no pressing need for him to observe her at the departure gate for the Dublin flight. Still, it would be no harm just to see what the journalist might be up to, if he could get to her gate before her flight began boarding. Pleased with his decision-making under pressure, Perez continued walking briskly towards the security check.

Steve sat back in his upholstered seat as the private jet taxied out onto the runway. The interior of the plane was comfortably furnished and he had far more space than on a normal commercial flight, yet he found it impossible to relax. So much had happened in the last couple of days – making love with Laura, the death of Vince Douglas, discovering the bugs, organising their getaway from Malaga – that his mind was still racing and his body felt charged up with adrenaline.

He could still hardly believe the extent to which things with Laura had taken off, yet counterbalancing the excitement of a relationship with such an attractive woman was the fact that now her welfare was a worry to him. He was relieved that she had eventually agreed to hole up at her remote cottage in County Clare and await the critical information that he hoped to glean in Torquay. It was as safe a course as he could envisage for her, yet the combination of knowing that they had been under surveillance and the untimely death of Vince

Douglas meant that he still couldn't help but feel uneasy on her behalf.

As for his own situation, he knew that he ought to proceed with caution. *And yet . . .* if he were honest, part of him wanted a confrontation with whoever had planted the bugs. He knew they were likely to be criminals – perhaps lethally so if they had been involved in the death of Douglas – yet such was his residual anger at what he had suffered at the hands of his kidnappers the previous summer that he wanted to take them on.

On one level he knew that it could be foolhardy to tangle with such people, even though his training with John Popovic had made him a much more formidable opponent, yet he felt a need to vindicate himself, even if only in his own eyes, after having slotted so unresistingly into the role of victim in his last encounter with criminals.

The sound of the jet's engines suddenly grew louder and Steve looked out the window, knowing that they would soon be hurtling down the runway. He had his mobile switched off at the pilot's instruction, and would have for the duration of the flight. After passing through security back in the terminal however, and while awaiting Captain Valdez's clearance of some final paperwork, he had excitedly rung a number of the Hollands on his down-loaded list.

Laura had previously begun working her way through the names on the drive to the airport, and with this second batch of calls he had managed to get to about the three-quarters point of the list. Being a Saturday morning several hadn't answered the phone at all, others had never served in the military, two were clearly much too young, and one elderly man had stated icily that he *had* been in the army but had served in the Grenadier Guards, not with a rag-bag unit of mercenaries.

The most promising replies had been two answering-machine messages, and Steve felt that either of them could possibly be the Dutchie Holland that he sought. Both of them sounded the right age, and one of them simply asked the caller to leave a message, whereas the other stated that Alfred Holland was away on holidays and would be back on the evening of Saturday the twenty-fourth – which was this evening.

All in all it wasn't a bad response, and Steve knew that even if the phone calls led nowhere he would pursue things on the ground in Torquay in a matter of hours. Just then the roar of the jet engines reached a crescendo, and the plane accelerated down the runway before smoothly rising in a swift climb. Steve looked down at the mountainous landscape below, then settled back in his seat, pleased to leave Malaga behind and anxious get to England and to find Dutchie Holland.

Come on, thought Laura as she sat near the departure gate waiting for the Dublin flight to be called. It was just after ten past eleven now, and with the flight scheduled for eleven thirty they should have started to board. She had seen no sign of the Latin man that Steve had described and as far as she could make out no one else seemed to be tailing her.

The initial sense of mild ridiculousness that she had felt in the outfit cobbled together by the Englishwomen had worn off now, and she reckoned that the radical change in appearance actually constituted a pretty good disguise. On the other hand if the people she was up against had guessed that she might return to Ireland then all passengers boarding the Dublin flight were sure to be scrutinised.

Would her impromptu disguise pass muster then? Maybe, maybe not. Either way there was nothing further she could do, and she had decided not to think about it too much. Dwelling on the possibility of being pursued by people ruthless enough possibly to have killed Vince Douglas was too frightening – better to concentrate instead on making her part of the plan work and on getting the story into a fit state to e-mail to the *Clarion*. Besides she did have one further card to play. If her disguise had failed and if she *were* in fact being tailed then presumably her opponents would want to follow her – which meant buying a ticket for the flight to Dublin. Laura however had purchased a ticket that would take her on to Shannon – only another twenty minutes by jet, but a hundred-mile journey by road from Dublin. The vast majority of the passengers on the flight would disembark in Dublin – and most people referred to her flight as the Dublin flight – but in fact the plane went on after a brief stop to discharge the small number of passengers who were travelling on to the south-west.

Apart from being much nearer to the cottage in Kilfenora, Laura hoped that the onward leg would throw anyone following her, with her pursuers likely to presume that she would disembark in Dublin, where she lived and where the *Clarion* was based.

Her musings were cut short by a tannoy announcement calling her flight, and she waited until a good number of passengers had congregated at the gate, then she unobtrusively joined the throng, handed over her boarding pass and went to board her flight.

Trenet was planning his tactics for the next board meeting when the phone rang. He was still at his desk in the IWS building and in the couple of hours since Perez had rung he had actually managed to compartmentalise the worries of the *Clarion* enquiries and to concentrate on business. Now however he saw from the caller recognition that it was Perez again and he picked up the phone. "Well?"

"Been some developments, said I'd keep you posted."

"What's happened?"

"Our American friend is smarter than I thought. It looked like he was taking the next flight to London, but it was actually a ploy."

"A ploy? For what purpose?"

"To put anyone watching him off the trail. He's actually taking a private flight, so he's going to get to Devon that bit faster."

"Damn!"

"It's a setback, not a disaster," said Perez. "So he gets to Devon a bit ahead of me. But I have an address so I know exactly where I'm going. And I checked with directory enquiries – our man is still living at the address your contact got."

"If you could check with directory enquiries so could they."

"Yes but they don't know his first name. All they have is a surname and a nickname and there's a lot of people with the surname in the area – I've checked. So it could take some time to find him."

"Or they could be lucky and find him pretty quickly."

"Possibly. But my flight will be boarding in a few minutes, so I won't be all that far behind. And also I have had an idea I wanted to put to you."

"What?"

"Supposing I ring the subject?" suggested Perez. " I give him a plausible story – and convince him not to open the door or take calls from any strangers till I get there."

"How would you convince him to do that?"

"I can be very persuasive. It worked with our friend in Spain."

"This is different. What would you tell him?"

412

"That some madman is stalking former mercenaries? I can say that Chavant, his old sergeant, sent me to talk to him, and I'll be there soon, but meanwhile talk to no one till I get there."

Trenet considered a moment. He had been worried about the opposition's head start, but he realised that Perez' notion might just work. "OK, it's worth a try," he said.

"Fine. I mean chances are I'll get there first anyway," said Perez. "But just in case the opposition strike lucky, this way we could still keep him out of the wrong hands."

"Yes – good thinking. And emphasise your links to Chavant. It'll strengthen your bona fides," said Trenet.

"Naturally. I'll call him as soon as I finish briefing you."

"What, you've more to tell me?"

"Yes. I'm afraid our friends have been playing games here in the airport."

"How do you mean?"

"They've split up. They know now about the surveillance, so presumably this is to throw us."

"So, what – the woman isn't going on the private flight?"

"No, she's returning to Ireland."

"What the hell are they playing at?" said Trenet.

"That's what I asked myself too. But the thing is, ultimately it doesn't matter."

"How can it not matter?" snapped Trenet

"Because all they have are suspicions. They've no hard evidence, and they've no story unless they get the information they need from our friend in Devon. And when they don't get that – they hit a brick wall."

"So what's she up to, going to Ireland instead of following the story?"

"I reckon that she's running a bit scared."

"What makes you think that?"

"The fact that she's making for Ireland. It smacks of going to ground."

"For all you know she might be meeting her editor as soon as she reaches Dublin airport."

"No."

"How do you know?"

"There are advantages to being a native Spanish speaker," said Perez enigmatically.

Perez felt his habitual irritation with the younger man suddenly increasing. "What are you talking about?"

"I spoke to someone on the airline desk – spun a yarn and was able to persuade her to check the passenger list. After the American's trickery I wanted to make sure our friend really was on the flight to Dublin."

"And is she?"

"Yes and no."

"What?!"

"Relax, it's all in hand. She's on the flight, but she's one of a small number of passengers travelling on to

Shannon. She's trying to give us the slip – and she's going to ground. I can feel it in my bones."

Trenet breathed out and consciously dampened down his irritation with the infuriating way that the Spaniard chose to impart information.

"She's going to lie low while our other friend confirms matters in Devon. I'd bet my life on it," said Perez.

"You may be right," conceded Trenet. "OK then, like you said, the priority is at the UK end. So make your phone call and then get there as fast as possible, all right?"

"Consider it done."

"And let me know how the phone call goes."

"Will do. Talk to you then."

Perez hung up, and Trenet put the phone down, then stared out the window of his penthouse office and tried to analyse all that he had heard.

CHAPTER 12

Steve checked his watch as the taxi pulled away from the terminal at Exeter airport. One thirty – he was making good time. The private flight from Malaga had touched down shortly after two, and Steve had turned his watch back an hour to be on local time, then he had paid the pilot and sought a taxi to take him to Torquay, a journey of about twenty-five miles. It was certainly an expensive way to travel but it would get him to his destination in the fastest possible time.

Assuming that he encountered no traffic congestion, he should be in Torquay by about two, and en route he planned to try ringing again those Hollands on his list that he hadn't been able to contact. If by the time he

417

reached his destination he still hadn't reached everyone by phone he would visit the addresses of anyone still unaccounted for. Torquay was a holiday resort, so he reckoned that there would surely be a tourist office where he could get a detailed street map, and no doubt there would also be car-rental companies in the town.

The optimum solution, of course, would be if he could alert Dutchie Holland by phone and simultaneously get the name of his one-time commanding officer. That was probably too much to hope for, however, and Steve suspected that instead he might end up driving to those Hollands in the general Torquay region that he hadn't already ruled out, and calling to their doors or talking to neighbours in an effort to find the elusive former mercenary.

Either way he was determined to find his quarry, and having persuaded Laura to seek the safety of her country retreat in Ireland he felt that he had to succeed in his quest, whatever it took. Still, first things first, he thought – maybe he'd be lucky and get his man by phone. He settled back in the taxi, took out his list of Hollands and switched on his mobile.

Perez negotiated the maze of interconnecting roads around Heathrow airport in his rented car, occasionally consulting a map of the south of England that was propped up on the dashboard.

He had travelled to the UK on a false passport that he

418

sometimes used when working abroad, and using a matching credit card, he had quickly paid for the car rental, then set out on the drive to Devon.

He planned to make it to Torquay as soon after five as possible but he kept his car just inside the speed limit despite his eagerness to get to the south coast. He knew that in other circumstances the head start that Steve Johnson had engineered might have been decisive, but in ringing Holland's number he himself had encountered his first piece of luck of the day.

The former mercenary was away on holidays and had left a message saying that he would be back on Saturday evening. That was *this* evening, which meant that Johnson would be unable to speak to him this afternoon, even if he were to establish Holland's location. Of course it could still be a problem if Johnson found the right house – the last thing Perez wanted was the American camped outside the door, awaiting Holland's return. But Johnson had a lot of other Hollands to eliminate, and with Perez aware of the correct address he felt there was still a good chance he would win the race to find his man.

While flying from Malaga to Heathrow, Perez had even worked out a scheme for dealing with the older man's disappearance. Handled skilfully it might be possible to give the impression that Holland had never come home. Or that he had come home and, unsettled by the holiday, had taken off again.

Trenet had told Perez that Chavant's contacts knew Holland lived alone, and Perez was confident that he could dispose of Holland's body in such a way that it would never show up. He knew enough of police procedure to recognise that Trenet had been right in claiming that the Missing Person's case would get nowhere near the attention a murder would generate.

Still, that was for later, he thought, as he approached the intersection of the M25 and the M3. He quickly consulted his map, then pulled out onto the southbound motorway. He took up a position in the middle lane, then he set the cruise control for seventy miles per hour, leaned back in his seat and sped southwards towards Devon.

Laura killed the engine of the car, then sat back in the driver's seat and breathed out deeply. She had parked the vehicle at the rear of her cottage in Kilfenora and after the tension of the journey that had begun in the Byblos Hotel, she now felt the relief of finally being on home ground.

She had landed in Shannon a little over an hour previously, and carefully following the steps that Steve had outlined for spotting a tail, she had seen nothing to arouse her suspicions. Nonetheless she had been unable to relax as she had quickly gone about renting a car, and she had frequently checked her rear-view mirror during the thirty-mile journey from the airport to Kilfenora.

Nobody had appeared to follow her however and she reckoned that the ruse of flying on to Shannon from Dublin had been a good one. The flight from Spain had been uneventful and even though Laura had surreptitiously observed her fellow passengers with great care she had seen nothing to suggest that any of them were on her trail. Eventually she had decided that there was nothing she could do anyway while airborne, and so she had taken out her notes and her laptop and tried to put some kind of shape on the Conn Lynch story as it had emerged so far.

Of course, nothing could be published until she had far more hard evidence, but she wanted to put together something reasonably polished to show Mac the direction the story was taking. In actual fact she felt a little guilty concerning the editor. On the journey from Shannon she had kept her mobile switched on so that Steve could ring from England as soon as there were any developments, and a few minutes ago Mac had rung, but seeing the caller recognition, Laura had ignored the call. She had felt bad about letting him go onto her answering service, especially since he had been supportive of her pursuit of the story, but she didn't want to talk to him right now for the same reason that she hadn't reported in earlier in the morning. The death of Vince Douglas and the fact that she and Steve had been bugged gave the story enormous significance for Laura, but she was unsure how Mac might react to it all. Maybe he would think it was too dangerous to carry on, or would want to report their suspicions to the police, despite the lack of hard evidence. Certainly he wouldn't be happy with the idea of Steve – one of the new owners of the *Clarion* – engaging in a potentially dangerous solo run in England.

Laura herself was far from comfortable with taking the more passive role, despite the logic of Steve's arguments concerning his training with John Popovic – which undoubtedly equipped him better than most to deal with conflict if it arose. Nevertheless this course of action was what she and Steve had agreed upon and until they had something more definite to report back, or at the very least until she got the rough draft of the story so far into better shape, she knew instinctively that it was better to keep the editor at arm's length.

She got out of the car now, gathered her belongings and made her way to the rear door of the cottage. She reached down and took the back-door key from its hiding place under a flower-pot, then she unlocked the door and stepped in, relieved to have finally reached the safety of her private haven.

Trenet looked at his false passport. The afternoon sunshine shone in through the windows of his mansion in Tervuren but even in the strong sunlight not even the tiniest flaw was visible on the passport. It was a superb reproduction, absolutely indistinguishable from the genuine article and he slipped it into his jacket pocket, knowing he should have no problems with the travel document. He had plenty of other problems, however, the chief one being that Perez was seriously stretched. Now that Johnson and Kennedy had split up, and with Johnson having taken the private flight, Trenet couldn't help but feel that the initiative had passed to the opposition. The one encouraging piece of news was Perez reporting that Dutchie Holland had left a message on his answering machine saying he was away on holidays and wouldn't be back until that evening. Even that piece of breathing space could still be negated however if Johnson were to locate Holland's house and wait outside until the subject returned from his holiday.

Trenet had reluctantly decided that Perez could no longer be expected to handle all the strands, and having taken the monumental step of deciding to intervene personally, he had gone from his office in IWS directly to Chavant's security premises to make the necessary arrangements.

His broken-nosed former sergeant had been aghast when Trenet had closed the office door and outlined his plan to go to Ireland.

"Daniel – this is madness. The point all along was to keep you well away from everything Perez did."

"Granted," said Trenet, "but the situation has changed. If Perez gets to Dutchie first, and the newspaper story hits a brick wall, then fine. I just come back from having a weekend in Ireland."

"Yes, but –"

"Hear me out, Alain. But if a problem arises – say Perez has to deal with Johnson – then he can't be in Ireland at the same time. If it's a thing we need to get to Kennedy as well, I want to be on hand."

"You're not seriously suggesting we whack the journalist? I mean, we said all along that that could create a huge stink."

"I know. And it's a last resort. But there's no going back now."

"Jesus, Daniel, I don't think –"

"Then you haven't thought enough," snapped Trenet. "There's too much at stake now."

"Look, I know a story could be damaging . . ."

"For Christ's sake, Alain, it's way beyond that! It wouldn't be *damaging* – it would be catastrophic. If we don't get the NATO contract I'm ruined."

"But –"

"No buts. The share price will drop, my debts will be called in and I'll end my days living on my pension in some dump of an old folks' home. And that's if we're lucky and only the Congo suspicions get aired. If they find out we had Vince Douglas killed, we could all end our days in prison."

"But how could what you're planning be hushed up? Just supposing Perez had to whack this Johnson guy as well as Dutchie – and then you whack Kennedy as well?

424

There'd be uproar. It would probably be the biggest story the paper ever printed."

"Not if their deaths were accidental. Or made to appear connected to something else. And we know from the bugged conversations that the only other person who's privy to this story is the editor."

"So what, we kill him as well!?"

"We do what has to be done, Alain," said Trenet coldly. "There was a time when you had the stomach to do that, regardless of the consequences."

"That was different. We were at war."

"We were fighting for our survival. And we're fighting for our survival here, make no mistake. If the Vince Douglas thing gets out, we'll both be done as accessaries to murder."

Chavant shook his head. "Jesus, I never saw it coming to this."

"Stop being so fucking defeatist! We've been in tough situations before and we've won out against the odds."

"Not situations like this. Planning hits on high profile journalists and newspaper editors?"

"Every situation has its own problem. Whether you're outnumbered by Balubas in Katanga, or double-crossed by some crooked arms-dealer, or being hounded by some bitch of a journalist, the principle is the same. If you want to win you take risks. Big risks sometimes, but you do what has to be done regardless of the risk, otherwise you lose. And in our world, Alain, losers end up dead.

425

You know that."

"Yes, but —"

"I'm not sitting back and doing nothing. I'll take whatever risks need to be taken. It's the only way, Alain. We're in too deep now. It's gamble everything on winning, or just hope against hope that we don't lose. I've never relied on hope — and I'm not starting now. Do I make myself clear?"

"Yes . . . "

"Good. And cheer up, man. The worst mightn't come to the worst. If Perez makes Dutchie vanish before Johnson gets to him, chances are we won't have to do anything further."

"Right . . . "

"But just in case, we must be ready. So, I'll need a silenced Beretta. Have it shipped immediately to Dublin packed in with a box of machine parts. For collection under the name on my false passport. I've already booked onto the four-fifteen flight to Ireland, so make sure it gets to Dublin by air express as soon as possible, all right?"

"OK."

That had been at lunch-time and Trenet had listed for Chavant the other items he wanted delivered in the box, then driven home, disappointed at how soft his old comrade had become. Still there was nothing he could do about that, and now he was preparing to leave his house to drive to the airport. He had paid for the flight

426

with a credit card in the same name as that on his false passport and using a slush fund that had been set up precisely for irregular activity such as this. And in spite of all the problems besetting him Trenet couldn't help but feel a touch of the adrenaline surge that he always got when going into action. He would much prefer if things had gone more smoothly in attempting to divert Kennedy and Johnson's enquiries, but now that it seemed that decisive action might be called for, part of him still exulted in the thrill of battle. He recalled the buzz of excitement and satisfaction that went with turning a difficult situation around or winning against the odds and he knew that in spite of Chavant's reservations he couldn't have sat passively in Brussels any longer. It was time to be at the heart of the action and to finish this business, one way or the other.

He finished packing his travel bag, then he strode off towards the basement carpark, eager to be behind the wheel of his BMW and to get to the airport.

Steve's pulses began to race as he walked up the drive towards the bungalow. It was after five o'clock now and he had spent the afternoon calling to those addresses in the Torquay region at which he had failed to get a response by phone. So far he had had no luck but he knew that each address was potentially the home of his subject, Dutchie Holland, and he couldn't help but feel excited each time to think that the meeting he so wanted could be just at hand.

He had found a Hertz office near the train station in Torquay and had hired a car that was now parked on a side road here in Brixham, a seaside town several miles to the south of Torquay. He reached the top of the drive, the blue waters of the English Channel sparkling in the late afternoon sunlight, then he crossed to the front door of the house. There was no car parked at the front and he figured that there was a fair chance that no-one was at home, but nonetheless he felt a flutter of expectation as he reached out and rang the bell.

He heard the bell echoing in the hallway, then there was the sound of footsteps and suddenly the hall door opened. A man in his sixties with slicked-back grey hair looked inquisitively at Steve.

Right age, thought Steve, then before he could speak the older man got in first.

"Not religion, is it?"

"Sorry?"

"You're not going to ask if I've let Jesus into my life, or any of that stuff?"

Steve realised that his well-cut blazer and slacks and the collar and tie that he had worn had made the man think that he might be a Mormon or some other kind of evangelical Christian. He allowed himself a small smile then shook his head. "It's all right. I'm not here to save your soul."

"It's not the double-glazing, is it?"

"I promise you, sir, I'm not selling anything."

"No?"

"Absolutely not. And I'm sorry to intrude on your privacy at all, but I rang earlier and got no answer so I thought I'd chance calling in later."

"I hope it's not a survey. Spent an hour last year answering questions about what we eat and how often we use the bus."

"It's not a survey, sir. I'm trying to find someone."

"Yeah?"

"I'm looking for a Mr Dutchie Holland."

"Look no further, son."

Steve felt a stirring of excitement but tried to keep it from his voice. "You're Mr Holland – Dutchie Holland?"

"Yeah. Why, have you been trying to find me?"

"I wanted to talk about Kaburi."

"Kaburi?"

"Yes."

"What the hell is that?"

Steve felt a stab of disappointment. "Kaburi – in the Congo?"

"Never heard of it."

"You're not – you're not the Dutchie Holland who served in the Belgian Congo?"

"Nah, got the wrong man, son."

"I'm sorry. It's just I was told he lived in the Torquay region. And when you said you were

Dutchie Holland . . . "

"Common nickname, mate. Half the blokes called Holland end up being called Dutchie."

"Yes, I suppose so. And you don't know another man called Holland, probably about your own age, who lives in these parts?"

The man shook his head. "Only moved here since I retired, don't know that many people."

"Right."

"Between here, Paignton, Torquay and Teignmouth there's droves of people – could be a good few of Hollands."

"There are. So I'd better push on. I'm sorry for bothering you."

"No worries, mate. Sorry I can't help you."

"Thanks anyway."

The man closed the door, and Steve started back down the drive. He felt disappointed, but told himself there was no reason to lose heart; it was a matter of continuing to work his way through the list. And there was still the Holland who had sounded the right age and whose answering machine had stated that he would be returning from holidays this evening.

In addition to which he could breathe easier now than before, having spoken by phone to Laura earlier in the afternoon. It had been a huge relief to know that she was safely ensconced in the cottage in County Clare and that she was confident that she hadn't been tailed.

Thinking of her now he felt a welling up of affection, and with it came a determination to show her that her trust hadn't been misplaced, and to succeed in his mission to find Dutchie Holland. So no more feeling disappointed, he decided – instead he would concentrate on finding his man.

He reached his parked car and slid in behind the driver's seat, then studied the map for a moment and worked out the best route to the next house on his list.

Perez felt a flicker of excitement. The old thrill of the chase, he thought wryly. It still kicked in every time. It was at moments like this that he felt most alive, that he felt vindicated in having turned his back on Port Boo and his family there – and the mind-numbingly mundane lives that he knew they must still be living. Many people would have felt the loss of family ties, but Perez had long since cut any links, the better to embrace the world of adventure and high living to which he had aspired ever since childhood. And now here he was, engaged in a manhunt and pitting his wits against worthy opponents while being well paid for his efforts. He smiled at the thought, then glanced at his watch.

It was five-fifteen now and despite a stiffness in his limbs after the long drive from Heathrow he reckoned that he had made good time travelling on the motorways that led to the south-west. He didn't know precisely how much of a head start Steve Johnson had on him but with

431

luck the American wouldn't yet have established which was the appropriate Holland residence. And if he had, then he, Perez, would simply have to play things by ear.

Now though he was finally approaching Torquay and he followed the A380 towards his destination, then pulled in to the side of the road on reaching the outskirts of the town.

He had stopped a little way back in Newton Abbot where he had bought a map of the region in a service station. He spread the map out before him, then checked the piece of paper on which he had written his subject's address. He studied the map carefully, eventually locating the area in which Dutchie Holland had his house.

Right, he thought, time to do a reconnaissance on the terrain. And then, all going well, he'd see to it that Dutchie Holland disappeared without a trace.

"Jesus, Laura, I don't know about this."

Although she was sitting in the kitchen of the cottage in Kilfenora, Laura could visualise perfectly the editor's sceptical expression as he spoke to her by phone from the *Clarion* office in Dublin.

"Trust me on this one, Mac, please," she said in her most persuasive tone, though in fact she knew that she was asking for a lot.

She had spoken to Mac earlier in the afternoon when she had rung to say she was e-mailing him a draft of the story as it had unfolded so far. She had managed to ride out the storm of Mac's initial anger at being presented with the *fait accompli* of Steve pursuing the story in England, but she had felt decidedly wimpish at having to explain that she had gone to ground in County Clare while Steve sought out Dutchie Holland. She had also been conscious that all of the evidence so far was circumstantial, and that even the indisputable fact of having been bugged didn't constitute proof of foul play in the death of Vince Douglas. Nonetheless she had asked Mac not to pass too many judgements until he had read the e-mail that she was ready to send him and she had waited anxiously as Mac had received and read the document, then called her back a few moments ago.

She reckoned that her position now was somewhat stronger in that Mac was an innate newspaperman who knew a potentially explosive story when he saw one. Still, she had played fast and loose in keeping the editor out of the loop, and perhaps even more worryingly from Mac's point of view, in allowing one of the new owners of the *Clarion* to put himself in danger – for which Mac might very well pay the price if anything were to happen to Steve.

In reality Laura herself was far more concerned about Steve's fate than Mac could ever be. The lovemaking that they had enjoyed back in the Byblos had seemed to cement a relationship that had been steadily developing since they had first met, and she was now feeling guilty

about not insisting on accompanying him to Devon –
notwithstanding the logic of separating to confuse the
enemy.

"It's not that I don't trust you, kid," said Mac, "but if
anything happened to Steve, there'd be hell to pay with
the new owners. I mean talk about getting off on the
wrong foot!"

"He absolutely insisted on doing it this way, Mac."

"I hope you have that in writing, kid."

"Come on, Mac . . ."

"And there's also the police angle. We need to weigh
up how they may react later on – when they find
we didn't tell them immediately about the threat to
Dutchie Holland."

"We don't have firm evidence yet."

"But you're convinced there's a risk to this man's life."

"Yes, I am, but the police may not share my view.
I think it's vital to warn him about what I think is a
genuine risk. But the police may well say it's all conjec-
ture on my part – and a lot of it is, admittedly – and
that there's no hard evidence. They may see it as a journalist desperately wishing for a big story, and not take
the threat seriously."

"Maybe."

"At least this way, Mac, as soon as Steve finds the guy
he'll put him in the picture. Then Mr Holland can
decide for himself whether or not to take seriously what
I think is a very real threat."

"Yeah . . . "

"It also means we don't get bogged down in police procedures and time-consuming questioning just when we're on the brink of trying to find out who's behind all this."

"There is that."

"Look, give us another day or so. By then Steve should have found our man. Once he's done that, we'll know who was in command at Kaburi. It's the key to the whole Conn Lynch mystery. So, please, twenty-four hours, OK?"

There was a pause, then Mac breathed out wearily.

"All right."

"Thanks, Mac."

"Yeah. And Laura – no more rabbits out of the hat, no more solo runs. I want to be kept posted on developments. Understood?"

"Absolutely."

"OK, ring me the minute there's anything."

"I will. And thanks, Mac. I think it's going to be worth the wait."

"Let's hope so. Talk to you then."

"Yeah. Bye, Mac." Laura hung up, then looked down at her mobile, tempted to ring Steve to find out the state of play. No, she thought. He had promised to ring as soon as there was anything significant. She herself hated to be hounded when she was working on a story, so better to leave it, she decided, and let Steve ring when the time was right.

She sat back in her chair, then looked around the sunlit kitchen. Just as Steve had suggested, she had locked all the doors and windows and had resisted the temptation to go walking outside. She felt pretty confident that she had shaken off any tail and that she wasn't in danger here in Kilfenora, but nevertheless she knew that she couldn't be too careful. After all, Vince Douglas had probably felt entirely safe in his cottage in the hills above Mijas and now he was dead. Sobered by the thought she rose from the kitchen chair, then went once more to check the locks on all of the windows and doors.

"Right, Boss, what can I do for you?"

Trenet looked critically at the assistant behind the counter of the air-freight company's Dublin office. An overweight man in his late fifties with dandruff on his shoulders, he was committing a cardinal sin in Trenet's book by chewing gum while dealing with a customer. The Frenchman dampened down his irritation however and handed over a docket with a reference number on it. "I'd like to collect this package. Addressed to Serge Launay. It should have arrived by air freight."

"Fair enoughski. Let's see the aul docket number there . . ." said the man, peering at it myopically.

It was twenty past five now and so far everything had gone satisfyingly to schedule. Trenet's plane had landed on time and he had gone through passport control and customs unchallenged, then made his way to one of the rental-car desks and hired a vehicle for two days. He had used the credit card that matched his false passport and that he had previously used to pay for his flight from Brussels, then he had picked up the car and driven the short distance to the offices of the freight company. If Chavant had done his job properly, the silenced Beretta should already be here in Dublin, having been express air-freighted under the description of machine parts.

"Right," said the man behind the counter, "I think that shipment's just come in."

"You think?"

"I'm fairly certain it has."

"Good."

"But I wouldn't be *sure*. Have a seat there, Boss, and I'll check it out for you."

Trenet wondered how it was possible to be fairly certain about something and simultaneously claim not to be sure, but he resisted the temptation to challenge the man. It was always better not to draw attention to yourself when on a mission, and the fewer people who remembered his face the better. "Thank you," he said, then took a seat as directed and awaited delivery of the Beretta.

Even as he did so, Trenet hoped that the weapon wouldn't actually be required. If everything went to plan it wouldn't be. But there was an old military saying that no plan survives first contact with the enemy. And if things did become messy, Trenet knew that his options would be considerably enhanced by having at his disposal a silenced Beretta.

He waited as patiently as he could, distractedly glancing every now and then at a television mounted on the wall. There was an afternoon programme showing in which a medium was gushingly explaining the accuracy of her Tarot card readings and it was with relief that Trenet eventually saw the gum-chewing assistant returning with a medium-sized box in his arms.

"Now, hot off the presses, what?"

"Sorry?" said Trenet.

"Just after arriving, like I thought."

"Good."

"If you could just sign your life away, on the dotted line there, please . . ."

Trenet quickly signed the delivery note, then the man pushed the package and a copy of the delivery note across the counter. "Now – she's all yours."

"Thank you."

"Machine parts," said the man, reading from his own copy of the delivery document. "Doing a few repairs on the aul washing machine, what?"

Trenet realised that this was meant to be a joke and he gave a token smile. "Repairing some components on an assembly line."

"Keep the aul assembly lines rolling – fair play to ye!"

"Yes, well, thank you."

"No problem, Boss. Have a nice visit."

Trenet nodded in farewell, then carried the box outside and strode towards his rental car. He pressed the zapper to take off the alarm, then opened the boot and placed the box inside it. He had parked in a corner of the carpark on arrival and had noted that there were no security cameras scanning the customer parking area, and so he now glanced around to make sure there was no one about, then used the car key to slit the heavy tape sealing the box. He quickly removed the packaging material and pushed aside a number of stainless-steel machine parts that had been inserted to make the parcel convincing, then he found the Beretta and the silencer, carefully packed with a spare magazine, and nestling in the centre of the box. He checked that the other items he had requested were present, then he replaced the packing material.

Excellent, he thought, already feeling the better for having such a trusty weapon at his disposal. Satisfied that Chavant would have provided a gun that was both reliable and untraceable, he resealed the box and closed down the door of the boot. He got into the car and started the engine, then he pulled out of the parking lot and made towards the centre of Dublin.

Perez drove along the road approaching Dutchie Holland's house. He made sure to pitch his speed at just the right level – not so fast that the reconnaissance would be unduly fleeting, yet not so slow as to arouse suspicion, should anyone look out from the house. Perez knew that Holland had stated on his answering machine that he would be back tonight from holidays, but there was always the chance that he might have made good time and arrived back a bit earlier, or even that he might have cut short his stay. Either way Perez knew that he couldn't automatically assume the house to be empty.

He drew nearer now, taking in his surroundings carefully. The road on which the former mercenary lived was inland from the sea and just past the outskirts of Torquay. The thoroughfare itself had an almost rural character, and Perez was pleased to see that the occasional houses set back from the road were spaced far apart.

Rounding a bend, Perez saw a small but attractive bungalow ahead, then his heart skipped a beat as he read the name: *Tradewinds*. He had found Dutchie Holland's house. He drove past, careful not to stare too obviously, yet taking in as much detail as he could. Although the house was small, it appeared well maintained, and it was on a beautifully landscaped and decent-sized site.

He drove on for about three hundred yards, then came to a halt at a rural laneway. Normally on a mission like this he would park a good distance from his target and then return on foot. In fact he had seen a suitable parking area on the Torquay side of *Tradewinds* and only about two or three hundred yards from the bungalow. It was a discreet parking spot near a public park, and if Holland's house had been overlooked by neighbours he would definitely have parked there and approached *Tradewinds* on foot.

As it was he was tempted simply to drive right up to the bungalow and if no-one was at home to park the vehicle at the rear of the house. That way his presence wouldn't be advertised but he would have the necessary transport at hand to remove his subject when Holland arrived home. Unless Steve Johnson also arrived on the scene before Holland got back from his holiday. In which case the car would be a giveaway and it wouldn't be possible to move it without alerting the American. No, he thought reluctantly, it would have to be the parking lot, and an approach on foot.

Satisfied that he had made the right decision, Perez quickly reversed the car into the mouth of the laneway, then he drove back in the direction from which he had come, this time going a little faster, in the manner of one who has gone in the wrong direction and is retracing his route.

He passed *Tradewinds* again, making a point this time not to glance over, then he arrived at the small parking area and tucked his car away discreetly in the furthest corner. There were two other vehicles parked there, their owners presumably off walking in the nearby park. Perez locked the car, then began to walk back up the road towards the bungalow. It only took a few minutes to reach his destination and to his relief he encountered no other walkers or vehicles along the way.

He drew close to the entrance to the drive, and now that he was on the brink of going into action he wished he had a firearm, but having flown to the UK there had been no possibility of getting a gun through security. Still, he had done lethal damage with his bare hands in the past, and could do so again if necessary.

He turned into the drive and walked briskly towards the front door. His senses were on full alert, but there were no twitching curtains, no barking dogs, nothing to suggest that his arrival had been observed. Which didn't necessarily mean it hadn't, he knew. Suddenly he was at the front door. He paused briefly, then he reached out and pressed the bell.

Trenet walked towards the *Clarion* offices with the air of a casual stroller. He had been to Dublin several times in the past and he had a reasonable knowledge of the city centre. Using the map supplied with the rented vehicle, he had found a carpark near O'Connell Street, the impressively broad main thoroughfare that he remembered from previous visits.

It was a bright summer evening and the pavements were full of Saturday shoppers, many of whom were now preparing to travel home after a day in town. Far too early for what he had in mind, Trenet had decided, but there was no harm in getting the lie of the land so that he would know exactly where to go if he had to take action later on.

He slowed down now, seeing the newspaper's office up ahead. It was an impressive three-storey building of cut stone. He drew nearer, purporting to look at photographs on display in the front window. In actual fact he was carefully observing the main entrance, but even as he did so he knew that he was unlikely to use it. If this were the main point of entry for the general public, then there was likely to be some kind of reception area inside, beyond which access would probably be limited by means of security cards or a number-operated keypad. Far better to check out the situation to the rear of the building where with any luck there would be far more coming and going, even later in the evening, as the print-run of the next day's edition of the *Clarion* came off the presses and was dispatched for delivery.

Trenet moved away from the front entrance and made his way towards a laneway that flanked the side of the building. It was a narrow thoroughfare, litter-strewn and smelling of urine, but Trenet ignored his distaste as he memorised the geography of what was presumably the *Clarion's* printing complex. He turned right again, taking in the layout of the rear of the premises. As he had expected there were a number of delivery bays, in one of which a van was being loaded with copies of an evening newspaper, presumably a sister publication to the

Clarion. There was a good deal of activity going on here and none of the workers bustling around the van paid any attention to Trenet as he walked past. He made sure not to catch anyone's eye, and with the image of the area implanted in his mind he continued on his way, satisfied with his reconnaissance and clear now on what would be his point of entry if he needed to take action later on.

CHAPTER 13

Steve killed the engine, then got out of the car. He looked over at the bungalow at the top of whose driveway he had parked. The lawns were beautifully manicured, and carefully maintained and colourful flower-beds gave the house a cheerful ambience, especially at this hour when the building was bathed in hazy late afternoon sunshine. There was a carved wooden sign above the door proclaiming the bungalow's name: *Tradewinds*.

It was the house at which he had gotten the encouraging message stating that the occupier would be back

that evening, but Steve had been hoping that the man
might possibly be at home, now that it was coming up to
evening time. The absence of a car in the drive however
suggested that he was going to be disappointed. Still,
better call anyway, he thought, just in case the owner
had travelled by taxi.

He started towards the house, aware that time was
moving on and that the head start his private flight had
given him over the Latin man at Malaga airport might
well be up by now. In which case it was vital to get to
Dutchie Holland before the opposition. He arrived at
the front door, then reached out and rang the bell. In
spite of the absence of a vehicle he still entertained a
hope that his man might have arrived home, and he
found himself holding his breath as he awaited an
answer. He waited a moment, disappointed but not
really surprised to get no response, then he rang again.
Once more he waited, but this time without any real
expectation of an answer.

Although there was nothing to indicate it, other than
the fact that the voice on the answering machine
sounded the right age, he somehow felt that this address
was the most promising of those on his list. And if this
were the house of a former mercenary who had been at
Kaburi, then he was tantalisingly close to discovering
who the mystery commanding officer was. Maybe . . .
maybe if this were the home of an old soldier there
would be photographs of past campaigns, he thought. It

was worth having a look in the window, he reckoned – after all there was clearly nobody home.

He moved to the nearest window, shaded his eyes against the sun's reflection in the glass and looked in. There were light net curtains on the window but Steve could make out that this was a bedroom. By shifting his position he could make out paintings on several of the walls but he couldn't see any photographs. More likely to be in the parlour or living-room anyway, he thought, and so he walked past the front door and looked in the window of the other room that faced at the front of the house.

Bingo, he thought, a parlour. And one with a number of mounted photographs, some standing on a table and others hung from the walls. With difficulty he could make out the subject matter of some of the wall-mounted ones – several appeared to be scenic and the rest seemed to be of a couple. The pictures on the table however were facing away from him and he couldn't see most of them but one was visible and it looked like a posed portrait of a young serviceman. Steve felt the hairs rising on the back of his neck. Maybe the other ones were also of the owner as a young soldier, maybe there were photos here of Holland and – if he were the Dutchie Holland that Steve sought – of his mercenary colleagues in the Congo. It was even possible that there would be names on them, thought Steve, his pulses starting to speed at the notion that maybe, just maybe, it would be possible to identify the commanding officer without having to wait for what could be hours for the owner to arrive home.

Steve's training with John Popovic had included security measures relating to doors and windows and while it had primarily concentrated on how they could be secured, Steve had also learnt the weakness of various systems and how trained operatives gained unlawful entries. Part of him shied away instinctively from even considering illegal entry, yet another part of him felt that the events surrounding the death of Vince Douglas made this, literally, a matter of life and death.

Before his nerve failed him he made his way around the side of the house. As he expected, the windows of the kitchen which faced both to the side and rear of the house were locked. The back door however was a light wooden affair and didn't seem to have a mortise lock. It wasn't all that surprising – Steve reckoned that a place like Torquay wouldn't exactly be a hotbed of crime – and it meant that picking the lock might well be possible.

Steve reached out and tried the handle and to his surprise the door swung open. Surely even in Devon people didn't go away and leave their back doors open, he thought. But then again, maybe they did. Maybe crime wasn't an issue down in this part of the world. Whatever the explanation he knew that this was a heaven-sent opportunity to check the photographs in the parlour. Damping down his sense of guilt at intruding into another person's home he stepped forward into the kitchen. It was a cosy room with built-in presses and on the far wall was another photograph, this time of a man and a woman. Steve stepped forward to look at the man in the photo, then he sensed a sudden movement to his left. He spun round, but the attack came too quickly, and he felt a searing pain as he was struck in the temple, then he slumped unconscious to the floor.

Laura sat at her desk, trying hard to keep her mind on what she was doing. She had set up a well-equipped study in one of the bedrooms of the cottage and she was going through her file on the Conn Lynch story, trying to list all of the loose ends that needed addressing.

She had already requested Janet, the researcher from New York, to bring to a close her enquiries in Dulwich, Connecticut, and there were also several contacts here in the west of Ireland whom she had checking out murder and manslaughter details in the Clare/Galway region over the last forty years.

All of that could be halted now, she felt, with the Kaburi angle on the story the one on which to concentrate. She made several notes of people to e-mail, but even as she did she found her mind kept drifting back to Torquay and the tantalising prospect of contacting Dutchie Holland.

Steve had rung in about thirty minutes previously to bring her up to date on his efforts to locate the former mercenary. He had said that he would ring again, when there was progress to report, and had once more requested Laura to err on the side of caution and to remain within the locked confines of the cottage until matters were resolved in Torquay.

She had been touched by his concern and had agreed to do so, and they had chatted for a couple of minutes, then Steve had said that he really had to be on his way to visit the next house on his list.

Laura had been delighted to hear his voice again, yet afterwards she found that the conversation had unnerved her somewhat. The very things that she found so appealing about the cottage – its remoteness and privacy – now seemed just a little daunting. She told herself that the likelihood of anyone having successfully tailed her without being seen was pretty slim, yet she couldn't help but feel uneasy.

Right, she thought, there was one way to deal with that. She knew from when she had cleared out the contents of the cottage after her Aunt Mary's death that Mary had always kept a shotgun in a press in the hall. She would get the weapon and load it, and thus she would banish what she knew was a foolish sense of vulnerability. She rose from her desk, pleased at having decided on a practical course of action, and went to get the shotgun.

Perez finished tying Steve's hands behind his back with

twine that he had found in the kitchen drawer and then bound his legs. The American was starting to come to, despite the heavy blow that Perez had delivered to his head with a hastily acquired frying-pan.

Perez had to consciously dampen his anger, knowing that the presence of Johnson was going to complicate things – it had already thrown his original plan to abduct Dutchie Holland without anyone being aware that Holland had had a caller to his house.

The intrusion of the American was all the more galling considering that up to now things had been going smoothly. Perez had gained access to the bungalow without difficulty, easily picking the lock on the back door through which Johnson had also entered.

Perez could see now that he had made a mistake in not locking it again after him, but he hadn't been expecting Johnson to come on the scene so soon after his own arrival.

Still, no point wasting time agonising over it now, he thought. His priority was still Dutchie Holland. And the reality was that just like the American before him, Holland too could arrive at any moment. The last thing he needed was Johnson regaining consciousness and crying out a warning to the returning owner. He needed the American silenced and out of view so that Dutchie Holland would enter the house unsuspectingly.

Perez glanced around then quickly crossed the kitchen. He opened a large walk-in cupboard in which a Hoover and cleaning utensils were stored, then he took a tea towel from one of the shelves. He opened the tea towel fully, then rolled it into a length before crossing back to Johnson and tying it tightly around his mouth as a gag. He saw the American's eyes flickering open but the man was still dazed. Perez quickly went behind him, lifted him under his bound arms and dragged him across the room. He bundled him into the cupboard, and closed the door behind him.

Perez crossed back to the table and sat down, taking out his mobile phone. He needed to contact Trenet and see how his client wanted to proceed. He was just about to dial the number when he stopped himself. A moment or two spent weighing up his options now would be time well spent, he decided. Yes, better to have figured out exactly what he wanted to suggest before ringing Trenet. That way he was more likely to retain the initiative. He placed the mobile back down on the table, then tried to clear his head as he figured out his best course of action.

Trenet picked at a chicken dinner in a quiet corner of the café. Normally he wouldn't have dreamt of eating in a fast-food establishment but he didn't want to dine in a restaurant where he might be remembered and so he had opted for the anonymity of a large, self-service café.

He was thinking again about what he had seen during his reconnaissance at the *Clarion* premises when his mobile rang. He answered immediately, seeing from the caller recognition that it was Perez on the scrambled line.

"Hello."

"We've had developments," said the Spaniard.

"Yes?"

"There's bad news and there's good news."

"Just tell me what the hell is happening!" snapped Trenet.

"The bad news is that Johnson turned up at the address before our friend arrived back from holidays."

"Damn!"

"The good news is that I have him."

"You have him?"

"Tied and gagged and out of sight for when our subject returns."

"That's supposed to be good news?"

"He found the place. What could I do?"

"You could have avoided engaging with him. Found some way to get to your subject before him."

"No, not possible," said Perez. "He actually got into the house – I'd no choice."

"Right . . ." conceded Trenet reluctantly, then he tried to weigh up the options.

"I can still make our friend disappear," said Perez. "But if I do, then obviously Johnson has to go too."

"*Merde!*" said Trenet. "*Merde, merde, merde!*" Even as he swore he knew that what Perez had said was true. Johnson's presence at Dutchie Holland's house meant that the game was up. It was time either to go for broke by eliminating both Holland and Johnson – and trying to weather the storm that the wealthy American's death would unleash – or to capitulate. Yet to capitulate could mean not alone the exposure of his skeleton in the cupboard regarding Kaburi – and the financial ruin that would follow the loss of the NATO contract – but also the real possibility of a murder investigation concerning the death of Vince Douglas.

Trenet's mind was racing as he tried to cover all the angles. The biggest worry was the *Clarion* and the degree of investigation and exposure of which they were capable. On the other hand he knew from the bugged conversations that the Conn Lynch story was a delicate one and that the details that Kennedy had unearthed so far had been restricted to her editor. If they acted boldly enough it might still be possible to keep a lid on all of this. It would mean taking a big gamble, certainly, but Trenet had frequently won out in the past in situations where the odds had appeared to be stacked against him. And besides, what choice had he really? He could go for broke and perhaps still get away with this, or merely stand by while Johnson and Kennedy brought ruination to his door. In reality that left only one choice, he decided.

"I'd like to act as soon as possible, in case our friend returns home," said Perez.

"Right."

"So do I take care of the American?"

"Yes," answered Trenet, "but first try to make him tell you where Kennedy has gone to ground."

"Making him talk shouldn't be a problem."

"Good. Ring me as soon as you find out – or if anything else develops."

"I will. And eh . . . you are certain you want me to do this?"

"I wouldn't be saying it if I didn't want it!"

"Just so long as you're certain."

"I am. So just do it, OK?"

"Consider it done."

Trenet heard the line going dead, then he hung up. He put the phone down and returned to his meal, but found that he had lost his appetite completely. Instead all he could think of was the need to stay off the front page of the *Clarion*. He pushed his plate away, then tried to focus his mind on what his next move should be.

Steve struggled to try and sunder the cords binding him. Despite suffering still from concussion and an aching throb in his temple, he was aware enough to know that too much movement within the cupboard would attract the attention of Perez, and that it would be disastrous if his captor were to open the cupboard while he was in the process of freeing himself.

He had heard Perez moving about in the kitchen while speaking to someone on his mobile phone and although he had missed the early part of the conversation he had clearly heard the other man asking the question: *"Do I take care of the American?"*

Steve had felt his blood run cold but had forced himself not to let fear paralyse him as it had during his kidnap the previous year. Instead he had allowed himself to experience a surge of anger at the Latin man from Malaga airport, whose face he had recognised on regaining consciousness. Of course, being angry by itself was of little use, but Steve knew that the work he had done with John Popovic was precisely for predicaments such as the one in which he now found himself. Admittedly all the training with Popovic had been for imaginary scenarios, whereas this was frighteningly real. Still, it had equipped him with a number of things that he hadn't had when abducted the first time. The most important was the item he was now attempting to use to cut his bonds. It was an adaptation of a weapon used by British Special Forces in World War Two. As originally designed it was a thrust-weapon with a really thin, needle-like blade, and a hollow pommel that rested in the palm of the hand and was used to add force to the thrusting movement. Popovic had had it cleverly adapted however so that the thin blade, now serrated on one side, was retractable and could be forced up into the hollow pommel, to be released at the flicking of a small switch. The pommel itself was small enough to fit into the hollowed-out heel of Steve's shoe, and, with the entire weapon made from toughened silicon rather than the metal of the original design, it enabled the wearer to pass through airport security systems undetected.

The problem now was keeping a firm grip on the weapon with his hands tied behind his back while simultaneously trying to saw the twine with the serrated edge. He was making headway but the awkwardness of his position and the need not to make a noise made the process nerve-wrackingly slow.

Steve felt beads of perspiration roll from his forehand down into his eyes and he shook his head, trying hard to concentrate on the business in hand. Every now and then he would get a stab of fear, especially when he recalled the words he had heard the Latin man use – "*Making him talk shouldn't be a problem*". It was a terrifying notion. They probably wanted to know exactly to what stage he and Laura had developed the story. An even more disturbing notion was that perhaps the other man was planning to extract from him the location to which Laura had fled. It would be unthinkable to betray Laura by revealing the address in County Clare, yet who knew what horrors his captor might engage in to make him talk? And if it came to that, how strong would he be in protecting Laura by not answering?

He felt the perspiration flowing more freely and he consciously stopped himself from thinking such disturbing thoughts. Such problems needn't arise, he told himself, not if he got himself free in time. But how much time had he got? He could hear the other man moving about the kitchen, and it sounded like he was opening and closing drawers. Steve had no idea what his captor was doing but whatever it was he hoped it would take some time. Meanwhile he tried to put all his fears from his mind and to concentrate entirely on sawing through his bonds with the serrated edge of the weapon.

Early evening sunshine shone through the kitchen window as Laura cradled the shotgun in her arms. She sat at the table, carefully polishing the stock of the weapon. It was an old firearm but she knew that it was in good working condition and that her Aunt Mary used to fire it occasionally when foxes tried to raid her hen coop. That would have been several years ago, but it was still in good condition, especially now that Laura had cleaned it, lightly oiling its components.

Years previously, when Laura had been a teenager, she had worked for a couple of summers in her father's chain of locksmith premises, and he had imparted to her a fondness that she still retained for well-oiled and smoothly operating mechanical devices.

She finished cleaning the gun, then loaded in two cartridges from a box on the table. The cleaning and polishing had been therapeutic, and the slight sense of unease that she had felt earlier had been banished. She wasn't sure if it was the distraction of the work or whether it was the sense of comfort that a loaded weapon brought, but either way she felt better.

Of course, having a shotgun was one thing, using it – even in self-defence – quite another. Come on, she thought wryly, you're getting way ahead of yourself. No-one other than Mac and Steve knew that she was here; the chances of her having to defend herself were pretty slim.

She rose from the table, put the box of cartridges onto a kitchen shelf, then crossed to the hall and replaced the shotgun in the press, pleased to have serviced the firearm, and comforted, despite herself, by the proximity of a lethal weapon.

Perez took a sharp steak knife from the kitchen drawer. Skilfully used, he reckoned it would almost certainly ensure that the American disclosed everything that he wanted to know. He placed the knife down on the kitchen table, then spread out a couple of large plastic refuse sacks underneath a wooden chair that he had pulled out from the table. It was a psychological ploy he had used in the past, when he had indicated to interrogation victims that the plastic sack was there because he didn't want their blood all over the floor.

It was the kind of graphic suggestion that could seriously undermine the will to resist and could speed up the breaking of a foe. And speed was of significance here. It was possible that Dutchie Holland wouldn't arrive back from holidays for hours yet, but it was also possible that he might arrive at any minute, and Perez wanted to have his business with Steve Johnson finished and tidied away before the former mercenary got home.

He crossed to the cupboard and opened the door. His bound victim looked up at him, startled, and with an expression of fear in his eyes. Good, thought Perez, keep him frightened and off guard. He reached in and grabbed the American by the lapels of his blazer, then dragged him roughly out of the cupboard and across the room. He hoisted him up, then tossed him back down into the chair underneath which the plastic sacks were spread.

He quickly undid the tea towel that had served as a gag, threw it onto the table and looked Johnson in the eye. The American nervously returned his gaze. Without warning Perez smacked the other man hard in the face, wanting to emphasise who was in charge and to keep his victim on edge.

Perez smiled humourlessly. "That was just to make sure I have your attention. Are you listening carefully?"

Johnson nodded immediately. "Yes."

"Good. Because I won't say anything twice." He took the steak knife up from the table and showed it to the American. "Nice and sharp – made for carving. Understand?"

"Yes."

"OK, here's what happens. I ask you some questions. And for every answer that satisfies me, I *won't* mutilate you. Any answers I'm not happy with . . ." He shrugged and indicated the plastic sack. "Let's just say that's there so the floor won't be covered in your blood." He saw the other man swallowing hard, then he drew nearer, the steak knife in his hand. He placed the tip of the knife on Johnson's cheekbone. "We'll start with your face – so answer carefully."

"OK, OK!"

"All right then. First question – where has your nosy bitch of a journalist gone to?" He saw what looked like a flash of anger in the other man's eyes and he smiled. "Sorry, I'd forgotten. You've become lovers, haven't you? Let me give you some advice. Don't make any big romantic gesture for her. Because I'll carve your face into slices if you don't give me an answer right now."

"All right, I'll tell you."

"Where is she?"

"Please, take the knife away! I'll tell you! I swear it!

Perez could see the terror in the other man's eyes and he lowered the weapon but brought his face nearer to his captive. "Where?" he repeated.

"Here!" screamed Johnson, and Perez drew back in shock. As he did, the American sprang upwards from the chair. Perez was taken completely by surprise and didn't respond quickly enough when the other man lunged forward, his hands now unbound. Before he could react further Perez felt a searing pain in his chest and he screamed in agony as Johnson pushed hard on the pommel of a needle-like blade that Perez saw with horror

461

to be embedded in his own chest. He felt an excruciating wave of pain and the taste of blood in his mouth. Mixed in with the pain was a fury that the other man, an amateur, had outwitted him, but despite being gravely wounded Perez retained the instincts of a street-fighter and he quickly brought up the steak knife that he had been holding in his right hand.

The American's legs were still bound together so that he couldn't move easily, and Perez had instinctively aimed for the other man's soft underbelly. Although in agony from his internal injuries Perez had jabbed the steak knife upwards with all his remaining might. A disabling blow to his opponent's guts could still provide the opportunity to regain the upper hand. To his surprise however the blow never landed. Johnson parried, expertly using his left arm to block the upwards motion of Perez' arm, then Perez felt another searing pain as Johnson took his right hand off the pommel he had been pressing on and brought it down in a vicious chopping motion onto Perez' exposed right arm.

Perez cried out in pain and dropped the knife, which Johnson instantly swooped to retrieve. Perez felt his strength ebbing and he hadn't the energy to try to grapple with the American, who quickly used the retrieved steak knife to cut the bonds on his legs.

Perez reached down to his chest, where the pommel of the embedded weapon protruded obscenely from his blood-soaked shirt, then the American spun him around and pushed him hard, knocking him back into the chair that Johnson had occupied up to a moment ago.

Perez felt another wave of pain and he nearly passed out when Johnson grabbed the pummel of the needle-like weapon and pulled it from his chest. He managed to remain conscious however and he could see that his shirt was sodden with blood, flowing more freely now that the offending weapon had been removed. Even in his agony a part of him couldn't help but wonder how a bound man could have got hold of a weapon while immobilised in the cupboard.

Before he could think anything further, he felt his hair being roughly pulled back, then the steak knife was pressed up against his exposed neck. "Make one wrong move, so much as fucking *blink*, and I'll slit your throat. Got that?"

"Yes," he answered shakily, recognising that the American had the psyched-up, adrenaline-driven demeanour of one capable of carrying out the threat.

"Who sent you here?" demanded the American.

Perez hesitated, then he felt a searing pain in his chest as the other man pulled his head back, further exposing his neck.

"Who sent you?!"

Despite his agony Perez hesitated. Betraying a man as powerful and ruthless as Daniel Trenet wasn't something to be done readily, no matter how threatening the present circumstances. And while Johnson had had the

463

balls to launch this attack, and would probably have delivered on the threat to cut his throat if he tried anything, Perez sensed that it wouldn't be in the American's character to murder him simply for not answering a question correctly.

"I don't know," he replied, "I was . . . I was hired by a detective agency."

"Bullshit!" said the American.

"It's true."

"It's not. Detective agencies don't murder people."

"I haven't murdered anyone."

"So, what – it was pure coincidence Vince Douglas died just before we could talk to him?"

"I never even met Vince Douglas."

"You're a goddamn liar. You probably killed him. Just like you'd have killed me. Just like you'd have killed Laura."

"No."

"Yes. Why else did you want to know where she was in Ireland?"

Perez felt lightheaded with the pain in his chest but he tried to think of a plausible-sounding reply. "I just . . . I was just told to report it back. I think maybe they wanted to make her an offer."

"You're a lying bastard and we both know it! But here's the thing. You'll soon be a *dead* lying bastard if you don't get medical treatment. And, if you want me to ring for an ambulance, you'd better start telling the truth. Just

remember the longer you wait the more blood you'll lose
– and the less your chance of surviving."

Perez could feel the metallic taste of blood in his
mouth and he knew that what the American had said
was true – he was going to bleed to death here if he
didn't get treatment. He raised his head with difficulty
and looked the other man in the eye. "Not calling an
ambulance . . . it's murder."

"Not in my book."

"Even in war – the Geneva Convention says –"

"Fuck the Geneva Convention!" snapped Johnson.
"You're not a soldier at war. You're a criminal, a corrupt,
preying scumbag. We've enough violent criminals
already in the world. One less won't be any loss."

"Please . . ."

"Don't *please* me, you sadistic bastard! You would have
happily carved me up. God only knows what you'd have
done to Laura Kennedy. So forget appeals to my better
nature. If you want to live, start talking. Unless, of
course, you feel that protecting some fat cat is more
important than living. Unless you want to sacrifice your
life so some big-shot keeps his skeletons in the
cupboard."

Perez tried to keep his thinking clear, knowing that
Johnson was trying to manoeuvre him into telling what
he knew. He slowly reached out and took the discarded
tea towel from the table and pressed it to his chest,
ignoring the pain as he tried to stem the flow of blood.

The tea towel quickly turned crimson and he realised that what the American had said was right and that he was losing blood at a dangerous rate.

Johnson looked at him. "You're going to die if you don't get help soon. So, last chance if you want me to ring an ambulance. I need the name of the commander at Kaburi – clearly that's who sent you. I also want to know who else is working with you, which of you killed Vince Douglas and what your plans are regarding Laura Kennedy."

Perez felt himself getting lightheaded again and he knew that he had to decide quickly on a course of action before he lost consciousness. All his deeply ingrained military instincts were not to reveal information to the enemy; it had been drummed into him in the Legion that no matter what the cost you don't betray a comrade. Except that Daniel Trenet wasn't a comrade. In truth he was an arrogant millionaire, exactly the kind of fat cat that the American had described. Was he really supposed to sacrifice his life so that Trenet's secret could be protected? He felt another spasm of pain and the taste of blood in his mouth became more pronounced.

"Daniel Trenet," he said. "Daniel Trenet was the commander at Kaburi – he hired me . . ."

"Why?"

"He . . . he wanted it all hushed up. Didn't want it known he was at Kaburi."

"Why?"

466

"I don't know. I didn't need to know to do the job."

"Who else is working with you?"

"No one."

"Don't lie to me!"

"I swear it's true. In Brussels I – I hired a couple of free-lances to tail you. But from Spain on I worked alone."

"So you killed Douglas?"

Perez hesitated instinctively.

"Answer me, man! You killed Douglas?"

"Yes."

"Is someone going to try to kill Laura?"

"No, I told you I worked alone."

"Why should I believe you?"

"I wouldn't have tried to get the information from you if I knew where she'd gone! I lost her . . . lost her in Malaga airport. For God's sake, ring the ambulance, *please*, I've told you what you asked for!"

Perez was hit with another crippling spasm of pain and he felt himself getting dizzy. He saw Johnson taking a mobile phone from his jacket pocket, then he felt his vision fading and despite resisting, he slumped into unconsciousness.

Trenet was determined that his visit to Ireland would be untraceable. He had had no option but to use the false-name credit card when buying his airline ticket and hiring the rental car, but other than that he was anxious to leave no trail. As well as deviating from his normal behaviour by eating in a fast-food restaurant he had resisted the temptation to check into a good hotel. It was too early to return to the *Clarion*, and he could have done with a rest in the comfort of a well-appointed hotel room, but instead he was killing time sitting in the driver's seat of his vehicle, in a multi-storey carpark.

He planed to revisit the *Clarion* in about an hour's time, at which stage he reckoned that the dispatch area might well still be bustling, but that the vast majority of the journalists should be gone from the editorial offices. Back in Brussels he had given some thought to how he might best gain entry to the newspaper building should that be necessary, and he had decided on an approach that Chavant never tired of hailing as a bedrock of security and surveillance work. It was the hide-in-plain-sight approach, the idea of being visible in a casual way – so as to be invisible – and the key to its success was the use of a uniform. According to Chavant, people seeing a postman or a traffic warden or a security guard usually saw just that – a postman, warden or guard. They tended to take the uniform at face value and not to see the individual wearing it.

Trenet hoped this was true, but there was no point fretting about it now. He had told Chavant to pack a security guard's uniform in his size along with the other items in the air-freighted package, and while there was no way of knowing what security company normally serviced the *Clarion*, Trenet was counting on anyone at the plant who noticed him not analysing too much the uniform of a passing security guard. It wasn't an entirely satisfactory arrangement, but Trenet knew in a scenario like this every contingency couldn't be taken care of and he reasoned that he could improvise his way out of most situations.

He looked out the windscreen now to see if there were any close-circuit cameras trained on this part of the carpark but he could see none. He got out of the vehicle and casually stretched while looking around. There was still no sign of any cameras and also nobody about on this floor of the carpark. No harm to change now while the coast was clear, he thought. Then when the time was right he could make for the *Clarion*. He glanced around one more time and listened to ensure there were no cars approaching, then he opened the boot and took out the black security uniform.

Steve rinsed the blood from his folding knife and dried its surface with a tea towel, then he retracted the blade up into the hollow pommel and replaced the weapon in the heel of his right shoe. He looked at the scene before him, still finding it hard to take in the magnitude of what had happened. Perez' dead body lay slumped in the chair, and Steve was torn between an instinctive horror at having killed another human being and a conflicting sense of survivor euphoria. In what was essentially a fight to the death he had won out, and in the process

469

saved his own life and that of Laura. For he had no doubt that had Perez prevailed and got the location of the cottage in Kilfenora, he himself would now be dead and Laura would be next on the hitman's list.

He had been just about to ring for an ambulance when Perez had suddenly slumped in the chair and, despite Steve's best efforts to revive him, the other man had made a rattling sound then stopped breathing altogether. Steve had tried mouth-to-mouth resuscitation but to no avail, and after a few moments he had had to acknowledge that the other man was dead. He had known at once that what he did now could have a profound effect on the rest of his life and so instead of ringing the police straightaway he had lowered the mobile and tried to think things through.

It hadn't taken long to realise that he was in a dangerous position. Sure, he could argue that he had killed in self-defence, but there were no witnesses. So how would the police react to discovering that he was a former kidnap victim, and someone who made no bones about his abhorrence of crime and criminals? Or to his carrying a lethal concealed weapon? He could find himself up for manslaughter. Or even murder. All he would need was some hot-shot public prosecutor who was out to make a name for himself. And a jury comprising ordinary working people might well be unsympathetic to someone who was a multi-millionaire. He could end up getting twenty years if it went badly.

Or he could leave the police out of it. It was a radical thought, but he remembered how the police back home had behaved at the time of his kidnapping and how he hadn't liked their approach. The investigating detectives had always made him feel even more like a victim, and his family had also revealed how the police had been opposed to a ransom being paid, even though Steve had been threatened with physical harm. He had sworn back then that he would never again rely on the system to protect him and had instead gone to John Popovic.

So could he trust the system here in England, now that he was the one who had actually done the killing? *No*, he thought – he simply couldn't. There were too many imponderables. The law was too frequently an ass to trust it in something of this importance. Plus if he went to the authorities there would no doubt be endless questioning and the likelihood of being held in custody, just when he most needed to be free to counter any further threats from this Daniel Trenet character.

Whatever way he looked at it going to the police carried too many dangers. Of course, the alternative entailed dangers too – and he'd be in huge trouble if he tried to cover up what had happened and was then found out. But why should he be caught? Assuming Dutchie Holland didn't land in on him in the next few minutes, what was to stop him from disappearing and getting the first flight to Ireland? No one had seen him coming to Holland's house. Almost certainly the man he had just killed would have taken similar precautions, so there was nothing linking them to this spot. If he were to make the corpse disappear – as the man had intended to do to Dutchie Holland – then there wouldn't be a murder investigation. It would simply be a missing person's case. And probably not even that – he hardly thought that Daniel Trenet would report missing to the British authorities an agent that he had sent to abduct and murder a British citizen.

For this to work it would be important that no trace of the body should ever emerge, but Steve's mind had gone into overdrive and already he had an idea of how to deal with that. There was an irony too in the fact that although the other man had bled copiously, the tiles of the kitchen had been spared much of the blood by the plastic sacks that he himself had spread out on the floor. If Steve quickly got the place back to rights he could be gone from here without Dutchie Holland ever knowing what had happened.

Time now to stop thinking and to start acting, he told himself, then without wasting any further time he moved towards the body, disturbed by its bloodstained state but determined to do what was necessary.

Trenet walked past the dispatchers who noisily loaded copies of the next day's *Sunday Clarion* into the backs of delivery vans. As he had hoped there was much toing and froing at the rear of the *Clarion's* printing plant and nobody paid attention to a security guard who went past, apparently studying a clipboard that he carried in his hand.

Trenet walked away from the delivery area and turned into a corridor that seemed to lead towards the main part of the building. His mouth felt dry and his heart was racing but to a casual observer he looked unflustered as he appeared to go about his business. Trenet continued along the empty corridor, still seeming to consult his clipboard so that he could avoid eye contact were he to encounter anybody.

He reached the end of the corridor unchallenged, then turned left away from the printing plant. According to his calculations this direction should take him towards the front offices of the *Clarion*, where presumably the editor's office would be. He continued on his way without encountering anyone, then came to a stairwell. He reckoned that if he were editor he would opt for a suite of offices on the top floor and so he began to climb the stairs.

On reaching the first floor he saw a sign stating: *News and Sports Departments*. He glanced around the stairwell and saw a large newsroom. Lights were on at a couple of manned desks, presumably those belonging to a skeleton staff of journalists who would take last-minute calls with copy for the late edition. Trenet resumed climbing to discover that the second floor housed Features, Fashion, Social Diary and Education, but no lights were on here.

Once more he started up the stairwell, pleased that his calculation had been right and that at a quarter to eight on a Saturday night hardly any journalists employed on a Sunday paper would still be at their desks. He had also counted on the fact that if the *Clarion* used a keypad or swipe-card system for security it would most likely be on entry points leading from the publicly accessible reception area to the editorial section. He had been banking on ready access being available between the plant and the editorial offices and he was pleased that in this regard his luck seemed to be in.

He was less pleased however with Ricardo Perez, who still hadn't rung back regarding where Kennedy had gone to ground, even though it was now an hour and a half since the two men's earlier conversation. Trenet found the Spaniard's power games infuriating – for there was no doubt in his mind but that Perez deliberately withheld and provided information in such a way as to try to retain the upper hand in their dealings. Despite his anger at the other man's ignoring of his order to report back, Trenet had reluctantly decided that he would ring Perez, just before he had set off for the *Clarion*. To his frustration the Spaniard had his mobile switched off, and notwithstanding the fact that Perez had done some excellent work, Trenet intended to give him a piece of his mind and to underline, yet again, the chain of command and the importance of reporting in as instructed.

For now though the priority was to locate the editor's office and he climbed another flight of stairs to find himself on the floor housing Accounting, Human Resources and the Editorial department. All of the lights were switched off but with late evening sunshine coming in the windows Trenet could see the layout quite clearly. Partitioned off from the open-plan office space were several individual offices that could be entered from either the open-plan area or from doors located in the far wall. Trenet reckoned that if he followed the corridor ahead of him and then turned left he should come to the entrance doors to these rooms.

Still clutching his clipboard he started down the corridor, then turned left. The first office had a plaque on the door stating *Head of News*, and Trenet moved on to the next door. *Deputy Editor, Martin Shaughnessy* was written on this one and Trenet felt his spirits soar. He moved on the next one and looked at the sign. *Editor, Eamon McEvoy.*

Excellent, he thought, then he slipped a pair of thin cotton gloves from his pocket, donned them and reached for the door handle. He reckoned that as there wasn't a security system preventing entry from the printing plant then they would hardly feel the need to lock office doors on the third floor, but it was still a relief when the handle turned easily, and he let himself into the room, quietly closing the door after him.

It was a smaller office than he would have expected for

the editor of a large newspaper and to Trenet's ordered mind it looked decidedly untidy. Along one wall was a blown-up piece of text stating *A Newspaper Is The Lowest Thing There Is!* Presumably an attempt at ironic humour, thought Trenet, then he looked at the desk on which there was a picture of man and a woman with four children. It was the only other thing in the room that didn't seem to be related to the newspaper business, and Trenet reckoned that McEvoy was probably the type of editor who was wedded to his paper.

There were overflowing trays of paperwork on the man's desk, and articles and typewritten sheets of paper in piles all over the room, and along one wall was a series of old-fashioned filing cabinets, but Trenet went straight to the personal computer that sat squarely on the middle of the editor's desk. He switched the machine on, then sat in McEvoy's swivel-chair as the machine booted up.

He knew there was no way he could get into the other man's e-mails without knowing his password but he reckoned there was a fair chance that McEvoy would have a *Word* file on the Conn Lynch story, and he was eager to see what had been written so far. He was also hoping that he might get an address for Kennedy, particularly now that Perez hadn't rung back with the information. He couldn't be sure whether the Spaniard had failed to make Johnson talk or whether he was simply making some kind of point by not ringing back immediately with the information. Meanwhile it seemed likely that the editor's computer might have the information stored away somewhere.

The machine finished booting up, and Trenet clicked onto the icon for *my documents*. The screen filled up with icons for individual documents and for files and he quickly scanned the names. None of the individual documents seemed to have names relating to Conn Lynch or Kaburi or the Congo and he hoped that McEvoy hadn't filed whatever Kennedy had sent him under some obscure codename.

He clicked onto a file marked *pending*, but none of its subheadings sounded like what he was looking for. He clicked on further files marked *miscellaneous*, *features*, *fillers*, and *human interest*, but to no avail. Come on, he thought, it has to be here somewhere. He tried another file marked *regional*, which again revealed nothing of any promise, then he clicked on a file marked *breaking*. Trenet's English was fluent, but not so idiomatic as to be familiar with the term 'breaking story', and so he wasn't sure what to expect. As soon as he clicked on it, however, his spirits lifted, for there in a sub-heading were the words *Conn Lynch*.

Trenet opened the file, then sat immobile, his eyes glued to the screen as he read everything that Kennedy had written so far. She was a tenacious little bitch, he thought, as he read how she had ferreted out so much of the story – yet his overall feeling was one of relief. For good as her detective work had been, it was obvious from the document that she still didn't know who had accompanied Conn Lynch back from the bush. And provided that Perez took care of Dutchie Holland, the last person who might be able to tell her should soon be unavailable. *It was all still to play for.*

He closed the file, then scrolled down until he found something that had caught his eye previously. There was a file marked *payment*, and it occurred to Trenet that staff members would be paid from payroll – which meant that payments might relate to freelancers. And he knew that despite her close relationship with the *Clarion* Laura Kennedy was technically a freelance.

He clicked on the file, which had lots of subheadings, and he quickly scanned them, stopping when he reached one marked *contacts*. He clicked on this and an alphabetical list, presumably of freelance contributors, came up on the screen with amounts paid in a column opposite each name. He scrolled down, holding his breath as he hoped fervently to see Kennedy's name under the Ks. And there it was: *Laura Kennedy*. *Bingo*, he thought as he noted her Dublin address, e-mail, and telephone and mobile number. And there, just below it was another address: *Lilac Cottage, Kilfenora, County Clare.*

Trenet had never been to that part of Ireland but he knew that the world-famous Cliffs of Moher were in County Clare. And County Clare was on Ireland's west coast – which was within easy striking distance of

Shannon airport, to which Kennedy had flown. He smiled to himself, satisfied that he had located her hideaway.

CHAPTER 14

Steve felt uneasy driving with a body in the boot of the car, despite the fact that nobody else would have reason to suspect anything out of the ordinary and that there was no reason why he should encounter road-blocks or police checks. He drove along the A380 making sure to stay within the speed limit as he left Torquay behind.

It was five to eight now, and the hour and a half since the death of Perez had been nerve-wracking, but at this point Steve finally felt more in control and he reckoned he was following a workable plan.

His initial priority had been to clean up the blood from the kitchen of Dutchie Holland's house, then he had securely bound the dead man's remains in a couple of large, black plastic sacks. He had been painstaking in ensuring that everything in the bungalow looked exactly as he had found it, and unless the former mercenary kept a tally on his plastic bags Steve was pretty confident that Holland would never know that his house had been entered.

Prior to sealing the remains in the black sacks Steve had examined the contents of the dead man's pockets and had made some interesting discoveries. The man had been travelling on a Portuguese passport, probably false, and he had a matching credit card and the rental papers for a hire car, leased at Heathrow airport.

The existence of the car had set Steve thinking. There had been no vehicle in evidence when he had called to the bungalow, so presumably the other man had taken the precaution of parking the car and approaching on foot. Which meant that the car was probably parked nearby, perhaps in the same small carpark that Steve had noted several hundred yards down the road. In a flash of inspiration it had occurred to Steve to use the London-registered car when disposing of the body.

He had taken the passport, car keys and rental paper-work, his mind racing as he made his way back to the secluded carpark. Sure enough a Renault Laguna whose registration number matched that on the key ring was parked in a corner of the carpark. An even better refine-ment of the plan had then struck him – namely to leave the car back at Heathrow tomorrow morning. That way there would be no search for an unaccounted rental vehicle, no suggestion that the Portuguese customer had gone missing.

There would be hundreds of cars rented in Heathrow, he reasoned, so he should be able to bring this one back without having to encounter the person who had originally provided it to the dead man.

And so he had driven back to Holland's bungalow in the Laguna, parked out of sight at the back door and loaded the remains into the boot. He had then made the short journey back into Torquay and left the Laguna at the railway station. From there back to the small carpark was less than half a mile, and he had travelled briskly an foot, collected his own car and driven it to the Hertz office that was adjacent to Torquay train station. The small rental office was closed for the night and so he had written a note stating that he had to return to London sooner than expected, and he had placed the note and the car keys in an envelope and posted them through the letterbox of the Hertz office.

Previously he had posted another, unsigned, note through the letterbox of Holland's bungalow, warning him that someone was stalking and killing mercenaries who had served in Congo and suggesting strongly that the former soldier should lie low for a while and should particularly avoid any contact with former colleagues from his mercenary days.

It was probably an unnecessary precaution, Steve

reckoned, for he believed that Perez had been telling the truth when he had stated that he was working alone, but in case this Daniel Trenet managed to unleash another assassin at short notice it was only fair that Holland should be warned.

For now though it was essential that he concentrate fully on implementing the next phase of his plan and so he consciously shut everything else from his mind as he drove his illicit cargo north and left Torquay behind.

Laura started when the phone rang. It had been several hours since she had last spoken to Steve but she had resisted the temptation to ring him. He had said he would call as soon as there was news, and if he hadn't rung then presumably it was because he was busy in pursuit of Dutchie Holland. Now though she was excited to hear the landline in the kitchen ringing, and she quickly crossed the room to answer it.

"Hello?"

"Hello, is that Deborah?"

It was a middle-aged male voice and Laura's heart sank.

"No, I'm sorry, you have the wrong number."

"That's not 091 821482?"

"No, you've dialled the wrong number."

"Sorry about that."

"No problem."

"Bye."

"Bye."

Laura put the phone back on its cradle. The call had been slightly unsettling but she told herself not to get paranoid. People dialling wrong numbers happened all the time and it would be ridiculous to regard the call as sinister just because her nerves were somewhat on edge. The only other call she had received since her earlier conversation with Steve had been from her sister Roisin. Roisin was a schoolteacher, married with two children and living in Dublin, and although Laura was close to her sister, for once she had been in no mood to hear about school sports or how her niece's drama classes were going. The call had been to her mobile and she allowed it to go to her answering service, wanting to keep both the mobile and the landline free for a call from Steve.

She thought again now about the wrong number and couldn't help but feel ever so slightly spooked. Yet the cottage landline was ex-directory and there was no way that anyone who didn't already know it should have been able to obtain the number.

Relax, she told herself, nothing would be gained by freaking herself out. She crossed to the television and switched it on, knowing that the Eurovision Song Contest was being broadcast tonight. It was corny television and highly kitsch in its presentation, yet she had a lingering affection for it and she thought it might banish her apprehensive mood.

When she was younger, she, Roisin and her brother

485

Alan used to watch the song contest together with their parents, paper and pens in hand, and they used to mark each country's song out of ten points. The scoring was taken seriously and her father always put up a prize of five pounds – a lot of money when Laura was a kid – for whoever chose the actual winner. Thinking now about the camaraderie and happiness of such innocent times actually made her feel a little more isolated and uncomfortable than she had been before, but she told herself to toughen up. And so she sat back and watched the song contest, yet even as she listened to the music she knew that she was only doing it with half her mind as she waited, anxiously, for Steve to ring from Torquay.

Trenet froze in the editor's office. He had had the upper floor all to himself and had worked undisturbed while examining the files on McEvoy's personal computer, but now he heard a sound that startled him. It was the whoosh of an approaching lift, followed by the tiny ping as it reached the appointed floor. The sound came from the other end of the corridor outside the offices, and Trenet heard the lift door opening, then he swiftly moved so that he was hidden from view behind the door of the editor's office.

He heard footsteps approaching along the wooden corridor and he found himself holding his breath, hoping the person would pass by. He had been careful not to turn on any lights and he was satisfied that there was nothing to alert anyone to his presence inside the office. The steps drew nearer, then slowed. Trenet dropped to his hunkers, still hoping that the intruder might enter one of the offices on either side, in which case he could remain down out of sight beneath the partition until the other person either left again or was sufficiently distracted for Trenet to make an exit himself.

The footsteps stopped, and to his dismay Trenet saw the handle of McEvoy's office door being depressed. He quickly rose from his squatting position and withdrew the silenced Beretta from the inside pocket of his jacket, then stood behind the door.

A man in his fifties with a shock of untidy grey hair entered the room. Trenet caught a whiff of beer as the man came forward, then the intruder wheeled around startled as Trenet pushed the door closed and levelled the gun at him.

"Jesus Christ!" the man cried.

"You'll meet him in person if you make any sound," said Trenet, aiming the gun at the other man's forehead. "Understood?"

"Yes! Yes!"

"Make sure you do."

"OK, OK. What . . . what are you doing here?"

"I ask the questions," answered Trenet. "So – who are you?"

"Eamon McEvoy – editor of the *Clarion*. What's this about?"

"I told you I ask the questions. Don't have me to tell you again!"

"All right!"

Trenet's mind was racing ahead, evaluating his options. Unfortunately there didn't appear to be that many. Although never one to shirk being ruthless when necessary, nonetheless Trenet didn't take pleasure in killing and had never done so lightly. But the law of the jungle dictated survival of the fittest and now that McEvoy had seen Trenet and could recognise him again, allowing him to live presented a real threat.

And yet . . . Trenet saw from the photograph on the editor's desk that McEvoy was the man in the picture with the woman and four children. No point creating a widow and orphans unnecessarily, he thought, then he gestured with the gun and ordered the other man to sit while he considered his dilemma

The editor obeyed him, sitting at the desk on which the personal computer was still switched on. Trenet tried to weigh up the situation. The problem was that now that Johnson had stumbled into the scene in Torquay, the American would have to disappear along with Dutchie Holland. Which meant that Kennedy and McEvoy would be sure to kick up a rumpus, despite having failed to discover the identify of the mercenary commander at Kaburi. And now to complicate matters further, Mc Evoy had seen Trenet face to face, and no doubt could publish a good Identikit picture of him in the *Clarion*.

As Trenet mulled it over, the editor slowly swung round in his swivel-chair.

"You've been looking up Laura Kennedy's address."

"That's right," said Trenet. "She really should learn to mind her own business."

"She's just doing her job. If anything were to happen to her –"

"What? You'd write a furious editorial?" interjected Trenet. He shook his head. "You people have no idea how things are in the real world. It's dangerous to stick your nose into what doesn't concern you."

"If you were to harm a journalist, there'd be hell to pay."

"I'm shaking in my shoes."

"You should be. There'd be such a hell of a stink, you wouldn't believe it."

"Angry words I can live with. But I can't live with what will happen if she keeps stirring things up. I'm sorry, but I have to put a stop to this. Permanently."

"*Please*," said McEvoy urgently. "She's a young woman with most of her life before her. She's just a journalist doing her job. If you're angry at anyone, be angry with me – I put her on this case."

In spite of his normal cynicism Trenet found himself admiring the editor's bravery in trying to deflect the blame onto himself. Especially when the man could have tried the father-of-four approach, indicating the picture on his desk in a personal sympathy bid. "You're a brave man," said Trenet. "I admire that, even in an enemy."

"We can work something out here," said McEvoy.

Trenet glanced again at the children who looked so happily and admiringly at their father in the photograph and he found his resolve slipping. Yet he really couldn't afford the luxury of being sentimental. He looked at McEvoy for a long moment, then he sighed, steadied the Beretta with both hands and shot the editor twice in the head.

The Irishman slumped to the floor and Trenet checked for a pulse but he knew he was only doing it for procedure's sake and that the nine-millimetre bullets fired at such short range would have done their job with devastating efficiency. In spite of all the combat he had seen in the past and the many lives he had taken, Trenet felt a guilty stab of distaste about what he had done, but he ruthlessly suppressed it.

Without further hesitation he reached into the pocket of his security guard's uniform and withdrew a floppy disc which he inserted into the editor's personal computer. He opened the file and typed in a command, then the disc went to work downloading a virus that would wipe everything off the dead man's hard drive. While it was doing so Trenet pocketed all of the editor's floppy disks, which were held in a couple of opened cardboard packs on the desk, then quickly went through the desk itself and its drawers.

As he expected Trenet found nothing further that related to the Conn Lynch story, and he checked the screen of the computer. He saw that the virus was already doing its deadly work and so he withdrew the floppy that he had brought from Brussels, then stood a moment considering his situation. Finally he took a large sheet of paper, and using a felt-tip pen from the editor's desk, wrote on it in capital letters. The scrawled message read: *STILL WANT TO DO AN EXPOSÉ ON THE DRUGS TRADE?*

Hoping that it would suitably misdirect the police, Trenet propped the sheet up on the dead man's chest, then he turned away from the body, crossed to the door and quietly let himself out of the office.

Steve scanned the landscape carefully as he drove across Dartmoor. It was only a short distance from Torquay, yet miles of wild moorland stretched in all directions here. He reckoned that it was probably as good a place in which to dispose of a body as anywhere in England, yet he realised that he still must exercise extreme caution. He knew from the map of the region that he had obtained earlier in the day that there were walking and cycling routes across the moors, and that with youth hostels and country inns to cater for visitors, the landscape was host to more hikers and birdwatchers than might be readily apparent.

Still, if he waited another hour or so for darkness to

fall he should be able to dispose of the body from the car boot without undue difficulty. At first he had toyed with the idea of seeking out some of the Dartmoor's abandoned mines and tipping his cargo down a deep shaft, but on reflection had discarded the idea. For safety reasons he imagined that the authorities would probably have sealed off the honeycomb of shafts, in addition to which he wasn't sure how close to the mines he could get by car. He had also considered weighing the body down with stones and dumping it in a river or lake but again had rejected the idea. What with anglers, swimmers and canoeists there were too many risks of the corpse being subsequently discovered. In the end he had opted for the most straightforward choice and had decided on a well-disguised grave in a remote area of thick woodland.

He had studied the map carefully and had chosen a forest that looked impressively large, that was off the beaten track, yet that still had a parking area. If he saw any place en route that looked more suitable, he would explore it, but otherwise he reckoned that the remote forestry area was as good as he was likely to get. He continued on across the wild landscape, careful to observe the moorland speed limit and to do nothing that would attract attention. The sun was beginning to go down now and its dying rays turned the wind-tossed heather into a sea of shimmering gold, but Steve failed to savour its beauty. Instead he drove on towards his destination, wishing for nightfall and the chance to dispose of his illicit cargo.

Laura felt her irritation rising as she watched the television. She knew it was foolish to take seriously something as innately superficial as the Eurovision Song Contest, yet she found the artificial bonhomie of this year's joint presenters wearing, and their relentless, self-indulgent attempts at humour were getting under her skin. She reached for the remote control and switched off the sound while they did yet another tiresome introduction, but she knew in her heart that it wasn't just the TV programme that had her on edge. It was after nine o'clock now and she still hadn't heard back from Steve. Why hadn't he rung her – even if only to confirm that he still hadn't located Dutchie Holland? It was over four hours since he had last been on. Perhaps on reflection he was less certain about continuing their investigation – and maybe even their relationship. Yet nothing in either his demeanour or tone had given any hint that that might be the case. Of course there was another possibility why he mightn't have rung: he could have fallen foul of the people who had killed Vince Douglas – for she was convinced that Douglas *had* actually been killed.

It was an explanation that didn't bear thinking about and suddenly Laura knew that there was only one way she was going to be able to put her mind at ease. She took out her mobile, then paused a moment. She didn't want to come across as being all needy and fretful, and Steve had said he would ring her when there was something to report. But, damn it all, that was four hours ago and in her book that was a long time, given all the circumstances. She would keep her tone non-hysterical, casual if possible, but she had to know where she stood. Without any further hesitation she pressed the speed-dial, then held her breath as she heard Steve's phone ringing.

She swallowed hard, willing him to answer and say that everything was all right and he had just been going to ring her, but instead the phone continued to ring, then switched to his answering service. She heard the beep, then tried to keep her voice up-beat while delivering her message. "Hi, Steve, it's Laura. Just . . . just wondering how things are panning out at your end. I hope all is going well and . . . eh, give us a call as soon as you get a chance. Talk to you then. Bye."

She hung up, thinking that maybe Steve had the phone switched off because he was talking, even now, to Dutchie Holland. She hoped that he would ring her as soon as possible, but there was no way of knowing what was happening in Devon, and she knew that fretting wouldn't help. Instead she picked up the remote control, turned back on the sound and watched the Eurovision Song Contest while she waited for the phone to ring.

Steve sat immobile in the furthest corner of the forest

carpark. From the passenger seat of the rental car he watched the disappearing tail-lights of the last other vehicle that had been parked there and he breathed a sigh of relief as it disappeared from view. With his mobile phone up to his face as though making a call, and with his vehicle parked almost fifty yards away from the Mercedes Jeep that had departed, he was confident that the hikers who had loaded their rucksacks into the Mercedes wouldn't have seen his face. It shouldn't actually matter, Steve knew, as he intended that the body should never be found, but nonetheless he felt that the less linkage there was between himself and the burial site the better.

He lowered the mobile, but didn't put it away, knowing that he really should make contact with Laura. He had had the phone switched off since the killing back at the bungalow, feeling that he needed all his concentration to be focussed on dealing with the aftermath of having killed the other man. Eventually however he had switched it on again and heard the message from Laura, but despite a strong desire to talk to her his instincts had held him back. He was sure that he had done the right thing in not throwing himself at the mercy of the police. Trying to convince them that he had killed in self-defence and against a man whom he suspected – but couldn't prove – to have already committed a murder in Spain was riddled with potential pitfalls. *Why was he carrying a lethal Special Forces thrust-*

495

dagger? Why hadn't he notified the Spanish police?

To say nothing of being held in custody, and the precious time that would be taken up on questioning, while this Daniel Trenet character was at large and possibly planning his next strike. And yet . . . he knew that Laura was at heart a law-abiding citizen who wouldn't have the same reservations about police forces that he had and who certainly wouldn't feel the same depth of animosity for criminals as Steve still felt.

No, best to present her with a *fait accompli* and explain face to face the reason for acting as he had. If he finished disposing of the body in the next hour or so, he could make for London, stop en route in a lay-by for a couple of hours' sleep, then drive on to Heathrow where he could leave the dead man's car in the returned-rentals parking area and get an early morning flight to Shannon. It would be much better to explain everything to Laura in person so that she could see why he had kept the police out of the matter. He reckoned too that she would also be excited that he had finally obtained the name of the mystery commander at Kaburi which might well provide the key to breaking the Conn Lynch story.

For now though he knew that Laura would be worried, and he couldn't let her fret all night, fearing that something might have happened to him. A text message was the best compromise, he decided, then he would switch the phone off until tomorrow morning. He activated the keypad for texting and thought a moment, then he wrote: *Safe and well. Can't talk – Holland story tricky and unfolding but looks good. Explain all tomorrow morning. Love Steve xxx.*

He pressed the 'send' button, then switched off the mobile. He waited a few more minutes till the dusk fully turned into night, then he got out of the car and went to the boot. He paused a moment, steeled himself, and opened it. He reached inside and removed a spade that he had taken from Dutchie Holland's well-equipped garden shed, then he reached into the boot once more and hoisted out the bound black sacks in which he had wrapped the corpse.

He closed the boot and locked the car, then he grasped the spade in his right hand, knelt down, and reached backwards to load the bound body onto his back. He reckoned that the dead man weighed eleven or twelve stone, but Steve was in good shape and despite the weight he rose and moved off without undue difficulty.

A quarter moon shone in a clear sky and by moving slowly he was just about able to follow a trail that he had scouted earlier. He continued along the trail through the woods, then he reached a clearing beyond which the forest floor sloped downwards to a gurgling stream.

This was the spot that he had ear-marked on his earlier reconnaissance and he lowered the body a couple of yards outside the tree-line, then paused to catch his breath. He had chosen the place carefully, not wanting to dig a grave among trees that might be felled and uprooted during future harvesting. Instead he had picked a spot that was just outside the trees but where the undergrowth was heavy.

His plan was to clear away the surface detritus and then carefully cut away a series of sods. After that he would dig a good deep grave, bury the body and then replace the sods on top so that the earth would quickly reknit with little trace of ever having been disturbed. Before leaving he would cover the surface with dead leaves and twigs so that nothing would be visible unless someone was actively looking for signs of disturbance. And in such a remote spot, and with nothing to alert anyone to the dead man having visited Devon, that seemed unlikely in the extreme.

He took up the shovel, cleared a space about six feet by two, then began to cut the sods.

Trenet drove across the bridge in Athlone, the broad sweep of the river Shannon flowing beneath him. He checked his watch. Ten thirty-five, he was making good time on his journey to Kilfenora in County Clare. He knew that once he reached the other side of the bridge he would be in the province of Connaught, the most western region of Ireland. He recalled having once read that this was the province to which the native Irish had been banished by the English general, Oliver Cromwell, with the infamous comment that his defeated enemies could go "To Hell or to Connaught".

Well, tonight he was going to Connaught – and Laura Kennedy was the one who would experience Hell for all the trouble she had caused. And he knew that there might well be more trouble to come, for at this stage four and a half hours had elapsed without contact from Perez. The Spaniard was supposed to report back on the Dutchie Holland situation, but had never called. At first Trenet had assumed that Perez was playing his usual mind games and establishing that while in the field he was the one in control, but now after such a long lapse Trenet was getting worried. With McEvoy dead and Johnson also having to be dealt with, the situation was now more complicated, but if Perez had reported back they could have filled each other in and made their plans accordingly.

Maybe the impression could be given that Kennedy and Johnson had met a similar fate to McEvoy – tying in with Trenet's inspiration back at the *Clarion's* offices when he had sought to link the killing to an imaginary exposé on the drugs trade. But with no word from Perez and no answer to his phone, Trenet didn't know what to think. At best the Spaniard might simply be busy dealing with both Dutchie Holland and Steve Johnson. – and indulging himself by using that busyness as a reason for not reporting in.

At worst things could have gone horribly wrong. Holland could have taken Perez by surprise, Johnson might somehow have escaped – the possibilities for disaster were endless. Trenet knew from experience however that it was better not to dwell on things that were out of his control, and so he tried to concentrate instead on the job in hand. Besides, once he got to Kennedy he would quickly find out what the position was with Johnson – assuming that he hadn't heard from Perez by then.

Meanwhile he wanted to get to County Clare as quickly as possible, though without risking police attention by speeding. He exited the bridge on the Connaught side of the river, glanced at the map on the dashboard to confirm his route, then headed westwards for Kilfenora.

Laura woke with a start. She looked at the illuminated figures on her bedside radio clock. One fifteen. She had gone to bed at eleven thirty but had taken almost an hour to get to sleep. She realised at once that what had woken her now was loud, insistent barking. She sat up in the bed, knowing the sound was coming from the boundary between her land and the neighbouring farm. The actual farmhouse was a couple of hundred yards away, but she knew that her neighbours' sheepdog was much nearer, and she realised that something must have disturbed the animal. Steve's warning about lying low with all the doors and windows locked had seemed slightly extreme the previous day but now Laura was suddenly glad that she had done as suggested.

She felt a tightening in her stomach that she knew was fear, but she had to investigate what was causing the disturbance. She swung out of bed, all tiredness gone now, and was about to switch on the bedside lamp when she changed her mind. Instead she took the shotgun from where she had placed it under the bed and slipped off the safety catch. She crossed the room in the faint glow from the radio clock and carefully parted a small opening in the curtains. She looked out, the landscape outside bathed in faint moonlight, but although the barking continued she could see nothing amiss at the front or side of the house.

She knew that if she turned on a light she would lose her night-sight and would be visible looking out, while unlikely to see anything in the darkness outside. Instead she made her way to the door of her bedroom, then felt her way along the familiar corridor and into the back bedroom. She moved cautiously across the darkened room then repeated the procedure with the curtains there. Again she saw nothing. The barking hadn't abated but Laura told herself that the dog's barking needn't necessarily indicate anything sinister. The dog might simply have picked up the scent of a prowling fox.

She considered a moment, then decided to switch on some lights. If there *was* someone prowling around outside, it would indicate that the barking had woken her and that she was no longer the unconscious occupant of a darkened house. She moved away from the window, then switched on the light in the spare bedroom. She moved out into the hall and went to the light switch, then opened the door of the kitchen and turned on the lights there and entered. She thought about whether she should go to the front door, shotgun in hand, and have a quick look outside, but rejected the notion almost immediately. While it might scare off a prowler to show that she was armed, it wouldn't frighten the kind of person who was prepared to kill an innocent man like Vince Douglas.

In reality Laura thought it highly unlikely that anyone would have discovered that she was here, but nonetheless she would exercise caution. She would leave the lights on in the spare bedroom and the hall for the rest of the night and she would stay up for a little while now that she was wide awake.

She would make herself some hot milk, she decided, then after a while go back to bed and try to get some sleep. She clicked the safety catch back on the shotgun, placed it on the kitchen table and went to the fridge to prepare her drink.

Trenet stood immobile in the shadows cast by a long line of mature beech trees. The trees were on Kennedy's side of what must have been a boundary with a neighbouring farm and he cursed the farm dog that had barked so excitedly when he had stealthily approached the cottage. Even before the dog had picked up on his scent however Trenet had realised that access to the cottage would not be easy. On arrival in Kilfenora he had driven through the late-night streets and had headed out of town in the wrong direction before finally locating Lilac Cottage, which was situated outside the village on the other side.

He had found a laneway about half a mile past the cottage and had parked the rented car there before walking briskly back to Kennedy's house. Dressed in the black trousers and jacket of the security guard's uniform he had known that he shouldn't be visible once he kept to the shadows along the edge of the drive leading up to Lilac Cottage. Halfway up the drive however he had rounded a slight curve and realised that there was a significant problem. Trenet had been counting on a house in a remote part of rural Ireland not to have an alarm system, but now he could see from a winking red light on a control box over the front door that Kennedy had an alarm system that was activated.

It was just then that he had heard the first barks from the approaching dog and he had quickly taken out his silenced Beretta. He hadn't needed to use it however as the dog had drawn near, then been blocked, presumably by some kind of boundary fence on the far side of the beech trees. Trenet had immediately retreated deeper into the shadows and stood immobile. After a few moments lights had come on in the cottage but nobody had emerged.

Now he reckoned that the priority was to extricate himself without being seen. If he waited a little longer and still no one emerged from the cottage he could quietly slip away. That way Kennedy would have no idea what had excited the neighbouring dog. With luck she should eventually relax again allowing him to retain the element of surprise when he struck. It would have to be in the morning, he decided, but already a plan was forming in his head. If he made his way back to the car unseen he could get a few hours of sleep, then early in the morning he would go into action. It was frustrating to have to wait, especially since he still had heard nothing from Perez and was really anxious to find out from Kennedy what had happened in Torquay. Still, a few more hours at this stage shouldn't make much difference, he told himself.

He waited a little longer, ignoring the dog's barking as he watched the cottage. Still nobody emerged and no other movement was evident. *Time to go.* Trenet slipped the Beretta back into his pocket, then moving slowly so as not to make any noise, he kept to the shadows and started back down the drive.

CHAPTER 15

Early morning sunshine gave promise of a fair day as Steve drove wearily into the rentals carpark at Heathrow airport. He had had a couple of hours of restless sleep in a lay-by somewhere in Wiltshire, then risen with the dawn and finished the second leg of the long journey from Dartmoor to London.

It was six thirty in the morning now and he planned to book a place on the first flight to Shannon. First though there was the matter of returning the dead man's rental car. He had filled the tank up at a nearby garage in order to return it as it had been supplied – thus avoiding any further financial transactions. Nevertheless he was feeling nervous now as he found a parking place, then switched off the engine of the Laguna.

Originally he had reasoned that a large number of cars would be rented each day at Heathrow and that he should be able to return the vehicle without attracting any attention. Now though, he was feeling less assured. Admittedly Heathrow was one of the world's busiest airports, but there were numerous rental companies and even on a busy day only so many cars would be hired out by each individual company.

He had gone carefully through the vehicle's paperwork and discovered that the car had been rented for twenty-four hours at two in the afternoon of the previous day. It also stated in the paperwork that the rentals office was open around the clock. Which meant that someone who had started an early shift yesterday could still have been there at two in the afternoon. Supposing the same person was on the early shift this morning and remembered the Portuguese customer who had rented the Laguna? How could it be explained that it was now being returned by an American?

I'm afraid my colleague got food poisoning and is confined to bed – so I'm returning the car for him . . . ?

It would probably pass muster, he thought, but would have the disadvantage of drawing attention to Steve and of linking him to the missing man. Still, there wasn't much choice but to return the keys, unlike with the small rentals office in Torquay that closed each evening, enabling him to post his own car keys in through the letterbox. But with the rentals office here never closing any ploy to avoid returning the keys in person would simply attract attention. Better just get it over with and hope for the best.

He got out of the car, picked up his hand luggage and locked the vehicle. He walked across the carpark towards the rentals office, breathing deeply to steady his nerves, then he entered the premises and walked to the reception desk.

"Morning," he said aiming for the kind of brisk tone that wouldn't encourage chit-chat. "Returning a vehicle."

The man behind the desk was a well-groomed Asian and he smiled cheerily. "Morning, sir."

"The tank is full and it's parked outside," said Steve handing over the keys. *This was the moment when the other man might remember the Portuguese customer if he'd been on duty the previous morning.*

"Ah, yes, '03 Laguna," he said, looking at Steve.

Steve felt his pulses racing but he just nodded curtly.

The Asian looked Steve in the eye and raised an eyebrow. "Everything all right?"

"Yes."

"It's a lovely car – just that some people find it strange starting the engine with a card rather than a key. Won't start up if it's in gear, for instance."

507

"I had no problems," said Steve, relieved that the other man didn't appear to be the person who had hired out the Laguna.

"Glad to hear it. Some nice design in the Laguna, mind you. I like the stereo controls on the steering column."

Steve realised that the other man was probably bored – there were no other customers in evidence at this hour – but he was determined not to get into a protracted conversation with him.

"I need to catch a flight, so . . ."

"Of course. I just need to have a very quick look at the car, sir," said the Asian, rising and taking up a clipboard.

"I'll show you where it's parked."

"Fine," said the man, coming around the counter. "Won't take minute, then we'll have you on your way."

"Good," said Steve, then he headed briskly for the door.

Laura luxuriated in the torrent of hot water that sprayed down from the power shower. She let the water play upon her face, waking her yet also soothing her with its warmth.

After returning to bed following the barking dog incident she had tossed and turned before eventually falling asleep. She had slept then until a quarter to eight, and on waking had risen at once. Immediately she had checked her mobile, in case Steve might have texted or rung earlier in the morning.

Nothing had registered, however, and as she soaped herself now she tried to imagine, yet again, what could have transpired in Torquay. She had read Steve's text message of the previous evening so many times that she knew it by heart. *Safe and well. Can't talk – Holland story tricky and unfolding but looks good. Explain all tomorrow morning. Love Steve xxx.*

It sounded positive, and she liked the *Love* and *xxx* parts, but it was also puzzling. Why couldn't he have given a quick ring? Or if he was caught up in something that was unfolding, then rung her later at night? Surely he could have guessed that she would have been more interested in hearing of developments than in sleeping? Still, he had said he would explain in the morning, so presumably she would hear from him shortly. And if by any chance she didn't, she would give him an hour – then if she had heard nothing by nine o'clock she would ring him.

She rinsed all of the suds off herself, turned off the shower and reached for a bath towel hanging on the wall of her en suite. She dried herself, then wrapped a smaller towel around her hair and stepped into her bedroom. The deep pile of the carpet felt soft beneath her feet as she towelled her hair, then crossed to the built-in wardrobe. She took out a pair of blue jeans and a white T-shirt, underwear, and socks. She rubbed in some body cream, then put on her deodorant and dressed, leaving her shoes for now where they lay under the bed. She noticed the time on her bedside radio clock. Eight o'clock. She switched on the radio for the news, turning up the volume so that she could hear it as she blow-dried her hair.

Neither of the first two stories registered strongly with her but the third item stopped her dead. She listened disbelievingly as the newsreader gave details of a killing in a newspaper office in Dublin. The victim had been identified as Eamon McEvoy, a native of Ballyhaunis in County Mayo and the editor of *The Sunday Clarion*.

"Sweet Jesus!" cried Laura.

The newsreader went on to say that the police were treating the death as suspicious, then went on to the next item of news.

Laura switched off the hair-drier and sat unmoving on the side of the bed. *Mac dead?* It seemed unthinkable, beyond belief. Yet even as Laura sought to grapple with the enormity of it she knew in her heart that it *wasn't* unthinkable. She knew instinctively what lay behind it, and she sat paralysed on the edge of the bed, over-whelmed by grief and filled with a terrible sense of dread.

Trenet felt the car shuddering and he swung hard on the steering to get it off the road before the engine died. He managed to get it onto the broad tarmac area in front of a set of pillars that flanked the drive leading to the modern-looking cottage. The engine then cut out completely and Trenet applied the handbrake. He got out of the car and lifted the bonnet, then bent down and reached forward, running his hand over the cables linking the spark-plugs to the distributor cap.

Although the rental vehicle was only a year old, the cables had a light coating of carbon, and when Trenet looked at his hands he could see that already they looked blackened and grimy. *Perfect*, he thought. He would leave the bonnet open so that it would be visible from the front door of the cottage and with his filthy hands he should look like a convincing breakdown victim when he presented himself at Kennedy's doorstep.

He knew that the likelihood of anyone glancing out the window of the cottage just as he had approached was pretty slim, but nevertheless he had deliberately stalled the car with the clutch, going through the charade of the car spluttering to a halt just in case he might be observed.

At five past eight on a Sunday morning there was very little traffic on the quiet country road but Trenet still felt uncomfortable at having to leave the vehicle like this. A car with the bonnet up was somewhat eye-catching for any other vehicle that might pass, but Trenet felt that he had little option. He knew from the previous night that a heavy closed gate precluded driving up to the cottage, and besides, if Kennedy was on guard, then everything that contributed to making his breakdown story look convincing would be important.

He would just have to gain access as quickly as possible, then he could neutralise Kennedy, open the gate and retrieve his car. Said like that it sounded simple, but he knew that in practice his plan mightn't be so easy to implement. Except that he *had* to implement it, especially in the absence of any word from Perez, about whom he was now seriously worried.

He had risen around seven after sleeping fitfully in the back of the car, and had changed out of the security guard's uniform and into a fresh shirt and his own smartly cut jacket and slacks. He had left his mobile phone on all night but there had been no contact from the Spaniard and now Trenet was convinced that things had gone amiss in Torquay. He had rung Chavant in Brussels but his security consultant had heard nothing from Perez either.

Chavant had once more begun to express doubts about the wisdom of being in Ireland and Trenet's patience had snapped. He had felt stiff and grubby after the night in the car and he wasn't in the mood for Chavant's negativity. He had told his former sergeant to stop acting like an old woman and to pull himself together. Then he quickly told Chavant about McEvoy and his own plan to contain things by dealing with Kennedy and Johnson, and he ordered the other man to call him immediately if Perez should make contact.

He had tried to gauge how soon he could call at Kennedy's doorstep without the earliness of the hour making her unnecessarily suspicious. Eight o'clock seemed like a reasonable time, he had decided. While he was waiting he had splashed his face with water, shaved with his electric razor then had a snack and brushed his teeth. It was a bright morning with hazy sunshine and he had felt uncomfortably visible while having to hang about. Fortunately though, the rutted old laneway in which he had parked was well off the beaten track and he had encountered nobody, then at eight o'clock had started the car and driven to Kennedy's gate.

Now he glanced at his watch. Five past eight. Time to go into action. He reached inside his jacket and slipped the safety catch off the Beretta, then opened the pedestrian gate and started up the drive.

Laura sat motionless on the side of the bed, still in shock as she tried to come to terms with Mac being dead. It was like a nightmare and she wished that she would wake up now and discover that it was all a bad dream. The image of Mac's face came into her mind unbidden with his sardonic grin and his air of cynicism – a cynicism that she knew was often a front for his innate sense of decency. She felt a sudden surge of loss, and her eyes began to well up. She knew that Mac had a wife, Helen, and four children, and she tried to imagine how this could be explained to them. *We were following a story and it all went horribly wrong.* It would be no consolation – what would it matter what they had been following up to a wife who had lost her husband and to children who had lost their father?

But it mattered to Laura, who sensed, with an instinct that she found frighteningly strong, that this was linked to the Conn Lynch story. Added to her sorrow and shock she now felt a burning anger. The death of Vince Douglas may been tragic but killing Mac somehow made the whole thing *personal*.

She lowered her head into her hands, struggling to deal with the confusing cocktail of emotions that gripped her when a sound from the front of the house startled her. It was the ringing of the doorbell, and automatically she rose from the bed and made for the hall without stopping to put on her shoes. She dabbed her eyes dry, then glanced at her watch. Six minutes past eight. Early for anyone to call, she thought, even in the country, where people tended to rise early.

She reached the hall door, pulled back the cover of the spyhole and looked out. A well-dressed older man with neatly coiffured silver hair was standing a yard or two back from the door wiping his blackened hands on a tissue as he waited for an answer to the bell. Laura looked past him and at the bottom of the drive she could see a vehicle with its bonnet raised.

Coping with a car breakdown was about the last thing in the world she needed right now, she thought. She let the spyhole cover fall back into place, then a couple of seconds later the bell rang again. Despite the confusing flux of all her other emotions she felt a stab of guilt at refusing to help someone in difficulty. The man with the engine-stained hands was about the same age as her own father. If *he* had broken down somewhere, she would expect someone to assist an older person who had run into difficulty. Still she hesitated, pulled in opposing directions by her conflicting emotions, then she allowed herself to be guided by instinct and reached out and opened the door.

"Good morning," said the man. "I'm very sorry to bother you but my car has broken down."

"That's OK."

"Could I use your phone please? I need to ring the fly-drive company – they'll send a mechanic."

"Sure. You can use the one here in the hall."

"Thank you very much."

Laura stepped back into the hall and the tourist followed. Although his English was excellent he spoke with an accent. French, Laura thought, or maybe Belgian. Suddenly she felt a chill run up her spine. The man had followed her into the hall, and in addition to the sound of the door closing Laura heard the click of the lock being engaged from the inside. The horrifying suspicion that was tightening her stomach with fear was instantly confirmed and she swung round to face him.

The man looked at her, the helpless tourist expression gone now. Instead he had a hard, angry look about him. "You just couldn't leave it, could you?" he said.

515

"What?"

"You had to be another nosy, muck-raking journalist, hadn't you?"

Laura swallowed hard, furious at herself for having been so naïve, notwithstanding that she had been badly shaken up and confused by the news of Mac's death. Her fury was short-lived however. Instead she felt a knee-trembling wave of fear sweep over her as the man reached into his pocket, took out a silenced pistol and aimed it at her.

Steve felt his stomach beginning to flutter as he shuffled towards the head of the queue at the security check in Heathrow. On entering the terminal he had booked an eight forty-five flight to Shannon. He had figured back then that he had plenty of time, and had showered, changed into fresh clothes and gone for breakfast.

He had miscalculated how long it would take to clear security however, and now it looked like he would probably reach his boarding gate with little time to spare. It would be important though that he should at least snatch a couple of minutes to ring Laura before boarding began. He had thought of calling her while he was having breakfast but had decided it was too early and instead had opted to ring her at about eight o'clock. At eight however he had been in the security queue where the presence of the other passengers ruled out the kind of conversation he needed to have.

516

It was a call he wasn't looking forward to, and he knew that Laura might well have reservations about what he had done with the assassin. Still, he really had to ring her and try to put her mind at ease – until he could get to Kilfenora and explain in person exactly what had happened.

The queue moved forward again now and he sought to focus his attention on the task in hand. Try to look relaxed, he told himself, relaxed yet slightly weary of security checks. The image to project was that of the seasoned traveller who realises that security must be undergone but who finds it a bore.

He took his passport out and held it ready for inspection and he forced himself to breathe evenly. The folding silicon dagger in his heel wouldn't activate the metal detector, he knew, yet there was always the off-chance of a spot check. And a thorough search by security or customs officers would certainly reveal the hollow heel in his right shoe in which the weapon was concealed. It was something that had never worried him much in the past but now that he had actually used the weapon he was much more conscious of its existence.

Thinking of the weapon reminded him again of the bloody confrontation with the Portuguese man in Torquay, but despite the fact that he had never killed before he found himself surprisingly free of remorse. It had been a kill-or-be-killed situation, and when subsequently there had been a choice between seeking

517

immediate medical help for the assassin and getting information that was essential for the safety of Laura Kennedy, it had been an easy choice. Which wasn't to say that the encounter hadn't been traumatic – he had thrown up shortly after the other man had bloodily expired – but looking back now he knew that if he could somehow relive the encounter he would make the same decisions again with a clear conscience.

Suddenly he found himself at the head of the queue. He felt his heart pounding but he reckoned that outwardly the image he was projecting was probably still that of the bored but co-operative traveller. He showed his passport, then slipped his loose change into a basket and placed his hold-all onto the conveyor belt of the X-ray machine. The security man handed back the passport, and Steve stepped through the metal detector without setting it off.

He had glimpsed random passengers being body-searched while he had been back down the queue and now he drew level with the security officer who did the frisking. Steve wondered whether, if he were selected, the man would examine his shoes. The security officer caught his eye, and Steve nodded casually, then continued confidently onwards as though not expecting to be stopped. He reached the belt on which his hold-all was now emerging. The fearful side of him half expected a tap on the shoulder and he swallowed hard. His bag arrived and he hoisted it from the moving belt, then turned to see the security man searching a young man in a buckskin jacket.

Steve breathed a sigh of relief, then he slipped his passport into his pocket, scooped up his loose change from the basket and moved away from the security checks. He glanced at his watch. Eleven minutes past eight. If he was quick he should still have time to get to the departure gates and ring Laura before his flight was called. Lengthening his stride, he set off briskly through the terminal.

Trenet forced one of her own scarves into the woman's mouth as a gag, then tightened it and began to knot it behind her head. He had used two other scarves to tie her arms to a chair in the bedroom and he knew it would be enough to immobilise her while he went back down the drive to retrieve his rented car.

He was close enough to her to smell her perfume and despite all the problems that she had caused him he couldn't help but be aware that she was a really attractive woman, and that in other circumstances the situation could be a turn-on. It conjured up images of sexual scenarios that he had played out very enjoyably – both on the giving and receiving ends – during his many visits to the Clinique Special.

Right now though he had more urgent matters to address and he consciously banished all thoughts of eroticism from his mind. He wanted to get back to the car quickly so that he could lower the raised bonnet before any passing motorist saw it. Then he could drive in through the opened entrance gates – he had seen their electronic control in the hallway – and park at the rear of the cottage. That way his presence wouldn't be evident, and he would have a helpless captive at his disposal. He would soon find out then what had happened between Johnson and Perez in Torquay.

For now though the priority was to retrieve the car and so he finished knotting the gag, checked that it was good and tight, then walked away from the firmly bound journalist and made for the front door.

Laura tried to fight down her sense of panic. Her head was spinning, what with the shock of Mac's death and the anger she felt with herself for letting a stranger into the house, but her overriding emotion now was fear. Trying to resist it, she forced herself to recall how a couple of years previously she had been held captive by a terrorist when following a major story in Harrogate. She knew from experience that the difference between being a victim and being a survivor was the ability to dampen down panic and to think clearly. She knew too that the chances were high that the man who had tied her up was also Mac's killer, and she realised that she would have to come up with a strategy to buy herself some time.

The one encouraging thing was that he had bound her to the chair. Despite the tightness of the scarves and the sense of vulnerability she felt, it suggested that he had no immediate intention to kill her. If she could keep it that way and somehow get free from her bonds then all was not lost. Her captor had the upper hand right now and was physically stronger and had a silenced pistol, but Laura knew that all of that could be overcome if she got to the loaded shotgun that lay hidden underneath her bed.

Before she had time to consider it any further the man came back into the room. He crossed behind Laura and she felt an easing on her gag as he loosened the knot in the scarf. The man removed the gag, then came around to face Laura. He stared her in the eye, then raised the pistol and aimed it at her.

"I'm going to ask you some questions," he said, "and you'd better tell me the truth."

The man had deep blue eyes that might have been attractive in other circumstances, but Laura felt a coldness in his stare and she knew instinctively that her captor would be ruthless.

"Understand?"

Laura nodded. "Yes."

"All right. What happened in Torquay?"

"I'm not sure, but –"

"You're not sure?" interjected the man impatiently.

"I'm waiting to hear this morning what took place. I swear, that's the truth."

The man sighed and shook his head. "I don't want to

hurt you," he said. "But you'll talk in the end, believe me. So do this the easy way and save yourself a lot of pain."

Laura felt a stab of terror at the idea of being tortured to reveal information that she simply didn't have and it took all of her courage to keep her composure. "I swear to you on my oath, I don't know the full story yet from Torquay."

"Tell me what you do know."

Laura paused, trying to gather her thoughts. She needed to maximise what she appeared to be revealing if she was to buy time with her captor.

"Tell me!"

"OK, OK. I got a text message from Steve. He was too busy to phone."

"You're telling me he didn't phone you since he went to Torquay?" said the man, clearly unconvinced.

"No, he rang me a number of times yesterday."

"To say what?"

"That he was calling to various houses, looking – "

"Looking for Dutchie Holland."

Laura nodded. "Yes. The last time we spoke was at about five."

"And he hadn't found him then?"

"No," answered Laura, "but he was about to drive to an address he had hopes for."

"And?"

"I heard nothing for a good while, so I rang him. His

phone was switched off, so I left a message."

"And you're telling me he didn't ring you back?"

"No, but he texted me. You can check it on my mobile. The message is still there."

"What was the message?"

"*Safe and well. Can't talk – Holland story tricky and unfolding but looks good. Explain all tomorrow morning. Love, Steve.*" It was a message that she could still remember verbatim, and now she watched as her captor gazed into the middle distance looking thoughtful. After a moment he turned back to her.

"Where is your mobile phone?" he asked.

"On the bedside locker."

The man went out of Laura's line of vision, then she saw him returning as he pressed the keys of the mobile to access the text message. She hoped that she had gained some points with him for having repeated the message so accurately, but he looked at her searchingly when he had finished reading. "It's morning now, so what has he reported?"

"He hasn't rung yet."

The man looked at her sceptically, and Laura couldn't be sure whether he was doing it to frighten her or whether he really did think that Steve had already rung.

"I swear he hasn't rung," she said. "It's early, it's only a quarter past eight."

"That's not that early."

"He'll probably call soon."

"I hope so for your sake. Because if you're lying to me . . ."

The man let the threat hang in the air, and Laura had to suppress a shiver.

"What was the plan once he found Holland?"

"He wanted to interview him," answered Laura, choosing her words carefully.

"You mean he wanted to get the name."

Laura hesitated briefly, but there was no point antagonising her captor when he clearly already knew their goal, and so she nodded. "Yes."

"Where did you and Johnson plan to meet up then?"

Again Laura hesitated and this time the man became angry.

"Where?"

"Here."

"In this house?"

"Yes."

"You'd better not be lying to me or you'll suffer pain like you've never known."

"I'm not lying," answered Laura.

Before the man could continue his interrogation, the mobile suddenly began to ring. Laura prayed that it would be Steve, as her captor held the mobile away from the morning sunlight to read the caller recognition.

"It's him," he said, his voice urgent. "Take the call and do exactly as I say. I have excellent English – if you give him any warning I promise you'll die slowly and painfully."

"OK, OK!"

Laura felt the bonds on her left hand being quickly undone, then the man thrust the mobile into her freed hand and pushed the silenced pistol painfully into the back of her head. "Answer it – and remember, I'm listening to every word!"

"All right!" She answered the phone and placed it to her left ear, conscious of her captor's breath on the back of her neck and the discomfort of the gun pressing against her head.

"Steve," she said.

"Hi, Laura."

In spite of her circumstances she felt a sense of relief at hearing his voice. "Are you OK?"

"Yeah . . . I'm fine."

"I was worried something might have happened you."

"I'm sorry, I'd a lot on. I'll explain it all when I see you."

Laura felt the gun pushed against her head, then her captor whispered in her other ear. "Ask where he is?"

"Where are you, Steve?"

"Heathrow. I'm just about to board a flight to Shannon."

"Right."

"I got the name, Laura."

"Yeah?"

"A Frenchman named Daniel Trenet is the man we're after."

Laura felt a tiny intake of breath from her captor as he listened in on the conversation and she sensed at once that the man keeping her prisoner was Trenet.

"Good work," she said, prompted by a short jab from the silenced gun-barrel to keep the conversation convincing. "Did you . . . did you warn Holland?"

"Not in person. He hadn't shown up when I was leaving, but I've left a letter warning him."

"Ask where he got the name then," whispered Trenet.

"So who gave you the name?" queried Laura.

"The guy from Malaga airport. He killed Vince Douglas. Tried to kill me too . . ."

"God . . ."

"What happened?!" whispered Trenet.

"What . . . what happened, Steve?"

"I . . . I defended myself. I'll explain when I see you."

"Ask has he gone to the police!" ordered Trenet.

"Have you been onto the police, Steve?" asked Laura.

"No, the police aren't involved. I'll explain it all when we're face to face. Listen, I have to go. My flight is boarding."

"Ask is the other man dead!" whispered Trenet urgently.

"The other man, Steve. Is he . . . is he dead?"

Although Steve hadn't hung up there was no answer. Laura got another jab from the gun and she repeated more pressingly. "Is he, Steve?"

Again there was a pause, then the American spoke. "Yes. Look, I'll explain it all when I see you – I have to go. Love you, Laura."

"Love you too. *Bí cúramach*, Steve, *Bí an-chúramach!*"

It was Irish for "Be careful, be very careful," but before she could even be sure that Steve had heard her the line went dead, then Trenet spun her around and smacked her hard in the face. The shock of the blow stunned her but before she could register the pain properly she felt her stomach tighten in fear as she saw Trenet raising the pistol and taking aim at her.

Trenet felt a surge of anger, then the woman cried out "No! Don't shoot!"

He brought the gun right up to her face and she cried "No! Please!"

"What the hell was that about?!" he demanded .

"What?"

"That last thing you said on the phone. What was it?"

"Just an Irish phrase."

"I told you not to try any warnings! I told you I'd use this," said Trenet brandishing the silenced weapon in her face.

"I know you did – it wasn't a warning! It wasn't a warning, really!"

"What did it mean?"

"It's . . . it's a declaration of love. It's what people say

527

in Irish to show their love."

"The second time you said it, you added something."

"The first part – it meant I love you – the second part, I love you very much."

Trenet looked searchingly at the woman but she looked like she was telling the truth. In reality he knew that his anger was only partly fuelled by her using another language. His real fury was at Perez for having been outsmarted somehow by an amateur – with all the complications that that could cause.

He needed to think this out carefully. Without another word he shoved the gun into the inside pocket of his jacket, then grabbed the woman's free hand and tightly bound it once more to the chair.

"I'm sorry about your friend," said Kennedy.

"Just shut your stupid mouth! Don't say another word unless I speak to you! Understood?"

"Yes," she answered fearfully.

Trenet turned away, not wanting to gag her for now in case further questions occurred to him. He had to control his anger and reason things out clearly, he knew, if he was to retrieve this situation.

He sat on the side of the bed and tried to weigh up what he had heard. Certainly Johnson having killed Perez was a bad blow, and an unexpected one at that. Critically though the American hadn't gone to the police – for whatever reason – so Trenet's identity was still undisclosed. And from the overheard conversation it was obvious that Dutchie Holland hadn't been party to the confrontation between Perez and Johnson. Which meant that with Holland still in the dark – apart from some kind of warning letter from the American – it must have been Perez who talked and revealed Trenet's name. *Bastard.*

Still, the more Trenet thought about it, the more it struck him that the situation was still retrievable. After all Johnson would be heading straight for Kilfenora as soon as he landed in Shannon. Chances were that he wouldn't know about McEvoy's death, and if it seemed that Laura was safe and well then he would arrive at the cottage off guard.

Trenet stroked his chin, trying to think through the possible complications that might arise. The biggest one obviously was Perez. But even if his body was discovered in the UK, he would have been travelling under a false name. And Trenet had never paid him directly; the Spaniard's fees and expenses had all been routed circuitously via Chavant's company. The more he thought about it the more satisfied Trenet felt that there would be no link made between himself and the dead Spaniard. And with McEvoy dead and the *Clarion* files destroyed by the virus, it simply required the silencing of the only two other people working on the story – Kennedy and Johnson – for the investigation to die a death.

Trenet continued to seek out any flaws in his

reasoning, knowing that there could always be imponderables in situations like this, yet the more he thought about it, the more he felt that he could still pull this off. Especially if he gave the impression that Kennedy and Johnson had been killed, like McEvoy, over some drugs exposé that had been ruthlessly suppressed by drugs barons acting to protect themselves.

He looked at his watch. Eight twenty-five. If Johnson was leaving Heathrow now it would be at least a couple of hours before he got to the cottage. Might as well put that time to good use, he thought. He remembered his days in the army and his golden rule during active service, both in Algeria and the Congo. Whenever in the field, avail of the opportunity to eat, drink and wash. He felt grubby after his night in the rented car. Time to shower and have something to eat while awaiting the American. But first he would gag Kennedy and secure her legs firmly to the chair. He rose from the bed, crossed to the chest of drawers and took out some more women's scarves, then made for the journalist.

Steve heard the roar of the aeroplane's engines rising to a pitch, then it accelerated down the runway and rose smoothly into the morning sky. He sat back in his window seat, idly looking down on the English countryside, but soon his mind went back to the telephone conversation with Laura.

She had sounded quite stressed, though on reflection

that was hardly surprising. The conversation hadn't gone as he wanted. He would have preferred to break the news about the killing when he was with her, but he had felt that there was no alternative to telling the truth when she had asked him straight out.

She would be worried now, yet what could he do until he got to Ireland? He would reveal all that had happened when they were face to face in a couple of hours but he knew now that he would have to be persuasive. Laura was aware of his loathing of criminals and it would be important to convince her that he hadn't acted murderously in the throes of an anti-crime hang-up. Instead he would have to explain how it had been an us-or-them situation with the assassin.

But was that the whole truth? He certainly hadn't *wanted* the other man to die, but in all honesty neither could he work up any sorrow at his death. It had been a bloody end to a human life, and although Steve had found himself throwing up afterwards he knew that that didn't necessarily prove anything except an instinctive revulsion. Had he taken pleasure in striking a blow against those who represented crime – and by implication taking a symbolic retribution for his own kidnapping and its attendant terror? It was something he had thought about a good deal since last night, but on balance he didn't believe that was what he had done. And as for demanding an answer regarding planned action against himself and Laura before calling an ambulance, on that he had no qualms. The man involved was someone who had already killed Vince Douglas – so if there was a choice between protecting Laura and allowing an assassin to die it was an easy choice. Apart from which, even if he had rung an ambulance straight away the man would probably have died anyway.

So no, he thought, no more soul-searching on that score. He would tell Laura the unvarnished truth and after that he could only hope that she would understand and that it wouldn't be something to come between them.

Thinking of her again, his mind went back to the telephone conversation, and he wondered once more what her final words had meant. *Bí cúramach. Bi an-chúramach.* She had said it with sufficient conviction for the phrase to lodge in his mind, but Steve had no idea what it meant.

He remembered their light-hearted conversation about the Boy Scouts and Girl Guides and Laura saying that "*bí ullamh*" was the Irish form of the Scout's motto "*Be Prepared*". So if "*bí ullamh*" meant "*be prepared*", then presumably "*bí cúramach*" meant "*be . . . something*". But what? Maybe it was some kind of greeting. Except that it sounded more intense than a mere greeting. *Bí cúra-mach . . .* he'd never heard the words spoken at any stage during his stay in Ireland. Then again the only Irish words he *had* heard were *Céad Míle Fáilte*, which meant a hundred thousand welcomes, and *Sláinte*, a drinking toast equivalent to 'Cheers'.

Just then the light indicating that seatbelts could be unfastened came on, and as Steve looked up his eye was caught by the airline's shamrock logo. Suddenly a thought struck him. He had booked with Aer Lingus, the Irish national carrier. If the mystery phrase comprised Irish words then presumably someone among the cabin crew would know what they meant. Pleased with his sudden inspiration he looked round, saw a steward coming down the aisle and raised his hand to attract the man's attention.

The scarves that bound Laura to the chair were uncomfortably tight but she had disciplined herself to ignore her aching limbs. At first it had taken all her resolve to overcome her sense of panic, but having convinced herself that she was in no immediate danger, she had tried to think things out.

The man had showered and changed his clothes, then gone to the kitchen, from where the smell of coffee now wafted back into the bedroom. His washing and food preparation had given Laura over half an hour to get her thoughts in order, and despite her predicament she felt a bit calmer now. She had replayed in her head everything that Steve had said during the telephone conversation, but no matter how she looked at it she found it hard to see why he hadn't contacted the police. She and Steve were the innocent parties in the whole affair, and if

533

Steve had had to kill someone in self-defence then surely the law would side with a highly respectable, law-biding citizen, as against a criminal who had probably committed murder the previous day.

Still, while there must have been a reason for Steve acting as he did, eventually Laura had decided that there was no point speculating endlessly about it – he had done what he had done. A more pressing consideration was what was going to happen now. She was still deeply upset by the death of Mac but she had tried to compart-mentalise her grief, telling herself that Mac would want her to focus her energy on surviving. Surviving, publishing the story and bringing these people to justice.

To succeed in bringing Trenet to justice however meant that she first had to outwit him. And to do that she had to try to get inside his head, try to see things from his perspective. The key consideration she reck-oned was that Trenet knew that only three people had been privy to the Conn Lynch story – herself, Steve, and Mac. And with Mac dead, the obvious course of action for Trenet was to silence Laura and Steve.

From Trenet's viewpoint it was obvious that Steve was the threat, being both lethal enough to have killed the assassin – if that was what had happened – and, even more dangerously to Trenet, still at large. But if the Frenchman just sat tight with Laura as the bait in his trap, then Steve would come straight to the cottage. And in case Steve might ring while en route, Trenet had to keep her alive if he wanted to be certain not to arouse the American's suspicions. So, she was probably safe for another hour and a half at least. Not that she intended to wait that long before making a move. If she could get Trenet to untie her – to use the bathroom, to take a tablet – whatever, then she stood a chance of getting to the shotgun under the bed. It was a risky strategy but still by far her best hope.

Of course, there was no way of asking to be untied while gagged as firmly as she was now, but she was planning to make noises of distress when Trenet came back from having his breakfast. With any luck, she reckoned that he would at least take off the gag to hear what she had to say.

She weighed up the various approaches that she might try with Trenet and had decided that the need for the bathroom was probably the best line to take, when suddenly the kitchen door opened. To Laura's surprise Trenet started towards the open door of the bedroom, carrying a small tray on which he had placed a glass of orange juice and a bowl of cereal. What was the thinking here? she wondered. To soften her up, to make her more biddable? There hardly seemed a need when he had her at his mercy, but nonetheless Laura breathed out in relief when her captor put down the tray, loosened the scarf that was tied behind her head and removed the gag.

What with the shock of Mac's death and the trauma of being taken captive Laura had little appetite, yet she knew that tactically it would be foolish to antagonise her captor by rejecting his gesture. Better to play meek and mild and thus get him off his guard.

"Thank you," she said gratefully. "Thank you very much . . ."

CHAPTER 16

Steve stared out the window as the aircraft cruised over the sunlit English countryside. Below him the southwest of England extended to the horizon like a patchwork quilt in shades of green and brown, but Steve barely took it in. The Aer Lingus steward had turned out to be from Northern Ireland and hadn't spoken Irish, but he had helpfully gone to get a colleague who did speak the language. Steve had felt a bit self-conscious about causing a minor fuss, especially when there was a chance that the phrase might simply be a salutation – *God go with you*, or some such thing. As it turned out however the Irish words meant: "*Be careful, be very careful.*"

Steve had mulled it over, wondering why Laura hadn't simply said it in English. It was hard to understand, unless maybe it was a catch-phrase – an equivalent of *take it easy* perhaps – and had simply sprung to Laura's lips. It had certainly sounded to Steve as though she had said it with conviction, and on reflection perhaps that was a good thing. Maybe it meant that she was instinctively aligning herself with him in the matter of his not having gone to the police. It would be really encouraging if that were the case, as Steve knew that her co-operation would be an essential part of the cover-up that he had already begun regarding the disappearance of the dead assassin.

Or was he reading far too much into her comment? Was she just saying be careful, as they had been careful ever since discovering the hidden listening devices back in the hotel in Spain? It was difficult to say, but in spite of trying to reach some kind of conclusion his thoughts went round in circles. Eventually he gave up on it, wearily closed his eyes and sat back in his seat, as the aircraft cruised through the morning sky on its westward route to Shannon.

Trenet watched his captive finishing her breakfast. For safety's sake he had kept both her legs bound to the chair. He had also been careful to provide her with no item of cutlery more lethal than the spoon with which she had eaten the cereal.

Initially he had pondered on whether to let her have anything at all to eat or drink, but having showered and eaten himself he had felt a good deal better and his initial outburst of anger when Kennedy had spoken in Irish had died down. All he had to do, he had realised, was to keep his nerve and wait until the American arrived at the cottage. Then he could find out exactly what had happened in Torquay, and how much Johnson and Kennedy knew, before dispatching them.

He still felt a residual irritation with the Irishwoman for pursuing a story better left in the past, yet a part of him couldn't but acknowledge that she was simply doing her job – and doing it with a fair degree of tenacity and courage.

He was sufficiently self-aware to realise too that providing her with breakfast was partly to appease his own guilt at having struck her in the face. There was no logic to it, of course, especially as he was going to have to kill her as well as the American, yet Trenet was of a generation of men for whom striking a woman was simply taboo. Despite having killed, and when necessary tortured enemies during the war in Algeria, Trenet had nonetheless been imbued with a code that said it was cowardly and dishonourable to strike a woman.

He knew the whole thing was wildly contradictory, yet he was glad that he had made the gesture with the breakfast. Perhaps it was to do with the warrior code of being ferocious in battle but magnanimous to a defeated enemy, he thought, then his musings were cut short as the woman put down the empty cereal bowl and turned to him.

"Thank you," she said.

"OK."

"Can I ask you to undo my legs, please? I need to use the bathroom."

Trenet hesitated briefly, then nodded. "All right. But don't even think of trying anything." He took out the Beretta and pointed it at her. "Understood?"

"Yes."

Trenet kept the weapon trained on his captive, then went behind the chair and undid each of the scarves, untying the knots with his left hand.

"Thank you," said Kennedy, briefly massaging each of her ankles, then rising from the chair. Trenet took a step backwards to be out of lunging distance, then indicated the open bedroom door that led to the hall off which the main bathroom was situated. "Walk slowly."

"Can I not use my own bathroom?"

"What?"

"My en suite, just through that door?"

The Irishwoman indicated a closed door at the far side of the bedroom, and Trenet felt himself becoming suspicious. A bathroom was a bathroom, what was it about the en suite that dictated using that? Perhaps there was a really sharp scissors there that could be used as a weapon, or maybe it had a large window out of which she hoped to climb. He looked at her searchingly. "Why the en-suite?"

The journalist hesitated, then gave a sort of embarrassed grimace. "That's where I keep my Tampax . . ."

Trenet felt slightly embarrassed himself. "All right," he said. "Go to the door but don't go in."

Kennedy looked at him quizzically, then nodded and did as instructed.

Trenet followed her at a distance, then indicated with the Beretta for her to step back a few paces. The woman complied, and Trenet opened the door to the ensuite. It was small room, with tastefully tiled walls and floors and Trenet saw at once that although there was a window that opened outwards it would be too small for Kennedy to climb through.

He stayed on the threshold of the en suite from where he could observe the interior of the bathroom yet still glance around to keep his captive in sight. He looked for other possible sources of difficulty without seeing anything that seemed to represent a threat. Just inside the door was a wall cabinet and Trenet opened it. Here indeed were Tampax tampons along with tweezers, tubes of hair gel, creams, moisturisers and all the other paraphernalia that he associated with women. *And a small but sharp-looking scissors.* Trenet reached out and took the scissors, slipping it into his pocket.

Satisfied that the house was too far from its neighbour for Kennedy to try screaming from the en suite window,

Trenet turned back to the Irishwoman to give her permission to use the bathroom. To his surprise she wasn't where he had left her in the brief moment that he had spent examining the bathroom cabinet. He quickly swung up the Beretta and aimed it at the journalist who was now several yards back across the room towards the bed. "Don't move!" he cried.

"What?"

"I told you to stay there."

"I've stayed in the room, I haven't done anything!"

"Why did you move? Why did you move?!"

"My ankles hurt from being tied, I was just trying to get the circulation going."

Trenet stared at her but she held his gaze.

"Honestly! The scarves were tight!"

Trenet looked at her, trying to gauge her demeanour. She seemed to be telling the truth but he couldn't be certain. Still, no harm had been done and he had confiscated the one item in the bathroom that could conceivably be viewed as a weapon.

"OK," he said, indicating the en suite, "go on then."

"Thank you."

"And don't lock the door – leave it slightly open."

"Right."

He watched her crossing the bedroom, then he stepped aside. The Irishwoman entered the bathroom and closed the door over, but left it slightly ajar. Trenet slipped the Beretta back into his jacket, then crossed the bedroom, sat in the vacated chair and awaited the return of his captive.

Steve stayed just within the speed limit as he cruised northward on the N18. His flight had landed in Shannon almost fifteen minutes ahead of schedule and he had quickly exited customs, hired a car and set off for Kilfenora. Back in Spain Laura had given him detailed directions on how to find the cottage, and with the light Sunday-morning traffic he reckoned that he should be there in about half an hour.

He was eager to see her again, yet part of him was also fearful about how she might react when she heard all the facts regarding the killing in Torquay. The reasons for not going to the police, which had seemed so instinctively right yesterday, now seemed a little less convincing. And yet, if he could travel back in time, Steve knew that he would do the same again. Until the mysterious Daniel Trenet was brought to book they wouldn't be safe, and Steve knew that he couldn't have risked being out of the loop because of police questioning in Torquay, while Trenet was at large and free to unleash another killer.

He would just have to explain his reasoning as persuasively as he could and hope that Laura would trust his instincts. He thought again about her '*bí cúramach*' comment, and once more he tried to convince himself that she was at least instinctively supportive, having made the comment after Steve had admitted to killing the man and not going to the police.

As for the actual admonition itself, he had been as careful as he possibly could be. He had covered his tracks meticulously, had been at pains to make sure that no one had tailed him – either in England or since his arrival in Ireland – and as far as he could make out he had left no loose ends that might link him to the killing. He would continue to be careful, then when he got to Kilfenora he would tell Laura what had happened and they could plan how to handle it from there.

Satisfied that there was nothing further that he could do, he breathed out, eased back in the car seat, and tried to enjoy the sunlit countryside of County Clare as he sped to this destination.

Tied once more to the chair, Laura glanced anxiously at the bedroom clock, knowing that she would need to make her move soon. It was almost two hours now since she had spun Trenet the yarn about needing the Tampax and she reckoned that enough time had probably elapsed for it to be credible for her to ask to use the bathroom again.

It had been frustrating the last time when she had nearly reached the bed, underneath which the shotgun lay, only to be caught just short when Trenet had turned around from the medicine cabinet and discovered that she had moved. Fortunately he had seemed to accept her explanation about moving to get the circulation going again in her ankles, but he had been on guard thereafter and there had been no opportunity to get to the bed on the way back from the en suite. Perhaps the next time he would be less alert, having already established that there was nothing of danger in the en suite. Laura certainly hoped so; the last thing she wanted was for Trenet to have both herself and Steve captive as the same time. The Frenchman had told her that he wasn't going to interrogate her further until Steve arrived at the cottage, and Laura had been relieved, and had reasoned that Trenet didn't want to take the time and trouble of having to go over the same ground twice. Her relief had been short-lived however for Trenet had off-handedly said that she would talk more effectively when Steve was also present. The comment had sent a shiver up her spine, something she suspected that her captor might actually have intended, notwithstanding his casual delivery of the line. Whatever the motivation, it was too frightening a line of thought to pursue, and so Laura had forced herself not to reflect upon it.

Trenet had retired to the kitchen and since then the time had dragged, with Laura's thoughts regarding Steve going round and round in circles. No matter how she looked at it she found it hard to see the justification for not going to the police in Torquay. The problem however was that he hadn't, which meant that nobody would be aware that Steve was now making his way to the remote cottage outside Kilfenora. And once Trenet had them both together the logic from his perspective was terrifyingly clear. He would find out how much they had discovered and then he would kill them. She *had* to get to the shotgun before Steve arrived – it was simply essential.

Without waiting any longer lest fear paralyse her, she called out, grateful that her captor had dispensed with the gag. "Monsieur Trenet!"

He came in from the kitchen and raised an eyebrow quizzically. "What is it?"

"I need to use the bathroom again."

He hesitated, and Laura felt a stab of panic. Her plan of getting to the shotgun depended absolutely on being freed to go to the en suite. Her captor looked at her searchingly for a moment, then he nodded assent, took out his silenced pistol, and with his other hand began to loosen her bonds.

Trenet cradled the Beretta in his hands as he sat back in the bedroom chair, waiting for Laura Kennedy to finish in the bathroom. He had spent the time in the kitchen carefully working out what his next moves should be, so that by now he had formulated his plan in detail.

The critical moment, he knew, would be when the door was opened to Johnson. The first few seconds would be vital in terms of getting the American into the cottage. Just in case any traffic should chance to pass on the road at that moment it would be important that there was no struggle and that the American entered the house voluntarily and still off guard. Once that was done Trenet would have the drop on him, and he could close the hall door, ensuring privacy for all else that followed.

Trenet reckoned that Johnson should arrive anytime in the next twenty minutes to an hour, assuming that the flight had been reasonably punctual. The key to getting him in safely was going to be Kennedy, and Trenet decided that he would only bind her by one hand and one foot when she came back from the en suite. That way he could quickly release her and she could get to the door briskly so that Johnson wouldn't have time to grow suspicious. He would have to put the fear of God into the Irishwoman just beforehand, so that she wouldn't be tempted to cry out or give Johnson any kind of warning. Once having done that though, he felt that his plan was sound and that there was no reason why the whole sorry affair couldn't be wrapped up permanently within the next hour.

He thought what a relief it would be to leave all of this behind, and even though he knew it would be dangerously premature to let his guard down, he couldn't resist savouring briefly the prospect of having turned a potential disaster into a victory. He pictured returning to Brussels with the Kennedy/Johnson situation over and done with and he imagined his run of good luck continuing by way of winning the NATO contract that he wanted so badly. It was a highly gratifying daydream, but Trenet was jolted out of it by the distant sound of a vehicle going over a cattle-grid.

He sprang from the chair and went to the window, taking care not to disturb the curtains. His heart pounded as he watched a Toyota Avensis wending its way up the drive. He stared for a moment but there was no mistaking the driver. It was Steve Johnson. The man must have made exceptionally good time, Trenet thought, even as he himself wheeled away from the window and darted across the bedroom to the bathroom door. Just as the reached the door he heard the toilet being flushed and he burst into the room as Kennedy was starting to rinse her hands at the sink.

"Jesus!" she exclaimed, a startled expression on her face.

"Out of here, now!" cried Trenet.

"What?"

Trenet pointed the gun at her while turning off the tap with his other hand "Don't argue!"

He manhandled her out of the en suite, then swung her around to face him. "Johnson's arriving. You're going to open the hall door, you're going to smile, and you're going to let him in. If you give him the slightest hint of a warning I'll blow away both your kneecaps! Understand?!"

"Yes . . ."

548

"Be certain you do. You've no idea how painful it is. And after that I'll kill Johnson even more slowly – got that?!"

"Yes! Yes, I understand. Listen, can I – can I put on my shoes, please – they're just under the bed?" She started towards the bed, but Trenet grabbed her shoulder and spun her around.

"Forget your shoes, out to the hall, now!"

"Please, I just – I just want to look my best so that-"

"Forget the shoes! Out to the hall, now!" snapped Trenet, pointing the Beretta at her.

"All right! All right!"

He grabbed the Irishwoman's arm with his left hand, kept the gun trained on her with his right and ushered her out to the hall. From outside he heard the sound of a car door slamming, then he warned the journalist one more time, stepped back out of sight behind the door and waited for the American to ring the bell.

Steve felt his heart beginning to pound. There was a car on the gravel in front of the house, so he knew that Laura must be here, and he was nervous yet excited at the prospect of seeing her again. He crossed to the door, then reached out and rang the bell. He had half expected Laura to come out to greet him on hearing the car coming up the drive, but perhaps she had had the radio on, he thought, as he waited for an answer. He listened for the sound of approaching footsteps from behind the hall door and he felt his pulses racing now that the moment of facing each other had at last arrived.

He heard the sound of the lock being undone, then the door swung open and Laura stood before him. Dressed in just a white T-shirt and blue jeans she still managed to look stunning, and he felt his spirits lifting.

"Hi," he said, smiling warmly.

"Hi, Steve."

Laura had smiled back, but Steve felt that she still looked pretty worried. Maybe his fears had been justified, and what he had done regarding the assassin *was* going to be a problem.

"Come in," she said, standing to one side.

"Thanks," answered Steve, a little disappointed that she hadn't taken him in her arms. He longed to reach out and hold her but he decided to take his cue from her and so he simply stepped over the threshold and into the hall. Laura turned back to face him but before either of them could speak the door was pushed closed and Steve was startled to see a well-groomed, fit-looking older man there. The man had a silenced pistol pointed at Steve's chest and now he adopted a sardonic grin.

"Mr Johnson, we meet at last." Before Steve could respond the man's smile faded and he looked Steve in the eye. " I'm afraid you've been causing me a lot of trouble."

Despite his shock Steve had no difficulty working out who the other man was likely to be. "So you're Trenet."

"Yes. And you're the man who killed my representative."

"Your *representative*? I think your *paid killer* might be more accurate."

"Brave words, Mr Johnson. But I'm the one with the gun, so you'd be wise not to make me angry."

"I'm sorry, Steve," said Laura again. "There was nothing I could do."

"It's OK," he said softly. "It's OK."

"Up against the wall, arms and legs wide apart," ordered Trenet. "Do it!"

Reluctantly Steve did as instructed, then the Frenchman ordered Laura to kneel with her hands on her head while he carefully frisked Steve. Trenet kept the gun pressed threateningly against Steve's head, and there was nothing the American could do as the older man satisfied himself that he was unarmed.

"Right, into the bedroom, both of you," ordered Trenet.

Steve hesitated, hoping there might be a chance to rush the Frenchman while Laura rose from her knees. The former mercenary was too experienced however and he kept his distance while keeping the gun trained on Steve as Laura arose.

"I said into the bedroom!" snapped Trenet, indicating for Steve to lead the way.

Not having any option but to obey, Steve crossed the hall and passed through an opened door into the front bedroom. He caught a faint whiff of Laura's perfume and realised that this was the master bedroom in which she had slept, then she followed him into the room with Trenet bringing up the rear. The room was tastefully furnished with a large double bed against the side wall but what caught Steve's eye was a chair with scarves tied to its legs and arms. He realised that Trenet must have used it to keep Laura immobile. He felt a surge of anger but dampened it down, remembering John Popovic's advice. *Anger is a hot emotion – use it sparingly. Calculation is cold – use that to cold-bloodedly outsmart your enemy.*

"Sit in the chair," said Trenet.

Steve's mind was racing and he tried desperately to think of some way to buy time and avoid being bound to the chair. His one hope of getting out of this alive was to gain access to the thrust-dagger concealed in his heel – something that would be impossible if he were bound hand and foot.

"Look, I'm sure we can come to some sort of arrangement, even at this stage," he said, forcing a reasonable tone into his voice.

"So am I," said Trenet, "and I'll tell you the arrangement. You're going to tell me everything I want to know. And if you don't, if you lie to me, or try to mislead me, or I think you're not co-operating – then I'll go to work on your lady friend here. And believe me, tied to a chair and helpless to stop me, you won't like it. So take my advice, and do this the easy way."

"That's not what I meant, " said Steve, drawing a little closer to Trenet. " I was talking about a business arrangement. You're a businessman; my family are extremely wealthy. If we print no story and compensate you for your –"

"Stop! Don't come any closer!"

"OK," said Steve halting. He still kept his voice reasonable. "Look, all I'm saying is we don't have to –"

"Silence! Not another word!"

Steve stopped speaking, recognising real anger in the other man's tone.

"The next time I give you an order and you don't obey, I'll put a bullet though your kneecap," said Trenet, his voice quieter, but no less menacing. "Now, for the last time, *sit in the chair*."

Laura's mouth was dry and her pulses were racing madly but she tried desperately to fight her rising sense of panic. *It was up to her – there was no getting away from it.* Trenet was giving most of his attention to Steve, but once he had him tied to the chair he would turn his attention back to her. *And when he was finished with her he would kill them both.* She had to act and it had to be soon. She felt a sickening sense of fear, and with it an anger that this murderous bully felt at liberty to end the life of anyone who crossed him. What could be worse, she thought, than to go along with Trenet's orders, yet still end up as another of his victims?

She began to cry, lowering her head into her hands as her body was wracked with sobs. Trenet looked around at her briefly, then turned back to Steve who was slowly lowering himself down into the chair. Laura continued to sob, sitting down distractedly on the edge of the bed and dabbing at her eyes. She could see Trenet was operating very cautiously with Steve, keeping the gun trained upon him while standing behind him and beginning to loop one of the scarves around his left hand. Trenet had obviously decided that having killed the assassin in Torquay, Steve was by far the greater threat, and as he concentrated on the scarf he briefly turned his back on Laura.

It was now or never she knew, and without stopping the phoney sobbing she quickly reached under the bed. Her hand closed on the barrel of the shotgun and she pulled it out, rising and aiming the weapon in one swift movement. Even as she was starting up off the bed, however, she saw Trenet beginning to turn, having caught her movement in his peripheral vision. He must have seen the shotgun for he instantly dropped behind Steve. Laura had psyched herself up to fire at the older man but now she hesitated, fearing to hit Steve with the shotgun blast. Already Trenet had his gun retrained on Steve, gripping the American around the throat with his left hand and pulling him back in the chair to make of him a human shield.

"Drop your gun!" screamed Laura. "Drop it now!"

"Drop yours!"

"Drop it or I'll shoot!" she screamed, her finger lightly on the trigger as she looked down the barrel.

"Do and you'll hit us both! Now drop the shotgun. Drop it right now!"

Laura knew that if she did both she and Steve would die. She tried to aim the gun so that she could get a clear shot at some vital part of Trenet's body, but the Frenchman had wrapped himself in behind Steve and the chair in such a way that he was too well shielded.

"Drop the shotgun or I'll blow his brains out!"

"Drop your gun or I'll blow you away!"

"You can't without hitting us both. Stop kidding yourself. Now put the shotgun down or I'll blow your lover's brains all over the wall!"

Laura made no reply, continuing to keep her eyes sighted along the barrel. She knew that what the older man said was true. The blast from a shotgun was too indiscriminate – she couldn't kill Trenet without killing Steve also. But if she didn't kill Trenet then the Frenchman was certainly going to kill both of them.

"I'm giving you one more chance," said Trenet, "and if you don't take it I'm going to blow his head off!"

Was he bluffing? she thought, desperately trying to calculate the odds. Would he risk shooting Steve and then trying to shoot her too, before she could open fire with the shotgun? He might, she realised – he had after all been a professional soldier and would be far more practised with weapons that she was. On the other hand if he did blow out Steve's brains then there was no reason for Laura to hold off any further, and she might well blast him away before he could turn from Steve to her and get off a shot.

"Put down the shotgun! Now!"

"Don't, Laura!" cried Steve.

"Shut your fucking mouth!" said Trenet, tightening his grip on Steve's throat, but without ever taking his eyes off Laura.

"Drop the gun, last warning!" said the Frenchman.

Still Laura said nothing, but her insides were churning. It was the cruellest of quandaries. If she lowered the shotgun to prevent Trenet from shooting Steve right now, Trenet would kill him anyway – and her too. Yet if she wanted to save herself by shooting first, she could probably kill the Frenchman with a close quarters shotgun blast – but only if she were prepared to kill Steve in the process. Could she sacrifice him to save herself?

"I'm going to count to five," said Trenet. "If you haven't lowered the gun by then his brains are on the wall!"

Laura kept her finger on the trigger and the shotgun aimed, but the Frenchman sounded like he meant what he had said, and Laura swallowed hard, uncertain what to do.

Trenet kept his eyes on the Irishwoman, trying to gauge her intentions. He was bluffing regarding shooting on the count of five, knowing that if he shot Johnson there was a real risk of Kennedy hitting him with the shotgun blast. His bluffing had worked well so far however, with his threats of knee-capping and slow deaths having the desired effect. This time though the Irishwoman didn't appear to be wilting

He could feel Johnson wriggling in his grasp but he kept his eyes locked on Kennedy while maintaining a firm grip on the American's neck. "One!" he said, watching for any sign of Kennedy's resolve weakening. There was still no indication of her caving in. "Two," he continued, making his voice as threatening as possible.

Still she held his gaze, and Trenet realised that he would only weaken his position if he reached five and then didn't shoot. Time to slow things down and somehow make it seem a better option to lower the shotgun. "Don't make me do this," he said. "It's in your interest to drop the gun."

"It's in my interest to let you shoot us?"

"It doesn't have to be that way," he said, improvising wildly.

"Of course, it does. You're not going to let either of us live, so why would I surrender?"

Trenet struggled to find a convincing answer, but he knew that it was essential to come up with something and that the longer he could keep Kennedy talking the harder it would be for her to hold up and aim a heavy shotgun. All he needed was her concentration to waver fleetingly in order for him to whip the Beretta away from Johnson's head and shoot her.

"You're right," he said, watching her expression carefully. "You're going to die anyway. If you do things my way I guarantee it will be painless. If you persist with this, I promise you agony like you've never known." He felt Johnson wriggling again and thought that perhaps the American was beginning to panic. "Stay easy," he ordered, tightening his grip on the other man's neck, but still keeping his gaze unwaveringly on Kennedy.

"How do I know you'd keep your word?" asked Kennedy.

"I promise you – it will be clean and quick," he answered, pleased at what he felt was the first softening in the Irishwoman's position.

"That's not much of a guarantee," she said.

Something in her tone sounded wrong to Trenet. It was like she was – what? *Stringing him along.* He stared into her eyes, trying to gauge what she was at, then he heard a click and he tensed. Kennedy's finger was still only resting on the trigger and she seemed no nearer to firing, and for a fraction of a second Trenet wondered what the sound was. Suddenly he felt a searing pain in his right thigh and he screamed in agony, his eyes wide with shock at the realisation that while he had been distracted by Kennedy, the American had managed somehow – unbelievably – to stab him.

Laura could hardly believe it had worked. She had watched, mesmerised, as Steve had swivelled the heel of his shoe, and she had deliberately kept Trenet occupied so as to enable Steve to do whatever he had in mind. Time seemed to stand still, then Steve cried "Shoot, Laura! Shoot!" as he dived away from Trenet, knocking over the chair.

The Frenchman had instinctively dropped the gun from Steve's head, both his hand going to his thigh, from where blood was pumping and in which a buried dagger jutted out obscenely.

Despite herself, Laura hesitated, finding it difficult to overcome the conditioning of a lifetime by snuffing out a human life. She saw Trenet recovering now from the initial shock of being stabbed and to her horror she watched him extending his gun-hand in her direction.

If she didn't fire now, she would die. Although it all happened in a split second, she saw the Frenchman quickly lifting his free hand to support his gun-hand and improve his aim. She swallowed hard, then pulled the trigger of the shotgun.

The blast sounded deafening and the recoil hurt her shoulder, knocking her backwards. She saw that Trenet had taken the blast in his stomach. He had been blown back onto the floor and his bloody torso had been horribly shredded and exposed. But he wasn't dead. Even as she realised that the blast hadn't killed him, he gave an animal-like cry and raised the Beretta in his bloodied hand, then quickly loosed off two shots at Steve, his nearest target.

The first shot missed, but Laura was stunned to see that second shot spinning Steve around, splattering the wall behind him with blood. She heard Steve cry out, then he collapsed behind the far side of the bed.

"No!" she screamed. "No!" Even as she roared the words of anguish, the stricken Frenchman was beginning to move again. Laura stood, paralysed with shock and sorrow and Trenet seemed to channel all his remaining strength into turning his blood-sodden body round to face her.

Although obviously in great pain and grunting and whimpering from the effort, he nonetheless managed to turn to Laura. He mouthed something that she couldn't catch. A pool of blood was forming on the ground beneath the mortally wounded Frenchman but he gathered himself for one last effort, locking eyes with Laura.

"Bitch!" he cried, audibly this time. "Stupid bitch!" He swivelled the Beretta in his wrist and shot at her.

Laura was caught unawares and she felt the bullet whizz past her temple, then her self-preservation instinct kicked in and she let him have the second barrel. There was another deafening blast, but this time she was ready for the recoil. This time too she had steeled herself for the results of her action and despite the horror, she didn't flinch. The Frenchman's chest cavity had been blown away and the wall behind him was crimson with his blood. Trenet's heart and lungs had clearly been shattered by the blast, and Laura knew at once that this time he was dead.

She stood a moment, shaken by what she had done, then she dropped the shotgun to the floor. She felt no remorse, and even the obscenity of the Frenchman's injuries seemed like no less than he deserved. He was a ruthless killer who had given her no option, and she turned away, knowing that she had to cross the room to where Steve had been felled, yet dreading what she would find.

She bit her lip, then breathed out and set forward. There was more blood on the carpet on the far side of the bed and Steve's body lay face down where he had fallen. "No!" she wailed. "No! No!"

Her cries of grief came from the depths of her being and she began to sob. Suddenly in mid-cry she stopped. Steve was moving, and she watched as he slowly and painfully turned his head. Laura quickly dropped to her knees as he managed to turn onto his back. "Steve! I thought . . . Jesus, I thought you were gone. . . "

"Not yet," he answered forcing a weak smile but grimacing then in pain. "Trenet?" he asked through gritted teeth.

"Dead," replied Laura. She looked at Steve appraisingly, anxious to find out how badly he was wounded.

"Shoulder," he said. "Hurts like hell."

Laura could see from the bloodied front of his shirt where the bullet had entered, but the blood loss didn't seem too severe and she knew that the important thing to establish was that the rear of his shoulder hadn't been blown away by an exiting bullet. She quickly checked and was relieved to see that there was no exit wound. "You haven't lost much blood," she said, "I know enough first aid to stem the bleeding, then I'll call for an ambulance."

"OK, Nurse," he said, trying again for a grin. "And, Laura?"

"Yeah?"

"You did well – you did really well."

"Jesus, Steve, I thought he'd killed you . . ." She hesitated, her emotions suddenly kicking in now and her eyes welling up with tears. "I thought he was going to kill us both."

"It's over," he said taking her hand and squeezing it with surprising strength. "From now on, it's all going to be OK."

"You really think so?"

"I promise."

He looked at her tenderly and Laura felt a welling up of affection for him. "I love you," she said.

"I love you too. Kiss me."

"Your shoulder, Steve."

"In a second. Just . . . just kiss me now. Please."

Laura bent down, then she kissed him lovingly. She felt her tears beginning to fall freely and in that moment of release she sensed that what Steve had said was true. In spite of all that had happened it was going to be all right. They were alive and together and it was going to be OK. She wiped the tears from her eyes, smiled at him, then leaned forward and kissed him again.

Epilogue

Dutchie Holland sat in a deck-chair in his back garden reading about the death of his old commander. It was three days now since Trenet's dramatic end in a house in the West of Ireland, but it had taken a couple of days for the story to break in the newspapers.

Dutchie had had no contact with the Frenchman since their days in the Congo but it hadn't surprised him that his former commander had gone on to be a highly successful industrialist. Trenet had always come across as a winner. As a soldier he had been tough, ruthless and tactically aware, the kind of guy you wanted beside you in a tight corner. He had been a good officer too, demanding, but fair with the men and loyal to those under his command.

Or so Dutchie had always thought. Now it seemed that he had been mistaken about Trenet's character. He had received a phone call from Laura Kennedy, who felt that he was owed more of an explanation than that provided by the short warning letter from Steve Johnson that he had found on returning from holidays. At first Dutchie had thought that the letter might possibly be a prank, or even the work of somebody deranged, but Laura Kennedy's call had clarified matters.

Difficult as it was to believe, it seemed that Trenet had been responsible for the death of Vince Douglas and that Dutchie himself would have been next on the hit list, as the Frenchman sought to ensure that his past remained buried. And now it emerged that Alain Chavant, Trenet's old sergeant and the head of a security firm in Brussels with links to Trenet's IWS, had suddenly fled the country.

At first Dutchie had felt shocked that former comrades would have been prepared to kill both himself and Vince Douglas, but then he reverted to this usual belief that nothing life threw your way should surprise or disappoint you. As a soldier and then as a mercenary he had seen people behaving nobly, crassly, selfishly, generously, with touching gentleness and with absolute savagery, and early in life he had realised that he lived in a crazy, unpredictable world.

Now it seemed that he was no longer in any danger, however, what with Trenet dead, Chavant forced to flee and the story in all the newspapers. He sat back in his deckchair, soothed by the birdsong that filled his sunlit garden. He had given up on soldiering shortly after returning from the Congo, and had spent the next thirty-five years working as a caretaker for a school in Torquay. It was a town he had fallen in love with, ever since seeing its pretty harbour as a ten-year-old while on a tour organised by his school in Bethnal Green, in London's East End. His daydream of running his own trawler hadn't been realised – he had seriously underestimated how expensive marine craft were – but he had settled happily enough for regular employment in a school in the town, and looking now at the inglorious end that was the lot of Trenet and Chavant, he reckoned that he had made a good choice.

He closed the newspaper, deciding that as far as he was concerned the matter ended here. He hadn't spent half a lifetime of normal and contented living in Torquay only to have his equilibrium shattered by feeling either bitter at Trenet for what he had planned or sorrow at his violent and untimely death. He folded the newspaper over, then rose from the deckchair and made for the garden shed to place the paper in the re-cycling box.

He entered the shed, its interior cool and shady after the warmth of the garden. The walls of the shed had rows of shelving on which were neatly-stowed garden implements, boxes of seeds, pest repellent and lawn feed – a testament to the love of gardening that Dutchie had shared with his late wife.

She had died two years earlier and they had never had

children, but working in the garden had been their passion and the beautifully kept gardens surrounding the bungalow were still Dutchie's pride and joy. Later today he would do some serious gardening, he thought. It would be therapeutic and would take his mind off the whole crazy business with Trenet.

He looked over at his garden tools, then stopped dead. It took him a couple of seconds to identify what was wrong, then he realised that his spade was missing.

It had been there the day before he had left on holiday – he had straightened the border of a flower-bed with it – and now it was gone. Could someone have stolen it while he was away? Certainly none of his neighbours would have borrowed it without asking, apart from which none of them would have lacked such a basic garden tool in the first instance. It seemed bizarre. Who would break into a garden shed to steal a spade? It just wasn't the kind of thing that happened in his quiet little corner of Torquay. Yet someone had.

He felt a sense of irritation at the invasion of his privacy, even if it was only his garden shed that was involved, then he consciously quelled his annoyance. What the hell, he thought, it was only a spade. He was alive, unlike Trenet, and he could get another spade. He checked that nothing else was missing, but everything seemed in order – they had taken a solitary spade. *Weird*. He shook his head, then turned away and stepped back out into the garden, closing the shed door behind him.

He had said it before and he would say it again, it was a crazy unpredictable world . . .

The harsh cry of the muezzin came from the speaker of the minaret as the evening call to prayer echoed across Tangier. Alain Chavant sipped a glass of red wine as he sat on the balcony of his rented villa and savoured the scents and lingering warmth of a Moroccan summer's evening.

He had flown from Brussels to the south of Spain on a false passport, then got the ferry from Algeciras to Tangiers, posing as a French Canadian. Although the business with Trenet and Perez had turned into a fiasco he hadn't fled empty-handed. Chavant had always been aware that after decades of shady dealing things might one day blow up in his face, and he had taken suitable precautions in case he ever needed to make a quick exit. It meant that now he had more than enough money salted away in his Swiss account to live comfortably in Morocco, although even here in North Africa he would need to change his appearance somewhat and keep a low profile until things quietened down in Brussels.

He knew that he could never go back, but as he was divorced with grown-up children who had long since moved away from home, enforced exile wasn't an unbearable wrench. And in reality he had seen this problem coming. As soon as Trenet had rung to say that Perez hadn't reported back from Torquay, alarm-bells had rung for Chavant. He knew Perez' style, and if the man had been successful in his mission he would have been quick to report it. Trenet hadn't wanted to accept such a bleak interpretation, but Chavant had felt that the silence from Perez meant that the Spaniard had come a cropper – and probably lethally so – during his assassination bid on Dutchie Holland. Holland might be in his sixties now, but Chavant remembered the affable Englishman as also being teak-tough, and well able to look after himself.

If it had been Perez alone who had died, it might have been possible to ride out the storm. Chavant knew that the Spaniard was single and had few close friends and no family ties in Belgium, so that there wasn't likely to be a big fuss over his death, or indeed over his going missing if Dutchie Holland had taken the law into his own hands and then disposed of Perez without involving the police. But once Trenet had also been killed, Chavant had known that the game was up.

Chavant sipped his wine now, a gentle evening breeze carrying the scent of bougainvillaea on the air as he pondered how things had played out. There had been a certain irony in word coming through about the NATO contract on the very day he had chosen to flee. Despite their lobbying, his contact at NATO had apologetically informed him that the contract had gone to a competitor of IWS, and Chavant knew that all of Trenet's efforts to protect his identity and avoid any hint of past scandal had actually been in vain. Such was life, he thought, yet all things considered, matters had turned out fairly well for him. Of course, it was a pity to lose Trenet, a comrade of over forty years' standing, yet Chavant couldn't help but think that it was largely Trenet's own fault for ignoring his advice not to go to Ireland. Yet despite the Frenchman's wilfulness and frequently arrogant approach Chavant had liked him most of the time. And there was no denying that he had done well over many years in hitching himself to Trenet's rising star.

He thought back affectionately to their early days in the Congo, where it had all started. There was another irony, he realised, in Trenet and his diamond cache enabling them both to leave Africa with far more money than they had before, and now, at the end of the partnership, in Trenet being the cause of his returning to Africa.

It was like coming full circle. Still, no regrets, thought Chavant. They had had more good than bad times together over the years. He raised his glass in a toast to Trenet, then he sipped the wine and sat back, lost in his thoughts as the setting African sun turned the sky to gold.

Laura sat back against the wall of the ruined church in Bishopsquarter cemetery, gathering her thoughts. She had been across the bay in Galway city and something had drawn her back to the graveyard at the northern edge of the Burren. This was where she had visited the grave of Conn Lynch at the start of the Congo story and somehow it seemed fitting to return here now that the episode was drawing to a close.

Three days had passed since the traumatic confrontation with Trenet in Kilfenora but it was only now that something like normality was returning to her life. This morning though had been difficult, with Mac's funeral being held in Ballyhaunis, about forty miles north of Galway in County Mayo. Upset after the burial, and having offered her heartfelt sympathy to Mac's wife and family, Laura had returned to visit Steve, who was still in hospital in Galway city.

His injured shoulder was responding well to treatment, the bullet having being removed after the ambulance had taken him from Kilfenora to Galway for emergency surgery. Before either the ambulance or the police had arrived, Laura and Steve had hurriedly agreed their story, and any reservations that Laura might otherwise have had about lying to cover Steve's actions with Perez were swept away by the knowledge that they had been up against ruthless opponents – opponents who had already murdered Mac and Vince Douglas, and who would just as readily have killed them too.

As it happened the police had accepted their story quite readily, the prior killing of Mac making it obvious that Trenet was the aggressor in Kilfenora also. The bullets removed from Mac's body during the post mortem matched those from the gun that Trenet had used against Steve at the cottage, and the police had made it clear that they regarded as reasonable Laura's explanation of using the shotgun in self-defence.

Neither Steve nor Laura had made any reference to the assassin whom Trenet had unleashed on their trail, and with Dutchie Holland unaware of what had happened in his house and with Trenet dead, it was most unlikely that anyone else would come forward and say that they had sent forth an assassin who was now missing, presumed dead.

It meant, of course, that Laura would have to write her piece for the *Clarion* in such a way as not to include the important fact that they had tracked down Trenet's lethal enforcer – but there was still plenty of drama in the story without that.

In actual fact Laura's first instinct had been to refrain from writing the story at all, the events being too recent and traumatic for comfortable reporting. She had had second thoughts, however, figuring that she owed it to the memory of Mac to break the story for which he had tragically paid with his life. Despite her heartache at his death, she knew that she shouldn't feel guilty about his murder though. It wasn't because she was a tenacious journalist that Mac was dead, but because Daniel Trenet was a murderer. That was how Mac would have seen it, and she knew that he would be disgusted if the *Clarion* didn't scoop their rivals with such a sensational story. Apart from which it would surely seem suspicious if a journalist at the heart of such an explosive story then chose not to write about it.

And so, on reflection, she was going to do a major piece for next Sunday's edition of the *Clarion*. She had made one other important editorial decision however. Over forty years after the events in the Congo and two weeks after his lonely death in a Galway hospital, she reckoned it was time to allow Conn Lynch to rest in peace. No one would ever know how much or how little he had been involved in what had happened at Kaburi in the matter of the missing diamonds and the death of his countryman Barrett, especially as much of the evidence was circumstantial. So she wouldn't be judge and jury either. She wouldn't reveal the source of the tip-off that had set her off on the trail that led to Daniel Trenet, and she would let Conn Lynch be remembered as a popular local employer who had come back from the States with his fortune made, and who ran a thriving business until his premature death from a heart attack.

But all of that related to an article that she had yet to write, whereas right now she had another decision with which to deal. She breathed out slowly, then leaned back further against the wall of the picturesque ruined church and looked out over Galway Bay. The sun was beginning to dip in the sky and the scene below her had a picture-postcard prettiness, the many shades of green being tinged now with gold from the sun's slanting rays. Was she willing to leave all this behind and make a fresh start in the States?

It was a suggestion that Steve had put to her in the hospital in Galway that afternoon, and despite never before wanting to live outside of Ireland her heart had lifted at the fact of his asking. It wasn't quite a proposal of marriage, but knowing Steve's style as she did, she knew it wasn't the kind of suggestion he would make lightly. It was obvious to Laura that he meant it when he said he loved her, and the trauma of her captivity and the eventual killing of Trenet had underlined for Laura just how much he meant to her too. Nevertheless it was a huge step to turn her back on the life she had made for herself in Ireland and to go to America. With the kind of presence that Media Group International had, she knew that doors would open for her, and she had enough confidence in her ability as a journalist to feel she could work there successfully. But still . . .

Starting a serious relationship was a big undertaking, especially since it was the first such relationship she had had since Declan's death. Moving country as well made it a huge decision, and she had told Steve that she needed a little time to think it over. He had said he understood, but as she was leaving the hospital he had looked at her and only half-jokingly said to take as long as she needed – but then please to say yes.

She smiled now as she remembered the look on his

face and suddenly she knew that she was kidding herself. She had felt the need for time to think it through, yet deep down she realised that such things were decided on an instinctive level. And her instincts were clear. Steve wanted her. She wanted him. She would go with him.

She rose to her feet, her heart suddenly light now that she had chosen what to do, and she wondered should she text Steve to let him know the good news immediately. No, she thought, this was the kind of thing that should be done in person. And she could be in Steve's hospital room in less than half an hour. She took one last look at the beautiful sunset unfolding before her, savouring the exhilaration her decision had brought, then she started across the graveyard towards her car, eager to get to Galway and to give Steve her answer.

THE END

Also available from Poolbeg

PAYBACK by Brian Gallagher

PROLOGUE

Gellert Hill, Budapest
January 2000

Abdullah Majid had finally tracked down his quarry. The search had been painstaking, but now the moment of reckoning was at hand; tonight he would kill his enemy.

It was a dark, moonless night, ideal for his purpose. Flurries of snow swirled in the wind that gusted up from the river, and the wooded slopes of Gellert Hill were deserted. Majid looked down the hill to where the broad expanse of the Danube flowed swiftly beneath the twinkling lights of the Szabadsag Bridge. Beyond that again he could see the floodlit buildings that stood like majestic sentinels on the Pest side of the river.

The lightly falling snow lent a fairytale air to what was already a striking view, but Majid hardly noticed. Tonight wasn't about scenery, it was about vengeance. For five years in an Israeli jail, and for almost two further years since his release he had imagined the moment when he would catch up with Moshe Avram. He had fantasised about it, played it out in innumerable ways in his head, and now, finally, it was about to happen.

Majid quietly stamped his feet against the cold, then scanned again all the approaches to the summit of Gellert Hill. He had read in his guidebook how Bishop Gellert, the Venetian martyr, had been thrown by pagans from this very hilltop, trapped in a barrel spiked with nails. It was exactly the kind of death Majid would have liked to inflict on Moshe Avram when he met him tonight.

Back in 1992 Avram, an Israeli agent, had led a Mossad team that raided the camp where Majid had been training in guerrilla warfare. The training camp, located in the Sudan, had been run by Mujahadeen, veterans of the war in Afghanistan. Everyone in the camp had considered the Sudan too hostile an environment and too far from Israel for a ground operation to be launched by Mossad. They had been wrong, and an audacious and well-executed Israeli raid had destroyed the camp, killing and wounding many of its occupants.

Majid and several others had been captured and driven by lorry to a remote spot on the Sudanese Red Sea coast, from where a Greek-registered, but Israeli-run, freighter had transported the prisoners to the Israeli port of Eilat.

Moshe Avram had interrogated Majid relentlessly during the two days of the voyage, and Majid still felt sick with shame and anger each time he recalled it. With Majid's hands and feet securely bound, Avram's henchmen had held him over a tub of seawater into which the Mossad officer had pressed his victim's face whenever he was displeased by his answers. During the interrogation it had reached the stage where Avram had only smirkingly to make a pressing motion with his thumb for Majid to feel his stomach tightening with fear. He had held out for as long as he could, but eventually the Israeli had broken him.

He had hated Avram for the brutality of the torture, but he had hated him even more for the self-loathing induced by being made to talk about the camp's command structure, staff and objectives. He had tried to blur the truth as much as possible and had mixed half-truths and evasions into the information they had extracted, but his pride had been badly damaged by the loss of dignity caused by being broken.

Now, seven years later and half a continent away, it was time to settle the account. On learning that Avram was in Budapest, Majid had suppressed his excitement and concentrated instead on devising an approach that he felt would hook the Israeli. It had to be something enticing enough to make a professional like Avram agree to a solo meeting at an isolated venue.

After much thought, Majid had opted for Hamas as his bait. He knew that the Israeli had a particular hatred for the Lebanese terror group, and so he had sent a note to Moshe Avram at the Israeli Embassy saying he had valuable information on Hamas. No point in pretending to be an Israeli sympathiser; a cynic like Avram would be more convinced by a commercial motive. He had offered therefore to sell first-class intelligence on Hamas, insisting first on a meeting alone with Avram to discuss money and communication methods.

Two in the morning at the Liberation Monument on Gellert Hill had been Majid's chosen rendezvous, and he had come an hour and a half early to scout the area and be in position long before the Israeli arrived.

On a snowy winter night the area had been deserted, with just the occasional car travelling up the hill and on towards the Citadel, a former military base now converted into a restaurant.

Majid had looked through his night-sight glasses every few minutes, scanning all approaches to the Liberation Monument. He had stood in a cluster of trees from where he could see the monument itself, the road to the Citadel above that, and the paths leading to the river below. Dressed in black and with his face encased in a woollen balaclava, he knew that he would be virtually invisible in the absence of moonlight.

As time had passed the cars threading their way up the hill had dwindled in frequency and, hearing one approaching now, Majid realised that it was the first vehicle that had passed in some time. He glanced at the luminous hands of his watch: one thirty, half an hour to go. Unless they come early, he thought.

The Liberation Monument, commemorating the Red Army's liberation of Budapest from the Nazis, consisted of a tall column on top of which stood a woman holding aloft what looked like a palm leaf. The significance of the imagery wasn't clear to Majid, but it was a good rendezvous point – near the city centre, yet off the main roads and surrounded by wooded parklands. On his arrival he had used a sophisticated infrared scanner to check the area carefully, but no body-heat images had shown up from any of the surrounding thickets, and he was reassured that an Israeli trap was not set in place.

That had been an hour ago and despite the cold he had waited patiently.

The car he had just heard had passed now, but in the distance he thought it sounded as if it had come to a halt. Instinctively his hand closed around the silenced Beretta in his pocket. Probably only a taxi going to the Citadel. Or Moshe Avram arriving early and approaching surreptitiously.

Still holding the gun, he lifted the night-sight glasses that hung around his neck and looked up towards the road. Nothing whatsoever was stirring there. And yet . . .

He had underestimated the Israeli once before and Avram had taken him by surprise. Tonight he had to be the one springing the trap. He lowered the glasses and took off his gloves, wanting to be ready for action. He slipped the pistol into his jacket pocket, then took out the infrared scanner.

Taking care to shield it from anyone on the road above, he switched on the screen. He pointed the scanner in the direction of the Citadel and immediately picked up an image. His heart began to pound, but he forced himself to breathe deeply. From the infrared image, it was clear that someone was walking down the road from the Citadel.

Majid strained his ears, but with the wind he could hear no footsteps.

Standing stock-still, he watched the image on the screen approaching, then slowing. He looked away from the screen and up towards the road.

Using the night-glasses again he stared hard, but he could see nothing in the swirling snow. He lowered the glasses, then from the corner of his eye he caught a movement and, looking back at the screen, saw that the target was moving again. This time the image was moving away, and he realised that the person was beginning to descend the road leading down the hill.

Majid breathed more easily. Probably just a late-night stroller who had slowed for a view over the city. He checked the infrared image again, but the person was still descending. One part of Majid was almost disappointed that it wasn't Avram arriving early to try to out-manoeuvre him. It would have been satisfying to surprise the Israeli as he tried to spring his own trap.

He glanced again at the screen and his pulses quickened. The person was no longer going down the hill. Instead the image was moving sideways.

Whoever it was had left the road and gone into the parkland. Majid felt the familiar thrill that always hit him when going into action, but he refused to give full rein to it. Whoever had left the road might have nothing to do with the rendezvous. It could be someone who had simply gone into the bushes to urinate. Except that the image was still moving. Slowly but surely the person was travelling in an arc that would eventually take him onto the main path below the Liberation Monument.

Majid looked away from the screen and down the wooded slopes, trying to gauge the area that the person would have reached. He used the night-glasses, scanning what he thought was the appropriate area, but failed to pick up any movement. Lowering the glasses, he shifted the scanner and gazed at the screen. What he saw caused him to swallow hard. A second image was now approaching from the direction of the Citadel. It could simply be a coincidence, but Majid didn't believe in coincidence, certainly not on operations like this.

A stab of fear tightened his stomach as it occurred to him that perhaps he had gone from being the hunter to being the hunted. No, he thought, they couldn't know who he was or what he had in mind. If the two images were of Avram and an accomplice, the chances were that they were staking out the area and providing a hidden back-up for Avram when he made the rendezvous.

They couldn't know that he knew there were two of them; he still had the upper hand. Plus he knew where they were, but they didn't know his location.

Unless they too had IR heat sensors . . .

No, he decided, there was no reason for Avram to assume that his contact would remain hidden in the woods. Even if they didn't know his whereabouts, however, he knew that the situation was going to be tricky. To do what he wanted with Avram he would have to kill the back-up, but without alerting the Israeli. Difficult, but not impossible. The problem was that he didn't know which of the two images was Avram. Probably the second one, he reasoned - that way Avram could appear to arrive normally along the path leading from the roadside, while his accomplice was in place to cover him from below the monument.

He would deal with the one in the bushes first. He switched off the IR scanner, then moved carefully along the snow-covered ground in the direction in which the first person had been heading. After a moment he reached a clearing where several paths met, then he stepped back into the cover of the trees and raised his night-glasses. By his reckoning the first person had been heading this way and would be exposed when crossing the clearing. He looked through the glasses and waited. Sure enough, after a moment he heard a slight rustle, then saw a figure moving stealthily through the trees.

The figure reached the clearing, looked about, then stepped back towards the bushes. As Majid had expected, it wasn't Avram. He hadn't seen the man's face properly, but Avram was over six feet tall, and this man was small and stocky. Majid kept the glasses trained on the figure as he moved into the shrubbery. It looked like he was taking up a position. The next moment all Majid's suspicions were confirmed. The man turned his head and, through the nightglasses, Majid saw that he was wearing a miniature microphone and earphones set.

It was good news and bad news. Good in that there could be no further doubt about what he was up to. Bad in that Majid couldn't kill him without alerting Avram. The dynamics of the situation had changed - he was outnumbered now, and the prudent course might be to retreat. Majid considered his options, recalling the rules that his trainers in the Sudan had stressed. Always consider the odds, always weigh up the possible gain and loss, never act just for the sake of acting. All things considered, the wise move now would be to withdraw. But Majid hadn't come all this way to be wise. His business with Avram was personal, a blood feud, and he wanted it settled, tonight.

Besides, he thought, maybe the radio mikes weren't an insuperable problem.

In his note, he had insisted that Avram come alone, that if there was anything untoward the meeting would be aborted. Which meant that Avram couldn't approach the monument wearing earphones and a mike. And if Majid used the silenced Beretta on the stocky man after Avram had removed his earphones, he could still take the Israeli by surprise. But it wasn't a sound plan, he knew. There were too many imponderables, the chief one being: when would Avram take off the earphones?

Majid realised that he would have to use the scanner to determine Avram's location and trust that on arriving near the monument the Mossad man would have slipped off the communications gear. Majid moved slowly backwards into the shrubbery, knowing that he couldn't switch on the scanner here, with its light being visible to the watcher in the bushes. He worked his way in a circle, taking care not to snap any twigs, until he was about fifteen yards behind the stocky man.

Majid switched on the scanner and pointed it towards the monument.

The image showed the second person moving slowly in that direction. Majid reckoned that he would have just left the road. If Avram were taking off the earphones, he would surely be doing it now. Majid slipped the scanner into his jacket pocket and withdrew the Beretta. Using his left hand, he held the night-glasses firmly to his eyes, then with his right hand he wedged the gun against the branch of a tree to steady his aim. He knew that the silencer would lessen his accuracy, but on the positive side he was an excellent marksman and the Israeli in the bushes was unmoving.

He held his breath, pressing the gun hard against the tree to minimise shaking, then squeezed the trigger twice. The noise of the wind dampened the thump of the silencer, and he saw his target slump to the ground. He fired two more shots into the body, then made for the nearby path, transferring the gun to his left hand and holding it just inside his pocket. He would have preferred to make absolutely sure that the first Israeli was dead, but he couldn't risk taking that much time. In case Avram was still wearing a mike, Majid knew that he had to get to him before he called in again with his colleague.

He moved swiftly towards the base of the Liberation Monument. Then suddenly he saw Avram. There was no mistaking the bulk of the tall Israeli standing in the snow-covered clearing. Majid felt his mouth go dry now that the moment had finally arrived, but his adrenaline kept him moving forward.

Hearing the approaching footsteps, Avram turned, and Majid saw his face in the faint light spilling down from the streetlamp on the road above.

There was no sign of any microphone or earphone, and Majid felt a surge of exhilaration. "Mr Avram, I presume," he said, holding out his right hand to shake as he drew near. He had worked out in advance exactly how he would play this.

Speak in English - Arabic would make Avram

instinctively suspicious. Hold out the right hand to shake hands - most people by reflex hold out their right hand in return. That way Avram would have to use what would normally be his gun-hand.

It worked perfectly. Avram held out his hand, and in one continuous movement Majid shook hands, pulled the gun from his left pocket and pushed it against Avram's temple. "One move and I'll blow your brains out!" This time he spoke Arabic, in which he knew Avram was fluent, and he saw the flicker of fear cross the Israeli's face. "Understand?" he said, pressing the gun harder into the other man's temple.

"Yes."

The Mossad agent's voice was steady, and Majid noted that he had seemed to regain his composure pretty quickly. He'd soon change that. Keeping the gun pressed to Avram's head, Majid moved behind him, then shifted the barrel to press into the back of the Israeli's head.

"Put your legs wide apart," he ordered.

Avram complied, then Majid took a step back, the gun still trained on the other man's head.

"Now slowly, very slowly, raise your hands onto your head."

Again the Israeli complied.

"Start moving forward. Keep your legs apart!" Majid enjoyed seeing the Israeli moving forward awkwardly at his command. He followed closely behind, his aim never wavering, then told Avram to halt. They were now out of view from the road above. "Keep your hands on your head, then turn around slowly," he ordered. Standing just far enough back to be out of lunging range, Majid reached up with his free hand and removed the balaclava.

"Face look familiar?: he asked.

"I can't see you properly," answered Avram.

Majid was almost going to move closer for the pleasure of seeing the Israeli's fear on recognising his face, but he stopped himself. This bastard was both cunning and dangerous - drawing near would be a mistake.

"Sudan ring a bell?" he said instead. "Little sailing trip up the Red Sea? Torturing a helpless man?"

Avram made no response, and Majid felt his anger rising. "Turn around," he snapped. "Turn around!"

The Mossad agent turned his back as ordered, and Majid quickly swung the Beretta, smacking the Israeli hard on the back of his neck. Avram stumbled and cried out in pain, but didn't fall to the ground.

"That's just for starters, you Zionist pig! Oh, and in case you're wondering - your friend in the bushes won't be helping. Ask me why. Ask me why, pig!"

"Why?"

"Because I blew his brains out!"

The Mossad agent said nothing, but Majid knew he

must be feeling sickened.

Frightened too, with no one now to rescue him. "You thought you were so smart, didn't you?" he goaded. Avram didn't answer, and Majid felt his anger rising again. "I'm talking to you, pig!"

"I'm not talking to you, scum!"

Majid felt a surge of rage at the Israeli's defiance and he swivelled the gun in one flowing movement and fired a shot. Avram screamed in agony, then stumbled to the ground, clutching his shattered kneecap. Keeping the gun trained on his captive, Majid kicked him hard in the ribs and was rewarded with another cry of pain. "Don't show disrespect again, pig. Understood? I said understood?"

"Yes . . ." Avram whispered, still holding his knee.

Majid looked at the Israeli contemptuously. "Not so good at taking it, are you? Really good at giving it out, when your victims are helpless - not so tough on the receiving end. Are you, pig?"

The Israeli stared up at him, but didn't answer. At first Majid thought the man was distracted by pain, then he realised that Avram was defying him. If he had any fleeting regard for the other man's bravery, it was swiftly overtaken by rage. Even when wounded and taken prisoner, the Israeli arrogance that Majid hated so much was in evidence.

"Answer when I speak to you, pig!" he said, but still the Mossad man held his gaze and made no reply.

Majid aimed the gun at Avram, his finger tight on the trigger, but still the Israeli refused to answer. Majid shot twice, the bullets aimed for the other kneecap, and Avram screamed.

Majid relished the sight of the prostrate and blood-soaked Israeli, but even as he did another part of his mind was operating objectively. Time to finish it. The scream and Avram's earlier cry might have been heard. He drew closer. He went behind the Israeli and buried his knee in his back, then jerked the man's head backwards with his left hand. "You've tortured your last Arab, pig. Time to die . . ." Majid slipped the gun into his pocket with his right hand and pulled out an ornate dagger. He quickly wedged the dagger-case between his knee and Avram's back and unsheathed the weapon with one hand, allowing Avram to see its finely honed blade. The Israeli's head was pulled taut to expose his neck, and Majid saw the flash of fear in his eyes.

Enough, he thought; then in one swift movement he slit the Israeli's throat.

Avram struggled and cried out as the blood spurted from his severed carotid artery, then eventually his struggles ceased and he went limp, and Majid allowed him to fall onto the crimson-stained snow.

Majid stared in triumph for a moment at his enemy's body before wiping the blood off his weapon in the snow and sheathing the knife. Exhilarated at paying off the first part of his debt so spectacularly, he took one last look at the body, then set off down the hill.

Also by Poolbeg

PAYBACK

BRIAN GALLAGHER

The most spectacular assassination ever staged –
and they've eight days to prevent it. Already the
clock is ticking …

When journalist Laura Kennedy breaks the law in chasing a story
she tells herself it's worth it to get a scoop. But she doesn't bargain
on making an enemy of Abdullah Majid. And enemies don't
come any deadlier.

A ruthless and highly resourceful assassin, Majid's mission is to kill
every Foreign Minister in the EU. Desperately seeking to stop him
are police officers Jack Thompson and Penny Harte who are
responsible for security at the Harrogate conference that Majid
has targeted.

As dramas are played out in Budapest, Dublin, Lebanon and
Marbella, Laura Kennedy finds herself on the trail of a truly lethal
quarry. And as the battle of wits develops and the hunters
unexpectedly become the hunted, Laura, Penny and Thompson
team up, only to be forced into the toughest of decisions. How
prepared are they to put their own lives on the line – if that's
the price for stopping slaughter on a terrifying scale …

ISBN 1-84223-110-3

Also by Poolbeg

FLIGHT

BRIAN GALLAGHER

For Mary Adams the choice is stark - betray her
husband if she wants her baby to live...

A moment of madness in the Yorkshire Dales creates
shock waves that will ripple out to London, Dublin,
Washington and Bangkok. For advertising executive
Dave Walker and his wife, actress Mary Adams, a chance
encounter sweeps away the certainties of a comfortable
suburban lifestyle and embroils them in the murky
world of cut-throat espionage...

Their dream of eagerly awaited parenthood turns into
a nightmare as they become targets for powerful and
ruthless opponents.

But Dave and Mary discover strengths they never knew
they had when their very survival is put to the test.
In a game of bluff and counter-bluff they pit their wits
against relentless adversaries in a world where nothing
is quite what it seems...

ISBN 1-84223-092-1